THE GREEN COUNTRY

BY
DORRIS MURDOCK

PROLOGUE
100,000 B.C.

Nora and Orem huddled together in their cave, she clinging to him; he cradling her, trying to shield her from the darkness that came sifting in, all but blotting out the light.

But there was no way he could protect her. Every breath filled their lungs with powdery, almost-invisible dust. A curtain of haze hung between them and the oval of light which was the cave's entrance.

The stillness was like nothing they had ever known before. Not the calm which came during the Harmattan season when the dust from the desert to the north crept in. No bird twittering, no small animal sounds, nothing but their muffled coughing as they tried to breathe through dust-clogged lungs. This was an eerier, unearthly quiet.

Fearful of confronting the creature who gave one sudden tremendous roar and blacked out the sun with his dusty breath, they remained deep in the cave for days, sleeping fitfully on their bed of pine boughs. He wakened over and over to sit up and listen he wasn't sure what for. He worried that he had heard nothing from his parents who lived nearby. No doubt they too were afraid to go outside.

Nora's mother, Anji, had come to visit shortly after Nora and Orem were joined to help Nora make the cave comfortable and convenient. The cooking was done outside with the cave used for storage and sleeping. Although Nora had watched her mother prepare food, she was only fourteen when she went to live with Orem so Anji helped her to make porridge without lumps and showed her how to cut the meat into very thin strips so as to be more tender when cooked. They gathered flowers and dried them which now hung on pegs on the walls

Their supply of firewood was almost gone, and Nora nursed the fire to life, then using only small sticks, burned just enough wood to cook their porridge for their one meal that day. Smoke from the fire added to the discomfort but she dared not go outside to cook. They shared their meager supply of dried meat and water, covered their nostrils with pieces of soft rabbit hide and waited.

How Nora wished her mother were here now. Fear, which had always lurked nearby, now moved into the cave with them. Fear of the creature who had roared but also fear of what lay ahead. Anxiously peering out at the still-dark sky, they knew there might be no food this year. There was seldom enough, even in the best of years. A black sky could mean no food at all this year. Their warm, protective cave where they had felt safe now seemed to be a prison.

They listened for sounds of their neighbors, Drik and Muni, who lived in another cave not far away. Once Orem called out their names but there was no response.

If Nora sat near the opening of the cave, just at the edge, there was enough light for her to work at braiding the sling of leather strips in which she would carry the baby. But would there be anyone to help when her time came to deliver the baby? Was the Medicine Woman still alive? Nora had left her tribe when Orem had chosen her as his mate, and oh, how she wanted to know if her parents were still alive.

She looked at her bulging stomach, feeling the slight movement there. Without adequate food for her, there would be no milk for her baby and it would die. She did not speak her fears. Her mate had worries enough.

One morning the cave opening seemed to be less dark. Orem tiptoed to the entrance and listened.

"Can you hear the others?" Nora whispered, trailing behind him.

"No"

"Would we dare go to see if —

"No!" he interrupted sharply. "The thing that did this might still be out there."

Nora had not allowed herself to cry after the first day, but now the tears came. Orem reached for- her quickly and folded his arms around her. "What if we are the only ones left?" she sobbed into his chest.

"Wait!" he said, putting his hand gently to her lips.

Nora instantly stopped weeping and heard what he had. A stirring. Perhaps wind. No, a slight breeze, then incredibly, it began to rain.

The raindrops came gently, covering the soft cushion of dust and turning it into mud..

"I can't wait any longer," Orem said. "I am going to see what has happened!"

"I'm coming too."

"No, it's not safe for you to go. The baby . . ."

"It's not safe for me to be here alone! The baby is safe in my body."

Grasping hands, they stepped through the small hole in the rock and lifted their faces to the warm rain. Muddy rivulets ran down their arms and faces. They opened their mouths and thrust out their tongues to catch the wet, slightly muddy drops.

Fearfully, they peered at the emptiness around them. They took a few cautious steps, and then a few more and found themselves standing at the center of what seemed like a room whose sides were formed by the dust, but even that was rapidly disappearing as the rain gently carried the bits of grit to the ground.

Orem guided Nora to a nearby tree and touched it. It was their tree, the tree where they hung gourds to dry to be used for utensils and storage. And the stools carved out of a tree trunk, still in their place beside the fire pit where she usually cooked their food. Somehow that made things less scary. At least, something was left.

Encouraged by the familiar tree, Orem called out. "Haloo! Is anyone there?"

The response was almost immediate. "Haloo!"

Voices called out again, and they waited without breathing. Shapes emerged out of the half-light. Mara, her husband Rini and their daughter Alta. They hugged and cried and hugged again.

Armed with his friends, Orem said, "Let's go see it!"

There were protests, but they were all too curious to hold out for long.

Orem took charge. "Let's go in the direction from which the breeze is coming. That should be the source. Be careful!"

As they walked through the drizzle, they looked at each other over and over, joyfully, and touched again, but no one spoke. Fear made them cautious still, their eyes constantly searching the edge of the horizon all around them. The drizzle continued to drip from a heavy gray sky.

Past the familiar pile of rocks called Devil's Slide, through groves of trees whose leaves were covered with dust, past places where they had hunted small animals for food, onward they followed the well-worn path now carpeted with the fluffy dust but fast becoming a muddy trail.

Rini, whose arm and face had been badly disfigured by a lion called for them to halt. It was too dangerous to go any further he said, but they ignored him, pushing on eagerly, moving more quickly.

As if at a signal, they suddenly stopped. Something was different, very different. They had reached the familiar plain where they picked berries to eat and gathered seeds from the heads of grain. This was the cave dwellers' gathering place, the place where they danced each month under the full moon. Mating ceremonies, blessing of the seeds, celebration of harvest, all happened here.

Perhaps their eyes deceived them. The misty dust had fooled them. They had gone the wrong direction. They questioned each other with a look. Was this the place they thought?

Orem confirmed it in a whisper. "This is the Gathering Place."

But it was no longer flat. From where they stood the ground sloped downward, gently at first, then more steeply to a spot that seemed to be the center, for the other side slanted up again the same distance. On the far edge they could see trees and bushes familiar to them. The rim of the depression formed a very large circle.

Orem picked up a rock and hurled it with considerable strength. They watched as it landed about half way to the center of the hole.

"It is so big," said Alta.

"Do you think this is where the dust came from?" asked Mara.

"A lot of dirt came out of here and went somewhere," Rini answered.

Everyone nodded.

Mara asked, "Do you think this was caused by the God of the Sky or by the God of the Earth? Who else could send such a thing?"

"There is no way of knowing," Orem answered. "I'm just glad the hole is no bigger than it is. See, there are still some heads of grain left at the edges."

"A good thing that it did not stop the rain or nothing would have grown for us to eat," Rini said.

They looked for water but the stream was muddy, so they went back to their caves and waited. The dust settled quickly, plastered down by the persistent rain. They caught some of the moisture to drink. Nora felt better after drinking, then she laughed at her foolishness in thinking it was the water that pleased her so much. It was not the water, it was the joy within her. The fact that her body was double was enough reason to feel good. And now that it was raining, there would be food. She hoped that the God who sent the dust was not angry because of her selfishness. The only thing she cared about was that she would have a strong baby and enough food to feed it.

CHAPTER 1

Somewhere over east Africa

They were off course, that much he knew. What he didn't know was how far off course. Hell, he didn't have the slightest idea where he was. Bert McEwen, the "best push pilot in east Africa" was lost!

They had left Nairobi, Kenya two hours earlier, heading for Blantyre, Malawi. He had made the trip so often he kind of put his mind on autopilot and now he couldn't get a fix on his position.

He had been proclaimed as "the best" in the latest issue of *The Pilot* magazine, published in the United States. It was a good thing he didn't listen to other people's opinions, otherwise he would be feeling guilty about being a phony. But fear was getting to him. If he didn't soon figure out where he was, he could end up dead, along with his passenger, Gui Manieux, a very important man in this part of the world.

His plane, a Cessna 210, was known as a workhorse because of the payload it could carry as well as its dependability and safety But it lacked the instruments he needed to fly in bush country, a fact that was becoming more obvious by the minute. His eyes were his instruments, and he constantly scanned the horizon for a familiar landmark.

But he had been in tight places before and always managed to escape, he reassured himself. Planes did funny things this time of year in this climate. A late harmattan, the fine sifting of dust from the Sahara, followed closely by the onset of high humidity as the seasonal rains began, could and sometimes did cause delicate instruments to register wrong. There was a strong tailwind today, and that in itself could throw them many miles off course. It had happened before, but usually he caught it before things got this bad.

This time he had other things on his mind, especially his intense aversion to Gui Manieux. It wouldn't have bothered him in the least if he did drop Gui into the bush country below. He really despised this guy even if he was the head of the biggest conglomerate farm organization in Africa. He oozed charm and had more money than he could ever use, but Gui's greed was legendary—and it had caused the death of Bert's friend. Gui Manieux was in Africa for no one but himself. This man would do anything to anyone to get what he wanted–power and money.

Bert glanced back and saw Gui was intent on his reading. He certainly seemed unaware of Bert's feelings toward him, and Bert would like to keep it that way. He needed the business Gui brought to him. And now he needed this man more than ever.

One reason Bert kept scanning the horizon, desperately trying to figure out his location was his own fault. He should have been thinking more about flying and less about money. For years he had sworn never to let money become more important than his flying, his safety or his dream. Now the dream was engaged in a battle for survival because of money. He had found the plane of planes, right there in Malawi just waiting for him to come up with the money to buy it. He could double his business and start doing some pro bono work, flying patients in from bush. He had never wanted anything as much in his whole life. It was all he could think about–almost.

Right now he had better tend to business or he wouldn't live to get that plane. His heartburn had returned, a sure sign of stress, and he was on his last antacid pill

Nothing below him looked familiar. He knew all the landforms up and down east Africa, but he didn't see one he recognized. His route was to take him from Nairobi, Kenya, to Blantyre, Malawi. He usually followed a route marked by large villages and definite landmarks. Obviously, he had strayed toward the center of the continent. He knew enough about the geography to know there were no landing strips in that area. Farmers and herdsmen here didn't use airplanes.

As much as he hated to, he had better alert Gui to the problem.

"Mr. Manieux," Bert called in a controlled voice, "we are having a bit of a problem." Then hurried to add, "We are going to be a bit late. I hope you didn't have an appointment this morning."

Gui Manieux laughed. "You know this country as well as I do, Bert." He spoke in easy, clear English with the French accent that made every woman's head turn toward him when he spoke. "A meeting starts when everyone gets there, even if it is the next day." He climbed through the space between the seats and eased his long legs into the right-hand seat.

Looking much younger than his early sixties, his thick silver-black hair crowned his dark eyes and olive complexion. His dark grey trousers were sharply creased, and the white polished cotton shirt looked fresh in spite of the ever-present humidity. The large unusually brilliant ruby ring on his left hand was his only piece of jewelry and the source of great pride. He did not even wear a watch.

"What is the problem?"

"Nothing serious—I think." Bert pointed to the console. "The weather messes up the gauges sometimes. We're a little off course." He hurried to add, "But I should have it figured out here in a minute or so."

Gui peered out his window. "I do not think I have ever been over this section of the country. Where do you think we are?"

Before Bert could admit he didn't know, Gui pointed ahead. "Put the nose of the plane down; I want to look at that area, whatever it is."

Bert pushed the nose down just a bit and adjusted the flaps to maintain the same speed. Everywhere below them the scene was the same, brown and bare. That was expected—it was the end of dry season. The rains had not yet begun. Sparse scrubby trees speckled the ground, kept short by the yearly burning by the farmers.

The one exception was the place Gui pointed to. A triangular-shaped piece of land, pointed at the north end and fanning out to a wide base at the bottom. Lush and green, it stood out in stark contrast to the surrounding barrenness. Bert nosed the plane down sharply to get a closer look.

"It looks like an oasis," mused Gui. "How long would you say it is?"

Bert measured with his eye against other landmarks. "Seventy-five, a hundred miles at the most. And maybe fifty miles across at the base."

"Looks like a land of master farmers. Just look at the trees, how large they are in comparison to those outside the area."

"That could be because they don't burn every year," Bert said.

"I suppose so." Gui sounded doubtful.

They flew in silence, peering intently at the unusual sight as they glided over the verdant green triangle.

"It looks like a virtual Garden of Eden," Gui said, "Mon Dieu! I swear they are growing guinea corn. In dry season!"

"Doesn't look like famine there this year!" Bert added.

They were not more than a thousand feet above the ground now. In the middle of a green area near a group of native compounds, a girl wearing a bright-colored scarf on her head waved to them. Bert dipped the wings, right and then left, as they passed over her.

As they crossed the southern border of the green triangle, the earth returned to drab, and the spot was immediately put out of mind as each man returned to more pressing matters, Gui to his cigarette and Bert to the problem.

Bert figured if he flew south southeastward, a familiar landmark would appear soon—it always did.

Bert's eyes moved from the gas gauge to the horizon and back as the plane hummed on for another half an hour, south by southeast. No gas pumps in this bush country. The knot in the pit of Bert's stomach was growing bigger. Too bad he wasn't a praying man, but he was ready to try most anything.

Then he saw it, unmistakably—Gar Girma—Mountain of the Goats. He knew where he was. He could relax!

He wiped the sweat off his face and promised himself a stiff drink when he got home where he could collapse.

As they landed at Blantyre, Bert turned to Gui. "Mr. Manieux," he said, "if you have any extra flights to make, I'd be glad to do them—any time. I need to earn a little extra cash—soon." Little—hell!

Gui nodded. "You are a good pilot, Bert,. I have several flights coming up, one to Salisbury before long. I will give you a call."

"Thanks," Bert said. *But where in hell am I gonna get ten thousand dollars by next week?*

CHAPTER 2

A Village Somewhere in North Central Africa

Saratu had not obeyed her mother. She ran out into the center of the grassy area in front of their compound as soon as she heard the sound of the aeroplane motor, retying the bright yellow scarf around her head as she ran. Her blouse and tightly tied braids were damp from the effort of grinding grain on the grinding stone, which was her daily job, and she hated it. She was delighted with the interruption.

She could clearly read the numbers on the wing. The only aeroplanes she had seen had been in books in school. Once in a while there would be one very high in the sky leaving a trail of white behind it. Saratu was fascinated with aeroplanes.

When the plane was almost overhead and quite low, she waved, and the plane seemed to wave back, dipping its right wing and then the left. *Who was flying the plane? What did he look like? Or did women fly planes out there in the Outside?*

She waved long after the plane was gone. Then she stood there for a long time, unmoving, staring at the spot where she last saw the plane. The plane represented what she wanted more than anything else in the world—to see the Outside, the world out there—to see it with her own eyes, and soon. Every other girl her age was either married or promised, but she had resisted it in spite of her father and mother's efforts to persuade her.

Saratu knew only that her homeland was a tiny spot in the middle of Africa—she had seen it marked with an X on a map in the village; it was never shown on any map in her schoolbooks. The elders of her tribe wanted it that way, fearful that outsiders would try to take away the gift given by the gods many years ago, the gift of good health and abundant crops. They gathered each day at sunset to thank the gods, at the spot where the gift had dropped from the sky leaving a huge indentation in the earth near their village. The elders still told the story of how the gods chose their tribe to receive this precious offering and how they were to safeguard it against all those who would steal the gift from them.

The aeroplane coming out of nowhere was like a sign from the Outside because planes just never, never flew over. Then and there she made up her mind that she really was going to see the world out there—the Outside. When she went to the Gathering Place for daily prayers, she would ask the God of the Earth to make it possible for her to do that. Maybe she would even get to fly in an aeroplane.

CHAPTER 3

March 2003 - London Heathrow Airport

D amn!" exclaimed the woman to herself. "Why don't they just bring up another plane instead of holding us here with the promise that the cargo door will be fixed soon!"

Malissa Taylor looked at her. "Might as well sit back and wait—there's nothing we can do one way or another." Malissa welcomed the conversation to relieve the boredom of waiting. She wished there were somewhere she could sleep, since it was already ten hours since she had turned off the alarm at three a.m. at her parents' home in Colorado. They lived a long way from the airport, and she could not afford to miss her flight.

Missing her flight might not have been so bad, it could have given her an excuse not to return to Africa at all. Instead, she could stay near her parents. They were in their sixties, and needed her; the temptation to stay near was very strong. Choices, always choices. She shut her eyes to staunch threatened tears of frustration, then hated herself for the lapse into self-pity. She was on her way back to Wamba and that was that.

Malissa scooted down in the hard, armless, straight chair, resting her head awkwardly on the unyielding plastic back. Part of her wanted to be left alone but another part wanted the companionship offered by this woman. Anything but the boredom of sitting around in this bare, noisy airport.

The woman said, "I just don't want to miss the flight from Rome to Nairobi. There's only one a day. I actually finished my business a day early, and I don't want to use it up sitting in airports."

Malissa looked at the attractive woman's face, the anxiety lines showing through her carefully-applied makeup. Her elegant, cocoa-colored tailored suit and peach silk blouse were set off by a single strand of pearls at her throat, and matching pearl earrings. Everything about her, down to the laptop computer bag at her feet, spoke of professionalism and poise.

Malissa noted the low-calorie health bar sticking out of the woman's purse. *Probably trying to keep her girlish figure.* Malissa didn't have to worry

13

about that. In fact, she was happy to have gained a few pounds while on furlough. The food in Africa was healthy, but certainly not high in calories.

A glance at the woman's expensive shoes made Malissa want to tuck her own sturdy walking shoes back under her chair.

"I'm going on that plane too," Malissa said, sitting up straight and self-consciously trying to pat her wayward waves back into place. Thinking about her complete lack of makeup, she suddenly felt dowdy in her wrinkled gray slacks, but where she had spent the last seventeen years, a mirror was seldom available, let alone having the time to use it.

"Do you live in Nairobi?"

"Actually, I live in Blantyre, but I have to finish up an assignment in Nairobi before I go on."

"Really, you live in Blantyre?" Malissa warmed to this woman, a white woman who lived somewhere in her part of the world. A fifty-year-old who obviously spared no expense on her effort to look thirty. Malissa liked the woman and wondered about the sadness in her eyes.

"Yes, I do," the woman said. "I probably would not choose Blantyre as my home, but Gui is there." A softness came into her eyes, obliterating the sadness momentarily.

Malissa felt a tiny twinge of envy. She would not object to having a man to return to, someone who changed the look in her eyes. But she had effectively prevented that. If there were eligible white men her age anywhere in Africa, they were certainly not in the small bush village she called home.

"You said you have an assignment in Nairobi. What do you do?"

From a side pocket of her purse, the woman pulled a small card which she handed to Malissa. "I'm Carol Walters, freelance writer."

"I'm Malissa Taylor. As you might suspect, I don't have a business card." She laughed ruefully. "Where I work I wouldn't know what to do with one. Do you write about Africa?"

"I live in Malawi when I'm not running around Africa and Europe or Asia," Carol said. "Periodically I have to return to London to meet with editors. Do you work in Nairobi?"

"Actually, I go on to Blantyre in Malawi. After Blantyre I have a day's travel by Jeep to Wamba country. I'm a nurse at a hospital there," Malissa said.

Carol looked at her with obvious admiration. "My mother wanted me to be a teacher and go to India or China, but I didn't want to. Actually, I don't think I could. I like to be around people. I don't think I could survive the isolation. How can you stand that?"

"Actually, I've been there seventeen years and it's become my home. I'm eager to get back."

"That's wonderful," Carol said. "How did you decide to be a nurse in the first place, and especially in this part of the world?"

Malissa didn't look at her as she spoke. "In college, I met a man whose dream was to be a doctor in Africa. I was to get my nursing degree and we would do it together." She stopped.

Carol waited. "And then?"

It had been years since Malissa had talked about this, and the sudden lump in her throat almost kept her from speaking. She swallowed hard and said, "I graduated with my nursing degree, and we were to be married when he told me he had changed his mind—about everything, including marrying me."

Gently Carol said, "But you are here."

Malissa nodded. "It seemed like a good idea—for seventeen years, but in a way I dread going back." she thought of how easy it was to speak of deeply personal matters with a total stranger in an airport.

"Why is that? Carol looked at her questioningly

"I am worried about the friends I have made there. I wonder how many have died while I was gone for three months."

"Wamba is in the drought area?"

Malissa spread her hands. "Drought, measles, whooping cough, dysentery, childbirth, snake bite, malnutrition, AIDS, the list goes on and on."

"But you should feel so good about yourself." Carol turned in her seat to look at her. "You are there doing something about it."

Suddenly Malissa was saying aloud what she had refused to admit to herself while she was with her parents. "I used to think that, but now I'm not so sure."

"Why is that?" Carol asked with obvious concern in her voice.

How could she explain to this woman how tired she was of the struggle against disease, death and loneliness? It would sound like she was whining.

"I guess I'm not sure I really am making a difference," she shrugged. "But if I had stayed in the States, how would I explain to people like Ladu and Yusufu? What would they think?"

"This part of the world is hard," Carol said. "I have the high-flown notion that I can do something about the problems of the world by writing about them."

"The pen is mightier . . . ?" Malissa smiled.

"Something like that, but the causes of the problems are so complex." Her eyes lit up again. "I'm just glad I have someone to go home to who cares as much about these things as I do."

"Your friend, you said, Gui, I believe, he . . . " Malissa began.

"My husband, Gui Manieux. I have kept my professional name, Walters."

Malissa looked away. The name Gui Manieux rang a bell. She had heard it before somewhere. Then she remembered the article in *Time* magazine in the African section. It said that Gui Manieux controlled the largest number of corporate farms in Africa. He was the man who held the life or death of millions of Africans in his hands as owner of Agricole Internationale. She had wondered if the person who wrote the story was just looking for something sensational to attract readers. The article certainly did not paint Gui as the caring person Carol did. In fact, it pictured him as a greedy man, counting success only in profits. Malissa wondered if Carol was aware of the magazine's description of her husband.

"It must be very difficult to try to deal with all those problems by yourself without a companion to go home to at night, share your day with," she said.

Malissa paused, thinking,. "I guess I am used to being the only one, so it doesn't — "

"Of course it matters, ":Carol interrupted. She leaned back in her chair and looked at Malissa considering, then sat up. " I know. There is someone in Blantyre you should meet. Bert McEwen. He's one of the nicest guys; he does contract flying for Gui. I think you two would hit it off."

"Don't even go there," Malissa said with a laugh. "I know this may sound strange, but I just don't have time to start a new relationship. My life is pretty hectic." She smiled ruefully. "And I can't quite imagine any man who would be the least bit interested in me."

"Nonsense!" said Carol. "Any man worth anything would appreciate what you are doing and who you are. But I can understand if you don't want to be bothered with the complications of having a man in your life. You seem pretty independent to me. You are used to looking after yourself and all those other people. But isn't it just an impossible job with the famine?" Malissa looked at the woman, a bit warily. She seemed to be interviewing her, but the obvious interest on the woman's face let her warm to one of her favorite subjects. "I believe hunger could be eradicated if only the lines of distribution were more effective. There are places that raise plenty of food, but their neighbors are going hungry."

Carol asked quickly , "Where, other than South Africa?"

"There is at least one area I know of that never has a crop failure and raises food year round, and they rarely get sick."

The words jumped out. "Where is this place?"

The loudspeaker blared announcing the flight to Rome. "We will load by seat numbers," the voice droned.

Malissa stood up quickly, throwing the strap of her bag over her shoulder. "My seat is in the back, so . . . " She turned to Carol. "Nice meeting you.

See you in Africa."

Malissa was sorry that the conversation had to end. Writers could influence what happened, and goodness knows, there were changes that needed to be made if illness and hunger were to be conquered in Africa. Maybe talking to Carol would have made a difference. If they were delayed in Rome, she would make a point of talking with her again. Malissa herself would like to know more about the small country that never has famine. Perhaps their methods could be used in other places.

As the plane touched down at Nairobi, Carol could think only of how quickly she could get a taxi to the hotel. She wished she had had more time to talk with Malissa. Most of all, she wished she could continue on the plane to Blantyre where Gui would be waiting. She had not made love for almost two weeks. Gui would be ready, as always, and so would she.

She grinned to herself as she hurried toward the baggage area. Who would have imagined that she would ever think about hurrying to go to bed with a man? It had certainly not been her style, not until she met Gui Manieux. She had had a good marriage, but it ended when Mark's plane crashed in Korea. She had been sure there would never be another man she would be even remotely interested in.

She had dedicated her efforts to excelling in her profession, winning prestigious writing awards and moving out on her own as a freelance writer. What she had said to Malissa was true – at one time. More than anything she had wanted to make a difference in the lives of the people she had seen and written about, the hungry, the poor, the sick.

Then she met Gui. It was almost like a fairy tale. The prince was handsome, wealthy and powerful. She knew she was smart, capable and dressed in designer clothes that hid some flaws, but she had always thought of herself as plain. The fact that this man actually wanted to marry her was almost beyond belief.

Gui was in a position to do something about all those things she cared most about, and incredibly, he loved her. They had been married for two wonderful years. It would be nice for Gui to meet her at the plane, but for some reason, that was just not something he would do. She would finish her work in Nairobi as quickly as possible and return to him.

In Blantyre, Malissa located the Jeep station wagon that had been left in the care of a missionary and awaited her arrival in the parking lot. She found the key to the car in her purse, and as soon as her luggage was stored in the Jeep, she headed across town to the narrow two-lane road that would take her back to Wamba and the familiar world of pain and famine. But at least she could usually do something about the pain; it was the hunger that made her feel powerless.

CHAPTER 4

Gui and Carol's home in Blantyre

That Monday afternoon the attractive young woman left in a taxi just minutes before Carol Walters appeared. Gui Manieux just happened to be looking out the window. In fact, he had been enjoying Danielle's abundant attributes by watching her walk from the front door to the cab. He was still reflecting on them when Carol's car turned into the drive.

Gui was so relieved at his narrow escape that he poured himself a gin on the rocks. Carol was not supposed to arrive until the next day. She would not have called from the airport because she knew he would not come to meet her. His method had always been to let the women come to him. He would never want to give them the impression that they were that important to him–- not even Carol.

She would not have been pleased to find him in bed with another woman. Thanks to his good luck, she would not know about his *diversions*. She might wonder if something was wrong when he declined to make love that night, but he would manage that somehow. Too bad that the years had slowed him down to no more than once in twenty-four hours.

But what was lacking in quantity was made up in quality. Slower love-making was certainly better. He had even discovered that the woman enjoyed it more at a more leisurely pace. At least, that was Carol's opinion. And he had come to value Carol's opinion above all others in the time she had been with him.

Of all the women he had met, known, or slept with over the years, Carol was by far the most interesting. She had taught him some things about love-making that he could not believe he had not discovered for himself. He was aware that not many of the women he had known truly enjoyed the experience, even though they usually said they did. He had never given it much thought. Carol insisted that a woman not only enjoyed sex, she appreciated the man who helped her enjoy it.

One reason he had invited the young woman who had just left was to test Carol's theory with other women. It was true. In fact, he had tested it quite a few times since Carol had explained it to him. It did enter his mind that over the years he must have missed many opportunities for increased enjoyment because of his own lack of concern in whether or not his partner liked it too.

But now that he understood; what he had missed in quality over the years would be made up. There had never been a lack of available beautiful women around Gui, and he had no reason to think it would change. Of course, Carol would always be the most important. He would make sure she knew that.

It had become vital that she stay with him. She had proved to be an invaluable asset. Although he held incredible power within his own circle, meeting ambassadors, artists, city planners whom Carol knew opened up a whole new world. Having access to that community had become crucial to him, and Carol was his key. As a correspondent for important magazines she brought influential people to their parties.

But more than that, in spite of her cosmopolitan air, Carol was basically naïve and took people at face value. She saw Gui as the handsome, intelligent, successful businessman that he appeared to be. She ignored the rumors about his personal life, assuming, of course, that he was no longer involved with other women. And the reports of his cruelty with his workers were dismissed out of hand, after all, she knew the true Gui Manieux.

Her declarations of love for him were real, and he drank in this first experience of real love. His only marriage had produced two children, and then four grandchildren. He had married because he wanted children to continue his family line. He was the only son. The marriage was wrong from the beginning; She simply did not understand his need for outside interests and they finally divorced.

His children insisted on sending him pictures of his grandchildren, which he tossed casually on a side table in the living room. He had little interest in offspring until they were old enough to go hunting. None of his children had visited him in Africa, but Brian, his grandson, now twenty and in college, had expressed an interest in working with him at Agricole Internationale in a few years. That was all the more reason to make sure that the company continued to do well.

It was not only doing well, it was doing extraordinarily well, especially now that food supplies for much of Africa were at such a premium. His corporate farms were a major supplier of guinea corn, peanuts, tea, coffee, and rice, the staples of life in every country in Africa.

He was the managing partner and the pay provided him with an adequate income to support the lifestyle that attracted the kind of women he wanted around him. There was always the wife or daughter of some prominent man who was pleased to go to bed with him. The young woman who had just left was daughter of the French ambassador.

Interestingly, his money was not what had attracted Carol. Carol was different. Hard to imagine, he thought, that one woman could be so different from all the others he had known. And she was almost his age! That was a surprise—he had always chosen women much younger than he.

He never tired of being near Carol, listening to her discuss her latest article for this magazine or that. And her childlike desire to "save the world," as she put it, was appealing. It was such a different concept than the one that motivated him. Not that he thought it was a valid reason for doing something—the real world was not meant to be "saved." His task was to keep the corporate farms producing, bringing in the money, and keeping control of the supply and the pipelines.

He told her a little about his work—very little actually. She had chosen to believe that he, like she, had a burning desire to help the poor in Africa. He had not told her any differently, he wanted her to stay.

Too many women in his past offered only a beautiful body—he wanted something more. Was that a sign of growing up, maturing at last, at sixty? That brought a momentary smile to his face. Whatever was the reason, he had everything a man could possibly desire.

The only thing he always wanted but never had, was the experience of making love with a woman who was a virgin. Somehow the thought of physically possessing a woman who had never had sex with another man was absolutely enticing.

It pulled at his thoughts at odd times. He would forget about it for a while, and then he would see a beautiful young girl, and the craving came back as strong as ever.

His housekeeper appeared at the door to his study where he was enjoying the gin among his considerable library of books and movies. "Miss Walters is here, sir. She says she will come as soon as she freshens up."

"Thank you, Flora. We will have dinner on the patio tonight."

"Esta bien, monsieur," Flora said without meeting his eyes lest he see the distaste there for what he was doing. Flora had been with him for twenty-five years and still insisted on the "sir."

She knew more about him than anyone alive, sometimes more than he wanted anyone to know. But in all those years, she had never so much as raised an eyebrow in judgment of anything he did. Jewels like that were hard to come by, and he rewarded her handsomely.

He heard Carol's steps in the hall and felt a twinge of desire but knew it would not happen. She would be disappointed. He would do something to make it up to her, although she would not know that was why he was doing it. She had a large collection of African art objects, collected over the years, he would add to it. She had some extremely valuable pieces in it, religious icons, and centuries-old handcrafted silver jewelry. What could he get?

He remembered her talking excitedly about a cross that was crafted out of a silver dollar, it would be a perfect addition. In the late 1800s Maria Theresa, of the Hapsburg dynasty in Germany and mother of Marie Antoinette, was commemorated on silver dollars which incredibly found their way to Africa. They were of little use to the Africans as currency, but were smart enough to turn them into profit. They pounded the silver into crosses of most unusual design and exquisite craftsmanship. Extremely rare, they brought a very high price. He would send out word that he was looking for one—at any price. Nothing was too good for Carol.

"Gui! I'm here!" The woman who sailed through the door on a wave of sensuous perfume took his breath away—again. Her exuberance, her joy, her own assurance that he was glad to see her. He wrapped her in his arms, and for just a moment he thought he might not have to make excuses tonight. Then he knew, alas, that it was useless. But there would always be tomorrow night, or maybe, just maybe, by about five o'clock in the morning.

CHAPTER 5

April in Mubi Village

In spite of the downpour of rain, Nomi did not stir from where she sat cross-legged in her compound with its mud huts and cornstalk fence, cradling the child in her arms, rocking back and forth. She was softly wailing the cry for the dead. Even if this shower was the beginning of enough moisture to grow a crop of guinea corn after three years of drought in the land of the Wambas, it would be too late for Kubili. Kubili, the name that was given every girl child when she was born; Anjikwi if it was a boy. To give a child a name of its own before it was two years old was to tempt the gods by daring to presume it would live.

Nomi grabbed the headscarf from her head and threw it away. Going bareheaded was a sign of mourning. Chilling, she pulled the shawl closer around her shoulders. She wore only a single wraparound cloth.

Nomi caressed her baby and began a lullaby in a husky, hushed voice. The lifeless form across her lap hardly looked like a human, with eyes sunken and skin stretched tautly across her bones. The hair changed from black to a reddish tinge, sure sign of end-stage malnutrition. For days the baby's cry had been like that of an animal.

Without enough food for Nomi herself, the milk in her breasts had failed, and there was nothing else for an eighteen-month-old child to eat. Dokwali, her husband, had gone everywhere, begging, searching for food, stealing it if he had to. But there was little to steal.

She had taken Kubili to the mission hospital. Miz Tayluh, the nurse there, had been so kind, giving her powdered milk. And she had mixed it for the baby, but instead of the usual amount, Nomi had doubled the water to make it go further. And she did not use boiled water as Miz Tayluh had instructed. Nomi didn't understand why the water should be boiled, and without much food, she had little strength to walk the several miles to gather wood for a fire.

And then the inevitable diarrhea took away whatever life left in the baby's body, and she died quietly. Even if the rains came, they would have no seed to plant—they had eaten it long ago.

Dokwali had gone to summon their families. There would not be a prolonged crying, not for just a child. There were so many deaths these days. Near their compound gate in the cornfield, another grave would be dug, near those of her other two children who had died from lack of food and from illness. For one it had been pneumonia, the other measles. It was true, she reminded herself, that the Wambas fertilized their fields with the bodies of their children. She was so numb that even that thought did nothing to alter her stare.

Dokwali paused in the gatehouse to summon his courage. How could he go through this—again? How could he face Nomi with another dead child in her arms? Nomi had been the prettiest girl in the village—at least he thought so, and she had consented to marry him. Him! But he had failed her. She depended on him to provide for her and the children, to grow enough grain to feed them. It was not his fault that the rains did not come for three years, yet it was a man's job to look after his family.

There was one thing he could do! The Defenders found food for those who joined them. Violence and lawlessness had never been considered in his family, but he could not go through this again!

He walked resolutely to Nomi's side. "Nomi! I'm going to do something about this—I'm going to join Usaman. He—the Defenders will make sure we don't go without food again!"

Nomi turned vacant eyes toward him. Unless she had food, good food, and soon, she too would die. She had not told him that her body was double—she was pregnant again.

CHAPTER 6

Blantyre, Malawi

D amn!" Bert McEwen repeated it with his fist against the fuselage of the
Cessna 172. "Damn!" If he were a praying man, he would be lighting
candles in the church. As it was, Bert was talking out loud, not to God, but
to his airplane. He and his airplane spent much of their time alone together,
and he carried on a conversation with her as usual. The African sun had
already turned his Kansas tan several shades darker, so he went to stand his
lanky frame in the shade of the plane's wings to ponder his dilemma.

It was three o'clock in the afternoon, and he had just returned from flying Gui Manieux in from Nairobi. He had pulled up near the passenger exit
because Gui was in a hurry to get home as he had been gone for several
days.

As always, Bert had given his plane a checkup before leaving it at the
airfield. "Couldn't you have waited a month—just one month to threaten to
blow your engine—until after I fly Mr. Manieux to Zimbabwe? It isn't even
time for your engine overhaul. Well, maybe just time. But look how I take
care of you! With this kind of TLC you should go another twenty, twenty-
five hours—easy!"

He glanced in the direction of the Cessna, patiently waiting for him to
find the money to buy her. This one just had to last until he could put the
deal together.

He removed the billed cap with "Potgeter's Elevator, Holcomb, Kansas"
written on it and tousled his sun-streaked brown hair to start the sweat dry-
ing. There was a permanent dent in his hair where the hat band went around
his head. The heat was oppressive, and he fanned himself with his cap for
cooling, while talking out loud.

"I can probably get by—by the skin of my teeth, if I put in a new gasket.
But the handwriting is on the wall—something major is going to have to
happen, and I don't have the time to fix this one, nor the money to buy the
Cessna." He frowned and sighed. "Maybe it's time I go back to Kansas and

find a job flying crop dusters again." He smiled wryly at the sweat-stained cap in his hand. "Anyway, it's time to get a new one of these."

And maybe, he thought, now that he was going to have to make some decisions, he should give some consideration to going back to the States to look for a woman to marry. Living alone was okay, but not as good as having someone there when he came home. Somehow he always thought it would happen, just naturally, but it never did. And he was getting older by the day.

He laughed. Who was he kidding? He was not going back to the States to live—he was not going back to the States to look for a wife. He loved Malawi, he loved Africa, he loved flying in Africa.

So, instead of running away to the States, he would go lie on the beach of Lake Malawi and watch the bathing suits. It was a poor substitute for having a woman of his own, but it was the only place in Malawi where a woman was allowed to wear anything less than a skirt covering her knees. No trousers for women either. Only people in tourist areas were allowed to wear shorts or bathing suits.

He liked the idea of having a wife, but the possibility of finding one in Africa was so remote as to be out of the question—not because there weren't women there, but because Bert was not the type to look for them. Once in a while one would find him, but she was never the kind he would consider marrying. And he never responded to their offers—sex should be only between people who had mutual respect—and, if possible, love.

"Not like Gui Manieux," he said aloud. "That man never seems to have enough women. What kind of a life would that be?" And with a wife like Gui had, who needed to look elsewhere? Bert had met Carol and was impressed with her charm and intelligence. It was just one more reason to detest Gui Manieux.

As he caught sight of his face mirrored in the side window of the plane, a slow grin spread over his face. The magazine article had also listed him as one of the most eligible bachelors in east Africa. He had always thought of himself as homely. His craggy face was deeply tanned below the bill of his cap; his intense deep-set blue eyes were usually smiling. He couldn't imagine any woman being attracted to him. He might be tall and lean, but so were scarecrows. His wrinkled shorts and almost-white T-shirt had never seen an iron and never would.

He hadn't sent the magazine article to his mother. He knew what she would say—that he should do something about being a bachelor if they were to ever have any grandchildren from him. Fortunately, his sister had two children.

He shouldn't have bought the house. It was a good deal, it was a great house for him, and he felt settled at last, but it took all of his money. He should have kept his savings for expanding his business. He was in this mess today because he needed a better plane, one with up-to-date instruments, more cargo capacity to take supplies where they were needed, airlift people whose very lives depended on him.

Now, incredibly, the plane he needed so badly was suddenly available at a give-away price. The late-model single engine Cessna Cardinal had everything he needed. One hundred and eighty to one hundred and ninety knots per hour with excellent fuel requirement. What especially appealed to him were the four-foot-wide doors that made entry to the low-slung cabin easy, even for patients on stretchers and medical equipment. Visibility from any seat was excellent. Its bright blue and yellow markings made it stand out among the other drab planes—and easier to spot if he went down in the bush. And it had the one feature absolutely required for bush flying—Short Takeoff and Landing configuration —with STOL the special wingtip offered a priceless capability for short airstrips in the bush as well as the need to get off the ground quickly in case of emergency.

The next most important feature was the very latest in instrumentation. If he had had that plane, he would not have gotten lost.

He had tried out the avionics but was itching to get his hands on the Flight Situation Display for real. It was a Pentium-based computer, showing maps, weather and traffic on a sharp color display. And the Global Positioning System was a must in his work. The present owner had been obsessed with the new technology and even had installed a Traffic Collision Alerting Device—hardly a necessity in the nearly empty skies of eastern Africa but it might alert him to other dangers.

An opportunity like this would never come again. He had to buy it now. He had talked with the seller the day before. The man was going through a divorce and needed to sell the plane quickly in order to give his wife half of the value in cash.

Ninety-six thousand American dollars was less than half of what it was worth. The owner would hold it for a week so he could come up with ten thousand dollars as down payment; the remaining money would be due in ninety days.

He was in Malawi to fulfill a dream. His father was a family physician in a small Kansas town who had always dreamed of going overseas to help sick people.. With a family to raise he never made it, but he urged Bert to become a doctor and fulfill the dream. Bert could not imagine sewing up holes in people or holding their head while they vomited. He liked airplanes. But the dream of the father was firmly implanted in the son. He had come to Africa with the plan to set up a successful charter business and then offer aid to doctors and hospitals in the bush country who needed his services.

At first his father had been skeptical until Bert showed him the number of clinics that were scattered around in east Africa. Before long, his father was talking about taking a few months off to work in one of the African clinics. His mother cried when he left but told him to find a nice daughter of a diplomat to marry. She made it plain that she wanted grandchildren.

He had talked with two banks, but they were not optimistic. It wasn't that he didn't earn a lot, bush flying paid very well. Perhaps hiding his earnings in order not to pay taxes on it had not been such a good idea. He could not prove his income.

In his mind, he already owned this plane. He thought about it all of the time. It was the one way he could be what he needed to be—not just some bush pilot flying rich old men to make yet another deal and another buck. He could be the pilot who flew desperately sick patients to decent medical care. He could save lives. He could enlarge his business, fulfill his dream of flying for the bush doctors and clinics, and be soaring in the most beautiful plane in the world.

Aside from his loftier ideals, what he wanted more than anything else in the world was a really good plane of his own so he could develop the best private flying business in central Africa. As it stood now, he could barely touch the need for air transportation. With a better plane, he could make a real impact, and start flying emergency flights for the missionaries.

He slapped his cap against his other hand. "Just when I thought this plane would last until I could manage to buy a different plane." He did some figuring in his head, muttering. "Three thousand dollars for an overhaul. If I could pay for it by the month—or borrow at the bank. It would take probably a week at least to do the overhaul—while I have no income. Besides, I really need a different plane, one that can carry more, go farther." The Cessna would do very nicely. Then he would keep this plane as a back-up and for smaller jobs.

The "Damn!" slipped out again forcibly, and he started walking back to the airport office. It was not very much out of the way to go by where *his* plane sat in its tie-down spot. He walked all the way around it, slowly touching it lovingly here and there. It was pure torture, to want something this badly. But there wasn't a chance in hell that he could come up with the money. He turned away.

A cool one at the bar in the Mount Soche Hotel would soothe his pain. He could visit with some of the men he knew—a couple other pilots and some of the town's businessmen. It was also the meeting place of the inter-national set—men and women from all over the world who had reason to be in Malawi, but were looking for companionship. One thing he had learned in Africa was to expect the unexpected. Who knows—he might even meet someone who had money to invest.

CHAPTER 7

Pennsylvania State University

Clayton Worthington, Ph.D., M.D., stared out the open window of his office at the campus below. It felt good to go without a jacket in the early spring warmth, to roll up his sleeves. He was glad he was not required to wear a tie.

Vivid flowering plum trees rained petals in a shower of lavender, and a sweet muskiness from the pure white blossoms of pear trees floated up to him on a light breeze. Students at the Pennsylvania State University at University Park were changing classes, walking without haste in the warm sunshine. But Clay did not really see any of them. He had a problem.

Somehow he had beaten the odds all his life. Without a father, but with a mother who believed he could do it, he excelled in school. He made it into college, then medical school, then a doctorate in genomics, and finally Assistant Director of the Genome Research Department at the Pennsylvania State University. And all that in spite of the fact that he was black.

But for several months now he had been spinning his wheels. The three point two billion genes had been mapped, and now each research department or medical research company was staking out its claim on a specific section of the genes. It was the most sensible way to do it. And incredibly, there had not even been much dispute about who would get what.

There had been some heated discussions here and there, but there really was enough work to go around, so they divided it up. And the Pennsylvania State University had its share, but for some reason, it had not excited him. They were working on Chromosome 16 which was involved in polycystic kidney disease. He should be interested in it as more African-Americans had the faulty version of the gene than others. He was doing his share of the work, but something was missing, he wasn't even sure what it was. He had been accused of looking for fame, but he knew himself better than that. He wanted to make a difference, not just in the kidney research, but something bigger, something unique, out of the ordinary. Common gene research had been fascinating and exciting in the beginning. It was still interesting and certainly valuable, but lacking excitement.

Was he jaded, merely tired of doing the same thing over and over? The work was so theoretical. He had the idea that there were examples of the effect of gene modification in everyday life. That was the kind of research he wanted to do.

So far his idea was strictly a theory, and until something showed up to support his theory, he would keep doing his job, but he would keep his eyes open. In this field of research surprises happened all the time, and if you weren't looking for them, you could miss them, until someone else pointed them out—too late. He wanted to get there first.

Perhaps he should have done what his friend, Jim Harris, had done, gone off to Africa where there was need for scientists. They could help where it was needed most—where people were dying of all kinds of illnesses, genetically-caused conditions among them. Jim kept telling him to come at least for a visit, but he never had. Maybe he should. He might get a different outlook on the world.

After all, it wasn't as if he was tied down with a family. Marriage just never seemed to happen for him. He never wanted to put a woman through the struggle he had experienced, and now that he was reasonably well off financially, he didn't know how to go about finding a wife. Sometimes when he was alone in bed at night, he wondered if it had been worth it.

CHAPTER 8

The Farm, Agricole Internationale, Blantyre, Malawi

The huge sign at the entrance to the compound was impressive *Agricole International.* The office building just inside the gate had several offices. The one for the General Manager, Gui Manieux, was elegant with a mahogany desk and chair inlaid with ebony and teak. Heavy burgundy wine-colored velvet drapes kept out the sun, and indirect lighting gave the feeling of pleasant coolness in contrast to the African heat outside.

Gui Manieux was taking five. As always he had arrived for work early, about seven o'clock, instead of eight o'clock when the others would show up, and now at ten o'clock he was ready for a cigarette and a little reverie. He poured out a glass of one of his favorite French wines from the decanters on the credenza, took it back to his desk and leaned back in his comfortable chair with his eyes closed.

As General Manager of Agricole Internationale, he divided his time between the corporate farms in Zimbabwe, Kenya, and Malawi. But he always spent the last of dry season and the coming of the rains in Blantyre.

Malawi was his favorite country in Africa, and it was home for him. With Lake Malawi running almost the entire length of the country, the climate was usually pleasant with a light breeze, even in the hot season. Unlike most African countries, this one had an abundance of food and the lake clean enough for swimming or boating, and especially the delicious chambo, the lake trout for which Malawi was well known all over east Africa. Expatriates living or working in Ethiopia to South Africa came to Malawi for vacations.

He sipped the wine and let his entire body slowly relax. He had learned an important lesson, crucial in doing business and in making love, his two favorite pastimes. "Do not rush it." It was wise to let things happen as they would, without trying to force them. An unforeseen event could turn into an opportunity.

He had to admit he had learned that bit of wisdom the hard way. That was not to say that hard driving and determination had not been the major factor in his being a millionaire by the time he was thirty-five, and now without doubt one of the most influential non-Africans in east Africa. But over the years, he had discovered that he had fared better by letting events happen in their own time rather than forcing things to happen on his schedule.

This method was being sorely tested right now as he needed desperately to find a breakthrough in the technology of food production. Agricole Internationale, had always been far ahead of all others in production and control of food commodities, but because of the widespread famine in Africa, due as much to failing governments as to the weather, the United Nations was committing millions of dollars to the problem. Rumor was that they would set up their own farms or merge many smaller food production companies into a large conglomerate. That kind of competition could be disastrous.

Gui smiled wryly. He and his partner, Roger LeFever, had had it all their own way for a long time. He did not really think there was any danger of their being out-classed, but he could not take chances. Such threats only spurred them on, making it necessary to tighten production and be on the lookout for new and better ways of doing the job.

It was a well-guarded secret that they had reached the top of their production capacity. Any improvement now would have to come from improved technology, or a miracle, Gui thought, wrinkling his brow in contemplation. He was on the lookout for either one.

Now he laughed out loud. Carol would probably tell him that "if you see it coming, it isn't a miracle. "

He realized again how vital she had become to his life, her philosophy, her optimism, and just as importantly, her body. He could not believe he had finally found someone who really cared about him with a completely trusting, childlike affection.

That had not kept him from spending the night with a favorite *diversion* in Nairobi. But that was different. Old ways died hard. And women were just part of conducting business. He enjoyed the variety and was always careful to use protection.

He remembered the day he met Carol. He had been complaining very loudly about a delayed flight out of Nairobi when Carol had appeared, equally upset about the delay. That time he had violated his own rule about letting women come to him first and approached the very pretty woman. Usually he never even gave woman over forty a second look, but Carol was different. She was not interested in him, did not know who he was and did not care.

The outcome of that had been that he rented a plane so that they could go to Blantyre together. That was when he met Bert, which had also turned out to be a lucky break, because in his business, a qualified and dependable bush pilot was indispensable, but hard to find.

Meeting Carol was probably the best thing that had happened to him. She was attractive, but there was so much more to her than looks. In addition, through her contacts as a writer for various business magazines, she knew all the important people on first-name basis. She was a valuable asset to his endeavors. And most of all, she believed him. She had been so angry about the article in *Time* about him that she refused to work for that publication.

Unlike other women, she was not particularly impressed with who he was, and she was not interested in having sex with no strings attached. The only way he could have her was to marry her. He did what he had never thought he would ever do again—get married. Persuading her had not been easy, and he had made promises. Most of the promises he had kept, except for one. He felt a little guilty about that, but not enough to stop.

However, he did have to be careful. In spite of the fact that Carol did say she loved him very much, he believed her when she said she would never stay with a man who slept with another woman. For the first time in his life he wanted something so much that he went to great lengths to keep her believing that he was the devoted companion. He knew she also believed he shared her same fervor for saving the people of this continent. That was important to her. It was one reason she had married him. She refused to believe anything that did not support her belief in him. He hoped fervently she would continue to do that.

To his surprise, he discovered Carol truly enjoyed lovemaking, which had made all the difference. For the first time since his divorce he had been with a woman for more than a year and still anticipated seeing her, like a young man with his first love. Life did not come any better than this.

With a wife like Carol he wondered why he kept going to other women, even seeking out young girls. He had to admit their supple bodies turned him on, that he enjoyed their inexperience. But sometimes there was crying afterwards. Treating sex casually could turn ugly. If only he could give it up.

He had decided that there were not very many virgins over eighteen, at least not in the society in which he moved. And now, to be realistic, it probably would never happen. But as he drowsed with the steady hum of the air conditioner, a beautiful young girl walked toward him, smiling, her arms outstretched. In his dream he did not wonder that she was black.

CHAPTER 9

Gui stood up, stretched and walked over to a window that overlooked the complex. When he pulled back the velvet curtain, what he saw transformed him instantly.

He grabbed open the door and yelled for his Japanese foreman who was just coming out of his office across the compound. "Yahara, get in here!"

Yahara came on the run. Gui was behind his desk when Yahara came in, closing the door behind him.

"Yes, Mr. Manieux?"

"If you cannot do your job, I will do it for you!"

"What . . . ?" Yahara began.

"I saw the men stealing grain!"

Yahara, the short, heavily tanned, muscular foreman stood in front of Gui. There was a defiant look in his eye, obviously considering his options.

Then dropping his eyes, Yahara said, "I will take care of it, Mr. Manieux." He strode resolutely toward the doorway, stopping just long enough to greet the man coming in the door. "Good to see you, Roger." He would never call Gui by his given name, only Mr. Manieux, but Roger was different— kinder, more human.

"Problems?" Roger LeFever leaned against the door of Gui's office as he coughed, a handkerchief over his mouth. He had come from another office just down the hall.

"Sorry," Gui said, "I did not mean to disturb you." The conversation continued in English, in spite of the fact these two Frenchmen had known each other since childhood. English was the everyday language of Africa.

"Time for a break," Roger said, straightening. "Running figures through the brain for hours dulls it—a short rest resharpens it."

"You know there is a bed in the bedroom here in case you would like to lie down," Gui said. "You can even stay here. It has all the amenities."

Roger knew why Gui kept a bedroom ready and did not wish to use it. He dropped heavily into the upholstered chair in front of Gui's desk and waited expectantly for a reply to his question concerning the confrontation with Yahara. Though the same age and long-time friends, the two men could not have been more different in temperament. Roger dressed casually, not particularly concerned about style, liking the comfort of shorts and T-shirt. Gui was wearing a cream-colored long-sleeved silk shirt and chocolate brown trousers. He never wore shorts.

Roger was fair-skinned in contrast to Gui's dusky complexion, declaring his Germanic background compared to Gui's Latin heritage. Roger was of slight build, almost fragile, moving without haste.. Gui too was slender but with obvious strength and quick movements.

Gui was slow in speaking. "Just be glad your job is cooking the books, Roger. Getting people to do the job on these farms is difficult to say the least."

"I thought you liked your job."

"I do, at least the part about making things grow, and figuring out how to take out more money than goes in. And I like living in Africa, but . . . " Gui stopped.

"But what?"

"Every time I get a foreman trained, he either decides to quit or he becomes chummy with the workers, and the profits start walking out the gate."

"This time . . . ?"

"This time the damned foreman does not have the guts to fire the men he found walking off with their pockets full of wheat."

"Pockets full?" Roger thought about that. "How much would that amount to?"

"What difference does it make how much? If they will take a pocketful, they will take a sackful."

"Oh, I see your point."

Roger was thoughtful, and Gui stared out the window.

"What happens to the men, I mean, they must need the jobs if they steal food."

"They are paid for their work—they can buy food. They will have a choice, be flogged in front of the rest of the workers or lose their jobs."

Roger grimaced. "I'm glad I'm not hungry and work here."

Gui strode around his desk, stood in front of Roger and shouted, "I have not noticed that you objected to the money you get from this operation! You do your job, and I will do mine!"

"Sorry, sorry! I was out of line." Roger pushed back against the leather chair. "You are absolutely right. The books look great, and the profits are up seventeen percent over last year."

Gui's tone was only slightly less brittle and as he spoke he became more animated, his voice getting louder and his words faster.. "If this famine keeps on, and it certainly does not show any signs of slowing down, the next months will see francs pouring into our bank accounts like you have never seen before!"

Gui's face was now flushed, and as he talked, his eyes darted everywhere as if his brain were disconnecting from his body, and his body quivered with excitement. "Some people think the way to get rich in Africa is with diamonds. They have come to me, offering to get me in on the riches of diamonds. But they do not know that something as mundane and everyday as food is really where the fortune is to be made."

He turned back to Roger, his hands waving in emphasis. "And I . . . we have it all right here in the palm of our hands. It has already started. People will come begging to us for food, because we are going to have it all tied up."

His face changed, and he sat down in his chair as he gave a hard laugh. "The only thing that could change that would be if the damned United Nations insists on sticking their nose into it as they are threatening to do, or a miracle—like someone discovering how to grow manna on thorn bushes."

Roger hurried to say, "You just keep on doing your job this well, Gui, and I will try to do mine."

Gui's voice softened slightly as he leaned forward. "I wanted to ask you, Roger, if you were feeling all right. You do not look very well. Anything wrong?"

"Just a cold that I can't seem to shake, several months now. It'll improve when I get back to Strasbourg, it always does. The mountain air, I think."

"How long do you plan to be here in Malawi?"

"A week, as usual. I have done a week at each of the farms in Kenya and Zimbabwe. I just came from Harare. The fourth week is for Strasbourg."

" That is a pretty rugged schedule.. "There must be some nice woman in Strasbourg, or in one of those spots, that you would like to spend more time with."

Roger did not look at him. "No, I'm really quite happy, like this."

"How about dinner Tuesday evening? Carol is back from her trip to London."

"You two are still together? That's great. She's an exceptional woman, Gui. Why don't you keep this one around." It was not a question. As he stood up to go, the cough returned. When it subsided, he said, "I will look forward to a very pleasant evening. Carol never lacks for stimulating conversation. I gather she is stimulating, in every way."

Gui just smiled.

"Well, I'll get out of your way, so you can take care of business." At the door he turned around. "I just finished my estate plan, Gui. If anything happens to me, this operation becomes yours."

Gui stared after him in puzzled surprise.

CHAPTER 10

Back at his desk, Roger sat in thought. He knew that Agricole International would never have become the mega company it was without Gui's skill and determination, but sometimes he wondered if he should be more involved in some of the management decisions. With the negative criticism of corporate farms that frequently circulated, they needed to be especially careful.

Gui's talk of controlling the food supply of Africa made him distinctly uneasy. Power had never been something Roger desired. Money, yes. He loved it, never seemed to have enough of it, but he would be content with the money without the power to go with it. He knew what Gui's answer to that would be. They had argued over this many times before. Gui would say that you couldn't have one without the other.

Thank God for Carol, at least she was there. There had been many women for Gui, none whom he bothered to mention to Roger. So when Gui introduced him to Carol, he could not believe that he was actually serious about a particular woman, especially one who was almost as old as himself. But that this charming, cultured, intelligent woman married Gui made a difference. Roger had sensed a change in Gui during the past year, which he attributed to Carol's presence. He assumed that she did not know all there was to know about Gui, and Roger would be the last to tell her.

CHAPTER 11

After Roger drove away later that afternoon, he stopped outside the foreman's office and went in.

" Yahara," Roger said when he entered the office. He closed the door behind him. "Looks like things are going well." It was a question.

"Well, I have to say, you know . . . " Yahara was weighing his words as if deciding how much to say. "I thought I knew all the ways to get the most out of workers, but Mr. Manieux, he's got 'em all beat. It's even hard for me to — "

Roger interrupted. "Is the job worth more than we are paying you?"

"Mr. Manieux pays good wages."

This was Gui's part of the operations, and Roger left it up to him. Moving closer, he asked, "Could you make my usual contact for me?"

"Of course. Markus will be glad to see you."

"Good. It is always a pleasure to come to Blantyre." He held out an envelope. "I thought it ought to be a hundred this time. The rest is yours. He's worth it, and I appreciate your discretion."

"Of course, Roger, of course!"

CHAPTER 12

Asta's Village in Kulanji

Asta studied the face of the troubled woman before. They stood behind a cluster of hibiscus bushes, sheltered from the view of people coming from Tuesday market in the Kulanji region. Kwarfaku's eyes were bright with intelligence, with cheeks rounded and full from fifty years of more than enough food, hair neatly and smartly braided in the current fashion. Large silver ornaments were at her throat and dangled from each ear. Her wrap-around zhebi, with matching blouse and head scarf were obviously expensive. She looked what she was, a wealthy, well-provided-for woman. The Kulanji women were proud of being smart, healthy, and attractive at any age.

"You are the only one who can do something about it, Asta." Pain and pleading were in her face.

The two women had been friends since childhood. They had always shared everything. Kwarfaku had become the chief's first wife; Asta's husband was on the chief's counsel and very influential in the tribe. The clothing Asta was wearing was every bit as elaborate and expensive as Kwarfaku's. And they shared something else. Kwarfaku's son, Pindar, was courting Asta's daughter, Saratu.

"Kwarfaku, I just can't believe Chief Inuwa would really consider this. Has he actually told you that he is getting rid of you?"

"Of course not. He tells me he is sending me to visit my family, with many gifts, of course. Then in a week or so he will send word that I am not to return to Bri since . . . " Her voice faltered. "I am being replaced." The last was barely audible.

Asta wanted to go right to the chief's compound and shake her fist at Inuwa. It was unfair! Kwarfaku was the chief's first wife, bearing his first child when she was sixteen—he had been a mere farmer's son then without even a farm of his own. Kwarfaku produced five more healthy children, along with training each succeeding wife as they came along. And now the chief wanted a new wife. But by decree of the Council of Men, he could have only four at one time. Since Kwarfaku seemed to have no inclination to die, in fact, was hale and hearty, his decided to get rid of her by deceit.

"What will happen to you?" Asta asked, grasping the other woman's hands.

"I will be given a house in the compound of my brother."

"Will you be allowed to see your children—and grandchildren? They can visit you?"

The other woman nodded, then spoke. "He is getting rid of me only because of the number of wives he wants. He must say that I performed a disgusting act, or broke one of the taboos. That is what I am crying about. Whatever he says will be untrue, and it is so unfair!"

Asta pondered the seemingly impossible situation. Women did not make the rules in the land of the Kulanji.

Kwarfaku exploded. "I'd just like to tell him to — !"

That triggered an idea. Asta grasped Kwarfaku's arm. "I think I know what to do! It's never been done before, so you will have to be very strong and very brave. Can you do that?"

"Whatever you say, just tell me! I do not want to leave under these circumstances.'

"Give me some time, tonight, to think it through. We'll meet in the morning at the well. Come early before the other women get there."

Kwarfaku gripped Asta's hands. "I knew you would know what to do!"

"Don't tell anyone, Kwarfaku! I'll do my best, but I can't guarantee we will get away with it."

"You can do it, Asta, you can do it!"

The "you can do it" stayed in her ears as she walked back to her compound, bowing in greeting to dozens of people on that busy market day. They thought she could do it because she had, over and over.

There was a medical dispensary and an elementary school because she had not given up until the Council of Men agreed. But perhaps this would be the time when she would fail, or worse, her own husband would finally say, "Enough, no more battles for the betterment of children, or the tribe, or now, women."

Well, this was a battle she would not retreat from. She had her own personal reason for wanting to win this one—a daughter who was being courted by the young man who could well be the next chief.

CHAPTER 13

United Nations Headquarters—New York

The statistics were devastating. Seventy-five thousand people would die this month from starvation. Another half million would die from Acquired Immune Deficiency Syndrome, AIDS. But Tomiko Hirokama had a greater problem—he just might lose his job—if he didn't do something about either or both of those other problems half a world away.

Just six months ago he had been hired as Special Assistant to the Director of the World Health Organization with a very special assignment. ,He even had lunch with Harara Oboji, the Secretary General of the United Nations. Mr. Oboji made it clear that Tomiko's task was to persuade as many countries as possible to do something about the number of people dying from starvation. And he was to coordinate international research on AIDS in order to slow the tide of destruction from that fatal illness.

Tomiko's usual studied calm was replaced with convincing enthusiasm as he responded, "I know I can do it!"

The Secretary General was so impressed that within the week the United Nations had designated fifty million dollars for Tomiko to *do it* with. It was such an important assignment that Tomiko was to report directly to Mr. Oboji himself.

The teeming city of New York lay beyond his window in the United Nations building. Not really different from any other big city in the world. Since he had become Special Assistant, he had traveled extensively to see first-hand the starving and the dying in countries around the world. Of course, he stayed at the best hotels and ate at the most expensive restaurants. He told himself he needed to see it all if he was going to do the job right.

He was Special Assistant to the director of the World Health Organization more by mistake than by design, or merit. He and Tomako Harakama worked in the same section of the United Nations International Children's Emergency Fund —UNICEF. Tomako, as program director, had a corner office and was in charge of millions of dollars in relief to children all over the world, while he, Tomiko, an accountant, sat in a room without windows and kept track of the money that came and went.

Not only did the American personnel director think that all Japanese looked alike, she couldn't keep the Japanese names straight either. When Tomiko was nominated to be Special Assistant,, he had a feeling that someone had made a mistake, but when he discovered the truth, he decided not to challenge fate, and kept his mouth shut. The personnel director was too embarrassed to admit her mistake, and besides, Tomiko was much better looking than Tomako. Tomako was even shorter than Tomiko and wore the thickest glasses the personnel director had ever seen. Somehow those were important differences.

Not that Tomiko was not capable of doing the job; he just could not muster much real sympathy for the recipients of the UN's charity. He himself had been born in one of the poorest neighborhoods in Tokyo and had been hungry lots of times. But at a very early age he had promised himself that he would be so successful that no one would ever think of him as poor again. He made top grades in high school and college; he married the right wife; he lived in the right part of Tokyo; he had the right friends. And now he was an important person, a very important person. He did not want that to change.

There was only one person to whom Tomiko ever revealed his real feelings—Matsuko, his wife. He was absolutely confident that it would never go beyond her.

Shortly after he was appointed Special Assistant to the Director of the WHO, at the evening meal in their New York apartment that looked out on Central Park, he told Matsuko, "They keep asking me what I am going to do about the countries where the relief supplies that we send are stolen by warlords and either sold or used by the people who already have food. I tell them that I would cut off all shipments to those countries. If the people who live there can't control their own neighbors and leaders, how do they expect the UN to do it?"

Matsuko nodded emphatically.

"And I am going to stop sending tractors to those countries. Hand-hoed farms make the most sense. Tractors require gasoline and repairs. I think we should send short-handled hoes, the kind people all over the Third World use. When they have put aside a little money, then we will let them buy oxen so they can increase the size of their farms."

Matsuko nodded again.

"And corporate farms. Some governments keep trying to make the owners give them back to the people they were taken from. I am in favor of letting them keep on producing food, but it is time for the United Nations to enter food production. A little competition will be a good thing."

Matsuko did not ask how he knew all these things. She just refilled his teacup.

What he did not tell her was the fact that he really had no idea how this was going to happen. As usual, he would go to the Shinto shrine again today to ask for help from a higher power. It might require a miracle.

"I will be gone next month to a conference in Zimbabwe. Representatives from all over Africa will be talking about ways to feed the starving people. I sure hope they come up with something I can use."

"I'm sure they will if you ask them, dear," Matsuko said.

CHAPTER 14

At the Kulanji Border

M ari stood a head taller than Dokwali, whose arms were pinned behind him. The metal badge on Mari's shirt pocket poked the prisoner's ear. The badge said "Chief: Kulanji Border Patrol."

"Where did you catch him?" Mari asked.

"Just beyond the stone tree," replied the border guard.

"Did you really think you could sneak into Kulanji territory?" Mari shook him. "Were you that dumb?"

"My family... they haven't had anything to eat since . . . "

Mari interrupted. "Well, you obviously don't know the rules in this country. Even if you succeeded in getting past the guards who are stationed everywhere along the border, you would get no food. No one, *no one* in Kulanji will give away food."

"But you have more than you need!"

"Our farms do better than the rest of the country, but we raise just what we need and a little extra." Mari stopped and then went on. "I'm curious, why did you choose that spot to try to get through?"

Dokwali looked away, as if he were not going to answer, and then pulled himself up proudly. Maybe if he were honest, they would still give him some food. "They told me it would be useless to try, but when your family is out of food . . . So I checked it all out. Your country is shaped like a leaf of the Lalia tree, pointed at the top and spreading out wide at the bottom, about half as wide as it is long. I know because I walked every step of it. The spot I picked looked like the best place because there are good hiding places, and no one can guard it all the time."

"So why did you get caught?"

Dokwali frowned. "I was just unlucky."

"Where are you from?" Mari tamped down his temper. Protecting their borders was a tiresome job.

"Mubi, in Wamba."

"There's a truck from Wamba picking up a load of grain today. Should be back through here before long. Maybe you can talk them out of some of it."

The hungry man who had been slumping suddenly stood up straight. "Maybe I can! It would be the only way to get any food. But if it reaches our country, the Defenders will probably steal it."

"Why doesn't someone do something about it?" asked the guard.

"They have guns."

The guard gave a knowing glance at Mari. "In Kulanji we don't need guns to make people do what they are supposed to do."

"Yeah?" Dokwali asked eagerly. "How do you do it?"

"Anybody who leaves the country, lets someone come in, or gives away food without permission is marked with a sign on their forehead and shunned for six months. No one in the whole tribe will speak to them or have anything to do with them. They might as well be dead."

"Is it really true that no one gets *kariya* in your country?" Dokwali asked.

Kariya, AIDS. Mari nodded, "And we are going to keep it that way. These rules have worked for generations. In fact, no one has been marked as long as I can remember. No Kulanji is going to break the rules. So tell everyone you know not to try to get into Kulanji country. Do you understand?"

"But . . . " Dokwali's words were interrupted by the roar of the truck approaching the checkpoint.

The truck lumbered under its weight, brakes squealing as it slowed to stop in front of Mari. On top of the bags of grain and vegetables, four men were perched, each holding a carbine. The driver slid out of the cab, papers in hand, and walked to where the three men were standing.

"What are you doing here, Dokwali?" the driver asked, recognizing him.

There was no answer.

The driver went on. "I thought every Wamba knew it was useless to try to steal food from Kulanji."

"He isn't very smart," the border guard said.

"Just hungry," Dokwali replied testily.

"Come on," the driver said, "you might as well ride with us." He looked at Mari. "Okay with you?"

"Sure, he can go," Mari replied.

They started toward the truck, but Dokwali turned and addressed Mari. "I know you Kulanji think you're better than the rest of the world, with your good farms and your good health, but if I were you, I wouldn't be the guard at this checkpoint—at least, not without a gun. One of these times, someone is going to take your food without asking."

CHAPTER 15

The hospital in Mubi

Malissa Taylor leaned against the doorjamb, every part of her body begging for rest. It was four in the afternoon, but she had been called in the early hours before dawn. This was the fourth delivery that day and it was not going well.. She had been back from her three months of leave for only a few days, and it was as if she had never been gone. She felt exhausted.

Very few of the Wamba women had prenatal care, and they appeared on the hospital's doorstep to deliver their babies with a hemoglobin of eight grams, a gutful of parasites, and a husband who demanded that the baby be a boy. At least the husband also arrived with a dozen chickens either in hand or on order from someone in the village. These were to be eaten only by the new mother, one each day for the first ten days. More recently because of the famine, the tradition had reduced the chickens to two or three, if the husband was lucky enough to find that many.

Even though this woman had been in labor for twenty-four hours, the baby had been delivered safely, but the mother was exhausted. She had nothing in her blood to stop the bleeding, no clotting factor. An iron-poor diet made it so. What she needed was blood, whole, pure blood. The lab technician, actually a man with a fourth-grade education and some training from Malissa, had taken the blood sample to type it. He would be back with the blood type soon, and maybe they could give a transfusion, maybe.

Malissa walked out onto the hospital veranda to look for the family. A group of two women, one with a baby on her back, and a man were seated on the cement among headloads of cooking pots and half-gourds holding food supplies. The older woman was no doubt mother of the woman who had delivered. The young woman was a relative who came along to do the cooking for the patient. Speaking in the Wamba language, Malissa addressed the man. "Are you Lemsu's husband?"

"Yes."

"The baby is fine—a boy. Your wife lost much blood before she arrived here. She is very weak. Will one of your people give her some blood?"

She knew the answer before she asked, but she always hoped that one day, after seventeen years of asking these people, one would say yes.

Each of the three persons shook their head. To give blood was the same as giving away their souls.

At that moment a Landrover roared into the hospital compound and screeched to a stop beside the small mud-block building that was the dispensary, sending the line of waiting patients scurrying to safety. A uniformed man was at the wheel. Malissa recognized the uniform and gritted her teeth. If the people who governed this town had any guts, they would outlaw the so-called *Defenders*. They defended nothing except their own families and terrorized the rest. Now why had this one come?

She walked the short distance to the dispensary as the man pushed his way through the line of people to where a hospital worker was measuring out pans of guinea corn, one to each family. Malissa recognized most of the people in the line, many of them she had delivered, them or their children.

The Defender yelled, "All right, that's enough. No more grain today!"

Malissa was furious. Who was he to interfere with the hospital?

"You! Dokwali!" Malissa said. "What do you think you are doing?"

"We need food," he replied without looking at her.

She was standing beside him now. "So do all these people. Stand in line for your share like everyone else!"

Suddenly Malissa was pinned by Dokwali's arm, unable to move and scarcely able to breathe, the muzzle of his gun thrust under her chin. "You can't keep me from getting food for my family!"

The crowd gasped in surprise and outrage.

"Leave her alone!"

"That's Miz Tayluh!"

"We need food as much as you do! Take your turn!"

Dokwali twisted toward the last speaker, growling under his breath. Unwilling to release the gun in order to turn it on the last speaker, he yelled, "Shut up!"

Furious now, Malissa said firmly, her words strained by the pressure on her throat, "Dokwali, stop this! I delivered all of your children. What do you think you are doing?"

"Getting some food, what does it look like?"

"Violence is not the way to do it!" Malissa said. She didn't think he would really shoot her, but she stood perfectly still, not wanting to give him any reason to think otherwise.

Finally he looked at her and said through clenched teeth, "My children are all dead—because they didn't have any food! That's violence enough for me!" His voice dropped to a whisper, "And now Nomi is pregnant again."

Malissa's gaze did not waver, and slowly Dokwali lowered the gun. Then turning but still brandishing the weapon, he grabbed up two pans, filled them with guinea corn, then strode past the crowd toward his vehicle.

One voice followed him. "Why don't you go to Kulanji and get food? They've got plenty!"

"And get killed?" he shot back. "I'll be back, here!"

CHAPTER 16

Asta's compound in Kulanji

"Mama, are we having tomato sukwar again? We had that last night." Saratu replaced the cover on the cooking pot over the fire. She stood, hand on hips, awaiting her mother's reply, a petulant frown on her face.

The warm aroma of spicy tomato sauce wafted upward. The sun was down behind the cornstalk fence, allowing the small breeze to bring a bit of coolness. The compound was neat and furnished with comfortable chairs and colorful woven hanging cloths, evidence of prosperity.

Busy stirring the guinea corn mush, for just a moment Asta considered not replying at all. Then she remembered that she had promised herself to be more patient with this seventeen-year-old part-child, part-woman. "There were just enough tomatoes for one meal. If I left them another day, they might spoil, and tomatoes are too valuable to waste."

"There are plenty more in the market," snapped Saratu.

"For a price," her mother replied steadily. "Only people who have dry season gardens have tomatoes to sell, and they are very expensive."

"I would rather have meat sukwar."

Asta gritted her teeth and said, "You know very well that meat is available only on market day, and that isn't until tomorrow."

"That's not true. If you really wanted some, you could find it. The canteen man often butchers in the middle of the week."

Asta could not hold her composure any longer. "The fact is that I don't want to find any meat," she said sharply. "There is nothing wrong with tomato sukwar to go with our diva tonight."

At that point Saratu's father stepped out of his house. He was wearing a long beige robe. He had changed from his shorts and shirt which he wore for work in his field. "Saratu, there was a young man, about your age, who was caught the other day trying to sneak into Kulanji to steal food. He said he was getting it for his children who had no food. I wonder how he would feel about having nothing but tomato sukwar to go with the mush for supper tonight."

51

"Let him have it!" Saratu said, under her breath. Giving her mother a withering look, she tossed her head and walked away. She did not dare challenge her father.

Yamta shook his head. "Asta, the other children were models. How did we get a child like this? Just today, I was talking with some men near the canteen when Saratu walked by. One of the men said, 'Yamta, that girl is a beauty.' And someone else said, 'Where are you going to find a man handsome enough—or rich enough—to marry her?'"

Yamta poured water into a large gourd and washed his hands, then sat down in his chair near the fire to await his food. As were most of the men in the Kulanji tribe, Yamta was tall, muscular, and strong. His beard was naturally scant, needing to be shaved only periodically. As one of the Elders in the tribe, he chose to retain a small goatee on his chin.

Asta shook her head. "Unfortunately people have been saying things like that to her ever since she was born. She has come to believe them. She may be old enough, but she certainly isn't ready to get married. She deliberately prepares food wrong and then says she doesn't know how to cook, so she won't have to do it. She is just plain lazy."

"Well," Yamta said with a grin, "at least we won't have to worry about coming up with a bride price very soon."

Asta laughed too, but she said, "I would not object to turning her over to someone else." She was quiet for a few moments. "One of my goals in life was to be a good wife and mother. I may have to find a new aim since I seem to have failed at this one."

"Let's not give up on her, or you, just yet," Yamta said. "I think you've done a good job, and whose opinion is more important than mine?" Their eyes met in a warm glance.

"There is someone else who thinks you do a good job," Yamta went on. "Chief Inuwa wants to talk to you about something he has in mind."

"Like what?" Asta stopped in the act of stirring the mush

"I'll let him tell you."

She laid down the stirring stick and stood in front of him. "Yamta, tell me!"

He said nothing.

She was pensive. "I don't know what I could do, I don't have any skills."

"No skills! You taught yourself to read; you can give a speech at the slap of a croc's tail. Everyone in this clan comes to you because they know you will do something about the problem, or collapse trying. A strong woman can be an asset or a liability. The chief is just smart enough to use you instead of trying to silence you."

"Oh!" She returned her attention to the diva. If the chief knew what was about to happen, he might not be so positive. Perhaps she should let Kwarfaku find her own solution to her problem. But Asta had promised. Even if it meant losing the chance to have an important position, she could not let Kwarfaku down.

She smiled at the thought of what she was going to suggest to Kwarfaku. This was going to be fun! Asta did enjoy a good battle, especially when it was fighting for someone who needed help.

"Things in this part of Africa are going to get much worse before they get better," Yamta was saying. "We've got ample grain reserves for our own people and some to spare, but there is a limit to that supply. The first rainy season grain won't be ready to harvest for at least two months, and the word from the Outside says there are thousands of people already out of grain. It's a rare day that someone doesn't try to sneak through the border."

"Do you think there will be violence?"

"The chief thinks so. He is doubling the guard on the border, and guns are supposed to be issued to the guards, maybe within the next month."

"What are they saying about that disease that is killing so many people," Asta asked, "I forget what they call it."

"*Kariya*, the name comes from some tribe east of here. It means 'the journey from which no none returns.'"

"Have they found medicine for it yet?"

"I don't think so. The United Nations has called a conference of all African countries to talk about food and *kariya*. Kulanji could send a representative if we wanted to."

"Did they ask us? I'm surprised. We have always tried to stay as remote from the Outside as possible."

"No, we weren't asked, but Chief Inuwa does hear about those things from the chief of the Higis, who he makes a point of keeping in contact with. He told Chief Inuwa that everyone is urged to send someone to the conference."

"Will we?" Asta walked over and filled a cup with water from the tall clay pot.and set it on the ground near Yamta's chair.

"I don't think so. It has always been our policy that the less contact we have with the Outside, the better off we are. There is a specially called council meeting tomorrow night to talk about it. The chief wants some help in making the decision. There are people who say we ought to be in on the decision-making since whatever happens will inevitably affect us sooner or later."

Using a gourd paddle, Asta dipped a portion of thick guinea corn mush into a half-gourd and then ladled the savory tomato sauce over it. Using both hands, she offered it to Yamta.

"I guess when Saratu gets hungry enough, she will come to eat," Asta said.

Yamta laughed. "She probably won't. She likes to pretend she is the one in control."

Yanta waited until Asta had served her own meal and had sat down in her chair near his. Then he lifted his arms and raised his eyes as he recited the centuries-old litany. "To the gods who have given us good food and good health, we give thanks. We will be neither greedy nor stingy but will repay these blessings by helping those in need and preserving the inheritance that is ours."

They each broke off a piece of the thick mush with their fingers and dipped it into the spicy tomato sauce. They ate in silence for a while.

"Yamta, why do you think our land is different from all the rest?" She had asked this question before.

"You know the legends as well as I do, Asta. The gods of the earth and sky chose this spot to bless. No one knows why; no one knows just how it happens, but from what the chief tells us, our guinea corn produces far more grain than other countries do. It grows taller, produces more and is virtually free of disease or insects. We can even grow guinea corn in dry season, which is impossible elsewhere.

"Many years ago while other tribes were being destroyed by hunger and disease, our ancestors were healthy, and because of that they were able to develop a vast workable system of irrigation. They began to add other crops and fruit trees that helped to keep us healthy. And for some reason, we have never acquired kariya. All I can say is, I'm glad I'm on this side of the border."

"I haven't heard from Ladu for months. I wouldn't be surprised to hear that she is coming."

"We will know when your sister reaches the border since absolutely no one passes without permission, especially these days, not even relatives."

"I can't remember when her baby is due. If it is soon, perhaps she won't come this year."

"From what I hear, Wamba is as hard hit by the famine as the rest of Africa is, so don't be surprised if she shows up, pregnant or not."

"It will be good to see her."

CHAPTER 17

Carol stopped abruptly and retraced her steps. As she was leaving the bathroom, for some reason she glanced back as something unusual caught her eye. On the floor a shiny object was caught in a nook under the sink. She picked it up, a lipstick. Definitely not her brand or color, and certainly Flora would not be putting on lipstick in that bathroom. Flora cleaned these rooms once a week, on Fridays. This was Tuesday. The lipstick had been left there in the last few days.

She closed her eyes and leaned against the wall. This confirmed her suspicions. Gui was bringing another woman to their bedroom while she was gone. The sigh that slipped from her was painful. It had been too much to hope for.

Years ago she had given up on having the one thing she wanted more than anything else, a lasting, loving relationship. She was sure she had found it in Gui. He seemed so completely delighted with her. He shared problems and successes in his business, something he apparently had never done with a woman before.

She had heard of this man before she met him, one of the most powerful men in east Africa. His reputation was of getting what he wanted without regard for other people, but his gentleness to her told her that people did not know the real Gui.

He was considered the most eligible bachelor in non-African society, never wanting for female companionship. After their chance meeting, he pursued her to Europe, finally persuading her to marry him. Not even her best friend would believe they had not gone to bed together before the wedding. Carol had explained that this was that rare pure relationship that superseded sex.

She was supremely happy. Gui was completely dedicated to her, not wanting them to be apart any longer than absolutely necessary. And at last she had found someone who shared her desire to do something about hunger in Africa, as well as AIDS; the two plagues which were killing off whole generations all over the continent.

As a writer, she wrote articles to explain or persuade, but he was where the action was, on the front lines of food production. At last she felt a part of the real effort to do something about the most serious problems facing Africa.

Lovemaking with Gui had been an unexpected plus. She assumed he was well experienced, and she was surprised at the things he did not know about a woman's body and about lovemaking, but she was a patient teacher, and he was an avid learner. She could see herself growing old with Gui, when lovemaking might happen only occasionally. It was a relationship of mutual joy and respect.

The old saying that a woman didn't care how many women a man slept with as long as she was the last, certainly was true for her. But there was the other side of that saying, that a man didn't care how many men a woman slept with as long as he was the first.

And now someone else's lipstick in the bathroom. Was Gui still looking for that *first* experience?

"In this day of AIDS, I am not willing to share my body with a stranger— and that's what it amounts to!" She said this aloud. Instead of easing the pain, it only pushed it deeper where it hurt more. In Africa, the disease was no longer that of only homosexuals or of just men. It was crossing all barriers.

Gui was out at the corporate Farm. His partner, Roger LeFever, was in Blantyre for his week's visit to the project and would be with them for dinner that evening. She wandered aimlessly through the mansion of a house, not even wanting the ease a drink of whiskey or gin might give her. She didn't want her mind dimmed. She wanted to keep the anger, but most of all, the pain of betrayal. He knew how she felt about AIDS and about a committed relationship.

Part of her wanted to pack her things and leave; the other part cared too much for Gui to give up. If she demanded that he not see other women again, what would he do? More important, what would she do if he refused, or worse, if he agreed and then did it again?

In the sunny kitchen she found Flora preparing a papaya for the dinner salad. Flora had known Gui longer than anyone. Carol needed someone to talk to, and there were things she wanted to know, had to know.

"Flora, tell me about Gui's mother and father. Did he have a normal happy childhood?"

"What is normal, what is happy?" Flora responded in slow, precise, heavily accented English, her hands moving expertly as she neatly cubed the papaya.

"What was Gui's childhood like?"

"Miss Carol, I have never ever talked about Mr. Manieux' personal affairs with anyone."

Carol interrupted. "Oh, I don't want you to . . . "

Flora didn't let her finish. "Gui could be my own son, but, it's time to talk about it. He has never mentioned his real mother. What I know I learned from his Aunt Nicole who visited a couple times. His mother died when he was three years old, at the birth of his little brother. The baby died a month later. The father was absolutely stricken, could not cope with caring for the little boy, and he just disappeared. Left Gui with another aunt."

"How sad, but still, he had a good home." It was a question.

"I have seen many children like this—after the war. If they lose their mother or father, they never really get over it. They live the rest of their lives being afraid to love anyone for fear that person will leave them like the mother or father did."

"And he lost both mother and father," mused Carol.

Flora nodded. "It is beginning to happen, again. Whenever a woman begins to get too close, he pushes her away, and looks for someone else. I know the signs. Gui wants love more than anything in the world, but just when it looks as if someone will love him, he pushes her away for fear she will leave like his mother did. And sure enough, she leaves, just as he feared."

"But why would he take such a chance, when we have such a great relationship?"

"I think he is pushing you, daring you to leave him."

Carol nodded. "I have a dear friend who had great emotional trauma, abuse, when she was ten years old. Her counselor explained that emotional development is stopped at whatever age the trauma took place. They remain that age emotionally for the rest of their lives, unless something just as traumatic happens to change it."

"Then Gui is five years old," Flora said.

Carol nodded her head slowly. "Five years old. He is still looking for the love he lost."

They both remained silent, staring into space, pondering the man they both loved.

Finally Flora spoke. "Of all the women who have come and gone in his life, you are the first one who has made a difference. You are nearer his age. All the others were little girls. You've been with him longer than anyone."

There was no point in holding anything back. Carol held out the lipstick. "I found this in the bathroom. It is not mine."

Flora nodded, pain in her eyes. "It seems to be the way of men."

Carol interrupted. "Not my man. Not the man I give my life to. I was alone for twenty years, and I can do it again. I do not want to die of AIDS because Gui can't control his appetite."

Flora nodded. "It may be the one thing that will finally make him change. He does not really want to lose you, of that I am sure."

"I am not hopeful. It may already be too late, but I am not quite ready to give up." She laid her hand on Flora's. "Thank you for being honest with me. Having someone else who knows, someone to talk to. Maybe we can . . . " She did not finish.

Flora nodded, relief in her face. "I hope so."

There would not be a chance to talk about it that evening since Roger would be there until late. Carol resolved to put it out of her mind until there was opportunity to discuss it calmly. Could she ever be calm about such a thing?

CHAPTER 18

In Kulanji village

Asta placed her hands firmly on Kwarfaku's arms. "Are you absolutely sure you want to try to do something about this situation, Kwarfaku? You could make matters worse."

"I am absolutely sure."

The two women were sitting on the seat next to the well. It was early, the sun was just coming up. They had come early but the other women would be coming for water soon.

"I've got an idea, and I will help get it ready. But you are the one who will have to stay the course until the last head of grain is threshed. I can't do it for you. I can't even be there when you do it."

Kwarfaku paused with a frown of uncertainty. "What do I have to do?"

"Well, here it is." Asta watched Kwarfaku's face as she spoke. "You are going to deliver a statement to Chief Inuwa saying that you no longer want to remain in his compound."

Kwarfaku interrupted, "But that is just like the decree of divorce."

"This is different. Instead of accusing him of terrible things, you say that you have accomplished your tasks as his wife, and list them. First wife to the Chief for twenty-three years, nourished five children to adulthood, prepared three other wives to be acceptable mates to the Chief. You feel that you deserve the reward of a comfortable old age. You then list your requirements: a house of your own in your son's compound, a yearly allowance, retain the title of Wife to the Chief, only it will be 'Retired Wife.'"

As she talked Kwarfaku's face became more and more animated. Now she burst out. "That's it! That will work! It will give him a way out and give me everything I want!"

"And," Asta added, "it will introduce a new era for women in the Kulanji tribe. It means instead of waiting for the men to decide our fate, we take our futures into our own hands."

Kwarfaku jumped up, clapping her hands. "That is so reasonable, so, so . . . "

"So right," Asta supplied.

"Why haven't women thought of this before?" Kwarfaku asked. She held her hand to her head, as if it were too much to take in.

"I guess they just weren't ready," Asta replied.

Kwarfaku sat down and said earnestly, "It was because they didn't have an Asta to show them the way."

"Let's just hope it works, Kwarfaku. Let's meet at mid-afternoon at the Garden, and we will compose it together. You will write it by your own hand. But you must be prepared to take complete responsibility for it, be ready to answer any question. You must be absolutely sure of yourself, or your husband will find an unguarded spot in your armor to shoot arrows at."

Asta paused, waiting to catch Kwarfaku's undivided attention. "And you must never say that you had help to do this. Can you do that?"

"Yes, Asta, yes, I can do it!" Kwarfaku grasped Asta's hands in her. "I can do it because I feel in charge. Not like I did, waiting to let something happen and feeling powerless. Asta, you've given me back my life!"

"No, Kwarfaku, it was not mine to give. You are taking back your own life."

"Maybe so, but if you had not demanded that girls be taught to read and write, I would not be doing this now."

"You were a fast learner," Asta said. "Now use what you learned."

The two women hugged in joy.

CHAPTER 19

It was almost impossible for Carol to concentrate on setting the table, arranging the flowers, handling all the minute arrangements for a lovely dinner. She had taken special care with the menu, finding lean pork chops in the market and having Flora prepare them with ndrum sauce, a local cherry. They would have candied yams and some wine she had brought from London.

It would be a difficult evening, especially since she usually looked forward to Roger's coming. Their conversations were always stimulating. The man had been everywhere, seen everything, knew everybody, or so it seemed. She had chosen a floor-length flowered sheath dress because she knew Roger would notice what she wore. Gui seldom did. Once she had asked him what kind of nightgowns he liked. He said, "The kind that come off easily."

Again she found herself staring at nothing. Her mind was going back over the past days and weeks, remembering little things. Like Sunday night. Making love was always especially pleasant after she had been away. But Gui had told her he wanted to wait until the next morning, something about making love at sunrise. It was supposed to call forth special hormones that early in the morning. But they had both slept until seven, and he had hurried off to the Farm.

Damn! Why did she let it get to her like this? Gui had made promises to her, and in return she had made a commitment to him. She had not realized how much of a commitment until now. She had found that which was the most important thing in the world to her, a relationship to which she could give unconditional love.

She gave, and he accepted, then treated it as an unimportant gift to be used when he felt like it and conveniently forgotten when he wanted to. She had been stupid to let it happen! She has wanted a good relationship so much that she made herself believe that this was it. Well, she would do something about it, and immediately!

But not tonight.

At five-thirty the telephone rang. Carol answered it since Flora was busy in the kitchen.

Gui was breathless. "Roger has taken suddenly very ill. I am at the hospital.

"I do not think it is a heart attack. It did not act like a heart attack.. They are examining him now."

"I'm on my way!"

At the hospital Carol found Gui in the waiting room, distraught, unable to sit, pacing the floor.

"How long have you known Roger?" Carol asked.

"Forty-five, fifty years. Too long to lose him now." Carol was quiet, waiting for him to go on. Talking might help. "He understands me. I'm . . . difficult to work with, but he lets me do things my way, as long as they work."

"And you do a good job."

Gui nodded. "Roger watched the money; I watched the farms. It was a good partnership." Gui ran his hand over his face. "They are trying to revive him, but they think it is too late."

"Oh, Gui, no!"

"That is not the worst." Gui stopped pacing and motioned for her to follow him through the door into the hall of the hospital. He led the way to the emergency room and pointed to the small window in the door. "This Seventh-day Adventist hospital is well-equipped and efficient. Three American-trained doctors and state-of-the-art equipment."

Carol had been in enough hospitals to recognize that the activity in the room was not normal. A doctor and two nurses surrounded the table on which Roger lay. One nurse was checking gauges, the other was monitoring body signs. The difference was the way they were outfitted. The gloves looked different, heavier than the usual rubber gloves, and on their heads were helmets. The scene resembled something from space travel.

The doctor pointed to the EKG monitor mounted above the table and said something. The nurses stepped back away from the table, and the monitor above the table was blank.

"He is gone." Gui said almost inaudibly.

They walked slowly back to the waiting room. Carol said nothing, only held on to Gui's arm. In a few minutes the doctor came. He was no longer wearing the helmet or gloves.

"I'm sorry," he said, "there was nothing we could do. But he was one of the lucky ones. He could have gone on for some years and died a slow, painful death. At least the hemorrhage in the lungs did it quickly."

Carol still had not grasped the significance of what she had seen. "Doctor, what — ?"

Gui interrupted. "He had AIDS, Carol. That is why all the special equipment."

Carol turned disbelieving eyes to the doctor.

The doctor nodded.

CHAPTER 20

Hospital at Mubi

If she felt one more abdomen full of worms, Malissa thought, she would just walk out and never come back. She had seen so many that she could diagnose the condition even without the laboratory report.

She glanced up to see the next patient, and she knew there were worse situations than a stomach full of worms.

The young woman sat down in the chair across from Malissa and eased her baby from her back to her lap, then pausing to cough a deep hacking cough.. Immediately the baby began to fuss, and the mother offered the ever-ready nipple. As the baby suckled, he followed Malissa with his eyes.

"How are you feeling now?" Malissa asked, knowing the answer.

"Tired. Tired all the time."

"How is your cough?"

"I try not to cough because it hurts, but sometimes I can't help it."

"Does it hurt to breathe?"

"Some of the time."

Malissa thought, at least it was not yet all the time. Should she tell her at this visit, or wait?

Pretending to be writing notes on a card, Malissa gave herself time to consider. Laraba, daughter of Ladu and Yohanna. was one of the first babies Malissa had delivered when she came to this hospital, almost eighteen years before. Her mother, Ladu, from the neighboring Kulanji tribe was healthy, never ill, and gave birth to the healthiest babies Malissa had seen among the Wambas. But now Laraba had kariya, AIDS.

Perhaps she should tell Ladu first. She and Ladu had become friends, as close as an American and a Wamba woman could be. Ladu was able to understand complicated explanations of how the body functioned and what made it sick or well. Then Ladu could pass on a simpler version to the other women. Many times Ladu had given personal information about this woman or that, so that Malissa could better understand the problems. Ladu often sent women to be in Malissa's prenatal care classes.

This kind of situation was not what Malissa had in mind when she volunteered to come to Wambaland as a young woman just out of nursing school. If anyone had asked her then what she could accomplish in seventeen years, she would have told them that all the people would understand about health care and preventive medicine. Mothers would deliver healthy babies, and there would be native nurses to take over the hospital.

Oh, her goal to save lives had not changed. The list was long of people who returned with a gift every year because she had literally saved them from any one of numerous deadly illnesses in this country.

And it wasn't that she had saved all who had come. She had failed many times but had come to accept her limitations.

But this problem was not due to her limitations. It was because of the refusal of a society to return to the standards of morality and safe sex practices required if the family unit was to be preserved. It wasn't that she had not told them—she had, over and over. But it was always in a class she taught to the women. The men were not there to hear, and would not have listened to a woman anyway. Unless something was done, an entire generation of young people would be wiped out.

But it was not an entire generation she had to face at that moment. It was one beautiful young woman who sat before her. She had to be told. At least Laraba had a strong mother to go with her through this.

Malissa steeled herself and said, "Laraba, you know what is wrong, don't you?"

Laraba looked away and then nodded. "Kariya." Her lips formed it rather than spoke it.

Malissa had to ask the next question, she needed to know. "Where did it come from?"

It was a rare Wamba woman who had sex with anyone but her own husband. Laraba's mouth contorted in pain as she tried to speak, but only jumbled sounds came.

"Your husband visits the House of Women."

Laraba nodded. Then her words came in a rush. "I refused to sleep with him when I was pregnant, so he went somewhere else. I should have . . . "

"No, Laraba!" Only with great effort did Malissa control her outrage. "No! It was not your fault! After two miscarriages, you had to be careful. You did what was best!"

Laraba just kept shaking her head.

CHAPTER 21

The Funeral in Blantyre

Pallbearers in black suits sat near the coffin in the Catholic church in Blantyre, Malawi, awaiting their appointed duties. Yahara was one of them, along with others. Some were familiar to Carol, some not. Ceiling fans slowly moved the warm air, giving a sense of coolness. But Carol felt her black dress dampening with sweat. Her hair under the black lace scarf was moist.

"Roger LeFever and Gui Manieux, two of the most powerful men in the world." She had heard that much of a whispered conversation as she waited in the foyer for Gui to come from parking the car. Now with Gui beside her, she wondered how powerful he felt at that moment.

She had not been able to bring herself to talk to Gui about the other woman since Roger's death two days ago. Gui went around as though he were paralyzed, not talking, not seeing. That morning she had a call from London requesting that she return immediately for an emergency meeting. Her talk with Gui could wait until she returned in a few days.

Gui stared, seeing yet not seeing. He had been in shock ever since Roger's death. Funerals were something to be avoided, yet here he was, telling his friend goodbye.

The priest from Roger's home parish had been flown in to conduct the funeral Mass. Roger had never admitted to having gone to church, but Gui had noted a St. Christopher medal on a gold chain around Roger's neck. Religion was another subject they had never talked about. People could go all their lives and never talk about the most important things, he mused.

Well, he was thinking about important things now. That casket bearing his partner and friend gave him a feeling of vulnerability he had never experienced before, ever. He had always had a pretty good idea of where he was going and how to get there. Now he was questioning his destination and the journey.

Carol's hand moved over to touch his, and he took her hand in both of his. All his life he had been hoping for someone who would care about him, stay with him. Not just a few minutes in bed, but really care about him. But he never got past the first sexual high before he had turned to another woman. Some of them would have stayed, but he was afraid; Afraid that if he showed them he cared, they would leave him, and he would experience the terrible anguish again. If he was the one to make the decision, it was less painful.

But Carol had not left. In spite of everything, she was still there. He had found someone who did not want to leave him. But, he was risking losing her! From the beginning she had made it absolutely clear that she would share his body with no one else. Not only because of AIDS, but that was reason enough, she said.

There was no one there that day to truly grieve for Roger, other than himself and Carol. The others were there for different reasons. What if it were he, Gui, in that casket?

The answer was incredibly simple, so simple that he almost laughed aloud. He still had time to make a difference in his life, to put the emphasis where it belonged, on the woman who cared about him. From that day on there would be no woman but Carol! Carol felt his body tremble and glanced at him with a question in her eyes.

This radical move would not come as a result of a late-blooming religious conversion; at sixty years old he had no fear of the hereafter. It was the now that mattered most. Nor would it be because his prowess had declined. In fact, he had often been told by women who should know, that his hardness was like that of a twenty-year-old. Nor was it that his desire had diminished. Far from it. While inspecting the tea farms in Malawi, or the coffee farms in Kenya, or the peanut farms in Zimbabwe, a pretty girl, or even one not so pretty, could stir longings that left him weak—as always.

The simple truth was that he was scared, scared of dying—from AIDS, of course, but more afraid of dying without anyone there to be with him. He could not risk losing Carol. There would be *no more* sex with anyone but Carol!

He gripped Carol's hand and held it so tightly that she looked at him in alarm.

When he walked past the casket with his friend now still, he spoke silently, "Sorry it had to happen, Roger, but you may have saved my life."

CHAPTER 22

Mubi Village

L adu was on her way out of the hospital after having her blood pressure checked by the African nurse and getting a supply of pills, something to improve her blood for the baby she was carrying, the nurse had said. Ali, her ten-year-old son, had gone with her to get their share of grain from the truck that came once a week when grain was available.

Suddenly, a motor truck, a small one, came into the hospital compound carrying a strange contraption in the bed of the truck. It pulled into the center of the compound, and two men got out. One man placed a hollow thing to his mouth and began to speak.

"Listen, everyone, listen! Come close and listen!"

People began to slowly edge toward the man. Ali had returned with the pan of grain and was standing with Ladu. Ladu took the grain and motioned Ali to go closer.

"You have nothing to fear," the man continued. "We are here to teach you how to stay healthy. Come close!"

Quickly there was a crowd around the little truck. The second man jumped up onto the bed of the truck and removed a covering from what looked like a wooden statue.

"You all know about the disease called kariya, that no one recovers from. Kariya is carried from one person to another when they sleep together and have intercourse. We are going to show you how to keep that from happening."

The two men had been trained in how to best present the information. There was no point in talking about AIDS as no one would recognize it.

Now the crowd gathered more closely, pushing against the truck. The statue seemed to be a huge finger mounted on a platform.

The man continued. "The way to prevent the spread of kariya is for the man to use something while having sex since the disease is spread by way of the fluid coming from the man's body."

He turned and pointed toward the statue. "This is a man's penis. Putting a rubber piece of cloth over it will keep the fluid from reaching the woman. Like this."

With quick motions the man who was not speaking unfurled a cloth bag and brought it down over the large statue, securing it tightly at the bottom.

Then the second man held up packages of condoms. "We will give these to you free if you will promise to use them whenever you have sex. Will you do that?"

Cries of "Yes, yes!" arose from the crowd as women and men alike pushed closer to get their package.

"And you can buy more very cheaply in your local canteens," the man said.

When it appeared that everyone had been given a package of condoms, the men covered the figure in the truck, waved goodbye and drove away.

Ladu had watched it all, not missing a word of the explanation. She had sent Ali up to get another package of the condoms. She would give one to her husband and the other to her daughter, Laraba, but she had the uneasy feeling that it was too late for Laraba. Something about the way she looked— pale and tiring so easily— worried Ladu, and the gossip in the village was that Laraba's husband had been sleeping elsewhere.

Ladu started walking away, but Ali had stopped to talk with a friend.

Suddenly another truck turned into the hospital compound, though this one was in a hurry and slid to a stop near where the grain was being distributed.

Two men jumped out, each with a gun.

"Defenders!" Ladu said under her breath, looking around for Ali. Her heart stopped as she saw Ali very near the men with guns, and in fact, looked like he was going to speak to them.

"Ali, come here!" she cried.

The Defender used the butt of his automatic carbine to send Ali flying through the air to where he landed in a crumpled heap in the dirt. Then the Defender, not much more than a boy himself, wearing a tattered khaki uniform, stood over the child, his gun raised above his head to bring it down again. The little boy cowered, speechless in terror.

"Dokwali, stop!" In one swift movement, the second man, also dressed in faded khaki, snatched the gun and punched the Defender in the stomach with the butt of it. He doubled up in pain. "It is not your job to hurt children!" the older man said.

The Defender gasped for air and dropped to his knees.

"Give you kids a gun and you think you are in charge of the whole world!"

The man pulled the young Defender to his feet, propping him against the wall of the building. The older man's uniform was in somewhat better condition than the young Defender's, and his gun was shiny, obviously new. "You shoot only men—women you knock down—children you leave alone! Is that understood?"

"But this kid . . . !"

"No training! No discipline! How am I supposed to keep things under control with a bunch of babies?" The man pointed to the sacks of grain, plainly marked *UNICEF, Gift From the People of the United States of America*. "Put the rest of those sacks into my Jeep."

The young Defender moved to obey, wincing in pain. Ali ran, stumbling and sobbing to find his mother.

"Usaman will not be happy about this!" the older man said, shaking his rifle in emphasis at the young Defender.

Shielded from sight now, Ladu gripped the slats of the lattice that formed the entrance to the small dispensary. If only she were a man! But even then, she would need a gun. Defenders! They defended no one but themselves and stole food from everyone else. Without those guns they would be helpless like the rest of us, she thought

Ladu grabbed for Ali as he staggered past her. Holding him to her, she whispered for him to be quiet. There was no need; he was still paralyzed by fear. The baby in her stomach stirred, and Ladu moved quickly, pulling Ali with her, out of range of the Defenders. She still clutched the small pan of grain, the meager portion each family was allowed from the supplies brought in by the relief people.

She knew the man who had stopped the attack on Ali. In fact, he was a relative, Dokwali, cousin to her husband. Perhaps he had recognized Ali. She hoped so. Surely there was something that would appeal to the conscience of the Defenders, make them stop the senseless killing and beatings.

They remained where they were for a long time, fearful of meeting the Defenders again on the road.

CHAPTER 23

Back in her compound, Ladu set about grinding the grain. Yohanna would be coming in from the field soon. The guinea corn this time was especially nice— large, plump, grains. If Yohanna saw it, he would insist on putting it away to plant. That would mean another day with nothing to eat but whatever leaves she could scrounge from the bush. She didn't mind foraging or eating the leaves again, but it was becoming increasingly difficult to walk long distances as she came nearer the time of birthing.

Ali was in a far corner of the compound, holding a stick for a rifle and shooting at imaginary Defenders. His language was loud and vulgar, but Ladu said nothing. It was a way for him to get rid of his anger.

Rahila, Yohanna's second wife, came out of her round mud house, carrying her nine-month-old baby, and sat on a short wooden stool near Ladu's grinding stone. "I don't want my child to grow up having to shoot a neighbor in order to have food!" Her baby pulled Rahila's full breast to him and began suckling hungrily.

Abruptly Ladu stopped moving the stone over the grain and sat back on her heels, panting from the exertion. "Of course! Why didn't I think of it before? I'll take Ali away from here. I'll go back to my people in Kulanji. It's my turn to visit Asta." The expression on Rahila's face made her instantly regret her words.

Rahila's look was withering. "Go to the Garden of Eden, huh? Leave us to starve while you eat all you want!"

Ladu lumbered to her feet, as quickly as a woman can when carrying such weight. Calmly she said, "I will bring some back."

"Sure you will! If the Defenders don't take it away from you on the way home." Rahila was still fuming. "It's not fair! I have to stay here and cook for Yohanna while you — "

"Ola!" a voice called from the gateway, and a young woman appeared, a friend of Rahila's.

"Ola to you," Ladu replied. To Rahila she said, "Finish grinding the grain and prepare the mush." Then she walked resolutely to the small grass-roofed mud building that belonged to her. No one was allowed in her private house without permission, except her husband and her own children.

Quickly she laid out a few items of clothing for herself and Ali. She was glad to get Ali out of there. What he was learning, no ten-year-old should know. And how great it would be to see Asta again! The thought of enough food to eat was pleasant too, very pleasant.

Rahila's friend squatted near where Rahila had taken over the grinding of the grain. "Ladu is going to Kulanji," Rahila whined.

"I'd like to see that place," her friend replied. "Have you ever been there?"

"Of course not. No one gets in unless they are Kulanjis."

"Just imagine. A place where there is always enough food, and no one gets sick," mused her friend. "But how come Ladu gets in?"

"She was born in Kulanji. The chiefs of the two tribes made a wager. Whoever lost would have to supply a wife for the other one. Our chief already had enough wives, so he paid a debt to Yohanna's father by giving Ladu to him as a wife for Yohanna."

"So Ladu didn't have a choice in the matter," the friend said, shaking her head.

" No," Rahila said.

They were quiet for a moment.

Rahila spoke. "The people from Kulanji are different. For one thing they are taller than everybody else." She paused and then said wistfully, "And their babies don't die like ours do." Rahila had already lost one child from measles.

"Why didn't Ladu go back to her family? Surely, for a price . . . "

"I'm sure she must have considered doing that. But Laraba was born before long, and if she had gone home, she would have had to leave Laraba here. She wouldn't do that. Her father had died after an accident; her mother was dead too. Asta is her nearest relative, a cousin."

"So she goes to visit?"

"Uh huh. One year Asta comes here; the next year Ladu goes there."

The friend lowered her voice. "I will never understand why Yohanna treats Ladu the way he does. She isn't even a Wamba, yet she is First Wife. Have you asked him why?"

Rahila shook her head. "I wouldn't dare. He treats her as if she were as smart as a man, asks her opinion about things. They actually sit together and talk about things."

"Is she smart?"

"All the Kulanjis are smart. Maybe always having enough to eat makes you smart, even if you are a woman."

When Yohanna came home some time later, the food was almost ready. Guinea corn mush with a sauce of green leaves, seasoned the way he liked it with sashu. The Wamba people didn't know how to make sashu. Ladu had brought the method with her from the Kulanji. Burn goat dung until it was a powder and add mamza, dried ground petals from a certain flower. It made anything taste better. Yohanna bragged about Ladu's cooking to the other men.

Whenever Yohanna and Ladu sat down together, Rahila disappeared. It was an understanding they had. Rahila was not happy about it, but she had no choice.

Ladu described the incident that had taken place that day at the dispensary and answered Yohanna's questions.

"Husband, I have decided to visit Asta. I do not like what Ali is learning here. And I'm not sure it is safe for the baby here. If I go now, I would not return until after the baby is born. Would that be all right?"

"Actually the idea had entered my mind, but I was afraid it was too close to your birthing." He took a drink of tea. "With the rains coming soon, you won't be able to return for several months. Do not try to return until the rains begin to taper off; I would worry about you." He smiled at her. "You will send word when the baby is born." It was a question.

She smiled too. "Of course." She refilled his tea. "Rahila will look after you. Ali and I will leave at first light. We will go by way of Laraba's compound. I couldn't go without seeing my only grandchild."

Yohanna nodded. "I will miss your good food, but Rahila can manage."

Ladu smiled at him.

She spoke again in a low voice. "The last time I talked with Laraba, she told me she had not been feeling well. She has had one cold after another, but this time it was worse."

She was interrupted as the dog that had been lying at their feet leaped up and ran, without barking, to the gatehouse, wagging her tail furiously. Ali came from where he had been eating his food and started toward the gatehouse also.

"Laraba?" Ladu called. Who else would the dog run to greet so eagerly without barking? "Why has she come this time of day? She should be at home cooking supper."

"Ola!" Laraba set down her son who started on wobbly legs toward Ladu and Yohanna. The dog raced in circles around them. "Pazhi!" Laraba called to the dog, "Stop that. You'll knock Anjikwi down!"

"Pazhi!" Yohanna commanded. "Come here. Lie down."

The dog lay down obediently beside Yohanna. Anjikwi toddled unsteadily straight for Pazhi where he sat down and began patting the dog, making pleased noises.

Half way across the space from the gatehouse, Laraba bent over in a paroxysm of coughing. It was deep and painful.

Ladu looked in alarm at Laraba. "Have you been to the dispensary?"

"Yes. That's why I'm here. I just came from there. I haven't even been home, to tell Husband." Her voice caught in her throat, and as she dropped to the low stool that was near, she began to sob, her hands over her face.

"Laraba!" Ladu cried. "What is it?" Ladu struggled to raise her awkward body from the low chair.

Barely audible, Laraba said, "Miz Tayluh thinks I have kariya."

Only Anjikwi's nonsense syllables were heard against Laraba's sobbing.

Kariya—the journey from which no one returns.

Ladu's response was instantaneous. "You will go with me to Kulanji. They have food—and medicine!" Her statement was more hope than certainty, but the sudden brightening in Laraba's eyes settled the plan.

Ladu looked at Yohanna, and he nodded, then she put her head in her hands and gave a deep painful sigh.

CHAPTER 24

Saratu's Compound in Kulanji

Saratu's worst fears were realized. Peering at the two men through the climbing vine that shielded her house entrance, she felt trapped.

"We are bringing a request from Chief Inuwa for permission for his son, Pindar, to marry your daughter, Saratu," they had announced to her father.

No girl had ever been allowed to wait longer than her eighteenth birthday to consent to a pact of marriage. Hers was not far off.

She should not have danced so many times with Pindar at the last market day festival. He was without doubt the most eligible man in the tribe, and was she not the most desirable woman? But it certainly did not mean she wanted to marry him. In fact, she had told him so the next day when he came panting to see her.

The fact of the Kulanji strict code of behavior for single women did not keep Saratu from wondering how to choose a man who was also a good partner in lovemaking. The talk among the women around the wells led her to believe that there were good partners and bad, mostly bad. What *bad* meant they never made that clear.

Her mother had begun what she called *growing-up* sessions—times they would talk about manners and responsibility. When Saratu had asked her mother about boys, Asta had started talking about sex.

"Young men have to prove that their bodies work properly, and the only way to prove it is with a woman's body. Remember, it is your body, and no one has a right to use it unless you agree."

But even more surprising was something else her mother had told her. "Making love should be as enjoyable for the woman as for the man, but it won't happen unless you insist. A woman teaches a man the art of lovemaking."

None of the other young women knew that. They laughed when Saratu said a woman should enjoy sex as much as a man. But then, most of them had been married by sixteen—and they didn't have her mother to teach them.

"If you want a good marriage," her mother had said, "be ready to make love when he is, but just as important, let him know you would like it. A man likes to know that he is desirable." At that moment, Saratu had understood some of the looks she had seen go between her mother and father. "When you have done that, you do not need to worry about him looking somewhere else to find sex."

And that had explained the guarded whispers she had heard about the hold her mother seemed to have over her father, because everyone knew that he never ever went to the House of Women.

The voices on the other side of the vine called her attention back to Pindar. He had told her she was the prettiest, in fact, *the most beautiful* girl in Kulanji, and he wanted her for his wife.

"So he can show off," Saratu said under her breath. She did not need Pindar to tell her that she was pretty, very pretty in fact. But she also knew she was intelligent—and destined to do something special with her life.

The boys in school were taught English because the headmaster said that English was the language of the future. She had borrowed one of the books so that she could learn on her own. But she was not satisfied with her choppy, hesitant manner of speaking English, so she had spent hours at the dispensary, listening to the American nurse who came once a month. Finally, she had courage enough to ask Miz Tayluh to help her with English. The woman had seemed pleased and stayed longer in Kulanji than she had planned, to teach Saratu English. Even her mother did not know about this.

She had not decided who she would marry, but it would not be anyone for a while. Once a girl married, there was no chance of ever doing anything but grinding grain, cooking food, going to market, and having babies. Her father would not agree to a marriage contract without her consent, and she was not about to give it.

"I am going to see what the Outside looks like before I get married," she told herself as she stared at the men.

Then an idea came to her. "Right now I'm going to have some fun."

With her head high and her back straight, she walked toward the group of men now seated in front of her father's house.

"Good evening, gentlemen," she said, bowing from the waist in perfect decorum. Then she walked with stately grace toward the gatehouse.

Exasperated as he was, Yamta could hardly hold back a smile. A woman did not interrupt a man's meeting—ever. But Saratu had done it—in style.

CHAPTER 25

Mubi Village

"You mustn't walk up the hill, Laraba, you must save your strength for the walk." Ladu set down her headload and checked the sleeping baby on Laraba's back. The trek would be long, and Laraba was already weak. "Ali, you wait here with Laraba. I'll not be long."

Ladu stepped warily in the half-light of early dawn as she climbed the small hill to Malissa Taylor's house; it was the time that snakes were looking for mice. She wore the usual wraparound skirt and blouse of a flowered printed material, but had added a heavy hand-woven guada cloth over her shoulders against the morning chill.

There was a light in the house. Hopefully Miz Tayluh would still be at home and not at the hospital this early.

"Salaam," Ladu called.

"Salaam to you," Yusufu, Malissa's cook, replied, coming to the kitchen screen door.

They exchanged the familiar greeting about family and health. "Is the dokita at home this morning?" Ladu asked. Every white person was given a nickname by the Wambas, and Malissa's was *dokita*, their corruption of the word doctor.

"Yes," Yusufu said, "She is eating breakfast. I'll call her."

Malissa returned with Yusufu. "Good morning, Ladu, how are you?" She bowed in greeting. Malissa wore a blue sweater over her white nurse's uniform, which was such a contrast in this world of dinginess and dirt where soap cost more than food.

Ladu bent from the waist in the usual manner but awkwardly. "There is much trouble in my family today. I did not want to go without telling you I would not be here for our meeting this week."

"For which trouble are you leaving, and where are you going?" Malissa asked.

"I am taking Ali to Kulanji to be with his relatives, to my family. It is a better place to raise a young boy. Wamba is not a safe place any more." She paused. "And Laraba is going also."

"Do they have medicine for kariya, Ladu?" Malissa's voice was low so Yusufu could not hear. She knew there were tribal remedies that the local medicine men used. Perhaps there was one they had not told her about.

"I don't know if they have medicine to cure kariya, but I know they have medicine to prevent it. Maybe it is the same thing. We will find out."

"Will you have trouble getting into Kulanji? They always let me in when I go to visit the dispensary, but they are very strict about where I can stay and how long."

"Family may enter, only family."

Malissa reached out to touch Ladu's arm. "Ladu, I will pray every day that they will have medicine to cure Laraba!"

"Thank you, my friend." Ladu hurried on. "I came for another reason. It is to warn you that you should take some time off, right away. There will be no opportunity again for many months. What has happened to Laraba is going to happen to many, many more. There will be no escape. And diarrhea season is upon us. You can't do it all, my friend. Go, go now. You think there is too much work to go now, but it will be worse."

"Thank you, Ladu, for taking time to think about me when your own burden is so heavy." Tears came unbidden to Malissa's eyes, and she turned away.

Then remembering, she turned back to the other woman. "Ladu, it is time for me to visit the dispensary in Kulanji again. I'm supposed to do it every three months. It has already been that long, so I need to go soon. Perhaps you could come to greet me there. You will be ready to deliver about that time. Or is your cousin's compound too far away?"

"That would be great if you could be there to deliver my baby! Their compound is not far from the dispensary."

"Babies come in their own time," Malissa laughed. "It will probably arrive just before I get there or just after I leave."

"Why don't you plan to stay a few days? I want you to meet Asta."

"Asta? Your cousin is Asta? I met her, she was the one who kept at the tribal council until they consented to setting up the dispensary." Malissa smiled. "And I met her daughter, Saratu. Very smart, wanted to learn English. Was doing very well the last time I talked with her."

"You could stay in Asta's compound," Ladu said.

"The public guest house should be finished by now," Malissa said. "They were hurrying to finish it before the rains come. Maybe I could at least stay overnight. It is extremely tiring to make the long trip in one day."

"A long journey—yes." Ladu turned to go.

Instantly Malissa regretted her words. A long trip in a Jeep meant infinitely longer for someone who was walking.

"Here, Ladu," Malissa said quickly. "Here is something for you to eat on the road. Yusufu has made biscuits for breakfast. And a couple oranges."

"Thank you," Ladu said, bowing as she turned to leave.

"May God take you in good health," Yusufu called after her.

Back at the road, Ladu placed her pack on her own head and checked the load Ali was carrying. They started walking at a fast pace toward the west. Ladu handed a biscuit to Ali and one to Laraba and tasted hers. "What do you think of it, Ali?"

Ali made a face. "White people eat strange food!" he said, laughing.

They walked on, munching on the biscuits, the baby's head nodding in rhythm to the steps as he slept on Laraba's back.

CHAPTER 26

Blantyre

Carol had left the afternoon of the funeral for an urgent conference with her magazine editor in London five days ago. Now as she approached her house in Blantyre, she dreaded the scene that was to come. She would tell Gui that it was all over.

Flora met Carol at the front door. "Welcome home, Miss Walters, Mr. Manieux is waiting for you in the library."

"Thank you, Flora." Carol wanted to go to her room before she saw Gui. She touched Flora's arm. "Is everything all right?"

"I think so, Miss. He's been in a crazy mood all day."

"Crazy?" Carol stopped her retreat to her room.

"I've never seen him like this before."

"Well, you may never see me again after tonight, Flora. I've got to tell him . . . "

Flora nodded; she knew. They had spoken of matters frankly, very frankly.

Carol took her time, changing out of her traveling clothes into her dressing gown. She would talk with Gui and then take her shower.

She wished she had questioned Flora closer on the kind of mood Gui was in. Having left the afternoon of the funeral for an urgent conference with her magazine editor in London, she had talked with Gui only on the phone. Her impression was that he was depressed and trying desperately to cover it up, because he kept saying he had great news for her but he would not say what it was. She just knew he was trying to pretend that things were great when in fact, he was devastated.

She had dreaded returning, and yet could hardly wait to see Gui. Her attraction to this man was something she could not understand, much less control, but for her own peace of mind, she could not go on with a relationship in which she was used when it was convenient and forgotten when he felt like it.

When she walked into the library, she feared the worst. Candles were the only light, giving a mysterious dimness. Was he having a wake for Roger? It would be so out of character for this man who had never before shown the slightest inclination to participate in symbolic gestures or religious rites.

"Carol."

It was the tone of his voice, low, sweet,— romantic? No, it couldn't be, she was interpreting it wrong. It was just different from anything she had heard from him before.

Gui was seated on the couch and motioned for her to sit beside him. The candles' flickering lights cast dancing figures on the walls around them.

"Gui, what's wrong? Are you all right?" She sat stiffly beside him.

He touched her arm. "I am probably more right than I have ever been in my life—ever since I was a little boy."

"Tell me, Gui! I want to hear about that—when you were a little boy."

He looked away now, his gaze coming to rest on the candle on the low coffee table in front of them, and remembering, his voice became softer. "They left me."

"Who left you, Gui?"

"They went away. Day after day I thought they would come back, but they never did. Sometimes, when the doorbell rings and I open the door, I think she might be there."

"Who, Gui? Who might be there?"

There was a long pause while Gui's eyes never left the candle on the low table in front of them. Carol waited. Was it his mother who went away and did not return—his father?

"And Roger went away too," Gui said.

"I'm sorry, Gui, he was your friend."

His eyes returned to her face, and the tone of his voice suddenly became bright, animated. "It is all right, Carol! Roger did not know what I know. Carol, I have finally figured out what is right!" Now he talked rapidly. "All my life I have been hurrying to find the right woman, the perfect sexual experience. Now I know what is really important!"

Carol eyed him closely. Was he ranting? Had he had a psychotic break? He was expecting her to know what he meant. Firmly, deliberately he took her in his arms. "I love you, Carol. I did not know that before, before Roger's death."

"I love you too, Gui, but . . . "

"You do not understand, Carol. I love *you*, I love who you are and what you are. I love your voice, your hair, the way you dress, your body, especially your body, all of it."

81

His hands traveled slowly, sensuously downward, starting at her lips, down her throat and inside the dressing gown, lingering gently at the silky mounds of her breasts, touching the nipples which firmed into hard little tips. He bent to wrap his tongue around one of them.

Carol tried to push him away. "No, Gui!"

He did not hear her as his fingers fondled one breast as his lips caressed the other nipple. " . . . your body, all of it." He pulled her close to him. "And because I love you, all of you, I am never going to have another woman in my life."

"What did you say?"

"Never again."

"Gui, how did this happen?" She pushed him away to arms' length. "Tell me!"

"It happened at Roger's service. I decided I simply could not take a chance on losing you. Nothing is worth that!"

"Are you sure?" *Was he still ranting?*

"I was never more sure of anything in my life."

Even in the dim candlelight she could see his eyes, and in them she read that what he was saying was true.

"Gui, do you know how happy that makes me?"

"Happy enough to let me prove it, I hope."

Now it was Carol whose hands were finding the soft places of his body. "Yes, Gui, oh, yes!" Her lips moved to his urgently. "Show me, darling. I have missed your body so much!"

"I'm not going to show you, my dearest. I'm going to let you discover it!"

He had never been so ready, and she had never been so eager to explore it.

CHAPTER 27

At the Well in Kulanji

The women of the village of Bri usually made a point of arriving at the well to draw their day's supply of water the same time Asta was likely to be there. Today there was a special urgency. Two close friends had arrived before the others.

One spoke excitedly. "I tried it last night!"

"Tried what?"

"You know, doing what Asta does and calling Husband by his name. I told you I was going to try it."

"I thought you were joking!"

"Well, I was, but the more I thought about it . . . "

"Tell me! What happened?"

"Nothing."

"He probably didn't even hear you."

"He heard me all right," She placed her bucket on the edge of the well and leaned against it.

"How do you know?"

"Well," She was suddenly embarrassed.

"Tell me!" Her friend gripped her arm. "If I'm going to try it, I need to know what is likely to happen."

She resumed. "When I served his supper, I called him by his name. He looked a little startled, but he didn't say anything. A little while later he came over and sat down beside me."

"Really?"

She nodded.

"And then?"

"He said there was something he had been wanting to ask me." Now she spoke quickly. "He went to his house and brought back a book he had bought in market. He, you won't believe this, he asked me to tell him some of the words!"

"Well, you are an excellent reader."

She shook her head. "But I've been a good reader for a long time. I think he was glad I had, well, sort of opened the door."

"Why didn't he ask one of the men to tell him the word?"

"You know one man can't ask another for help like that!"

"I'm going to try it!" declared her friend. "Tonight! I'm going to try it tonight."

"Good morning." Other women were arriving, chatting about the usual things while watching to see if Asta was coming yet.

Asta was privy to the goings-on in the realm of government because her husband was a member of the tribal council. No woman, not one, would ever admit where she learned certain facts. If their husbands learned that Asta was their source of information, Asta would be castigated, but more importantly, their supply of news would dry up. But in spite of trusting Asta to be their leader, it was not without resentment.

"I wonder what would happen if I called my husband by his name like Asta does," mused one woman.

"I would be sitting outside the compound with Husband throwing my belongings at me," answered another.

The two young women smiled at each other and said nothing.

"Ola!" called out Asta, approaching the group, her water gourd in hand.

One woman immediately asked the question they had all been waiting to ask. "Asta, is the council going to send a representative to the conference next month?"

Asta had told them the week before about a conference on food to be convened by the United Nations.

"How did the invitation come?" another woman asked. "I thought we didn't have communication with any other government, especially international groups."

Asta smiled. "You know, Mardi, a year ago you would not have even known enough to ask that question. I'm proud of you." She set her water gourd down on the well edge. "Chief Inuwa does meet with the chief from Wamba now and then, and that's how he heard of it. But the council decided that if we send someone to that conference, the whole world will soon know about us. They think it is better to say nothing, and no one will know we are here." Asta waved her hand to include all the women. "What do you think?"

"Absolutely."

"We've kept out of sight this long, let's keep it that way."

"If we start letting people know about our land, we might not be able to keep them out any longer."

84

There was a dissenting voice. "They already know about us. I saw two trucks loaded with grain and potatoes going out of here yesterday."

"And goodness knows, enough of our young men slip out to get beer."

Another woman broke in, "And don't tell me they don't meet women out there."

"Asta," one of the women addressed her, "I overheard my husband and some of the men talking last night. I couldn't hear it all, but it was something about you taking Pinta's place as Director of Education."

Gasps went up everywhere. "Pinta's place! A woman!"

Asta had not intended to tell them—let them find out some other way. As much as she enjoyed seeing things happen, she had never felt like telling of her accomplishments—it was too much like bragging. But they were waiting for her response.

She turned away, not looking at them."Chief Inuwa asked me to come to see him. He told me that Pinta was resigning from the position of Director of Education and asked me to take it."

"Are you going to do anything different?"

"Maybe," Asta said. "Do you have any ideas?"

"How about women teachers?"

"Let girls into secondary school."

"Mama!" Their discussion was interrupted by Saratu who entered their midst without ceremony.

Asta frowned. Her daughter refused to observe the usual courtesies expected of offspring of the Kulanji. Why was it that a child could pick the moment to be contrary when it would cause her mother the most embarrassment? But, of course, that was why she did it.

"Yes, Saratu?" Asta's voice was strained.

"I've finished grinding the grain. Now what do I have to do?" Her voice was whiney.

Asta smiled, albeit with some effort. "I'll be right back, Saratu." She hoped that would be enough to send Saratu back to the compound. She was wrong.

"Sure! You will stay out here and talk forever, as usual!" Saratu plopped down on the well edge, her pretty face in a pout. "If we don't get my zhebi made today, it won't be ready for the dance. And I'm not going if I don't have a new zhebi."

Asta was wise enough to know a losing situation when she was in one. "Excuse me, please. It seems I have work to do."

When the two were out of earshot, the buzzing began.

"Nkwargai!" It was the word for brat.

"I'd never let a daughter of mine talk to me like that!" A murmur of assent went around the group.

"Look, all of you," a woman Asta's age said. "Asta certainly has worked hard to see that we have things better than we used to. You know how kids are, they do what they know will hurt you the most.."

"I'll be the last one to criticize. There's no guarantee that my daughter won't act the same way."

"I don't think we should be surprised that Saratu is acting like that," another woman said. "She is using the very things Asta has taught her in order to get her way."

"Saratu is too young to understand these things."

"A girl is supposed to be mature at seventeen! Why, I was married and had a baby by that age."

"I don't think we have seen the last of problems from Saratu. She is beautiful, intelligent, and immature—a dangerous combination for her right now."

CHAPTER 28

Mubi

M alissa was furious. The mail arrived only once a week during dry season and less often during the rainy season, depending on whether the roads were passable. She had received an invoice at least a month before listing an order of plastic gloves. She had sent the order many months before, knowing how long it took for an order to finally arrive.

But there was no box of gloves in this day's mail. That meant one of two things. Either she went without gloves altogether or she took time to sterilize the ones she had. The first was not a choice. She had used her last throwaway gloves that morning. Her supply of the gloves that could be autoclaved was down to less than a dozen.

AIDS was on the rise in her area, and one thing she did without exception was to wear gloves whenever she touched a patient.

Now what was she to do?

The gloves could arrive next mail day, supposedly a week from that day, or the week after. And then again, they might never arrive, having been stolen or lost somewhere en route. This was a serious matter. What should she do?

"Miz Tayluh," the dispensary assistant stood in front of her. "Everything is put away."

Rising, she walked robot-like out the door.

"Miz Tayluh." The men's ward nurse hurried to catch up with her. "The man with the snake bite, he just died."

Nodding, but without looking back, Malissa walked up the hill to her house. Yusufu had prepared pork chops and rice. The pigs never put on much fat, so the pork chops were lean. They were baked until brown and tender, and the rice tasty—if one didn't mind a quartz rock now and then. She had learned never to bite down on rice. But actually, she wasn't paying any attention to what she was eating. She left half of the food on her plate, knowing Yusufu would finish it.

She climbed under the mosquito net and prayed for sleep that did not come. She was the only trained professional in the entire hospital of a hundred beds. The midwife who had been with her for almost ten years was at home with her new baby. The midwife-in-training was still learning, so Malissa had to handle all of the deliveries—and be slowed down by teaching the midwife. The dispenser had been ill for several days, which meant she had to run the dispensary and examine and prescribe medicine for each in the long, long line of sick people. And, to top it off, it was diarrhea season!

At the end of the dry season, some time in April, the rains began. They were sporadic at first, then increased in frequency and intensity. With no toilets, people squatted wherever they happened to be, so that the rains came, the refuse and feces was washed into the river and the shallow wells where people drew their drinking water. The bacteria that caused dysentery was set loose again, and the mothers began arriving with their ill babies on their backs, dehydrated and weak to the point they could no longer nurse.

Malissa covered her ears with her pillow to shut out the high-pitched wail of a woman carrying her dead baby home on her back. It would be buried before morning.

It was the middle of May. Rainy season could start in earnest any time after the first of June with daily afternoon rains. If she was going to get a break before rainy season set in and the roads would be impassable, she should do it soon. But who would look after the hospital? She had asked the mission board for a helper but had heard nothing. While she was in the States for three months, they had sent someone from another station, but now it was her responsibility.

There were other missionaries who lived about a mile away, but she saw them only rarely, at their prayer meetings or get-togethers for someone's birthday. There was just no time left over for socializing. If she finished work early, she would just go to bed. The only lights available were her kerosene lamps, and she liked to save her resources. She did manage to keep up with her month-old newsmagazine on the weekends.

This morning, the nagging problem of the gloves returned. They were a must. It would require at least a month to get a reply from the company where she had ordered them. The nearest telephone was 400 miles away. She could not continue to assume that they would surely come in the next mail, because one of these mornings she could reach for a glove and find the box empty. She could not do her work without gloves!

Ladu's words came back to her: "You can't do it all, my friend. Go, go now."

She sat up in bed. Ladu was right! She would go away for a few days—just a few days—before the rains started coming every day. The people would have to get along as best they could. After all, they had a dispenser and a midwife, which was more than they had before she came.

Usually she had gone to resthouses built especially for the mission staff, on a high plateau where the temperature was cool. There were other missionaries there to visit with and books to read, and there was a dining room where they took their meals. No one went anywhere else because that was the least expensive place, and on their small salaries, cost was a consideration.

She remembered overhearing a conversation in the airport at Blantyre. Two people were saying that the lake perch out of Lake Malawi was a delicacy, and very cheap. She had never stopped in Blantyre but had seen the pretty hotels on her way through. Wouldn't it be fun to stay in a nice hotel and eat in restaurants?

She turned from her back to her stomach. There was no way she could justify making a trip to Blantyre just because she was tired. It would be too expensive, although with her simple lifestyle, she had managed to put back a little nestegg.

But there was another consideration— the gloves! Medical supplies for her hospital came from England or the States, but she did know that Blantyre had a large hospital. She could no doubt pick up a supply of the gloves there.

She convinced herself that obtaining gloves would be reason enough to make the trip. And to heck with the cost. She would leave immediately.

The decision made, she slipped into sleep, which while not completely restful, did release her from the day's events, and allowed her to dream. She saw herself sitting at a table with a white tablecloth and crystal goblets with a plate of browned fish before her. And strangely, there was a tall man sitting at the table.

CHAPTER 29

At the Well

You would think Asta was a man, the way she gets included in all the business that goes on in this village." Wahir jerked the rope on the bucket, causing it to tip and spill most of the water she had just pulled from the well. "Shegeh!" She muttered the curse under her breath and dropped the pail down again.

"I don't think you need to worry about Asta," her friend Kwalaku, replied. "She allowed her cousin, Ladu, to come from Wamba into Kulanji country."

Wahir interrupted, "She's done that before, and no one said a thing. I think they should have . . . "

"Shut up and listen!"

The tone of voice stopped Wahir in the act of pouring out the water into her large gourd.

"Ladu brought her daughter, Laraba," Her voice dropped, "who has kariya!"

"She didn't!"

Kwalaku enjoyed her moment of triumph.

Kwalaku went on. "Now what do you think will happen to Asta?"

Wahir's eyes were suddenly wide. "What will happen to us, all of us? We will get kariya too!"

Kwalaku shook her head. "Probably not. No one has gotten it so far. Not a soul in Kulanji has kariya."

"That's because no one goes out of here and has sex with anyone outside."

"No? Then you haven't been listening. Just the other morning the women were talking about how the men sneak out to get beer supposedly, only of course, that isn't all they do out there."

"But there still isn't any AIDS here."

"That's right. For some reason no one gets it when they go out there. But bringing someone in, that's different!"

Kwalaku was thoughtful. "If Laraba has kariya, that means she slept with someone who has it. Was that her husband, or did she sleep around? In the Outside, people don't have the strict rules we have."

"I think we deserve to know the answer to that. I don't want her sleeping with my husband!"

"A lot you would have to say about it," Kwalaku said. "If she's pretty, your husband would be interested."

"So would yours!" Wahir snapped. Then she added wryly, "She wouldn't even have to be pretty."

They shared a momentary glance of pain. Kwalaku hurried to move away from it. "Why would Yamta allow Asta to invite Ladu when Laraba has kariya?"

"Maybe Asta did it without asking—only this time she isn't going to get away with it! My father is really going to be upset when I tell him about this." Wahir picked up her gourd of water to leave.

"Nobody talks about what it's like, out there, on the Outside," Kwalaku said. "But wouldn't you think that the fear of getting kariya would be enough to make a man stop sleeping around?"

"I could sure do without sex if it meant not getting kariya!" Wahir stated emphatically.

"But men don't feel that way. You know what they say, 'it's the . . .'"

". . . last thing to go,'" Wahir laughingly interrupted. "It's too bad it's the only way to get babies. If Husband didn't insist, I'd never . . . "

"I think I'll ask Husband." Kwalaku had an impish grin on her face.

"Ask him what—to help you enjoy it too?"

"Oh, he does that. I'll ask if he would give up sex rather than risk getting kariya."

"You wouldn't dare!" Her look confirmed her disbelief. "You would really be asking if he would want to sleep with another woman!" She drew back in horror. "I could never, never ask Husband such a thing! He would kill me!"

"Maybe you couldn't, but Husband and I have been having some very interesting conversations recently."

"You keep this up and you will be like Asta!"

CHAPTER 30

The Farm

It was three weeks since Roger's funeral, and Yahara had something to say to Gui. He was waiting at the office door when Gui arrived that Friday morning.

"Yes, Yahara, what is going on?" Gui asked in his usual brusque manner.

"I think you knew that Mr. Lefever had a partner here in Blantyre."

"A partner? What kind of a partner?"

"Whenever Mr. Lefever came to Blantyre, he asked me to contact Markus, always Markus, no one else."

"So?" Gui still did not understand.

"Markus is ill."

"So?"

"He has AIDS."

"Oh!" Abruptly Gui understood, and for a split second he looked away. But then his gaze returned, cynical and defiant as before. "So?"

"The man needs medical care."

"What do you want me to do about that?"

"I supposed, since Mr. Lefever was your partner, you would want to take care of this man's medical bills."

"The man who gave AIDS to my partner?" His voice grew loud. "Never!"

Yahara's voice remained steady, calm. "It is possible that Mr. Lefever gave it to Markus."

Gui stared in horror at Yahara for a brief second then stepped through the door and slammed it behind him as he said again, "Never!"

CHAPTER 31

Kulanji

"Asta!" It was Yamta's voice, urgent, angry. It was the first time in a very long time that Yamta had spoken to her like that. She knew why, and she was not surprised, but she was prepared.

"Yes, Husband?" Instead of usami, master, which women were expected to use in addressing their husbands, she used nankula, husband. She stepped into the dimness of his house, the largest building in the compound; it was square, not round like all the rest.

"Why did you do this?"

"What are you referring to, Yamta?" Women did not call their husbands by name either, only Asta.

"Kariya! Here in our compound!"

"They were given permission to come by the tribal council."

"Only because Ladu is your cousin and therefore must be granted entry if you request it. But they didn't know about the sickness."

"Neither did I, Yamta," Asta said firmly. "Ladu should not have brought Laraba without informing us first, but I can understand why she did it. What if Saratu had kariya? We would do whatever was required to try to save her. Right?"

Yamta spoke with authority. "The whole idea is that we isolate ourselves from the rest of the world precisely to keep from altering our lifestyle, and, since kariya came to live in Africa, to keep any of us from getting it."

Asta needed to distract him. "I still wonder why the Kulanji are blessed with good crops and good health."

"That's just the way it is," Yamta replied testily.

Asta persisted. "What makes the difference? Are our bodies created different? We still get measles and the cough, and colds, and even some cancers, but as far as we know, not one in Kulanji has ever had kariya. Why? And our guinea corn crop always does well. Why?"

"All I know is that is the way it is! I am not interested in testing the gods to see if they might change their minds and let us have kariya after all," Yamta said.

"Maybe there is something in this place, in the air, in the earth, in the water. Ladu was born here, lived twelve years as a Kulanji. She is taller than the Wamba women; the children she bore were healthier; she is rarely ill. All that is true about the rest of us too. Why is this?"

Now Yamta answered thoughtfully. "It's not the air; the same wind blows across many countries. The water, it could be the water, although our rivers come through other countries. Perhaps there is something in the soil."

He has been looking at Asta, but now he turned away. "Those are the wrong questions. The right question is why do you do these things without asking me?"

"So that is the problem, Yamta." She paused. Was this the time for this argument? It had been brewing for many months; this was only the crocodile's nose above the water. If she was going to be of any help to Ladu and Laraba, she could not alienate Yamta. The argument could wait.

Asta's voice was calm, soothing. "I will make sure they do not leave this compound. I will send for Birama, the Wiseman, immediately. We will do whatever he tells us to do. If Laraba is not better in a month, I will escort her to the boundary and send her home."

"Laraba will not go to the well for water." He held up a hand and pointed to one finger.

"That's right."

"She will not go to the dances." He pointed to the next finger.

"She will not."

"She will eat by herself, and her utensils and clothes will be kept carefully separate." The third finger.

"Yes."

"In a month we will discuss this again."

"Yes, husband."

Asta returned to her own house and let drop the curtain that covered the door. She loved Ladu, but why did she have to come just now? Ladu did know that Asta could not refuse to take in a member of her family. Only if the tribe would forbid it could Asta send her away.

No one knew if coming to Kulanji would erase kariya, or if instead, the Kulanji would contract it, but they were about to find out.

CHAPTER 32

Salisbury, Zimbabwe

The conference was turning ugly. Twenty-five top leaders from all over Africa were in Salisbury, Zimbabwe, to talk seriously about the problem of hunger. Not a country north of South Africa was untouched by hunger. The presence of South Africa at the conference had made some of the representatives unhappy, but without them there, others would not have come at all.

"Why do you in South Africa think you have a right to tell us how to feed our people?" A robed man from Zaire was speaking. "We don't have the fertile land or industrialization you have, and we aren't going to get it overnight, so don't tell us what to do!"

The representative from Tanzania jumped up. "South Africa is the one who should be helping us. They have drained us over the years, taking our best products for the least money, knowing they were our only market. They owe us more than they can ever repay. They should start turning loose of some of their food."

Another man interrupted. "If we had good sense, we would ignore South Africa altogether and form trade agreements among ourselves."

The chairman, Tomiko Hirokama of Japan, Special Assistant to the Director of the World Health Organization stood to speak. "We are here to find answers to the immediate problems of food for hungry people." Then he added with a wry smile. "And if anyone has a cure for AIDS, please come forward."

Gui was not a delegate, but any time a group got together to talk about food, he was always invited. After all, Agricole Internationale supplied more food and more jobs than any single country in Africa.

As he was arriving at the hotel, Gui had met Tomiko Hirokama on his way to the conference after the morning break. His first reaction was to avoid Tomiko. After all, he was the enemy. But Gui was not where he was by being afraid of enemies. The first step to controlling an enemy is to know him.

They exchanged an affable, if somewhat strained, greeting.

"May we have lunch some time?" Tomiko asked.

"Sure. How about today?" Gui responded. "At the Neam Tree Café.."

"Very good. Lunch today."

After Bert tended to his plane, he wandered into the meeting. Since it was a topic of interest to him, he had taken care to forego his normal flight uniform of shorts and t-shirt for khakis, button down shirt and tie. When Gui questioned him, he admitted his interest. Gui gave him a pass.

Entering the room, Bert spotted Gui near the back of the room and slipped into an empty seat near him. Gui leaned over and whispered, "These conferences usually turn out to be boxing matches and sometimes brawls. No one wants anyone else to have more power. There is plenty of food for everyone. The problem is getting it to the people who need it."

"I've flown all over eastern Africa," Bert responded. "I've seen the farmers scratching with hand hoes. Seems to me a lot could be done to improve production."

"No," replied Gui, "we do not have the years it would take to discover methods that work here. What works in the States or in Europe will not necessarily do the job here. And the second problem is convincing farmers to change. Using a technique that works even now and then is preferred to one that they have never tried."

For some reason, into Bert's mind came the scene over the nose of the airplane, the green triangle in the midst of brown arid land. "Whoever lives in that green triangle knows how to make the land produce."

Gui turned sharply to look at him. "What green triangle?"

"You remember, that place we flew over that had all the trees and fruit?"

Gui's eyes narrowed as the scene replayed itself in his mind. The green triangle surrounded by seared earth. An incredible idea came into his mind.

Gui stood up. "Bert, I need to return to Blantyre."

"We just got here. I thought you came for the conference."

"Do you think you could find the green triangle again?"

"Sure." Bert spoke with more confidence than he felt.

"We will leave—now. I will meet you in front of the hotel in half an hour."

On the way out, Gui stopped to send a conference page with a note of regret to Tomiko.

CHAPTER 33

Bert shifted from one foot to the other, impatient to be off. They couldn't leave soon enough for him. The clock over the concierge's desk said eleven forty-five. They could be back in Blantyre by eight o'clock at the latest. Good! He could be at the Credit Union when it opened tomorrow. He had not originally considered that possibility since his account had less than one hundred dollars in it, but who knows, they might loan him the money. He told himself he was almost desperate enough to steal the money at this point—if he could find a place where ten thousand dollars was waiting to be stolen.

Bert had not unpacked his bag, but apparently Gui had to repack his. Or else he was taking time to eye the local sights. Gui always seemed to have time for that.

Evidently the conference was taking its noon break, for a stream of delegates was coming in the door.

"Aren't you with Mr. Manieux?" It was Tomiko.

"Yes."

"I was sure I saw you sitting with him in the conference. I'm Tomiko Hirokama. I am supposed to have lunch with Mr. Manieux."

"Oh, well, in fact, we are leaving immediately. Something came up."

"I'm sorry about that. Please convey to him my regrets also. I was looking forward to having a chat with him. I would like his ideas on the problem of effectively distributing food."

"Yes, I'll do that," Bert hastened to assure him. He was not interested in prolonging the conversation. He was not at all sure he could find the Green Country again, and he wanted to be left alone to try to recall everything he could about the original flight.

Mr. Tomiko was in no hurry to leave. "How was your flight this morning? You did fly up from Zimbabwe today, didn't you?"

"No. Actually we came from Blantyre."

"That's in Malawi, isn't it? That's just about the only country in Africa I haven't visited. I hear it is very pretty—with excellent lake perch and beautiful tourist accommodations on Lake Malawi."

Bert suddenly had an idea for some help in finding the green country, and he interrupted. "I thought I had seen them all, too," he said. "But there was one we flew over a couple weeks ago that was new to me. Here at the end of dry season, it was lush and green. I call it the Green Country. Do you know the name of it?"

"Green—now—at the end of dry season?" Tomiko was amazed. "Where was the place?"

"Somewhere north of Malawi, to the west, I think."

Tomiko shook his head. "I don't . . ."

"Mr. Hirokama, I want you to meet . . . " They were interrupted by two gentlemen, and Bert quickly stepped away. He obviously would not get any help from Tomiko. The three men walked together toward the dining room as Gui appeared.

Together Gui and Bert hurried out the door. Tomiko watched them go, a frown on his face.

CHAPTER 34

Blantyre

Once they landed and made plans for the next day, Bert lied to Mr. Manieux, telling him that the weather would prevent them for taking off to look for the Green Country until eleven o'clock. Actually, early morning would have been better, but Bert was not going to let anything get in the way of being at the Credit Union office when it opened at nine o'clock. Gui had wanted to look for the Green Country on the way back from Nairobi, but Bert convinced him there was not enough time before dark.

The interview at the Credit Union lasted only a few minutes; the answer was no. Now he had only five days left to come up with the money.

His plane was sitting on the tarmac when they taxied for takeoff. What a beauty!

Gui was in the co-pilot's seat.

"Mr. Manieux, see that plane off the left wing tip?"

"Yes."

"I'm going to buy that one."

"Good looking plane."

"If—I can get the money together."

Gui made no response.

Finding the Green Country was not as difficult as he had feared, but it was not particularly easy. It was not shown on any flight map he could find, and he had to guess how far off course they had been that day.

Gui glued his eyes to the nose of the plane and saw it first. "There it is! Take the plane down—as low as you can."

There were no police around to arrest him for flying too low over a populated area, so down he went. They flew from the upper tip to the lower edge of the green area, then turned around and flew around the entire border.

Gui wrote down what he saw on a paper in his lap, naming them off. "Citrus trees, all kinds, mango trees, guava, dry season gardens of vegetables, trees just for shade, flowers, lots of flowers, even some dry season guinea corn." If they could do this in dry season, what must their crops look like in rainy season?

Children ran out into the open to stare up at the plane, then adults ran out to grab the children, sending them scurrying back to cover.

"Just like kids," Bert said. "I remember running out to watch planes when I was young. Do you remember doing that?"

Gui was more interested in something else. "Their borders are airtight. Thorn fields that not even Brer Rabbit could get through."

"I suppose you could burn you way through them," suggested Bert.

"That is a thought, but probably not a good idea, considering what would be waiting on the other side."

"Do you see anything to indicate why this piece of land is different from all the rest?"

Gui peered through the window. "No. But there has to be a logical reason."

"Shall we go around again?"

"Yes, and then once more straight up the middle; then let's go home."

Bert could see a young woman standing in the middle of a compound, like the first time. They were so low he could see the colors in her headscarf. She waved, so he dipped his wings to her. He wondered what she looked like—was she pretty? Why didn't she run to hide like the rest of them?

Gui was obviously deep in thought, scribbling on his pad of paper, and Bert said little during the two-hour flight.

About ten minutes before they landed, Gui seemed to come out of his preoccupation. "Damn! Nothing adds up. How in the world can we find the answer to that riddle?"

"You mean the riddle of the Green Country?"

"The Green Country, good name for it."

"But don't you think it is just because they have a good supply of water and understand how to use it better than their neighbors do?"

Gui thought about that. "I do not think so, but . . . "

"You don't think they are just master farmers?" Bert asked.

"Well, if they are, I want to take lessons from them." His voice was loud now. "If I had the answer, I would have the key to the problem of enough food for the whole world! Do you know what that would mean?" Gui, usually extremely close-mouthed about business matters, especially this important, was too excited to keep quiet. "That answer would be worth a lot of money!"

Bert listened in astonishment at this usually reserved man who was anything but quiet now.

"More money than anyone ever dreamed of, ever in the history of the world. It will revolutionize the food industry!" He drummed his fingers on the map of the Green Country he had drawn on his pad then slapped his hands together. "I am going to solve that riddle!"

A different feeling about this man began arising in Bert's gut, only this time it was not distaste, but fear. Such information in the hands of this man was dangerous!

Bert's look must have conveyed his disapproval.

Gui waved his hand toward Bert. "I suppose you are worried about the hungry people in Africa. You and Carol! But it is okay, there will be enough to feed them too."

CHAPTER 35

The Farm

Racing into his office that Tuesday afternoon, Gui grabbed up the phone, punched the numbers, then yelled into the phone. "Yahara, get in here *now!*"

He hung up and paced the floor until Yahara arrived, panting.

"Yahara, this may be the most important question you will ever answer in your life, so please think carefully before you tell me you do not know." Yahara dropped to the edge of the upholstered chair in front of Gui's desk, his eyes never leaving his employer's face.

"This morning Bert and I flew over a piece of land that is different from any other land around it. Now at the end of dry season, it is still green, and it is filled with fruit trees, flowers, and dry season gardens. It is about an hour and a half as the crow flies northwest of here. There are no main roads leading to it; there are no air routes that go near it. It appears to be a forgotten land, and apparently the people keep it that way.

"You have workers who come from all over to work on the farms. Has anyone mentioned a place that blooms all year round?"

Yahara wanted nothing so much as to say he knew about the place. Gui did not have to draw him a picture of what it would mean to find a spot like that. His own battle with nature to produce quality crops taught him the value of a kind environment. He frantically searched his mind for any chance conversations that he might have overheard.

"You don't think they are just good at dry season farming?"

"It surpasses anything I have ever seen in dry season farming, and I have seen it all."

"I'm sorry, Gui, I have never heard of such a place."

"It is one of the best guarded secrets ever," said Gui. "It has obviously been there a very long time. I was so sure that one of your workers would have wandered in from there."

Yahara laughed, "You mean someone got tired of the Garden of Eden and decided to see what Hell was like?"

"I see what you mean," Gui said wryly. "There would not be much point, would there? Yet, it always seems that someone is dissatisfied and wants to leave Paradise. However, if it is as difficult to get out as it is to get in, it is no wonder we've never heard of the country." He described the thorn boundary.

"I'll be glad to ask around among the men." Yahara began.

"No! Do not do that! I do not want anyone to know that I am looking for this. If you can ask discreetly, okay, but do not tell *anyone* about it. Understand?"

"You bet, Gui. Not a word."

After he left, Gui paced the room. He wished he had not mentioned it to Yahara. The fewer people who knew about it, the better.

With the knowledge of how those people do it, he could be the most powerful man in the entire world! If he could just get there first and make an agreement with them before anyone else found them. Time was of the essence! Someone could stumble on that triangle of green land any moment. If Tomiko Hirokama learned about this...!

"'I' must get there first!"

Who would know? Where could he go to find the name of that place? Who could he trust to do some research?

Then it came to him. Of course!

Not bothering to put on his raincoat, he raced to his car in a downpour, throwing a spray of mud as he sped away to find Carol.

Yahara watched him go as he too experienced an intense excitement at the thought of a Green Country. Such knowledge could be used to set him up in business on his own—and he would no longer have to follow Gui Manieux's orders. But more than that, he might actually be able to do something about making food available to hungry people.

CHAPTER 36

C arol! Carol!" He ran through the house, frantic to find her.

"I'm in the sunroom, Gui."

She sat at her computer, which was on the low table in front of her and a glass of iced tea beside it. A silk robe, splashed with brilliant flowers, was more revealing than concealing. She moved to draw it around her. Gui did not notice.

Carol saw his face as he came toward her and cried out, "Gui, you found whatever it was you were looking for!"

"Carol, I have the most important research assignment you will ever undertake. And when you hear about it, you will die for a chance to do it!"

"I'm listening."

"Listen to this riddle. There is a country shaped like a triangle, a hundred miles long from the point of the triangle to the bottom of it and about fifty miles wide at the base. It has been there for thousands of years, but no one knows about it. Yet it produces fruits and vegetables and grain in abundance, even in dry season. From the air it looks like a lush garden. No one knows the name of the place or the people who live there. A wide band of thorns surrounds it so no one can get in." He stopped. "What do you think so far?"

"Have you found the Garden of Eden? Some anthropologists believe it was in Africa, you know."

"All I know is that it does exist and that if I could find the secret of its productivity, I would hold the Midas touch in my hand!"

Suddenly Carol understood his excitement. "Gui, it could mean the end of hunger!"

"You are absolutely right!" He dropped down beside her chair, his hand on her arm. "Carol, you know how to do research. You could find this place for me. Will you do it?"

She touched two keys and then turned off the computer and gathered her robe around her. "I love riddles, especially one that could change the world. I will go right down to the library and see what I can find." She headed for her room to change. "I'll be back in a little while."

CHAPTER 37

Blantyre

M alissa had never really looked at Blantyre before. She knew it was one of the more progressive towns in eastern Africa with a fairly up-to-date hospital and some impressive hotels and public buildings. In fact, a pamphlet in her hotel room had described Blantyre as the business center of east Africa. Out of curiosity Malissa had looked at the phone book and found several pages of businesses and professionals such as attorneys and accountants. She recognized some American companies with subsidiaries in Blantyre. There was even an American Express office.

It was obviously a town of contrasts because just outside the center of the town the homes were built of mud bricks with tin roofs. Water was a spigot on each block. She had seen the women carrying water in buckets on their heads to their houses. Goats and dogs were everywhere, even downtown.

Blantyre was another example of what she called the "African syndrome." Well-built, even beautiful public buildings and hotels to serve the upper layer of society surrounded by mud-walled houses on dirt streets, open toilet trenches and swarms of flies and other flying insects. Now at the beginning of rainy season the mosquitoes were just beginning to be a nuisance. She had not forgotten her malaria medicine that morning

The inevitable traders flocked around her with their wares in boxes on their heads. .Malissa had lived in Africa long enough to know what was qual-ity ivory or wood carvings, and she gave a quick glance at each trader, just in case there was something worth keeping. The graceful birds made from cows' horns were clever. The ubiquitous but pretty ivory bracelets, earrings and pins, no doubt from pig ivory, not elephant ivory. She knew how to tell the difference. Carved heads in mahogany and ebony, from three inches tall to actual head size. Maybe she would look at those later. One had to watch carefully for quality workmanship. Unfortunately some carvers were putting them out wholesale for the tourist trade with little concern for quality.

If she found a really well-made chest set, she might buy it for her father, but later. Today, she was in another world. It was hard to believe that this was Wednesday, market day in Mubi, and she was not staying late to see the added load of patients who came by on their way home from market.

Somewhere between Mubi and Blantyre, the pain, the death, the hunger, had dropped away. "A person can take only so much," Malissa had said to herself as she had set the thermos of coffee on the seat of the Jeep and waved farewell to Yusufu, her cook..

Now the hospital was only a dream, a bad dream. The ten-hour drive was exhausting over dirt roads roughened by holes left from the last rainy season and not repaired, and she had not had much sleep the night before she left Mubi. She had arrived at the hotel late the night before and went right to bed after a refreshing shower. Even if the water was cold, it actually felt good after the hot sticky ride.

Malissa was used to walking wherever she went, and the hospital in Blantyre was not that far. She did not relish the idea of driving among bicycles and animals. The world got up early in Africa, and there were many people also on their way to somewhere. It was a ten-minute walk to the Blantyre Hospital, an imposing two-story white-stuccoed building run by the Seventh-day Adventists,.

The supply room manager was most generous and let her have enough disposable gloves for a couple of months. He would not even take payment for them.

"We just have to be very careful," he said. "Don't ever go without these."

She was relieved to get that out of the way. The gloves were not heavy in the knitted bag that she carried over her shoulder.

Then she had gone walking from the hospital down the main street of town. Mercedes vied for space with the Deux Cheveux and 4-wheel drive vehicles with horns blaring. Bicycles darted between cars, not waiting for the only traffic light in town to change. Malissa knew that the native Africans would do most of their buying in the big market which was several blocks away. She would go there perhaps tomorrow because she actually felt more at ease bargaining with traders there. The people she saw here were mostly foreigners who lived in the gated section of town in big houses with servants. They were all intent on their own errands and Malissa was glad to be left alone.

Most of the shops were just open spaces that would be enclosed by shutters at night. The wares were scattered on tables or hanging from wires. The shops would be closed from 12 o'clock to 3 o'clock to avoid the midday heat. She paused at some of them to imagine herself buying whatever was there, plastic dishes from China, metal cookware from India, blouses made by the seamstress on site, pretty pillows, but she would not spend money on such things. She wandered on, careful to step over the toilet trench at the side of the street.

The last block before the hotel had nicer shops with proper doors and front windows. She was surprised by a little shop, a boutique. Mannikins in the big front window wore lovely creations. Again she considered the contrast between home-sewn blouses and Paris-designed dresses. She didn't even pause to question if she should go in.

"Miss, that is your dress!" purred the young woman in the boutique. Malissa saw the Paris label and bought it. An elegant bit of peach silk and lace—she deserved it! It gave her complexion a glow. Then she tried on, of all things, a bathing suit, one-piece to be sure, but a striking turquoise with a ribbon of pink flowers going diagonally from the left shoulder. It accented her curves nicely. In fact, as she stood in front of the mirror in the bathing suit, she felt elegant and yes, sexy.

She started to dismiss the thought when the clerk said, "Miss, you have a very nice figure! Are you going to the lake?"

"Yes," Malissa replied quickly, even though she had no idea where the lake was or that she would be going there.

"There are many single men at the lake resorts, Miss. Enjoy your lovely bathing suit!"

It was madness, she told herself, but she bought it.

It was a thought that had long been absent in Malissa's mind—that a man might find her attractive. She was usually impatient with the errant waves in her medium brown hair and gave no thought to the deep tan of her well-formed legs. But she had to admit that the woman she saw in the full-length mirror was definitely attractive. She didn't even need the padding in the bra of the bathing suit to fill it out.

By the time she left the boutique she had bought two other dresses, little summery sheers that matched her mood and were in sharp contrast to the utilitarian cotton print dress she was wearing.

Malissa ambled slowly on the way back to the hotel. Hotel Mount Soche, the nicest, most expensive hotel in Blantyre. She was sparing herself nothing this time. She was delighted to find a bookstore, a real bookstore with international newspapers and world-class books. She browsed quite a while there and bought a novel. She would actually have time to read. Next to the bookstore was a sandwich and ice cream shop. She did indulge in a dish of chocolate ice cream, sitting in the little garden patio in the shade. She was glad the hotel was close as her packages were getting heavy.

When she reached the hotel, she would lie down for a few minutes and then go have a lovely dinner in the dining room. Some of the Lake Malawi perch, just like in her dream.

CHAPTER 38

"I tell you, Gui, that place is just a figment of your imagination!" Carol said. "I searched through every map in the library; I tried every possible reference work. If it exists, it is indeed the best kept secret in Africa."

"We have to find it, and quick, before someone beats us to it!"

Carol was pouring their after-dinner wine as they sat on the couch Thursday evening in the spacious, open living room, enjoying a slight evening breeze refreshed by the afternoon rain.

Carol laughed. "I read about a syndrome that occurs when a person finds something new. Even though it may have been around for centuries without anyone knowing about it, suddenly the person is sure that dozens of people are on the verge of knowing about it also. What makes you think anyone else is trying to find this place?"

"Something that could change the entire world is just too important not to be found. I just want to be the first."

"Why, Gui? Why do you want this?"

A half-smile came over Gui's face. "I think it is because it is a riddle. I want to be the one to solve the riddle."

"And when you have solved the riddle, you become a very powerful and a very wealthy man, right?"

"Right."

"I'll let you be powerful and rich—if you solve the problem of hunger when you solve the riddle."

"It is a deal!"

Carol pulled him to her, his face against her breasts. "What I really want is to keep you just as you are," Carol said softly. "Every morning when I awaken, I savor another day with you."

Gui's response was immediate. His lips caressed her soft mounds as he closed his eyes and breathed in the heady scent of her perfume, of her body. "You are all I want," he murmured, "and I want all of you."

Flora was already in her room, and they missed the rap at the front door at first. It was Carol who finally realized there was a visitor. "Gui," she said softly, "someone is at the door."

"Damn!"

As Gui opened the door, Bert blurted out, "I'm sorry, Mr. Manieux, but I need to speak with you about . . . " It had been perhaps the most difficult action of his life, deciding to ask Gui Manieux to loan him the money. This man who he despised was nevertheless his last resort.

Suddenly Gui saw a possible answer to his problem. "Bert! You are just the person I want to see. You hang around bars and the market and places like that, don't you?" He did not wait for the answer. "You said you needed money. How much money do you need?"

"At least ten thousand kwacha," Bert blurted out. He had planned to approach the subject gingerly, finally getting to the amount he needed. Now he was sure he had blown his chances.

Gui spoke quickly. "If you can find the name of the Green Country and the name of someone who lives there that we can contact, you will have your ten thousand dollars."

Bert's astonishment was almost greater than his need to find the money, but not quite. He parroted back, "The name of the Green Country, and the name of someone we can contact."

"Correct."

Reeling, but still on his feet, Bert said, "You've got it!"

As Bert turned to leave, Gui stopped him. "Don't discuss this with anyone. Be very, very discreet with your questions."

Bert nodded. "Of course, Mr. Manieux."

CHAPTER 39

Mount Soche Hotel, Blantyre

Tomiko was tired and hungry and more than a little bit exasperated. Getting something done in east Africa had to be the most frustrating experience in the world. And he should know. Few people had visited as many countries as he in just a few months ..

At least here he could open up his laptop computer and communicate with someone on the other side of the globe. Providing laptop computers for himself and a world system of communication through World.net was one thing Tomiko had accomplished since becoming Special Assistant to the head of the World Health Organization.

In fact, he had taught his wife, Matsuko, how to use World.net E-mail, and they communicated daily.

It had taken most of the day on Thursday at the airport to gain absolutely no information about Gui Manieux's pilot. It was not that they did not know it; it was just that this man was away from his desk, one was gone for the day, or was on holiday. It all depended on who you talked to. The last person he tried to see never did quit talking on the phone. And, of course, there was the three-hour break for lunch.

He had come away without even learning the pilot's name. Oh, they were all most polite—that was the infuriating part of it. Each person who had delivered the message that the person he was looking for was not there would inevitably say, "Come back tomorrow. He will be here tomorrow." He knew it was not so—it was their stock answer.

Tomiko plopped his perspiring body into a wicker chair in the Kapeni Cocktail Bar at the Mount Soche Hotel. At five o'clock the room was already filling up with the international set that seemed to be drawn to Blantyre, and especially to this hotel, according to the American Express agent he had questioned after his unprofitable day at the airport.

Oh, for a small drink of sake! He knew without looking at the row of bottles behind the bartender that there was only the liquor that Americans,

Europeans and Indians drank.

He muttered under his breath, "This would be a great place for a bar." If he waited long enough, a waiter just might ask him what he would like to drink. That was another thing he could not understand—how restaurants or bars in Africa could stay in business. The service had to be the worst in the world, just a step below the food.

Time was running out. He needed to do something significant, something spectacular if he was going to keep his job as Special Assistant to the Director of the World Health Organization. And it had to happen soon. All kinds of projects had been tried with a little success here and there, but nothing that effectively addressed the hunger problem in Third World countries. If he could even come up with a small idea, just something that would make a small impact on a small area of the world. If there was possibly any truth to there being a place called the Green Country, maybe someone there would know of an idea that he could use.

How was he going to find Manieux's pilot, and if he did, was there anything to the story? And would he learn it in time to forestall catastrophe at World Health—catastrophe being the loss of his job.

If there was such a thing as a telephone book—and if he could find one, he could call Manieux himself, but he did not want to alert the man to the idea of a country that had an answer to the problem of hunger. The off hand way in which the pilot had mentioned the Green Country made Tomiko believe that he attached no significance to it. Manieux's reputation was well-known in international circles. He was not anyone to get involved with unless you held all the aces, and even then, you would have to insist on keeping all hands above the table. No, contacting Manieux was not an option.

Surely pilots came to this bar, since most of them were expatriates, having come to Africa to fly, as very few Africans acquired pilot's licenses. Foreigners tended to seek other foreigners. He would strike up a conversation with every man who looked anything like a pilot. Someone would know the pilot's name.

Tomiko had a keen ear for languages and spoke several himself. He had learned them with the idea it would help him find a better position, and it certainly had. From here and there, and as people passed him, he heard bits of English, French, Pakastani, Spanish, German—but no Japanese.

After he had managed to get a whiskey, he would find the dining room and order some of the perch that Malawi was famous for. Surely they could not ruin fish. Several times he tried to hail a waiter, and finally he walked to the bar where he waited another fifteen minutes before the lone bartender could take his order.

The bartender said something unintelligible in English, something about did he want . . . what? Finally the bartender reached for a bottle. It was sake! "AWA," Tomiko said under his breath. AWA stood for "Africa Wins Again." Over and over in Africa just when one expected something to be one way, it suddenly was changed, either completely wrong or completely right, and there was never any predicting which it would be. Like the taxi driver who was objecting loudly when Tomiko paid him, only to finally discover that the taxi driver was telling him he had paid too much.

Imagine the bartender having enough sense to offer him sake. Tomiko nodded emphatically. Another thought struck him as he watched the bartender pour the drink. There had to be another Japanese person in Blantyre.

Incredibly at that moment he spotted the man he was looking for. He was standing at the door of the now-crowded room, peering at each person there as if intent on finding a particular one.

"Monsieur!" For some reason that Tomiko could never explain, when he needed to speak quickly to someone who did not speak Japanese, he spoke in French. "Monsieur!"

Bert's ears picked up the sound of someone calling out in French over the noise of many voices, and his glance followed the voice. When his eyes found Tomiko, his brain responded quickly. Tomiko was the last person he wanted to talk to. He had done the incredibly stupid thing of mentioning the Green Country to Tomiko. He did not want to discuss it with anyone except someone who knew where it was. Ten thousand dollars was too important to take a chance on Tomiko's remembering their conversation.

By the time Tomiko pushed his way through the crowd, Bert was nowhere to be seen.

CHAPTER 40

Mount Soche Hotel Dining Room

M alissa's brain was hazy—nothing seemed real. The nap had served only to dull her senses. Which come to think of it, was just what Malissa wanted. What a relief that the only decision she had to make was whether to have the perch baked, broiled, or fried. Even her mission friends were not on hand to raise an eyebrow at her lavish spending on a bathing suit that she might never wear, or at the forbidden drink of wine that waited at her fingertips.

This was gracious dining; linen tablecloths, cloth napkins, candles, quiet music, and flowers in huge bouquets all around the room, not just on each table.. The scent of blossoms was heavy, and wonderful. Heavy drapes in cool blue-green seemed to shut out the sluggish heat as slow-moving fans teased her curls.

She smiled at the thought of her curls which she had allowed to bounce out around her face, making her feel younger than she had in years. The dress was one of her new ones—crisp cotton sheer in soft turquoise with tiny clusters of pink flowers. She had noted in the mirror that the dress and her eyes were the same color. Not that it mattered. Who was to see them, her dream notwithstanding?

She had chosen a table off to one side where she could have a clear view of the room. Watching people was half the fun. A polite waiter who spoke reasonably clear English took her order for chambo, pan-fried with parsley and a dill sauce, with oven-baked tiny potatoes. She was in no hurry, she told him, and she would have the mixed-fruit salad first.

The dining room was filling up, and as couples went by, she felt just a twinge of self-consciousness at being alone. By the time the waiter came to clear her salad plate, she was ready for a second glass of white wine. Having had nothing to eat since the ice cream earlier that afternoon, her head already buzzed pleasantly from the wine.

The service for the other place at her table had not been removed, and she found herself thinking of friends that she might like to have with her, enjoying this lovely place. Alas, she had been gone from the States too long. All of her friends were out of touch, except for maybe a card at Christmas. A sense of sadness overwhelmed her, and tears filled her eyes. More than a little surprised by the emotion, she daubed at her face quickly with her napkin.

This was not like her—she was usually quite unemotional, or at least well in control. Here she was, having the time of her life and suddenly she tears up. Perhaps she had been under more of an emotional strain than she had realized, but then again, the first glass of wine always did loosen her emotions.

There was a sound of quick steps and sudden movement, and Malissa blinked rapidly, trying to see through her blurred eyes. A man had seated himself in the other chair at her table. Alarmed, she started to say something.

"Please!" His voice was urgent but low. "I hope you speak English." She nodded, and he rushed on. "I know you don't know me, but could you pretend for just a little bit?" His words tumbled over each other in his haste. "There will be a man coming in here any moment. I don't want to talk with him. If I am with someone, he will not bother me. Could you, would you mind if we looked like friends?"

She was now speechless.

"I'll buy your dinner, okay?"

She could not refuse the panic in his eyes. It was for real. "You may stay— a few minutes." In college Malissa had been labeled "Malissa the Lip" by her close friends, and now she stated solemnly. "In fact, I just realized that my wine glass is empty and that I surely will want a dessert and . . . probably a coffee."

For just a second he stared at her, then seeing the unmistakable gleam in her blue-green eyes, he grinned. "Anything you say! And thanks, thanks a million.

CHAPTER 41

There was a momentary awkward silence until Malissa said, "My name is Malissa Taylor. Even if we are going to be acquainted only a few minutes, names would be nice."

"Oh, oh, sure! Sorry, I'm not quite with it. Bert McEwen." He started to put out his hand and as quickly pulled it back as his eyes darted around the room looking for the expected visitor. Grinning, he said, "We would not be shaking hands if we already knew each other, would we?"

"Where are you from?" Malissa asked. "Your accent . . . "

"Kansas. Some call it a twang. Been here almost fifteen years and haven't lost it yet, have I?" He indicated his jeans and blue and white striped cotton shirt. "And I still dress like a ranch hand."

As his eyes again searched the room, Malissa said, "What does this person look like? I can watch for him too since I can see the door and you can't without turning around."

"Japanese, only the second one I've seen in Blantyre."

"That should make it easy."

The waiter arrived with Malissa's fish and looked inquiringly at Bert.

"Would you mind if I ordered?" Bert asked. "It would make it more believable."

"Of course, go ahead."

"I'll have the same," Bert said to the waiter. "And a bottle of Carlsberg beer." The waiter nodded and left.

"Don't wait on me—your food will get cold." Bert said.

"I'll eat slowly," Malissa smiled. As she took the first mouthful, a nagging memory suddenly popped out clearly. "Tell me your name again."

"Bert McEwen."

The name of the pilot the woman at the airport in London had said Malissa should meet had incredibly stuck in her mind. "Are you perchance a pilot?"

A sudden boyish grin lit up his face. He relaxed against the back of his chair and said, "Not only did I pick the prettiest woman in the room, she is also a psychic."

Malissa flushed at the compliment. "You, you are a pilot," she repeated, trance-like.

He reacted quickly with a puzzled frown. "Wait a minute, how did you know I was a pilot?"

She shrugged.

"Actually," Bert said, grinning now, "I'm the best, or does it matter how good a pilot I am. Are you just looking for a pilot?"

Now she was flustered, and again a wave of pink flowed over her face. Rather testily she said, "I wasn't looking for anyone at all. You found me, remember?"

But Bert seemed not to hear her. "A woman who can still blush. Where have you been hiding for the past twenty years?"

She could not help but smile. "I guess you could call it hiding. I am a nurse with a mission in the Wamba tribe, northwest of here."

Bert was instantly interested. "A missionary nurse. Northwest? How far?"

Malissa's gaze did not leave Bert's face. "I think your expected guest has just come into the dining room."

Bert reached for one of the dinner rolls. "May I?"

Malissa nodded.

Bert was studiously spreading butter onto the roll as Tomiko stopped at their table.

"Good evening, sir, lady," Tomiko said, bowing to each in turn.

Bert's expression was not one of welcome.

"I am most sorry to interrupt your dinner."

"As a matter of fact," Bert said firmly, "we are eating."

"I will take only a moment of your time," went on Tomiko. Turning to Malissa, he said, "I am Tomiko Hirokama, Special Assistant to the director of the World Health Organization." Then to Bert he said, "You are Mr. Manieux's pilot." He waited for a response.

Bert did not answer but took a bite of the roll. Malissa waited, her curiosity mounting.

"When we were in Salisbury, you mentioned something about a green country. I would like very much to know where it is."

Bert frowned and appeared to be trying to remember. "Green country? I don't remember anything like that."

Tomiko was not to be put off. "But you told me you had flown over a green country. You even asked if I knew where it might be."

Bert shook his head emphatically. "You must have been talking to someone else. There were a lot of people at that conference."

"No, it was you," Tomiko insisted.

Bert's eyes hardened. "Mr. Hirokama, I don't know what you are talking about, and my friend and I are having dinner." He stood up, rising far above Tomiko. "Please, " he said, but please was not in his voice. He motioned for Tomiko to leave.

Tomiko looked helplessly from Bert to Malissa, finally backing away.

As Bert sat down, the waiter arrived with the drinks.

They watched as Tomiko made his way through the tables of diners to where the head steward stood. After a conversation, the steward led Tomiko to a table across the room where he sat down. Any move they made would be in his full view.

"Looks like we're stuck, Malissa—I can't leave now."

"You can't leave now anyway. You promised to pay for my dinner, and I'm not even sure what all I am going to have yet."

"I certainly am not going to complain about having dinner with a beautiful woman. This is a rare treat for me," Bert said.

Her face burned pink, and furious with herself, she reached for her wine glass. She could handle almost any crisis, but this was one she had had no experience with.

But speaking of attractive, the man across from her was certainly that. Not handsome, just good looking. She had noted early on that he was not wearing a wedding ring—if that meant anything these days.

Quick to rise to any occasion, even this one, Malissa told herself to relax and enjoy the dinner—he would not be there very long. And it was not unpleasant to have people see her with a gentleman friend.

She did wonder about Bert's treatment of the man who was with the World Health Organization, obviously a rather important person. Bert had seemed frightened, or angry, she was not sure which.

"Mr. Harakama, or whatever his name was, asked about a green country. Was he talking about one in this area?"

Bert hesitated, still fearful of losing the secret. But, he figured, this was a woman from bush country who was certainly not a danger. Besides, she was attractive, and it had been a long time since he had sat across the table from any woman, much less one this good-looking. No point in being rude by refusing to reply.

"I think he meant in this general area."

"Could he have been referring to Kulanji?"

He stopped with his beer in mid-air.

Only with great difficulty was Bert able to keep his heart out of his throat long enough to say, "Tell me about Kulanji."

CHAPTER 42

"Kulanji lies about 500 miles northwest of here, bordering the tribe where I live. It has been called various things, Garden of Eden, The Garden Spot, The Farm. I have never heard it called the Green Country, but it is certainly an appropriate name."

Bert started to speak so quickly that his breath caught in his throat, causing a hiccoughing sound, but he gulped and asked, "Why is it green when everything around it is brown?"

"No one knows for sure. There are legends about something happening long ago that caused it to be different. The Kulanji still give thanks to their gods for treating them different from other people."

"That must make other people envious of them."

"Definitely. But more than just raising good crops, they are just more healthy than other people. They stand a head taller than their neighbors, perhaps from heredity, but probably due also to generations of enough food and fewer illnesses. They are less likely to have certain diseases, although they do get measles and some of the rest."

"How do you know all this?"

"I set up their dispensary for them about five years ago. I make regular visits every three months to see that the dispenser is following correct procedures and if he needs medicines. I also trained their dispenser and keep him up on new techniques or procedures. Once every three months is really often enough because they don't have nearly the incidence of illness that we have in Mubi."

Bert shook his head in disbelief.

Malissa asked quickly, "What is it?"

"I can't believe this. While I am trying to avoid Tomiko, I stumble onto the very person, perhaps the only person in Blantyre at this moment, who could answer my questions. This has to be one for the books, or maybe the gods have decided to be nice to me for a change." He motioned with his hand.

"Go on, tell me more."

"The Kulanji are a most unusual people, and they guard their people with unceasing caution. "

"You don't mean that *no one* gets in or out. Someone is going to sneak out just to prove he can do it."

"I am sure that does happen, but apparently that does not result in a greater incidence of disease."

"Is there no communication with other tribes, even between chiefs?"

"There is limited contact with chiefs of neighboring tribes.."

"But you get to go in."

"Under strictest supervision. Someone is with me at all times."

"And there isn't even any . . . " Bert paused, looking for the right word. "fraternization?"

"One thing I do know, there is no premarital sex within the tribe, so it is logical to suppose that the young men do go elsewhere."

Strong skepticism was registered in Bert's eyes. Malissa nodded to reinforce her words. "The men demand that they have only virgins as brides, and there is strict enforcement. Of course, the women are married very early too, shortly after puberty begins."

"Oh." That made it easier to believe, but he was too curious not to ask the next question. "Do you mean there are no unfaithful wives or husbands and no prostitutes?"

Malissa smiled. "I doubt their difference from other people goes quite that far. I have never asked, but as I have begun to know their language better, I hear whisperings about such things." Malissa took a sip of wine, savoring the heady sensation that was invading her brain. "But the most surprising thing, I suppose, is that in the five years I have been going there, I have never seen a case of AIDS."

A rocket went off in Bert's brain. Growing super crops was one thing, but knowing the answer to AIDS was something else again. "You've got to be kidding! No AIDS?"

"I've never seen a case. Of course, I haven't seen every person in the tribe, but . . . "

"That must be because they don't intermarry with other tribes."

"It's possible, but I don't think so. I think they have an immunity to AIDS."

The impact of what she said was overwhelming, and only a glance at Tomiko restrained him from shouting. Instead, he said as calmly as possible under the circumstances, "Malissa, do you realize what you just said?"

Malissa looked bewildered. "What did I just say?"

"That there is something that will prevent AIDS."

"Ye—s?" she said slowly, still not understanding.

"Don't you realize that that secret would be worth millions and millions of dollars?"

"I never thought of it that way." She added thoughtfully, "I guess I've been too close to the forest to see the trees."

"People would kill for that secret and sell it to the highest bidder."

Suddenly there was fear in her face. "Is that why Mr. Hirokama wants to know where it is, so he can exploit those people, steal their secret?"

"I don't think he knows all of what you have just told me. He is probably just looking for an answer to the problem of enough food for starving people, and he thinks such a country might know something no one else does. After all, that's his job."

Now her voice was harsh. "Those people have been safe for centuries. Their lives should not be invaded now." She looked at him with suspicious, insistent gaze. "Why do you want to know where it is?"

Bert could not look at her. He had come face to face with what was undoubtedly the greatest dilemma of his life. All he had to do to receive his ten thousand dollars was tell Gui Manieux the location of Kulanji and give him Malissa's name. It was that simple, he could walk away.

But in the past few minutes he had also come to know a woman who looked at things differently. To reveal the location to Gui also meant the end of life as the Kulanji had known it for generations, because one thing he did know, Gui Manieux would have no qualms whatsoever about doing anything that was necessary to acquire the secret. Those gentle people, and this gentle woman, would be safe no longer.

Bert felt Malissa's warm hand touching his and her voice demanding, "Why do you want to know, Bert?"

"Sir, here is your dinner." The waiter set the steaming plate in front of Bert.

"Thank you," Bert said fervently, picking up his fork to eat. "Malissa, is this as good as it looks?"

He would remember to give that waiter an extra large tip.

CHAPTER 43

Thursday morning Gui himself hurried to open the door to Bert, leading him into the study. After a sleepless night, Bert had made up his mind about the Green Country secret. He would tell Gui only the bare essentials. It was obvious that Malissa would not talk to Gui when she realized why he wanted the information. He would get his ten thousand dollars and leave.

Gui greeted him and said, "Do I assume your early return means you succeeded?" Carol appeared behind Gui.

"In an amazing stroke of luck, I bumped into the person who was probably the only one in Blantyre who actually knows anything about the Green Country. She goes there every three months to visit the medical dispensary. She described it in detail."

"Good work!" exclaimed Gui. "Did she tell you why the crops are so productive?"

"She doesn't know why, just that they are."

"Can you take me there by land?"

"It wouldn't do any good, you know."

"I want to see it for myself!" Gui said adamantly.

"Any effort to force your way in will only be met with resistance. There simply is no way to get in there."

"Are you saying I cannot find out why their crops are better than anyone else's?"

"I don't see how you can. Those people have secluded themselves for centuries."

"That is just too bad!" Gui almost shouted. "They cannot hide away any longer!"

Carol was shocked at Gui's outcry. "Gui, you can't just go in and seize the knowledge of how they do it."

"Why not? It must be pretty obvious to someone who knows what to look for."

"It won't work—unless you want a full-scale war on your hands." Bert knew Gui would not take no for an answer easily, but he was determined to halt the whole thing if at all possible.

"Then you are saying I should just give up?" Gui was shouting now.

"That's up to you, Mr. Manieux. I have brought you what you wanted to know."

"You expect me to pay ten thousand kwacha for you to tell me to forget it?"

"The agreement was that I would find the location of the Green Country and the name of a contact person. I have done that."

"No way! You do not get paid if I cannot get into the country."

Carol intervened. "Gui, you told me yourself that for ten thousand kwacha Bert was to locate the country and find a contact person. He has done that."

"No! I will not agree to that!"

Bert spoke in a controlled voice. "Then I won't tell you where it is or give you the name of the person. And there is no way under heaven that you would be able to find the information yourself."

Carol placed her hand on Gui's arm. "Gui, I will go and talk with the woman. I'll tell her how important it is if hunger is to be erased in Africa. I can persuade her, you know I can." Gui's face relaxed a little. "Pay him the money, Gui—he earned it."

Gui was not quite ready to surrender the ten thousand dollars. "Sure, he probably slept with her, and now . . . "

Normally slow to react, something exploded as the image of gentle Malissa flashed before Bert's eyes. Anger pent up from his first encounter with this scoundrel burst forth as Bert hit him hard. Gui went down, blood gushing from his nose. Bert stared in surprise at his own hand, bleeding from the blow.

Carol grabbed a small towel from the bar and held it to Gui's face. "You asked for that!" she said without sympathy.

Still dazed, Gui pulled himself into a chair, holding the towel on his nose. Carol spoke in a low voice to him. Gui nodded and she turned to Bert. "Come by this afternoon with a map of the country and the name of the person. Your ten thousand kwacha will be ready."

"Make it between five o'clock and six o'clock," Bert said on his way to the door.

CHAPTER 44

On Thursday, Malissa saw Tomiko coming onto the patio of the hotel where she was stretched out on a lounge chair reading a book. She was enjoying the morning coolness, surrounded by flowering hibiscus and bougainvillea. She felt gloriously sinful to be here instead of at the hospital back in Mubi She sipped on a minted ice tea.

Bert had asked her not to discuss Kulanji with anyone else, absolutely no one, especially Mr. Hirokama. He never did give a satisfactory reason. After all, Mr. Hirokama was with the World Health Organization. Perhaps some good would come out of his knowing about Kulanji, and surely he could be relied upon to use the knowledge for the good of everyone, not some special interest group.

But she had promised Bert, and she would honor that promise. Malissa covered herself with a beach towel and hoped Tomiko would not see her.

"Miss," Tomiko began. "I'm sorry, I did not get your name last evening."

Malissa did not raise her head. Giving her name to the head of the World Health Organization did seem the polite thing to do. "Taylor," she replied.

"It is very important that I find out about the green country. I am wondering if your friend, Mr, oh, dear, I have forgotten his name."

"Bert."

"His last name?"

She should not be doing this, but how does one avoid giving such information without being rude? "McEwen."

"Of course, now I remember. Bert McEwen. Did he happen to mention the Green Country?"

Now she sat up. "Mr. Hirokama, if Bert wanted to talk to you about that, I am sure he would have done so last evening."

"Oh, no, I think he just did not want to be bothered when he was dining with a friend. It was rude of me to interrupt. It is of the utmost importance that I learn the location of this country. It could mean the difference between life and death for a great many people. You see, I am in a position to do something about hunger in Africa if I had certain information."

She was tempted to tell him, but she held back. Her dinner with Bert had been altogether delightful. Their conversation had very quickly left the Green Country as they comfortably shared bits of their lives. They had lingered over dessert and then coffee, waiting for Tomiko to leave. Then they danced until the band stopped playing, around midnight. By that time Mr. Hirokama had given up and left. Malissa still could not believe she had spent the entire evening with a stranger and felt so comfortable about it.

Bert was coming to take her on a sightseeing trip this afternoon, and she could hardly wait.

"If you will excuse me, Mr. Hirokama, I have an appointment."

"With Mr. McEwen, I trust."

She did not answer but walked across the patio and into the hotel feeling approving glances following her, including Mr. Hirokama's.

CHAPTER 45

"Let a woman in your life . . . " The musical phrase from "My Fair Lady" kept repeating in Bert's mind as he drove to the Hotel Mount Soche. If Malissa had not been the person with the information, it would have been so simple to give Gui all the information. He would even have asked to help carry out the next steps in securing the secret of the Green Country—for more money, of course.

But the image of gentle, trusting Malissa was something he could not ignore. He had never known a woman like Malissa. In his teens he had experienced puppy love. What he felt now was respect and admiration and desire, all of them.

A woman sure did complicate a man's life! He almost lost ten thousand dollars because of her. He had not realized how he felt about her until Gui made that nasty remark. Funny, he thought, that my brain didn't know, but my fist did!

He arrived at the hotel early, and rather than take a chance on running into Tomiko, he went in a side entrance and straight to Malissa's room. When she opened the door and saw him, her face flushed like it had the night before. He liked that. He longed to take her in his arms on the spot, but he did not want to embarrass her. How could she know how he felt? After all, they had met only the night before. .

Wearing a pretty soft pink cotton dress with a bright scarf tied around her head, she looked younger than the day before. "When I bought this outfit, I didn't even know I would have a use for it," she laughed.

"It looks very nice," he said sincerely. "I like your hair that way."

"Thank you," she said as she stuffed some things into a small cloth bag. "The sales clerk told me to buy the bathing suit in case I met a man on the beach."

"Take it, maybe you'll meet one."

"Maybe one will trip over my lounge chair—or fall over my umbrella. It could happen, you know. One fell into a chair at my table last night."

Bert grinned. Fell was the right word. He would give a lot to know how she felt about him.

"I'll be right with you," Malissa said, heading for the bathroom.

While he waited, Bert glanced around. The closet door was open, and he walked closer, taking note of the obviously new peach-colored dress still hanging in its plastic bag with the name of the dress shop,

The two-hour drive to Lake Malawi did not seem nearly that long—they had a lot to talk about. They passed small farms where men and women were sweating as they worked at clearing patches where they would plant guinea corn or tomatoes. They had to slow down several times for goats being herded down the road. The young boys herding the goats waved gaily at them and held out their hands for money. In the small villages they passed through, tall trees sheltered small houses where people sat in the shade with children playing nearby. One group was kicking a plastic ball back and forth and shouting at each other. Each village had its canteen, or little store, where one could buy matches, hard candies, canned beans , and some medicines such as aspirin, malaria medicine or Beano

At a restaurant in Chipoka on the lake they had grilled chambo that had been pulled out of the lake only an hour before. Large French fries came with the fish.

While they were eating on a veranda overlooking the lake, a young man asked if they would like to see the hippopotamuses. Bert said they would.

The boy sat in the back seat of the car, showing them points of interest and answering their questions in his stiff, broken English. About five miles up the lake road, the boy pointed to a side road. After bumping over a rutted road for half a mile, they came to the lake's edge where nine or ten hippopotamuses were splashing around in the water.

Malissa wondered why Bert seemed to be looking at her more than at the animals. Was something out of place? She did not ask. She also noted that he looked at his watch now and then.

"Do you have to be somewhere this afternoon?" she asked.

"Between five o'clock and six o'clock. We have plenty of time."

There was no place to change into their swimming suits, so Bert held up a towel while Malissa changed in the back seat of the car. Then he changed into a pair of shorts. He had had the presence of mind to bring snorkeling equipment, and they took turns watching the myriad of colored fish in Lake Malawi.

"Ninety-five percent of the tropical fish for aquariums in the world come from Lake Malawi," Bert told her.

When it was her turn, she paddled slowly through the crystal clear water. Suddenly she was transfixed by a large round orange fish with five little round orange fish following it in precise formation, like pictures in a child's math book. Count the fish. Malissa moved her hand, and suddenly the large fish opened its mouth, and the five little fish darted inside. Then the mother snapped her mouth shut and swam away.

They had a lime coconut drink under one of the umbrellas on the beach and talked. It seemed like there was no end of things to talk about, airplanes, medicine, flying in bush country, her work.

Bert drove home more slowly, reluctant for the time with Malissa to end. At the hotel, he followed her into the lobby where she turned to him and said, "I usually walk up instead of taking the elevator. I need the exercise." It was obvious that she did not expect him to follow her.

"Dinner tonight?" Bert asked.

"Won't that be a bit much—being together all day and then for dinner?"

"Not for me." Then he said before he could stop himself, "I just want to be with you."

An alarm went off in Malissa' head. He sounded like a little boy, and while that was touching, it was also less than twenty-four hours since she had met this man. She liked him—a lot, but she was more than a little overwhelmed by his attentions. Better to take it easy. She would be here for four more days—plenty of time.

"I would rather have you take me to see the artisans at work tomorrow. I just want to collapse tonight and read or do a crossword puzzle."

"Oh, all right." The disappointment was apparent in his voice. "I'll pick you up at say, eleven o'clock tomorrow?"

"Make it after lunch, say one o'clock." She stepped inside her room. "Thank you for a lovely day, Bert."

He stared at the closed door. "Damn!" he said to himself. "I frightened her. Now I've got to spend tonight alone thinking about her."

CHAPTER 46

Gui was no place in sight when Flora opened the front door and led Bert into the living room late Thursday afternoon. Carol came from the back patio.

"I'm really sorry about last night, Bert."

"It's okay. I've known Mr. Manieux for a quite a while—I wasn't really surprised. What surprised me was that I hit him. I've never done that before—to anyone—since I was a kid."

"You felt strongly."

"Yes, I did."

Her eyes looked for what he had brought. He unrolled a paper showing the location of the triangular-shaped country in relation to its surrounding territories. A rough drawing but essentially accurate, with Kulanji colored in bright green. He handed her another piece of paper on which Malissa's name and hotel room number was written.

She held out an envelope in exchange for the papers he had brought. Opening the envelope, he counted out ten thousand kwacha in one hundred-kwacha notes. One kwacha was roughly equal to one American dollar.

"Thank you, Miss Walters. It's a good thing you are around. You make things go better."

"Thank you, Bert." At that point she opened the piece of paper and glanced at it. "Malissa Taylor, Malissa Taylor! That's the woman I met in London as we were waiting for a plane." The conversation came flooding back to her memory. "I had completely forgotten, but she talked about a country where they grew great crops. This is going to be easier than I thought."

Bert did not like the sound of that. He just wanted out of there. He started toward the door. "I don't know if she will talk with you," Bert said.

Carol followed him.

"I really appreciate your doing this. This may be a momentous step for the people of Africa, Bert."

"I hope you are right. Africa sure needs help." He wanted to make sure she understood. "I don't know if Malissa, uh, Miss Taylor will talk with you."

"Oh, I think she will." She stopped him with a touch on his arm. "When I saw Miss Taylor in London, I told her you were someone she should meet. I'm curious, how do you happen to know her now?"

If Gui had asked that question, he would not have answered, but he liked Carol. "We happened to sit down at the same table at dinner last night."

"How nice." She hurried on. "Bert, Gui isn't angry with you. In fact, today he laughed and said he didn't know you felt so strongly about such things."

"Now he knows," Bert said firmly, without a trace of a smile.

CHAPTER 47

Tomiko was out of ideas. He had exhausted every avenue he could think of, and it looked like he would have to wait for matters to take their course.

News via his E-mail from his office in New York would indicate that he was on a short fuse to destruction if something didn't happen soon. News releases coming out of the conference in Zimbabwe did nothing to stem the tide since there had been virtually no progress toward solving the problems of hunger or AIDS.

He wished he were at home with Matsuko. She would give him a massage and a wonderful dinner, and they would make love. No doubt he could find a willing, or paid, companion in Blantyre, but he was old-fashioned in that way, or maybe just spoiled by Matsuko. He wanted nothing less than what Matsuko could give him.

At least he could have a glass of sake. It was five o'clock, time to be cutting out for the day anyway.

At the Kapeni bar in his hotel he found a quiet corner where he could enjoy his sake in peace. It was still early for people getting off work, and there was only a handful of people, all men in business suits with their suit jackets removed.

But to his surprise, a Japanese man walked in and was waited on at the bar almost immediately. Tomiko walked over to him and greeted him in the Japanese manner then invited him to his table. The man readily accepted.

"I am Yahara Harakawa," the man said as they were seated.

"Tomiko Hirokama."

"Most pleasant to see Japanese here," Yahara said.

"Most pleasant to share your sake," Tomiko returned.

Three hours later they had finished dinner in the dining room and felt like old friends. Hoping Yahara might know something that would be helpful, Tomiko shared his concern about his job and the Green Country, only to learn that Yahara already knew about it because Gui had asked his help in finding it.

When they parted it was with the promise to keep in touch, and Yahara pledged his utmost help in Tomiko's project, but he also gladly promised to not share anything about the Green Country with Gui Manieux.

As he left the hotel, Yahara smiled to himself. If he could help Tomiko find out about the Green Country before Gui did, maybe it would make Gui Manieux suffer, at least a little. A man who would refuse to help Markus, Roger's sexual partner, could not be trusted with the knowledge of something as important as the Green Country's secret.

CHAPTER 48

Friday morning Bert sat in his Landrover outside the office where he was to deliver the ten thousand kwacha. He had the ten thousand all right, but if he failed to come up with the remaining eighty-seven thousand kwacha, he would lose the first ten thousand.

Be realistic, Bert, he told himself, where are you going to get eighty-seven thousand kwacha? These ten Gs dropped into my lap, but the next eighty-seven aren't going to be that easy.

Why kid himself, he knew what he had to do. Somewhere, somehow, he would find the rest of the money.

He got out of the car, envelope in hand, and headed for the office.

CHAPTER 49

Friday morning, and Malissa did not have to rush off to the hospital. Instead she would luxuriate in bed, have a late breakfast and be ready when Bert came at one. How different this vacation was turning out to be! And how nice!

Malissa jumped in surprise when the phone rang. Living in bush without such amenities made one forget they existed. It must be Bert, no one else knew she was there. She picked up the phone with trembling fingers.

The voice on the phone was a woman's, quiet, assured and non-threatening. "Miss Taylor, my name is Carol Walters. We met in London airport when you were returning from furlough."

Malissa paused, then, "Yes, I remember." now she was even more surprised.

"I am associated with the firm which employs Mr. Bert McEwen. When he mentioned your name, I thought perhaps we could have lunch. Would that be possible?"

Malissa was instantly on guard. This was happening too fast. What had Bert told her—or was it about the Green Country? "I— I'm not sure. What would be the reason for that?"

"Well, as you know I am a freelance writer for international magazines. I seldom get the opportunity to talk to someone who knows about Africa intimately as you do. Bert mentioned that he had met you, and I remembered our conversation and would like to follow up on it. Would you be free at lunch?"

Malissa had to admit she was flattered by such attention, and she remembered her feelings in London about Carol being someone who could write about Africa's problems. "To talk about—what?"

"Just about your work and the people you work with." She said it so glibly.

Malissa said, "It, it would need to be early. I have a one o'clock appointment."

"Shall we make it eleven o'clock? I will pick you up, and we will go to a little restaurant I know of."

It was a reluctant response. "All right." This was a little too fast, but then Malissa did not have to discuss anything she didn't want to talk about.

"See you a few minutes before eleven."

"I'll be in the lobby. I'm not sure I will remember how you look."

"I think we will know each other instantly," the warm voice said.

Carol was right—Malissa recognized Carol immediately. They could have been sisters, she thought, each in suit dresses. Carol's was a soft rose; hers medium blue, each with a scarf at the neck. It was the one business dress Malissa had brought with her from the States, and this was the first time she had had occasion to wear it.

The little restaurant had only a few tables and chairs in a room that looked out on a small garden of bougainvillea and hibiscus, shaded by papaya trees laden with fruit. From somewhere drifted the scent of hyacinth.

"You may think this is a strange place for lunch," Carol said, "but they make the best grilled cheese sandwiches in Malawi. I thought that just maybe that would sound good to you."

"Sounds wonderful," responded Malissa. "What a lovely little garden."

"That's the other reason I come here—it is a restful place to sit for a little while."

A young woman in a white full apron over a dark blue dress came for their order. Her hair was plaited into tight rows with the shiny scalp showing through.

"Two grilled cheese, two hot chocolate." Carol waited for a nod from Malissa, then added, "We will want ice cream later."

"Did you notice her hairdo?," Carol said. "It is the latest style, called the Star. If you look at the crown, the parts for the braids form a star. Very pretty."

"Believe it or not, the Star has made it to bush country. The young girls are scrambling to sport the latest fashion. Most people don't realize that there is fashion in the African bush as there is anywhere," Malissa said. "It just doesn't change as often."

"Tell me about your people, Malissa. Is the hunger bad in your area?"

Malissa's reluctance was breaking down. Here was a journalist who could write stories that could make a difference, and Carol was obviously honest in her desire to learn about African problems.

Malissa warmed to the subject she knew so well. "The famine this year is very, very bad. Every year, starting in May, people get only one meal a day, but this year that started in March."

"The first new grain will be available—when? Early August?"

"Yes, *if* the rains come as they should. Otherwise, the first crop may not even mature."

"What are the people eating now?"

"All reserves of grain are gone. They have only what is brought in by the relief agencies, and even much of that is stolen and sold on the black market."

"Malissa, I am a writer. It is my job—and my opportunity—to tell people things they did not know before. I can help make things happen. Do you remember when we were in the London airport you started to tell me about a country where people knew how to grow crops better than anyone else. The plane was called, and we never did get back to the subject. Now Bert brings us together. Please tell me about that place."

Malissa had no reason to mistrust this woman who obviously had a close connection with Bert, and Malissa began speaking. It was a pleasure to tell about what she knew well—the people of Kulanji, their gardens, the farms, the dispensary. She mentioned no names of people she knew there, having decided it would be best not to involve specific people.

The sandwiches arrived, smelling delicious and looking crusty golden brown the way grilled cheese ought to. The hot chocolate was rich and almost hot.

Malissa did not start on her sandwich but lowered her voice now. "There has to be something unique about Kulanji, and just possibly, knowledge of what it is could help others. I'm sure Bert told you that he thought the fact there is no AIDS in Kulanji might mean that there is something in that area that would prevent the disease."

Carol had been only half listening as she took a bite of her sandwich. She stopped with her sandwich in mid-air. "What did you say?"

The sound of Carol's voice and the look on her face made Malissa instantly sure she should not have mentioned it. Obviously Bert had not told her the most important bit of information, and he would have had his reasons. After all, he knew Carol better than she did.

"Did you say there is no AIDS in Kulanji?"

Was it too late to change what she had said? "I could be wrong, there probably is some there."

"But you said there is none. Is that what you said?"

"Ye—s. As far as anyone knows, there is no AIDS in Kulanji."

Carol was excited—the way Bert had been. "There must be a reason!"

"No doubt there is, but no one has ever done any research."

"Then it must be done!"

Suddenly Malissa wanted out of the conversation. If only she had not mentioned it. "They will let no one into the country."

Carol interrupted, "They let you in."

"Someone stays with me at all times."

"But you could . . . " Carol seemed to search for ideas, "bring out samples."

"Samples of what?" Malissa asked.

"Of soil, of water. There has to be some reason for the extraordinary crops and the absence of AIDS. Don't you see, Malissa, this is the most important breakthrough in the history of AIDS!"

"But they don't allow anyone in or out without permission. No one can remove water or dirt."

"I am fascinated, Malissa," Carol said, leaning forward. "Tell me about this tribe, about their customs, their food, anything."

With great reluctance, Malissa began, choosing a subject that she thought would be safe. "They have no delinquency. Their daughters are guarded absolutely so that they are virgins when they marry, usually shortly after puberty."

"Fascinating!" Carol said. "But you are the key to the puzzle! You are almost the only person from the outside who can go in." Carol rushed on. "Do you know anyone in Kulanji?"

"Carol, I know them well, and that is the reason I do not want to talk about this. We have no right to interfere in their lives. There is a reason why they have isolated themselves over the centuries."

"But they can't keep the secret for themselves forever!" Carol actually gestured with her sandwich for emphasis.

"The secret is in their country. It probably wouldn't work anywhere else."

"But we don't know that, Malissa."

"No, Carol."

Suddenly there were tears in Carol's eyes. Embarrassed by her loss of control and struggling to manage her trembling voice, Carol spoke in low tones. "Malissa, all my life I have wanted to do something about the pain and suffering that I see people going through. I have been so fortunate, so blessed, but I could never forget the misery that I knew was out there. That is why I came to Africa. I couldn't be a missionary—I'm not religious, but I do care about people. It tears my heart out to write about the plight of the children in Africa, but write I do—because I keep thinking maybe, just maybe, something that I write will make a difference."

She put her hand over Malissa's. "I don't have to be the one to do this. You have the answer, Malissa! You could make the difference!"

"But I can't, no one can get into Kulanji."

"There has to be a way, Malissa, and you are the only one who can do it!"

Malissa had barely touched her sandwich. She sat there shaking her head, pain and indecision in her eyes.

"Think about it, Malissa. There has to be a way. I'll help—I'll do anything—anything. But you are the one with the key to the secret!"

Malissa stood up. "I will have to think about this."

"Good! You think about it. I'll call you tonight, would nine o'clock be all right?"

Malissa frowned and without replying walked away quickly.

CHAPTER 50

After she left Malissa at the hotel, Carol drove like a race car driver, sliding through stop signs, honking at dogs in the street. It was Friday afternoon—she would have to drive out to the Farm. Gui would still be at the office, she was sure. She skidded to a stop in front of the office door, bumping the log marker.

Before she reached Gui's office door, it opened and Gui was standing there. "Carol! I heard your tires screaming in the gravel. What in the world . . . ?"

"Gui! You won't believe what I found out!"

"Not unless you tell me."

Gui pulled her into the room and shut the door. Carol stood where she was, exclaiming with her hands. "Not only does the Green Country have the secret of how to grow enormous crops, they have the secret of how to prevent AIDS!"

"Are you sure? Bert did not say anything about that."

"I don't know why Bert didn't tell us—he knew it—she told him."

"Prevent AIDS!" Gui grabbed Carol and swung her around. "Tell me more about these people!"

"Well," Carol paused to remember. "They don't let anyone in or out of the country without special permission. No one is ever allowed to remove even a tiny bit of their soil or water. They have no juvenile delinquency. Their daughters are all virgins when they marry." She paused. "What more is there to say except that they don't get AIDS."

Gui was still grasping her arms. "Do you know what that means?" he exclaimed.

"Yes, Gui, yes! It means the world can be free of AIDS!"

He did not hear her. "It means everyone will have to come to me for the answer, and . . . " His look was distant. "and I will be very, very rich," he said.

She stopped the dancing and put her hands on his arms. "Gui, this isn't the kind of thing you get rich from. This is the gift you give the world! Imagine a whole tribe of people who are free of AIDS!"

As Gui looked at Carol, a light turned on in his brain. "A whole tribe of people who are free of AIDS" went through his mind over and over, along with the other bit of information that was of primary interest to him, that all the young women were virgins. He responded automatically, "Of course, Carol, of course."

Carol did not notice his distraction as her mind considered a very different future. "Malissa is going to think about it. I am going to call her tonight to see how she thinks we can go about uncovering the secret and bringing it out."

Unaware of her own actions, Carol was clasping and unclasping her hands. "Malissa has to be one of the most selfless people in the world— gentle, caring. She will do it, I know she will do it. She has to do it!"

"That's great news, Carol, great news!" He sat down at his desk and picked up a folder lying there. "Thank you for coming to tell me. We will talk about it tonight."

Finally, Carol became aware of a change in Gui's demeanor. "Gui," she began.

"We'll talk about it tonight." He was almost impatient with her.

Carol left, more than a little perplexed by his unexpected response, it was not like him.

Gui waited until he heard Carol's car start. Quickly he dialed a number. Roger's death had meant that suddenly Gui had more money than he was likely to spend in his lifetime. By damn, he was going to use some of it for the one thing he had always wanted.

After several rings, Bert answered.

"Bert, I must see you!"

"Sorry, Mr. Manieux, I was already out the door when the phone rang. Can't talk to you now."

"Would thirty thousand kwacha change your mind?"

"Thirty thousand dollars?" He had to catch his breath. "For what?"

"Meet me at Independence Arch in ten minutes, and I will tell you."

CHAPTER 51

Independence Arch, Blantyre

Bert was not happy. Fortunately Independence Arch was on the way from his home to the hotel, but it would mean he would arrive late. He did take time to call Malissa, but that was not what bothered him. He did not want to talk with Gui. The whole thing was turning into a nightmare.

At least he had his ten thousand kwacha or rather, had. He would pick up the temporary title papers to his plane later that day. One thing he wanted to do was take Malissa to see the plane. He hoped she liked flying. And all he wanted right then was to see her.

He had not thought anything could ruin his mood, but Gui's call had sure put a damper on it. He should have just refused, but thirty thousand kwacha was hard to ignore. It was one step closer to the eighty-seven thousand he needed, but he knew enough about Gui Manieux to hear warning bells going off all over the place.

Gui was waiting for him under the arch. Bert took his time getting out of his Landrover and walking to where Gui stood. He said nothing, waiting for Gui to speak.

"Bert, there was one item of information you neglected to pass on to us—the bit about a way to prevent AIDS. Any good reason for that?"

Damn! He should have told Malissa not to mention that. He thought quickly. "No one knows for sure that people don't get AIDS in that country. Frankly, I don't believe it," he lied. "It doesn't make sense, now does it—any spot in Africa that doesn't have AIDS?"

"Maybe, maybe not. But just on the chance that it is true, and there certainly is something unique about that country, I think we should find out more about it, don't you?"

Bert's tone was still guarded, defensive. He would not look at Gui. "You obviously have something in mind."

Gui sensed Bert's reticence. "Look, I am sorry about yesterday. I was out of line. I forget that you are—different. Can we forget that?"

Bert raised reluctant eyes to look at Gui. "Okay. So what?"

Gui spoke slowly and deliberately now. "If you find out the truth about whether or not the people in the Green Country have AIDS, I will pay you thirty thousand dollars—cash." He waited for his words to soak in.

Bert seemed unable to respond. Gui went on. "I do not care what you have to do—I will leave that up to you. As long as you bring that information to me, I will ask no questions. If you have expenses—flying your plane out there—whatever, those will be paid on top of the thirty thousand. Just present the bill."

"How long do I have to get this done?" Still suspicious, Bert was by no means ready to accept the assignment.

"Is two weeks long enough?"

"Maybe, maybe not. I'm not even sure what I'm up against."

"All right. Give me an update at the end of each week—on Sunday."

"And if it turns out to be impossible?"

"Your expenses will have been paid. There just will not be any thirty thousand."

Bert made a rule to never take a first offer. "It may turn out to be a full-time job for several weeks, so I couldn't do any contract flying. I would need some kind of advance."

Gui nodded. "Three thousand now and more if it goes longer than two weeks. Fair enough?"

What was he getting himself into? Everyone knew Gui Manieux was not to be trusted. "Five thousand up front, and that is in addition to the thirty thousand and expenses." He waited for Gui's nod, which came after a frown of hesitation. "When I pick up the five thousand kwacha tomorrow, we sign an agreement. I'll write it up."

"Fine. Come early tomorrow morning, about seven o'clock."

Bert considered that. He almost said it would have to wait until tomorrow afternoon when he and Malissa returned from their outing but changed his mind. As he started to walk away he said, "I'll be there."

"When will you start?"

"Today."

"Just one other thing." Gui's tone was urgent, and Bert stopped. "Do not call me at my house or my office about this. Do not speak of this to me at any other time than when we meet on Sundays. Do not under any circumstances mention this to Carol—or anyone else. If you do, the whole deal is off. Understood?"

"Understood." Bert's eyes narrowed. "Why do you want this so bad?"

Gui looked straight at Bert. "Carol has convinced me that my destiny is to save the African from AIDS."

"Then why isn't she to know about it?"

There was just a hint of hesitation, then, "I want it to be a surprise."

Bert could not get away from there fast enough. He felt as if Gui's sticky fingers were all over him. The man had no interest in saving anybody but himself. But there was much more to it, something sinister about the whole thing. Bert knew all there was to know about the situation, and yet he had the feeling that there was something Gui knew that he did not.

Bert set his jaw. He would proceed only as long as he felt comfortable about what was happening. The instant he felt otherwise, the instant it posed a danger for Malissa, he would drop the whole thing, even if it meant losing the plane. That was a promise.

How did he get into this situation? He had made a pact with the one man that he utterly disliked and mistrusted. Was he selling his soul to the devil? Actually, as he thought about it, he grinned. He just might beat Gui Manieux at his own game.

CHAPTER 52

Malissa went down to the lobby to wait for Bert. Seeing people from countries all over the world was one of the fun things to do in Blantyre, and the Mount Soche Hotel was the place to watch them. Women shrouded in saris and women in skimpy skirts,, men in turbans, bush coats, or robes, all crossed through the lobby. She did note that there were very few suits and no ties at all.

As she stepped out of the elevator, she glimpsed Tomiko just entering the coffee shop. Malissa had never met anyone as important as someone high up in the World Health Organization. Yet, he seemed like just an ordinary man. There were things she would like to know. The laboratory facilities at the hospital at Mubi allowed only the most elementary tests. Every now and then she would like to order more sophisticated tests. Perhaps the WHO had a laboratory in Africa that she could send blood samples to. It would not hurt to ask. Of course, she would say nothing about the Green Country.

Quickly, she followed him into the coffee shop where he had chosen a table near the windows.

"Good morning, Mr. Hirokama."

He was surprised. "Yes, yes, good morning, Miss Taylor." He motioned to the empty chair.. "Won't you join me for breakfast?"

"No, I have an appointment. I'll just sit here a couple minutes." She took the chair opposite him and shook her head when the waiter asked if she wanted coffee. "My ride will be here soon, but I would like to ask you a question."

"Of course, Miss Taylor. How may I help you?"

"My hospital in the bush has only the simplest facilities for doing blood work. Is there a place in this part of Africa where I could send a sample now and then for a more complete report?"

"As a matter of fact the World Health Organization has established a state-of-the-art laboratory in Lilongwe, right here in Malawi, precisely for such needs as yours. You have only to send a sample, and they will give you whatever you need." He went on quickly, taking a small notebook and pencil from his suit jacket pocket as Malissa wondered at his wearing a suit and tie in this heat. "I will write down the address, but you must give me your full name and address so that I can tell the director of the lab who is a friend of mine to expect your work and to get the report back to you quickly."

"I would really appreciate that," Malissa said, again pleased by this man's kind helpfulness. But she needed clarification. "If I send lab samples by special messenger, could they send the report back the same way? Mail service is so slow and undependable."

"You have only to ask," he assured her. "And again, I will make sure that my friend takes good care of you."

As he wrote her name and address, she said, "Lilongwe isn't that far away. Having a lab that close would be a tremendous help."

"Miss Taylor, I would like . . . "

"I have to go, I don't want to keep my friend waiting, Mr. Hirokama. Thank you so much!"

Tomiko watched her go with a feeling of relief. At last he was making some progress. He had a name and an address.

CHAPTER 53

Kulanji

Asta found it hard to believe that the young woman in front of her was her daughter, Saratu. This was not the whining, irritating child of yesterday—or even that morning when she had demanded more sugar for her tea. This young woman stood straight, assured, and determined.

"I will marry someone, maybe even Pindar. He's probably as good as anyone. But not until I am ready, which isn't going to be until some other things happen in my life."

With a sense of dread, Asta laid down the knife she had been using to chop onions and gave her full attention to Saratu. "Such as?"

"I want to see the Outside. I've read every book in Kulanji. I want to see a library, and a movie, out there. I want to visit a hospital, and use the English I've been learning." She rushed on before Asta could respond to that. "Then I would come back and read the books that would teach me how to be a nurse, or a teacher. I want to go out there, just once, and see what it is like."

Asta shook her head sadly and looked away. This child was a generation, maybe several generations, ahead of her time. What she was asking was not allowed a Kulanji woman, and was illegal for any other member of the tribe except the chief. But the fact of the matter was that she had every right to want what she wanted. Asta knew her own daughter well enough to know Saratu would not be put off. Better to offer a compromise than to have complete rebellion.

"Mama, are you listening to me?"

"I'm listening, Saratu. I was just remembering another girl who stood before her mother . . . " Asta's voice trailed off.

"Yes, Mama, what happened? What did you want when you were eighteen?"

"I wanted only to be allowed to learn to read. If they would let me do that, then I would marry your father."

"All you wanted to do was learn to read? That was nothing big. Every woman can learn to read."

"Not then!" Asta broke in. "It was unheard of and not allowed."

"What did you do?"

"I said if I could not learn to read, then I would not marry anyone." Asta laughed. "How brave I was!"

"What happened?"

"Your father said if I would marry him, he would let me learn to read. Everyone told him he was crazy to let a woman like that into his compound. There have been times since when people have reminded him of that."

Saratu pulled a stool close and sat down, peering into Asta's face. "All I want to do is see what the Outside looks like. Is that so terrible?"

"Yes, Saratu, according to tribal rules, that is terrible. Just like a woman reading was terrible back then. You know why, the Kulanjis absolutely must protect themselves from the Outside. It is a daily promise to the gods in return for the incredible blessings that are ours by virtue of having been chosen to live in this Garden."

"But I just want to take a look."

"Is that all?"

Saratu stood up now and started walking back and forth. "Mama, I have never wanted anything so much in my life! It is like a hunger, eating at my stomach. Sometimes I think I will be sick, sick enough to die, if I can't see what is out there."

Asta's memory did not fail her. She remembered becoming physically ill with the longing to read what was on the pages of the books on the shelves in her father's house. Or perhaps it was the anger in her stomach at being treated with less consideration than the men in the tribe.

She never forgot that it was her husband, Yamta, who had made it possible for her to discover a whole new world, and become a new person because she could read. She also remembered that it was her own mother who steadfastly refused to give in. Asta was not going to let Saratu remember her own mother that way.

Asta picked up the knife and started chopping onions. "Saratu, I can't make any promises, only that I will see what can be done. That is the most I can offer."

"Oh, Mama, thank you, thank you!" Saratu ran to her mother and hugged her, like a little girl.

CHAPTER 54

Malawi

I have to have that one!" exclaimed Malissa, pointing to an end table sitting prominently among smaller carved stools. It was carved out of a single piece of wood from a king ebony tree, a two-inch thickness of wood was left for the top and another two inches for the base with a head carved from the wood between. A wide layer of ivory-colored wood made a ring on the outside of the tabletop. It was that ivory ring that distinguished King ebony from all the rest.

All around them in orderly rows sat wood carvers, each intent on his specific project, each one different. Some were special orders; others were original designs, most of them from ebony, a few from mahogany.

"Come here, Bert," Malissa motioned. In a low voice she said, "See that table, the one I want. The face looks just like that man, that one—there. Don't you think so?"

"You're right! I suppose they do use each other as models."

"Maybe it is a self-portrait. Oh, I would like that!" She leaned down to get a closer look. "It's a good thing I drove a car by myself to Blantyre. At this rate there isn't going to be any room left over when I start back on Sunday." She stood up.

"Sunday!" Bert reached for her hand and pulled her away from the line of artisans. "Did you say Sunday?"

"Yes, I have to go back, that's as long as I can be gone. I need to be there for work on Monday."

"But that is—there is only one day left!"

"Bert, we've been together every day since I got here!"

"But I wanted to show you the lake, lots more of it, and take you for a plane ride, and visit the Zomba plateau and go to greet my friend at my favorite place in all of Malawi, Mr. Stephen's Inn."

"Bert, I have a job waiting for me! I shouldn't have left, and now I have to go back."

Bert looked at his watch. "It's three o'clock. Let's get going. We've got lots of things to do. Let's get the table you wanted."

She would not be hurried, and an hour later they were finally on their way back to Blantyre with Malissa sitting close to Bert.

Bert was glad he had gone to see Gui that morning instead of waiting until this afternoon. He had the five thousand securely stowed away, and his level of stress was somewhat less with the thought that another thirty thousand might be his very soon.

"Malissa, you haven't said anything about your conversation with Carol Walters. It's none of my business, but you have seemed distracted at times today. Does it have anything to do with that?"

"Of course it does. You already knew that. She is going to call me tonight to see if I will work with her on it." Malissa paused in thought. "This is not going to go away, is it, Bert?"

"You mean the secret of the Green Country? No, it isn't." He was glad for the subject to come up at last, he had to get started toward accomplishing his assignment. "Too many people know about it. It seems to me that the better part of wisdom would be to try to contain the damage, to control what information actually gets out of Kulanji."

"I am afraid you are right. I just keep thinking there must be some way to let those people go on living their idyllic life a while longer."

"It isn't going to happen. Believe me, Malissa, it isn't." He spoke emphatically.

She looked at him in alarm. "Why do you say it like that?"

"As I said, too many people know about it. Someone will crash the gates, and it will be all over. At least, if we find out what there is to know, we can decide who will have access to it." Was he making it possible for Gui Manieux to be the one to decide?

"Bert," her tone was wistful, "it would be great to find a solution to hunger and a cure for AIDS, wouldn't it?"

"That would be the best of all worlds. And maybe, just maybe, it can happen and let the Kulanji go on living in peace too." He was raising false hopes and knew it, but he needed justification for what he was doing, and a part of him even believed it—or wanted to.

There was one other thing Malissa needed to know. "When I met Carol in London, she mentioned her friend, Gui Manieux. I want to know, is he going to have anything to do with this?"

The tone of her voice told Bert that he had better answer no, but he dodged.

"Do you know Gui Manieux?"

"I know only of him, and it isn't good."

"I . . . I don't think you need worry about Gui. Just stick with Carol. You can trust her."

If she realized he was dodging the question, it was not apparent.

They had arrived at the hotel where Bert pulled into a parking space and turned off the motor. Malissa laid her hand on his. "Bert, let's promise each other that we will do everything possible to try to make that happen without hurting the people in Kulanji."

He took her hand in his. "I promise, Malissa." It was a tender moment, the first time they had held hands. Neither was quite sure what to do next. Again Bert wondered what she would do if he kissed her.

Instead, he said, "You will have dinner with me tonight, won't you?"

She grinned at him, "Unless I get a better offer between now and six thirty."

"You just might. I imagine Tomiko is still around."

"You know, Bert, he did seem like a very nice man. He has a tough job as Special Assistant to director of the World Health Organization. Maybe we should let him in on the secret when we find it."

"I'm afraid I don't trust him not to give control of it to some big international company who would demand exorbitant returns on their investment. No, we must keep this as simple as possible, known by as few people as possible. That is the only way we can hope to not damage those people."

Inside he cringed as he thought of what Gui Manieux would undoubtedly try to do with the information. The only consolation was that Carol was apparently going to be involved. She seemed to be the only person who had any influence over Gui.

He opened his door and came around to her side where she was already standing by the car. "I've known you for three days," Malissa said. "How do I know you are to be trusted with the secret?"

"You don't," he laughed mysteriously. "I even have some other secrets I am keeping from you."

To his complete surprise, she stood on tiptoe and kissed him unhurriedly on the mouth. "I love secrets," she said.

* * * * *

When the phone rang in her hotel room that night, Malissa was ready ..

"Hello, Malissa, this is Carol. I've been thinking about the Green Country, and it would mean so much if . . . "

Malissa interrupted. "I am going to see what I can find out. I make no promises. I will be in touch with Mr. McEwen."

"Oh, but . . . "

"Goodnight, Carol."

Malissa hung up the phone firmly.

CHAPTER 55

Bert was at the airport at six o'clock that Saturday morning, going over his new plane again, looking into every opening and tube. It was beautiful— just as beautiful as the first time he saw it. But now he wanted it to look its best because he was taking Malissa for a ride that day. He hoped she would not be afraid and get sick or something. She seemed like a pretty strong female to him.

He leaned against his new aircraft, savoring its smell, but remembering another scent—Malissa's perfume when he had kissed her goodnight. God, it was wonderful! He could not even remember the last time he had kissed a woman. It just was not something he did lightly, and since he was very much of an introvert, women did not come looking for him, at least, not the kind he would want to kiss. Finding Malissa had been a stroke of luck. Come to think of it, he should be friendlier to Tomiko. If it had not been for him . . .

Dinner had been at the Mount Soche Hotel again, there really wasn't any other place as nice in Blantyre. They had lingered over dinner until almost ten o'clock and then walked through the hotel gardens. They found a bench in a secluded corner and held hands while they talked. There was so much to talk about, so many things to find out about each other.

Finally Malissa said she was tired and started to stand up. But he pulled her to him and kissed her. Her response was immediate and fervent. When they finally released each other, neither could speak. They walked quickly to the hotel, and Malissa hurried away up the stairs, not waiting for the elevator, waving goodnight at the landing. He managed to say, "Nine-thirty in the morning, I'll be here."

He did not sleep very well, in fact, didn't sleep much at all. His mind was full of Malissa, as was his body, wanting her there with him. He would never suggest that to her, but he wondered if she ever had such thoughts. Did a woman have the same desires he had? Probably not. And yet, her response that night had been pretty strong.

It had been so long since he had had serious thoughts of making love with a woman that he had wondered if he was too old, if that part of him had atrophied. If nothing else, he was glad to know it was definitely alive and well.

Suddenly he sat straight up in bed. That was it! He would ask Malissa to marry him. If she said no, then she would at least know he cared about her. And if she said yes . . .

The rest of the night was spent sleeping fitfully but with intermittently envisioning his life with a woman in it, Malissa. Did he dare believe he could be so fortunate?

CHAPTER 56

B ert arrived at Independence Arch a couple minutes before Gui that Saturday morning. It took only a few minutes to exchange the hastily drawn agreement for the five thousand dollars. The paper stated that Bert would endeavor to discover whether or not it was true that people in the Green Country did or did not have AIDS. For that he would receive five thousand dollars up front with thirty thousand dollars to be paid when the information was delivered to Gui.

Gui was all smiles but Bert was sober and puzzled. Information concerning whether or not the people in Kulanji had AIDS seemed harmless enough, but Bert was haunted by his realization that thirty thousand dollars for that piece of information was out of line. There was more here than met the eye, and he would be on the lookout for whatever underhanded reason Gui had for doing this.

In the meantime, it certainly made things easier for Bert. It was thirty thousand dollars less that he had to come up with for his plane. But the only way he was going to secure the information was to use Malissa, and that made him distinctly uncomfortable.

CHAPTER 57

He picked Malissa up at the hotel at nine-thirty that Saturday morning. In jeans and a cotton shirt, she looked ready for anything, he thought. His arm went around her naturally as she went ahead of him through a door. Her hand touched his easily as they walked together. And his heart jumped ahead of itself at each contact.

He opened the car door for her and bounced around to his side like a twenty-year-old. As he turned the key in the ignition, he said, "By the way, why did you come to Blantyre? I never see very many mission people here on vacation. I understand they go to Lilongwe or Nairobi."

She grinned. "I had a dream that if I went to the hotel where they served the fish out of Lake Malawi, a strange man would sit at my table. And I believe in dreams, don't you?"

He reached over and squeezed her hand. "I'm glad you came to Blantyre."

"So am I," she said.

"Can't you stay at least another day?"

"No." It was not to be argued with.

"Where are we going?" Malissa asked as the plane glided smoothly off the runway. This was the first real flight for his new plane, although he had done several local hops.

"I'm curious to see where you live. Would you like to fly over it?"

"Oh, I'd like that!"

The plane was gassed and ready, and their take-off was smooth. He asked a number of questions about just where she lived and then turned the plane north by northwest. "If you see anything familiar, let me know," he said.

The array of gauges was fascinating, and she looked them over one by one, asking questions about each one. With obvious pride Bert described their function.

"It is a four hundred mile drive from Mubi to Blantyre," she said, "How long a flight is that in this plane?"

"About two hours each way. We'll be back in time for a nice dinner."

"Where are we going to eat tonight?" Malissa asked.

"That's one of the secrets. It is probably my most favorite place to eat in East Africa."

" By the way, I am assuming there is no place to land out here. What are we doing for lunch? I'm hungry already."

"And that is another secret," he said, grinning.

Shortly after take-off Bert pointed below to carefully laid-out plots of ground, some ready for planting, some already with small plants started. "I fly for the guy who owns those corporate farms," Bert said. "Gui Manieux,"

That name again, thought Malissa. "What do they raise?" she asked.

"Tea, peanuts, yams, guinea corn." He nodded his head. "A big operation. They hire lots of workers."

"Are corporate farms a good thing?" Malissa asked, still surveying the fields that extended for miles.

Bert shrugged. "Depends on your point of view, I guess."

The noise of the plane did not encourage conversation, and they flew mostly in silence, Malissa intent on the view below and Bert checking gauges periodically.

An hour slipped by.

"Want a turn at the controls?" Bert asked. They were scooting along beneath fluffy clouds, the flight smooth and stable.

"Sure," Malissa replied. She had watched closely as Bert manipulated the various controls and gauges.

He was surprised at how readily she took the controls, but he said nothing. After all, there was nothing to do but keep the plane's nose going straight ahead.

Another hour passed as they flew over bush country, called bush because the vegetation including trees were burned off periodically in order to keep land cleared for farming, The trees never grew very large and remained small bushes. When the rains began in late May or early June, a mat of green would appear, but now the horizon-to-horizon color was dirt brown, broken only by compounds here and there. They were low enough to see small herds of cattle being followed by herdsmen and goats that were free to wander. Very soon the animals would be tied up or in enclosures so as not to destroy crops

On the right appeared an unusual formation. "Could we take a closer look at White Woman Peak over there?" Malissa asked.

"So that's what the natives call it. Is that near where you live?"

"It isn't far from there, perhaps thirty miles beyond."

She made the proper change of heading to bring the plane closer, trimming the nose to descend a little lower.

"All right, confess, you've flown a plane before, haven't you?"

"My father was a commercial airline pilot and flew his own Cessna 172. He insisted that if I was going to fly with him that I be able to land the plane. So I learned."

"Well I'll be damned! Why didn't you say so?"

"You didn't ask." She nodded toward the mountain they were approaching. "White Woman Peak is a good place to climb, but I've never had time."

"When I come to visit you, we will do that."

She looked at him, surprised, as if this was a new idea. "All right," she said.

"Let's go down," Bert directed.

Malissa pushed down on the controls, and the plane descended smoothly. "You take the controls now, Bert. I want to look."

They continued on for another few minutes.

"While we are at it," Bert said, "let's look for a spot that could be a landing field. This plane has STOL design, which means Short Takeoff and Landing, so the space available could be fairly short."

She pointed. "There, almost hidden in that grove of trees is the hospital. My house is on the little hill beside it."

"Is that a water tank?" Bert asked.

"Yes, I have running water."

"Electricity?"

"Just when the hospital generator is going. And since I have to be at the hospital when it is being used, I never get to use the electricity at my house."

"Don't suppose you do much reading in bed," Bert grinned.

As they circled the area, they discussed this or that spot for a landing field. "It wouldn't be easy, but there . . ." Bert pointed. " that would probably be the best. That is a road, isn't it?"

Malissa laughed. "Granted it is hard to recognize, but yes, it is a road."

As they passed over the hospital, Malissa said excitedly, "I can see Garba. He's the dispenser. I'm glad to see he is at work. He was sick most of last week which meant I had to see the dispensary patients as well as all the hospital patients and do the deliveries."

"Do you really want to go back to that kind of a schedule?" Bert asked. Without waiting for her answer, he hurried on, "I know there would be a job for you at the hospital in Blantyre. You, you could live in my house. There's lots of room."

The look she gave stopped him in mid-sentence. Instantly he was furious with himself. He had blown it completely. He fully intended to ask her to marry him, and now he had suggested something he did not at all intend.

He opened his mouth to repair the damage, but Malissa pointed as she said, "That is the way to Kulanji. Straight west from here. Kulanji has a common border with Wamba for about fifty miles."

"The entire eastern edge," Bert hurried to say.

"I believe so. I've never driven the perimeter."

They flew in silence, Bert desperately trying to think of something that would show what he had really meant to say, but he could not bring himself to try again for fear he would really mess it up.

Malissa did not look his way but watched the ground slide by beneath. Her heart was pounding. She knew he had not said what he intended to say. It did not come as a surprise that he was serious about this relationship. Even a woman who had spent twenty years in the bush could see that.

Then an incredible thought pushed its way into her brain. *What if he had asked her to marry him?* A white man in the African bush surely did not have many opportunities for a suitable mate. He might even be a little desperate since she understood that most men wanted sex in their life.

She willed the idea away. She was not prepared to think about that just then.

Before long an unusual pattern appeared near the horizon, different from anything around it. As they moved closer, ahead of them stretched a dark line running from north to south. Bert pointed.

"The thorn barrier," Malissa said. "It doesn't look so formidable from up here, but down there, it isn't something I would like to try to get through!"

As they neared the thorn barrier, Bert said, "Let's do a couple fly-overs while we do some serious thinking about what makes this section of the earth unique. We can't really talk while we fly. When we get back to Blantyre, let's put our heads together and see what we can come up with."

Malissa nodded in agreement. At least she was not going to have to do this alone.

CHAPTER 58

Kulanji

Asta waited until everyone else had gone to their sleeping houses for the night. It had been the day to make quasis, the little crispy black-eyed pea cakes, frying them in peanut oil to a crunchy brown. She had kept a special supply of them aside for Yamta, as she always did, but today she had taken special care to be sure they were the way he liked them, with grated onion in them and peppery hot.

She sat down next to him, placing the bowl of quasis between them. As she removed the lid, the aroma surrounded them.

"Ummm!" Yamta exclaimed. "If these are quasis, it must be Tuesday." He popped one into his mouth.

They sat in silence, eating quasis. Asta had rehearsed what she would say over and over, but she still was having trouble actually beginning the conversation.

"You're quiet tonight," ventured Yamta. He knew his wife well; something was on her mind.

Might as well get it out into the open. "Do you remember how much I wanted to learn to read?" she began.

"Enough to refuse to marry me if you didn't get to, as I recall," he said dryly, then laughed as he added, "Are you sorry you learned to read?"

"I'm not sorry I married you, if that is what you mean," she said, then went on quickly. "There is something Saratu wants as much as I wanted to read."

"Really? Whatever could that be— having a new zhebi to wear every day, have meat sukwar every night?" He paused. "I know, fly in that aeroplane that came over the other day."

"Almost," said Asta. "She wants to go see the Outside." There, she had said it.

He did not respond immediately, then finally, "I hope you aren't serious."

"You know I am, and you know our daughter would come up with something like this."

"Not in my worst dreams did I expect this!"

"Yamta, it has to happen some time. I guess Saratu might as well be the first."

"The answer is no, no, and no. How could she ask this seriously? She already knows the answer."

"How about if she didn't go alone?"

"And who . . . ?" He sat up straight in his chair. "Was this your idea?"

"No, Yamta. It was hers, but she can't go alone."

"Why are you talking as if she were going?"

"Because she probably will." There was complete silence, then Asta said, "I married you, didn't I?"

He sensed he was losing the battle, so he thought of a way to solve the problem. "There are too many stories that filter in from the Outside about people getting killed when they ride on the lorries or buses. The only way she can go is if she doesn't go in a motor vehicle."

"Yamta, that is unreasonable. You know she can't . . . "

"That is the only way," Yamta said with finality.

CHAPTER 59

When they arrived back in Blantyre at four o'clock that Saturday afternoon, Bert tethered the plane and put it to bed, carefully writing down the hours on the plane when they left and when they returned. That would go on the expense bill to Gui. And the bill would be higher, now that he was flying the bigger plane.

"I've saved the best for your last night here. I'll pick you up in an hour. This is the night to wear that new dress you bought."

"How did you know about that?"

"I peeked into your closet, and it was still in its wrapping from the French boutique."

"Just for that, snoopy, you have to pick up one of those beautiful orchids that I saw in the flower shop window."

"Why didn't I think of that?" he asked.

He left her off at the front door of the hotel. As she passed the concierge's desk, the woman behind the desk called to her. Malissa walked over, and the woman handed her a florist's box. In it was a perfect lavender orchid. She hid her smile. So, he had already thought of it.

The shower was wonderfully refreshing after the hot sticky flight and the dusty drive from the airport. A warm glow of pleasure enveloped her, as much from her state of mind as the scented oil she rubbed on her body. This had been the right place to rest and escape. Bert had made it possible for her to do both.

She did like Bert, and he had certainly made her vacation one to remember. In her journal the night before she had put Bert down on paper: tall, good-looking in a rugged sort of way, bashful, intelligent, thoughtful, gentle, the quintessential man. She had laughed as she wrote the big word. But there was a lot she did not know about him.

She had the feeling he had not told her everything about his wanting to know about the Green Country. In that matter she would be absolutely unyielding, no one would be hurt if she could help it. The thought of a man in her life was not unpleasant, but she told herself firmly that some time later she and Bert could perhaps have a serious relationship, but it was not something that could happen now. It was enough to feel her way through this and make no decisions about anything in regard to him just yet. There was plenty of time.

Or was there? Here she was, completely removed from anyone and anything that was in her normal world. Here was an opportunity for her to enjoy this to the fullest. There was no doubt in her mind that Bert would be glad to spend the night with her. She had only to let him know.

She had never been to bed with a man in her life; maybe it was time. Would there ever be a better opportunity, or even any opportunity? She was looking at herself in the bathroom mirror, and slowly she shook her head. She could not go against the person she had always been. Without real caring, she could never go to bed with a man just because it was a unique moment.

She grimaced at herself in the mirror. Was she to go on always being the sensible one in the crowd? Maybe this was the time to let her feelings be in charge for a change. She stood looking at herself for a long moment, then sighed, and turned away. She was who she was; it was too late to change that now.

Always ready ahead of time, Malissa had a few minutes to sit on her balcony which overlooked the garden and the busy streets of Blantyre beyond. Her thoughts returned to the quiet village of Mubi. She wondered how many babies had died of diarrhea since she left, and how many of them were babies she had delivered, her children, she called them. Who had come in to have their babies, who had been bitten by snakes as they worked their farms in readiness for planting as soon as there was enough rain, and who else had discovered they had AIDS? It was time for her to go home, back to where she was needed. It was her life after all, the only life she knew.

She decided to walk down instead of taking the elevator, and as she passed a full-length mirror in the hallway, she paused to view the woman in the glass. An insistent little voice said, *Are you sure?*

She paused at the top of the stairs that led into the lobby. Almost immediately Bert came through the double doors and headed for the elevator. Malissa was not sure Bert was the same man who had left her an hour before. This man could only be described as sophisticated, in a dark blue suit, ivory silk shirt open at the neck and black shoes polished to a high shine. Now she knew why she had chosen the peach dress. She waved to him, and he stopped.

Bert stopped because he couldn't do anything else. He hardly noticed that she waved. He was transfixed. She was beautiful! The peach dress touched her face with a glow and followed the shape of her body in perfect detail. As she reached him, he leaned down and kissed her lightly on the lips.

"Careful," she laughed, feeling like a high school girl at the senior prom, "you'll crush my flower."

"Then we'll throw away the flower," he said seriously.

She put her arm in his. "Thank you for the flower. I've never had an orchid before." She moved toward the door. "I'm starved. Those peanut butter and jelly sandwiches were gone by two o'clock."

In the car he handed her a bottle of white wine and two glasses. "You do the honors while I drive," he said, "but only one glass for me. I want us to get to this dinner safely." The way he said "this dinner" made Malissa wonder what was going to be special about this occasion.

It was five-thirty when they turned onto the road which led up to the Zomba Plateau. Before long, the sun on its way down touched the clouds clustered at the horizon and turned them into glorious tints of reds and golds. At the next wide shoulder of the road, they stopped to view it, with majestic Mount Mulanje on the horizon to the right and the sculptured hills spread out below, now in variegated shades of gray to black against the brilliant sunset.

"Now you know one of the reasons this is my favorite drive," Bert said.

A uniformed waiter met them at the front door of the Ku Chawe Inn with a welcoming cup of tea. Bert had chosen this place for dinner that Saturday evening for two reasons. One, there was little chance that Tomiko, or anyone else, would happen onto them there. And two, it would allow for an uninterrupted intimate interlude with Malissa. The place was famous for couples who went there for romantic dinners, even honeymoons. And he had every intention of saying what he had fumbled earlier that day.

He would have to get Malissa to help him find out whether or not people in Kulanji did or did not get AIDS. But more important, he was going to ask her to marry him.

In the midst of dirt and poverty, the KuChawe Inn was an oasis for the business people and dignitaries from Llilongwe and Blantyre. It was about half way between the two cities. The dining room was subdued in candlelight with hand-hewn tables and chairs of dark wood. They did not mind the slowness of the waiter. An appetizer of fresh vegetables came first, along with crusty rolls followed after while by a salad of fresh greens and tomatoes. They talked of African foods, flying, of nursing, of hospitals, of their respective homes and families in the States.

This time the chambo was oven-baked with tiny potatoes and fresh parsley sprinkled over all and thinly sliced carrots that had known hot water for only a few minutes before being bathed in butter. Bert ordered a bottle of wine. And all the time their eyes rarely left each other's face.

After a long while Bert said, "I recommend the crème caramel, and coffee, of course."

"Bert, I have the feeling you are prolonging this dinner as long as possible," she said somberly.

"You are right, I don't want this to ever end. I don't want you to ever go away."

She flushed. "I thought it was because when we finish eating we have to talk about difficult decisions."

He reached across the table for her hand. "Decisions I can handle, your leaving won't be as easy."

This time she smiled as her cheeks grew pink. "It's too soon, Bert, you don't know . . . "

"Too soon! I've been waiting for you for years, I just didn't know who you were."

She laughed, a lilting laugh. "You don't know me yet!"

"But I know myself, that's all I need to know. Malissa, I want . . . will you . . . ?"

She broke in quickly. "Bert, there is plenty of time for whatever is to happen. You see, I have learned that everything has its time and its season. I do believe that."

"Yes, but I think this is the time to . . . "

"Bert, this is the time to decide the fate of a whole tribe of people."

"But I've been waiting twenty years!"

"Then another month or so won't make a whole lot of difference," she said calmly, smiling.

"I give up!" He fell back in his chair, resignedly. "But not before I have some dessert and coffee. Okay?"

"Of course."

The créme caramel was finished and their coffee had been served. Bert had to get on with what he had to do. "Tell me, Malissa, what do you think is the secret of the Green Country?"

"I've been thinking about that, a lot. It stands to reason that there is something in the soil and-or the water that is unique to that triangle of earth. Wouldn't a chemical analysis of soil and water within that triangle compared with surrounding soil and water show the difference if there is one?"

Bert nodded. "It would certainly be the place to start. It shouldn't even be particularly difficult."

"Bert, you don't seem to have gotten the message. Nothing leaves Kulanji without their permission, not even, or should I say, especially, dirt. It is a priceless commodity."

"They are serious, aren't they?" Bert mused. "Are you allowed to take dirt into the country?"

"Perhaps, I hadn't thought about it."

"Could you take in a bowl of dirt so that when you went out with a bowl of dirt, no one would think anything of it?"

"I'll think of some way to obtain a cup or two of dirt," Malissa said, "but where do we send the dirt for analysis?"

Bert frowned as he pondered the question. "There are agricultural companies that routinely test soil." His mind remembered Gui's establishment. There was a soil lab there, he was sure. But how to get the soil tested without Gui obtaining the results. "I will find the answer to that one, Malissa. Send the sample to me."

"But," Malissa went on, "there is a much more difficult problem. In order to know whether or not the disease-preventing element is in the soil or in the genes, a human being would have to be tested. That is infinitely more difficult."

"Any ideas?" Bert asked.

"Absolutely none. You see, the Kulanji believe that blood is sacred, and they have never allowed blood transfusions. They will allow blood to be taken for testing but not for giving to someone else."

"Don't they lose a lot of people who need blood?"

"Of course, especially women in childbirth, although they are so much healthier than most African women that their death rate is naturally much lower."

"So they do allow themselves to be stuck for taking a little bit of blood?" Bert asked, grimacing at the memory.

"A little bit, yes, but we need a couple vials of it for adequate testing this time."

He could wait no longer, he had to ask Malissa to do something for him. "Look, Malissa, could you write me a statement that says the people in Kulanji don't have AIDS?"

"I don't know that for sure," she responded.

"Could you find out?"

She thought about that. "I suppose, I could check some people." She frowned. "But why do you want such a statement?"

"Let's just say that that piece of paper would ensure our future."

His answer did not make sense, especially the *our*. Who did he mean by that? She did not think she wanted to pursue that line of thought just then. The seriousness of his expression made her respond. "I suppose I can do that, maybe. They might refuse if I asked to take blood from healthy people without any good reason."

"Please, Malissa, it is important."

Still frowning, she nodded.

Bert had what he wanted and now changed the subject. "How in the world do you know what is wrong with the patients? Whenever I go to see the doctor for my annual exam, he takes a couple vials of blood and then tells me what is wrong with me."

"Actually, stool specimens tell most of the story in this country. The Kulanji still have all the intestinal parasites."

"Parasites?" Bert did not understand.

"Worms."

"Oh! Sorry I asked," Bert grimaced.

They dropped into a prolonged silence as each considered the problem. Finally Malissa said, "Getting a large enough blood sample is going to have to await my trip to Kulanji. You will have to trust me to work it out. At this moment I haven't the slightest idea. But then," she smiled at Bert, "four days ago I didn't know you existed, and now look."

Bert's voice was low and intense as he took both of her hands in his. "I have been looking, and I want to keep on looking—at you. We've talked enough about other people. Let's have another cup of coffee, then an after-dinner drink, then . . . " He stopped, his eyes resting on her lips.

"Another of your secrets?"

"It's not a secret, Malissa. I love you. I want you to marry me."

CHAPTER 60

Malissa could not speak. She looked at his face, so serious, so intense. She shifted her gaze to the candle flickering beside them and made no effort to remove her hands from his. Her world was suddenly a different place. He loved her, and she knew as surely as anything she had ever known that she loved him.

"Will you, Malissa, will you marry me?"

And just as surely as she knew she loved him, she also knew she could not fail to return to Mubi, to the people who were expecting her. "I can't, Bert. Not now. "

"Go back to Mubi, go look after your job there. Find someone to take it over and then come back to me."

"Bert, we've got a problem to solve. Let's do that first. Then we can talk about our problems, about us."

"Having you in my life would solve problems, not make them."

"Wanna make a bet on that?" Malissa laughed.

She sat very close to him on the way back to Blantyre. Traffic was very light with few bicycles and no goats on the road. They spoke very little as their newfound joy washed over them in ever increasing waves. It was as if they had entered a place that was unfamiliar to both of them, and they did not know the language. Several times he looked over at her and smiled. Finally he reached for her hand and held it as she swore electricity raced through her body. With the fingers of her other hand Malissa gently traced his fingers. They said little after that as they reached the outskirts of Blantyre.

At the hotel Malissa again took Bert's hand, and without a word between them, they walked up the stairs to her room, unaware of the slight figure in the shadows.

In the room Malissa did not turn on the lights but put her arms around him as she said, "I have a secret too, Bert."

He kissed her as he said softly, "Yes?"

"I've never made love before. I really don't know . . . "

His lips on hers stopped her in mid-sentence. He knew what to do, but now his own fear of not being able to perform after all the years of abstinence made him move slowly and deliberately.

"First," Bert said, reaching for the zipper on her dress, "clothes are just in the way. I'll help you and you help me."

It was a dance, as he helped her slip out of the peach dress and she unbuttoned his shirt.

"We takes turns," Bert directed softly. "Now it's my turn." Her slip came off over her head, and they paused for a long kiss. Her fingers fumbled with his belt buckle, but instead of helping her, he kissed her nose, her forehead, her cheeks.

She laughed. "Hey, I don't know how to do these things. How about some help?"

With a quick flip Bert undid the buckle and pulled the belt free. Another twist and his trousers fell to the floor.

With one movement he swooped her up in his arms and laid her gently on the bed.

"Bert, I... I'm not sure . . . " Malissa began.

"Shhh," Gently, deliberately he began massaging her toes, running his fingers lightly between them, then moving up gradually without any haste at all. A long while later, first his fingers and then his lips found the taut nipples. The long years of abstinence had not dulled her senses, and she cried out in sheer pleasure.

For one quick moment she wondered what the other missionaries would say if they could see her now, but she could only smile and cling to this wonderful, incredible man in her bed.

Sometime after midnight, Bert let himself out of the room. Malissa drifted into dreamless sleep.

CHAPTER 61

When Bert arrived at seven o'clock Sunday morning, Coolness hugged the ground as if trying to avoid being swallowed up by the inevitable heat that was sure to come. Malissa was standing by her car, packed and ready.

He took her in his arms, announcing, "I love you, did you know that?"

"I know that!" she said gleefully, hugging and kissing him at the same time.

"I still think you should . . . "

"No, Bert, I'm leaving. Tell me goodbye."

Bert gave her a copy of the map he had drawn of Kulanji and the surrounding area, including Wamba.

"I thought you would like to have a map of the Green Country," Bert said. "It might come in handy—when you are trying to escape with a cup of dirt under your hat and a bottle of water in your ice chest."

"You are a pretty good map maker. And the names are clear and easy to read." She peered at it closely. "You even have White Woman Peak on here."

"That was to remind you that we are going to climb it one of these days." He motioned toward the hotel. "The coffee shop will be open in a few minutes. I think you should have a decent meal and a cup of coffee in your stomach before you go. It will help keep you awake."

"The bumps in the road will take care of that," she assured him.

He put his arm around her. "Come," he begged, "give me a few last minutes, please?"

"Breakfast does sound good," she smiled. Opening her car door, she laid the map on the front seat beside her thermos and a small ice chest with cans of pop for which she would buy ice at a market on her way out of Blantyre.

"I might as well get some coffee here," she said, reaching for the thermos.

Checking to see that her keys were in her pocket, she pushed down the latch and shut the door.

CHAPTER 62

Tomiko watched as Bert and Malissa walked together toward the coffee shop on the main floor of the hotel. He had observed them at Malissa's car. It was obvious that she was leaving. He had to smile at their prolonged embrace. He loved a love story like anybody else did.

When he was sure they were out of sight, he sauntered casually over to the car and peered inside. The map on the front seat was plainly readable with a triangular piece of land colored in bright green. The Green Country! It was true, and the fact that Bert was hiding it from him made him even more sure that he was on to something extremely important.

With a pencil and paper from his briefcase he quickly sketched a copy of the map. Bert had done an excellent job, even to using a dark marking pen, which made it possible to read the names of the towns and rivers.

"Kulanji," he said. "That must be the name of the Green Country."

Tomiko was quickly out of sight.

Tomiko knew all of Malissa and Bert's activities of the past few days, although he had been very careful not to be seen. His journal contained a complete accounting of their activities, including their midnight tryst. He had made several trips to the airport, finally gleaning some information.

From the clerk in the hotel he had confirmed Malissa's address, which meant nothing to him until he spent half a day in the library viewing maps with a magnifying glass until he found the tiny village of Mubi.

The luncheon of Carol and Malissa sent him scurrying to learn Carol's identity, and upon discovering that she was Gui Manieux's wife, he was even more convinced that something was going on that he needed to know. Gui Manieux did not waste time on insignificant matters.

He learned that Bert owned an airplane, actually two airplanes now; he knew their registry numbers. He confirmed the fact that Bert and Malissa had made a trip of about four and a half hours on Friday by computing the number of gallons that plane would use per hour and dividing it by the number of gallons required to fill the tank upon their return. It required another hour, and fifteen kwacha to the attendant in the flight room, to learn that they had flown northwest from Blantyre.

The one fact he did not know was where they went, until that Monday morning when he went for his usual early morning walk and spied them in the parking lot. What a stroke of luck!

But now that Malissa was leaving Blantyre, his only contact would be Bert. That was all right. In the course of his investigation he had discovered some ways to obtain information that would be helpful.

Tomiko had carried out his promise to Malissa to contact Doctor Jim Harris, the head technician at the laboratory in Lilongwe, but it was with instructions that Miss Taylor had requested that copies of all lab reports be sent to him via E-mail with hard copies to follow. Doctor Harris had questioned the necessity of this, but Tomiko was insistent that they should be sent by E-mail first. Given the undependability of the mails into bush country, Doctor Harris did not object further.

Tomiko had never actually met Doctor Harris, although he had looked over the resumes when he was hired. The man came definitely qualified for the job. Tomiko had the feeling the United Nations was lucky to have found someone willing to take on the task of running a laboratory in Africa.

Tomiko had managed to stall Mister Oboji, the UN Secretary General, for a little while longer. And now he could sound a bit more sure of himself, could even hint that he had found *someone* who had the secret to high crop production.

He would stay here in Malawi because obviously this was where the action was. Known as *the warm heart of Africa*, Malawi was the vacationland for people all over eastern part of the continent. There were worse places to be stuck in June than Malawi.

CHAPTER 63

H ere are your sandwiches, sir," the waiter said.
Bert had insisted on sending ham and cheese sandwiches with
Malissa. It was nice to be looked after, and she would miss it, but right now
she was eager to be on her way. It was a long trip. If she was lucky, she might
arrive by suppertime.

"I just wish there was some other means of communication than the mail,"
Bert said. "Even at best it is unreliable."

"It's the best we have, although I have had some luck sending a message
by someone who is going by lorry. If I have news of great importance, I will
just send a special messenger."

"Look, this is important enough that I might just might fly out. Until the
rains make it impossible, I could land on that road near your village."

"Because it is up to me to say when I will visit the dispensary in Kulanji, I
have yet to decide when to go. It will be this week if possible. It is better for
me to be gone on weekends, so I could drive over on Saturday and return
on Sunday. That is what I plan to do as of now. If that changes, I will let you
know. And, in any event, I will write."

They were standing beside her car. "If you had not bought so many provi-
sions, you would have to come back sooner," Bert said.

"At least I shall have canned cream for my coffee every morning, and a
wonderful supply of Toblerones." She pointed to the orange and blue triangular box that stuck out of a sack in the back seat. Milk chocolate with bits
of honeycomb through it, made in Switzerland.

"You have my address." He pointed to the paper in her hand. "And my telephone number just in case you find a telephone out there somewhere." Then
the most important thing . . . "Malissa, don't forget the statement on AIDS."

Again she wondered about his insistence on this, but at that point she
could refuse him nothing. "I'll do it if I can."

He took her in his arms then and kissed her, long and fervently. They were both breathless.

"I love you," he said.

"I love you, too."

He watched until she was out of sight.

CHAPTER 64

Kulanji

Usually Malissa made her visits to the Kulanji dispensary only when it was a comparatively slack time in Mubi, but not this time. In spite of the fact that she had been home only five days, she packed her Jeep with supplies, and with Yusufu, her cook, she set out very early Saturday morning. Her head dispenser was actually quite capable of looking after things at the hospital for a day or two. He had declared, in fact, that no more people had died while she was gone than would have died had she been there.

In addition to taking care of Malissa's household, Yusufu was a driver, a good one, and Malissa was glad to let him herd the Jeep around the animals and people in the road and especially the potholes in the road.

She had sent word by messenger to Tomas, the dispenser in Kulanji, to expect her Saturday morning. That way, if there were special cases he wanted her to look at, he could get word to them to be there on Saturday.

The cool May morning was ideal for people working on their farms, preparing for the expected and hoped-for rains, and many people waved to them as they passed along the road which lead through the village. She had lived there so long and treated so many of the people that everyone recognized the Jeep of the Dokita Tayluh.

The first part of the trip went rather quickly because the road was reasonably smooth, but after turning off the main road onto the one leading to Kulanji, they could drive only half as fast. People were discouraged from going to Kulanji by the simple fact that absolutely nothing was done to keep up the road. It remained a two-wheel path through the bush country.

Many small bushes grew by pushing long roots into the earth. However, not many trees survived the burning so there were few groves of trees, and solitary monkeybread trees or neam trees continued to grow near springs of water. Now and then they passed clusters of earth-colored houses surrounded by cornstalk fences, and always people who watched them go by waved.

After more than two hours bouncing over rough dusty roads, they approached the guard station at the border to Kulanji. The thorn barrier stretched as far as eye could see to north and south.

Malissa knew what to expect, and as soon as she stopped in front of the pole gate, she climbed out of the Jeep, as did Yusufu.

The guards greeted her by name. "Nice to see you again, Miz Dokita," the head guard said, smiling and bowing. Malissa returned the gesture and asked about his family and his health. Then she stood close by while they searched the Jeep, answering their questions about each item. By now they were familiar with the usual supplies that she brought.

Her hope that they would pass over the can of dirt was not to be realized. The guard held up the can, and as he carefully removed the plastic lid, he asked, "What is this?"

Malissa was ready with her answer. "That is a special powder that I use in treatment of snake bites."

He nodded solemnly, and replacing the lid, he set the can down exceedingly carefully. Malissa thought it was odd, the way he was acting. It was as if the can was, what? Then it came to her, like someone would handle something that was sacred. But then, she thought, every African had a healthy respect for snake bite remedies.

The inspection was soon finished, and they drove away, waving at the guards.

At the dispensary, Mallam Tomas, the dispenser, was already at work but stopped when he heard the sound of the Jeep's motor. Word had gone out that the Dokita would be there that day, and the crowd of waiting patients was already twice its normal size. Any visitor to Kulanji was a rare occasion and one not to be missed, so villagers as well as patients gathered around as close as they could as soon as the motor died.

Malissa greeted Tomas in the Kulanji language. Tomas' English was poor but passable, and he liked using it because it was a sign of importance. Malissa knew that and usually spoke in English, resorting to Kulanji now and then when it was obvious he had not understood.

They went into the dispensary where Malissa talked with Mallam Tomas about how things were going for him and his dispensary. He was probably the most important man in Kulanji, after the chief. Anyone who could cure disease was no less than a miracle worker. Malissa brought out a supply of fingerstick blades, microscope slides, and several bottles of a special solution.

"Tomas, it is important that we check some of these people today for a special disease. First, I want you to put on these gloves. Do not go without them. Then I want you to pick fifty people and take a bit of blood from each person's finger, then mix it with one drop of this solution. Then write down patient's name and the results on this form. If it turns blue, check this box. If it turns red, check this box. Then carefully place the slides in here to dry." She indicated a box with a lid on the worktable. "Is that clear?"

"What do I tell them it is for?" Tomas asked.

"Tell them a new disease has appeared, and we want to make sure they don't have it. We want only one drop of blood from each."

Tomas carefully chose a few of the people standing nearby and explained the situation to them, only he told them that by mixing their drop of blood with a very special medicine, they would become very healthy and strong. After that, he had no trouble getting people to give the one drop of blood because those in front of the line passed the word back along the line. In fact, the ones who were not asked to give a drop of blood were unhappy.

As soon as she checked in the supplies she had brought, Malissa began seeing the special patients that Tomas wanted her to see. Some had never seen a white person before, as this was the only dispensary in the Kulanji area, and some of those people had walked many miles to be there. At Tomas' command, the people remained behind a line marked by the dispenser's desk and came one by one as the young man who was Tomas' assistant called them.

What a difference from the dispensary in Mubi! There she knew ahead of time that each patient would have three kinds of intestinal worms, malaria, and either constipation or diarrhea, in addition to whatever specific complaint had brought them that day such as an injury, cough, anemia, or measles.

Here they came mostly for infected cuts, broken bones, or persistent cough and chest congestion. There were the inevitable intestinal parasites, but for some reason they did not overwhelm the body as happened elsewhere. And dysentery, the disease so prevalent elsewhere, was uncommon here. That would have to be because rules forbade polluting of ground water with human body products. Toilet facilities were found in each compound and in common areas.

Mallam Tomas had explained to Malissa that this was not because the people understood that disease was caused by germs, but rather that the earth and water were sacred. They had been taught from early childhood that their good crops and healthy bodies were due to the soil and water, which produced the crops, and those gifts from the gods were therefore to be treated with great respect.

The day went quickly, and by five o'clock the line of waiting patients was gone. Malissa was ready for what she knew awaited her, a tasty dinner and a quiet evening to read or rest. There was nothing else to do, but she would not have been allowed to leave the resthouse anyway, at least not without an escort. She was not free to come and go as she wished.

She turned toward the resthouse as Tomas locked the dispensary.

Yusufu had her meal ready, and with a sigh of relief she dropped into the lounge chair with its hand-woven seat. Beside the chair on a low stool waited a pitcher of cool water and a glass. It reminded her of what she had to do, exchange the water in her thermos for some of this water. The men at the gate had not given her thermos a second look, knowing it was her drinking water.

Yusufu brought her dinner, rice cooked with bits of meat in a rich peppery sauce. It smelled heavenly. There were even two still warm small loaves of bread. The Africans ate only two meals a day, so she and Tomas had not stopped for lunch. Her stomach was complaining loudly. "What a great meal, Yusufu. Where did you find meat today?" Malissa asked. "And who baked this lovely bread?"

Yusufu came from where he had been tending the fire built between some rocks. "The chief's wife sent you a gift of pig meat, and the rice came from the dispenser's wife. There is a village baker who heard you were coming and scheduled his bread to come out this afternoon in time for your evening meal. I borrowed the spices from Asta Yamta's compound."

"Asta, Ladu's cousin?"

"Yes."

"Did you see Ladu?"

"No." Yusufu's voice dropped to almost a whisper. "She and Laraba and the children are not allowed out of their house except when no one is around."

"Ladu too, not just Laraba?"

Yusufu nodded.

"Is the compound nearby?"

"Not very far."

"While I eat, I would like for you to take a message to that compound that I would like very much to see Ladu, and Laraba too, if possible."

Yusufu nodded and turned to leave. "Do you need anything else before I go?" he asked.

"I'm fine," Malissa replied.

She ate quickly, savoring the fresh bread and dipping it into the spicy broth. She had not tasted anything better than this in the fanciest restaurants. She was suddenly transported back to Malawi as had happened dozens of times a day since she returned home. She was with Bert in the Ku

Chawe Inn where he had in his charming boyish way asked her to marry him. Her body became warm as she followed the next events of that evening. In spite of the fact she could never admit to her fellow missionaries what had happened there, she had no regrets.

In fact, her thoughts had returned to Bert so often over the past few days that she wondered if she was really taking care of her patients adequately.

As soon as she finished eating, she found a spot where the soil was soft, dumped out the can of dirt she had brought, and replaced it with fresh dirt. It was different soil, extremely fine granules, almost a powder, and a rich dark brown. Obviously over the centuries they had discovered its restorative and medicinal attributes. What elements in it could reverse AIDS, or was it just the good food and loving care? Or was it because the soil was not polluted with human wastes?

She smoothed out the area and returned to her lounge chair and her thoughts. Yusufu had returned from his errand and then disappeared to wherever he would spend the night.

"Salaam," interrupted her musings. She looked up to see a young woman whom she immediately recognized as Saratu. Malissa had taken time to help her learn to speak a little English the last several times she was in Kulanji.

"Welcome," Saratu said. "How are you?" Her English was stiff and stilted, but clear.

"I am fine. Come and sit down." Malissa removed the water pitcher from the stool and motioned toward it. Saratu moved the stool a few feet away and sat down. It was not polite to be too close to an important person. Then she went through the usual Kulanji greeting with Malissa responding. It was a ritual not to be omitted.

"I understand my friend, Ladu, is staying at your compound," Malissa said. "How is she?"

"She is well. Each day she thinks perhaps her baby will come. She said she was waiting for you to come so you could deliver it."

"I would be happy to do that. Just send a messenger if it happens tonight," Malissa laughed. "And how is Laraba?"

A painful look crossed Saratu's face, "She is—not well."

"I know what her illness is," Malissa said quietly.

Saratu's face brightened. "They have been here for six weeks, and she says she feels very good and is not having some of the symptoms that she had when she came."

"Is that right?" exclaimed Malissa. "I am eager to talk with her about that. I sent Yusufu with a message."

"Yes, I met him on the path. If you are not afraid, you could return to the compound with me."

" I would like to do that." Malissa started to get up.

"Wait, please," Saratu said, holding up her hand. "There is something I want very, very much. I am hoping you can help me." She was no longer attempting to speak in English, but had dropped back into the Kulanji language. The Wamba and Kulanji languages were similar, enough so that Malissa could follow fairly well.

Malissa waited for her to go on.

"I have to see the Outside!" Saratu's voice was suddenly urgent but not loud. "It is something I must do. Do you think you could help me?"

"But I thought that was not allowed." Malissa frowned.

"My mother says she will give me permission, but she does not know how to make it happen. We need help from the outside. I thought maybe you . . . "

Suddenly Malissa's predicament did not seem so impossible. But she would have to go about this very carefully. In addition to water and soil, they would need human blood if they were to ever know for sure what was going on in Kulanji.

"Perhaps I can help." She paused. "I know you have been reading many books. You know that there are things in our bodies that cause disease or prevent disease. These are found in the blood."

She waited for Saratu's nod of understanding.

"I will help you get to the Outside if you will let me take some of your blood for testing, not very much, just a little."

Again she waited. This time she was not sure what the answer would be. Blood was sacred to the Kulanji. No one had ever consented to give more than a drop or two of blood before, and then only for their own health.

Saratu did not look at Malissa but stared at her hands. Then she gave a little laugh. "I guess if I'm going to violate the sacred law about leaving Kulanji, breaking another rule would make little difference."

Malissa did not answer, but immediately reached for her medical bag, which was never very far away and found the necessary equipment.

"You just look the other way," Malissa said. "Most people don't like to see this."

At first Saratu did look away but then was too curious and turned back to watch.

Unhurriedly with smooth precision, Malissa went about collecting two vials of blood. She made three slides with three different reagents, then added the necessary reagents to the vials and wrapped them securely. Saratu observed each step with great interest.

Malissa was elated. This had been easier than she could have imagined. Saratu was more interested in other matters. "How do you think we could do this, get me out of Kulanji?"

"I am more concerned about what would happen to you. Would they let you back in? Would you not be marked for disobeying tribal laws? And most important, what does your father say?"

"My mother says it is time, that we cannot live like this forever, that it is just a matter of time until someone demands to be allowed to go outside."

"You did not answer my question about your father," persisted Malissa.

Saratu did not look at Malissa. "He says I may go if I don't go on a lorry, or a bus, or an automobile." She turned back to face suddenly, "But there isn't any other way, is there? That was just his way of saying no without saying no." She rushed on, "Miz Tayluh, I want this so much that sometimes it almost makes me ill. I can't eat; I have no appetite. I will not be happy until I have seen some of those things I read about in the books."

"May I suggest that it isn't all that great, that perhaps what you have here is better after all?" Malissa said.

"But until I have seen it, I won't know, will I?" She bounced on her stool like a small child. "Please, Miz Tayluh, help me do this."

Malissa was quiet for a few moments before she replied. "Saratu, there would be one absolute requirement. Without it I would not even consider helping you."

"Anything, just anything!" Saratu cried.

"Your mother would have to go with you."

A look of panic came into Saratu's eyes. "Oh, no," she said, "I don't think she will."

"You ask her and let me know," Malissa said as she stood up. "Shall we go?"

CHAPTER 65

As Malissa walked with Saratu along the winding dirt path to the compound, she was much more optimistic about their chances of discovering the secret of Kulanji than she had been before. And she was even more convinced that there was a secret to be learned.

The evening had cooled down somewhat but Malissa started sweating. Saratu led the way past compounds where she could see families gathered around a fire eating their evening meal. Dogs ran out to bark at them and follow them down the path a little way before turning back. The scent of peanuts and onions waved past them.

When they arrived at Saratu's compound, Asta came quickly to greet Malissa. Then word was sent to Ladu who came immediately, moving as quickly as she could with her protruding belly and awkward gait. Ali, her son, came with her, smiling broadly.

"Hello, Ladu, hello, Ali," Malissa said, bowing.

"Welcome, Miz Tayluh, welcome!" Ladu said, bowing also.

One look at Ladu's face, and Malissa said, "Laraba is better, isn't she?"

"She is much better! In just six weeks she is feeling better, she isn't tired all the time, she is eating well, and best of all, she isn't so depressed."

That was better news than Malissa had dared hope for.

She followed Ladu to the shelter of the little house Ladu, Laraba and the children were staying in.

"What is being done for you, Laraba? Do you take medicine?" Malissa asked after greeting the other girl.

Ladu responded. "Birama, the Wiseman, came to see her and said she must take a small spoonful of dust every day."

"Dust?" Malissa said wonderingly. "What kind of dust?"

"It comes from the Gathering Place here in Kulanji. It is used in special ceremonies and for certain illnesses."

"Is that all?" Malissa asked.

"I make sure she has good food, lots of green leaves, sweet potato, fruits."

"Promise me you will be extremely careful with the new baby when it comes, Ladu," Malissa said. "Laraba, you must not kiss the baby and you must wash your hands carefully many times a day."

"Yes, I know," Ladu said, and Laraba echoed it.

"I am so delighted that you are feeling better, Laraba. I would not have believed it could be, although you must remember that the disease acts like this. The person gets better, then worse, then better."

Tears started in Laraba's eyes. "I am so grateful that Mama brought me here and that the people here are so nice to me. I wish I could live here forever."

The women asked about their families in Mubi. Then Malissa returned to where Asta and Saratu were waiting near the fire as the evening was growing cool. They all sat on hand-carved wooden stools. After a few minutes, Malissa said quietly to Saratu, "Hadn't we better talk about this matter?"

Saratu nodded, but looked unsure of what to say next.

"Did you tell your mother the conditions, Saratu?" Malissa asked.

Asta replied without waiting for Saratu. "At least if both of us are marked, we will have each other to talk to."

"When could you be ready to go?" Malissa asked calmly.

"Are you serious?" cried Saratu.

Malissa nodded.

Saratu and Asta looked at each other. Asta spoke. "Just tell us when."

"We will plan to go on Saturday, two weeks from today. Listen carefully. I will come to Kulanji that morning. About noon a plane will fly over. That will be the signal for us to get through the entry gate and a half mile down the road where the plane will land."

"How will we get past the guards?"

"You will need to think of a way to do that. Can you do it?"

They looked at each other and both nodded solemnly.

"You are to take nothing with you. We can get clothes or anything else you need in Blantyre."

"Blantyre," Saratu interrupted excitedly. "I have read about it, now I get to see it! And cars, and buses and white people, and yellow people, and . . . "

"Saratu, I have to warn you," Malissa said firmly, "if you go out of Kulanji, you will never be the same again. You may never truly feel at home here again. Are you ready for that possibility?"

"Oh, yes, yes!"

Asta met Malissa's gaze, and they both smiled, but there was sadness in their faces.

Saratu caught the glance that went between them. "Tell her, Mama, tell her about you learning to read!"

Asta was silent for a moment and then explained to Malissa about her own girlhood dream. "Perhaps I started this whole thing after all," Asta said. "Each generation must have its own dreams."

"Let's just hope her dream does not destroy the Kulanji culture," Malissa said.

"And yet, it is possible," Asta said, "that my dream was the beginning of it."

They were all silent, staring into the fire until Asta said, "If a dream destroys its maker, then perhaps it is time for it to happen."

There was a murmur of assent.

"But, Saratu," Asta went on, "there is one thing you must do before this thing goes any further. You will go to the Gathering Place at dawn and take a gift to Gwara and tell him what you are planning to do."

"Gwara?" Malissa asked.

"Gwara is the god who gives us health and happiness," Asta explained.

"Must I?" Saratu asked, obviously upset by this.

"You cannot go alone to the Gathering Place. Birama must go with you," Asta said.

"What do I tell Birama?" Saratu asked.

"Nothing. Gwara knows your heart, but you must tell him at the altar where he is sure to be."

"All right, if I must," Saratu conceded.

"Yes, you must. You will say nothing to Birama, only that you are troubled and need to talk with Gwara. I will send word to Birama right now."

Ladu called to Ali who came running.

On the way back to the resthouse Malissa was full of questions. "Saratu, tell me about the god, Gwara," Malissa said. "I have heard only bits and pieces so far. My understanding of your language is still small."

"Gwara has been the all-powerful being for our tribe forever. He is the God of the Sky."

"Surely you have stories about how he came to be called your god," Malissa urged.

"Yes, we hear them from the time we are very small children. Gwara was upset that the earth and the humans on it were not doing the right things, so one day he screamed very loudly and caused that hole to appear in the ground at the spot which our people had called the Gathering Place. It was a reminder of his anger at humans for not doing what he wanted them to.

But then he was sorry and sent a healing cloud of dust which settled all over this land.

"Ever since then bits of the dust have been used in sacred ceremonies, and whenever anyone becomes ill, they are given some of the sacred powder."

To Malissa's mind came the way in which the guard at the gate had handled the can of dirt. He understood healing soil. "

"Where is the Gathering Place?" Malissa asked.

"It is where I will be going with Birama in the morning." Saratu added, "I am sorry you are not allowed to go also."

"Perhaps," Malissa looked for words. "Perhaps I could follow at a far distance?"

Saratu thought about that. "Only if you do not follow closely." She went on. "I would like to do something for you for saving my life," Saratu said.

"Saratu, no one can save your life; you do it for yourself. I am just glad to help if I can."

Malissa had considerable difficulty getting to sleep that night. She went over again the rationale for what she was doing and again concluded that if she did not do it, someone else would. That wasn't an excuse but it was a reason.

She had the sample of water in her thermos and had exchanged the dirt sample. All that remained was to get a message off to Bert to make arrangements for the flight out. She went over and over every aspect of the maneuver. That afternoon she had overheard people talking about the news that guns would be given to the border guards in the near future. She hoped it would not be for at least another two weeks.

She had been asleep about an hour when she was awakened by Yusufu's voice. "Miz Tayluh . . . Miz Tayluh, they want you to come. They want you to come now!"

She knew without asking that Ladu's baby was on the way.

CHAPTER 66

In spite of the fact that Malissa did not get to sleep until well after midnight, she was ready when Saratu called softly at the guesthouse door at dawn the next morning.

The baby had delivered without incident, a healthy girl.

Malissa remained at a distance as Saratu met Birama at the crossroads where the two main roads of the area crossed. He was perhaps fifty years old, tall and straight, wearing a blue embroidered robe and turban against the morning chill. The sky became brighter as they walked, and now Malissa could see clearly. The sun would not be visible for a little while yet as it would have to climb over a low range of mountains pushed up in the east. She followed as they walked, Birama in front, Saratu following at a distance, for perhaps a mile and a half until they came to a place where they halted. Malissa moved silently to where she could see that the earth suddenly slanted downward.

The earth sloped down for a distance and then rose the same distance on the other side. Odd, Malissa thought, how could an indentation in the earth be so nearly perfectly round. It was a natural amphitheater, close to a mile across. Many bushes and trees were scattered throughout the bowl, and Malissa kept out of sight by moving from one bush to another.

Birama and Saratu walked ceremoniously with Birama leading, to the center of the depression where Birama knelt in front of the altar of stones that had been built there, motioning for Saratu to do the same. Malissa had moved closer but could not hear what was said. Then Birama stood, waved his hand over Saratu's head, obviously saying something. Then he knelt again, remaining there for perhaps a minute.

Malissa leaned over and ran a bit of dirt through her fingers. She was standing on the spot where all this began. What riches did the soil hold? What mysteries that had been guarded for centuries were about to be revealed?

From behind her a very light breeze picked up the powdery dust which swirled and enveloped her. For just a moment as Malissa looked over the ancient crater, she had a feeling of fear, wonder, and exhilaration, but more than that. It was as if she were not alone, that there was a presence all around her. An involuntary tremor traveled through her body.

CHAPTER 67

Bert had not slept well since Tuesday, the day Malissa left. As long as she was there, things seemed to make sense. But with her gone, he began to question everything. He wanted nothing so much as to have her close to him again. How clearly her face appeared to him, and if he closed his eyes he could remember how her body felt next to his.

Then he would panic. What if this whole thing about the Green Country got everyone in trouble, especially Malissa? At one moment he was sorry he had ever made the first move to do anything about it, and in the next he was wishing he could find the secret so that Malissa would have some better ways to aid the people she was trying to help.

At the heart of it, finding the secret should be a positive thing, providing ways to better the lives of millions of people. But with the secret in the hands of Gui Manieux, it was likely to better no one's life but Gui's. And why did he want to know for sure if the Green Country people did not have AIDS? It had a sinister feel to it, and Bert wanted to somehow separate Gui from this whole thing. Gui was involved in food production, not AIDS eradication.

Of course, there had been the story going around about Roger LeFever having had AIDS. Maybe Gui actually was interested in a cure for AIDS.

But then he remembered the thirty thousand dollars. How could it possibly be worth that much to Gui? That was troubling. That's what made it seem menacing and malevolent. Gui's intense desire to know that bit of information and his willingness to pay that kind of money was out of proportion. Was he going to try to sell the cure or prevention of AIDS to the world by corncring the idea? That sounded like something Gui would do. But why keep it from Carol? Maybe she would try to keep him from selling it.

If Gui were doing this for Carol, the whole thing would make sense. Whenever he had seen Carol and Gui together, it was obvious that Gui was entranced by the woman.

Then it came to him that he did not have to do this for Gui. Malissa could get the soil and water sample and test blood for AIDS so that the secret could be discovered. They could do that without Gui.

But the money? He had a ball of pain in the middle of his stomach as he thought about giving up the plane. But he wanted to do nothing that would make Malissa displeased. Doing this without involving Gui was the only way to be sure of that.

It was Sunday afternoon, May thirtieth, and he had to meet Gui to give him an update on his progress. What would he tell him? That he wasn't going to do it? Well, why not? Was the plane really as important as the possibility that Malissa would be hurt? The more he thought of it the more he realized that was what he had to do, plane or no plane. He would tell Gui that he would not do it!

He rushed through light Sunday afternoon traffic to the Arch, hurrying so he could get this over with; tell Gui to forget it. The beautiful plane had suddenly become ugly in comparison to helping Malissa. They would use the knowledge from the Green Country to help people and leave Gui out entirely.

It wasn't as if Gui had found the idea first. In fact, it was Bert who had remembered the Green Country. He had absolutely no obligation to Gui Manieux.

Gui pulled in right behind him. Bert started toward him, his mouth open ready to tell him.

Gui beat him to it. "Carol tells me that Malissa will be contacting her through you. I told Carol there was nothing to the no-AIDS thing, but she is still excited about finding out what makes those people so healthy and why their crops grow better."

"Mr. Manieux."

"Thirty thousand dollars is not the end of it, Bert. After you get me this bit of information, if it is true, and I will bet my bottom dollar that it is, there will be another project, only this one will be worth more."

Bert couldn't help himself. "How much more?"

"More than you already have been paid."

Bert was suddenly angry at Gui, at himself, at the whole thing. "What in the world is that important to you?"

"I want just one more, one more, Bert, a safe one."

"A safe what?" He almost yelled it.

Gui suddenly took a step backward. "I forgot, you do not . . . "

"I don't what, Gui, I don't what?" Now he was shouting.

"You do not understand, that is what." Gui started walking toward his car. "See you next Sunday. You should know something by then, right?"

Gui didn't wait for the answer. He was gone in a swirl of dust.

"Damn!" Bert said. "Damn, damn, damn!"

CHAPTER 68

Blantyre was more than a tourist center in eastern Africa, it was also a major business center. It had attracted a group of top-rated medical doctors. Since businessmen and women from all over eastern Africa came there for vacation, they would plan to have their yearly physical checkups. Gui was no exception.

Doctor McGuire was an American doctor who came originally to work with the Seventh Day Adventist Mission Hospital, but liked living in Malawi so well that he opened a private practice on the side. Gui's appointment was for Monday afternoon.

The doctor had looked him over, checked his prostate, had the nurse draw blood for lab tests, and now he was in the doctor's office for the final word.

"Healthy as usual," Doctor McGuire said.

Gui moved as if to leave.

"Except," the doctor went on, "you are still smoking. I hear some sounds in your lungs that I don't like. Do you get short of breath with exertion?"

"No, not really."

"Do you exercise regularly?"

"I get lots of exercise, but nothing regular."

"There are lots of reasons to stop smoking, Gui, but at your age one of the most important is that it affects your blood vessels and usually leads to impotence. Have you been having any difficulty with erections lately?"

In fact, he had recently had some problems maintaining an erection. He thought he was just tired.

"I thought maybe that came with age," Gui said.

"It needn't. Half of the men over thirty who smoke will have some degree of impotence, and as you get older, it becomes much more pronounced."

Gui was staring at the doctor, his mind racing. He had smoked since he was fifteen, at least a pack a day. He was a man of quick decisions, and now abruptly he pulled the package of cigarettes from his shirt pocket, reached into his pants pocket and took out a lighter, both of which he laid on the doctor's desk. "I have just quit smoking, Doc."

"Just like that?" Dr. McGuire asked.

"Just like that!"

"There is nothing you can do for yourself that would be more important to your physical or mental health, Gui. I hope you stick to it."

"You can count on it." For just a second he considered telling the doctor just how important it was that he not be impotent, but decided against it.

CHAPTER 69

When Gui arrived home that Monday evening, Carol met him at the door, glass of wine in hand.

"Dinner is almost ready," Carol said. "We will have a drink on the veranda first. What took so long at the doctor's office?"

Gui dropped into a lounge chair and automatically reached for a cigarette, then remembered and pulled his hand back.

"I stopped off at the Fitness Center and signed up for a workout time three times a week."

"That's great, Gui! We can go together. What days are you planning to go?"

"Probably Tuesday, Thursday and Saturday. Thought I would go early, like seven o'clock in the morning."

"I like early morning workouts. I will just arrange my schedule to go at the same time you do."

"And you can throw away the ash trays, I have stopped smoking."

"Gui! That's wonderful! You can't guess how often I have wished you would do that! Let's celebrate, or aren't you drinking any more either?"

"Doctor. McGuire says smoking makes men impotent. That was enough for me. But drinking I can still do, in moderation."

Carol dropped into his lap and put her arms around his neck. "What a great anniversary present, Gui, undiminished sex for the rest of our lives!"

The look on his face told her he had forgotten their third anniversary.

She kissed him long on the lips. "I'll forgive you, sweetheart, if I get to enjoy some of that undiminished sex tonight."

But it was not to be so. When Carol slipped into bed beside him, naked and smelling of Chanel Number 5, Gui was unable to perform. "It's okay, sweetheart," Carol soothed, "a few weeks off of cigarettes should take care of that."

Gui was not convinced, and he awakened numerous times in the night, wondering.

CHAPTER 70

Malissa arrived back home in Mubi Sunday about noon. The workers at the hospital had obviously been listening for her motor as a young woman in a white shirt was running toward her when she got out of the car. A woman had been brought in bleeding heavily from childbirth.

Carrying the precious blood, water and soil samples that she had held all the way home, Malissa walked into her house and put the blood samples into the refrigerator. Then she hurried down the hill to the waiting patient.

She did not get away from the hospital until almost seven o'clock that evening. The bleeding woman had finally stabilized about three o'clock, but then a man with a compound fracture of the leg was brought in. By the time she finished setting his leg and splinting it, it was dark.

Yusufu had a sandwich ready for her, which she ate gratefully.

Monday morning as soon as she could break away from the hospital, she carefully placed the blood slides and the vials in a box surrounded by frozen packs and then in the middle of a bigger box with wadded newspaper all around it. She had to keep the size of the box as small as possible since a messenger would carry it. Malissa had learned that wadded newspaper was the best packing if she wanted something to get through safely over rough roads.

The vials needed to be kept cool. She gave the messenger a large amount of money with the instructions to go as fast as possible, and he would be paid the rest when he delivered the package.

She was not going to trust the dispenser's judgment on the slides he had collected from the fifty people. She wanted the slides checked again by the lab in Lilongwe, and she wanted the precious vials of blood to be tested for everything including DNA values. She only hoped that Tomiko's friend did indeed exist and that he would send the report as quickly as possible. However, there was a letter in the package requesting that the report be sent to Bert McEwen in Blantyre. Perhaps there was less chance of it being lost that way.

The soil and water samples were packed equally carefully and dispatched with another messenger to Bert along with a letter. Fearful that the messenger might think it was valuable and try to sell it, she told him it was stool and urine samples to test for a new disease. The look on his face would seem to indicate that the sample was safe from theft.

CHAPTER 71

Thursday evening Bert had just sat down to enjoy a beer before he ate his evening meal. He wasn't even sure what he was going to have for supper yet.

When the doorbell rang, he waited until it rang the third time before he got up. Maybe they would go away.

At the door stood a young black man. "Mister Uwen?" the young man asked.

"No." Bert started to close the door when the man pushed toward him a package to which an envelope was taped. He recognized his name on the outside. Uwen was a corruption of McEwen.

"How much?" he asked.

The young man shrugged. "Dokita Tayluh say you pay."

Bert recognized the way Africans pronounced Taylor, and suddenly his mouth went dry. A message from Malissa! He smiled as he realized that, of course, they called Malissa a doctor.

He reached into his pocket and pulled out a couple bills. "Okay?" he asked.

The young man's eyes went wide. "Okeh!" he said as he turned to leave.

"Thanks!" Bert called after him.

Tearing the envelope raggedly, he opened the letter.

Dearest Bert,

Incredible breakthrough. I will be bringing a young Kulanji woman, Saratu, and her mother, Asta, to Blantyre. But they must go by plane. Can you pick us up? I know it is rainy season, and you may have difficulty finding a good day to fly.

If you can, come on Saturday next, June twelfth. Fly low over the Kulanji village that is nearest to the entry gate then land a half-mile down the road from the gate. Give us fifteen minutes. We will no doubt have to leave in a hurry, so don't turn off your engine.

I am sending the samples of soil and water. I will leave it up to you as to what to do with them for testing. I will be most interested in learning what they find.

I have included that statement about AIDS you wanted. We did a preliminary check on fifty people and found not even one incidence of AIDS. However, I really do not trust either my dispenser or the reagents we use in the tests. They could be wrong. So I am sending them off to Lilongwe for confirmation or otherwise. I hope this is good enough for what you need.

I had the incredible good luck of getting Saratu to consent to giving enough blood to do some definitive testing for everything in the books. That is off to Lilongwe also. Because of the difficulties of mail delivery, I have asked that the report be sent to you rather than to me.

One other thing, you need to make an appointment with a doctor, either internal medicine or gynecology, for a thorough examination of Saratu on Monday or Tuesday.

I cannot state too strongly that the only way I will consent to bring Saratu to Blantyre is that she must never be left alone at any time. Either you or I must be with her at all times, so please arrange your schedule accordingly.

If you don't come on Saturday, we will expect you on Sunday. If you can't come on Sunday, let me know, and we will try another time.

I love you. Malissa

Unbelievable! Malissa was going to accomplish his mission for him. Bless her! The airplane was his!

Suddenly the guilt came rolling back in. Poor Saratu would be dropped into a completely alien world and subjected to all kinds of tests, questions, probing, not to mention Gui's guiles. He was selfish to want the plane so much that he would let this happen. And putting Malissa through this ordeal, was it worth it? But it was Malissa who decided to bring the young woman out of Kulanji. He was very curious as to why and how she had managed to accomplish this.

But the plan was in place now, and no amount of guilt or fear could keep him from savoring the prospect of actually owning that gorgeous plane. It had regained its place of importance in his mind, and having it would most certainly make the difference in his accomplishing this mission which required landing in a difficult area and needing a quick takeoff.

Later in bed when he could not go to sleep, he wondered to himself which was his greater desire at the moment, wanting Malissa or wanting the airplane. Would it anger the gods if he asked for both?

CHAPTER 72

On Friday morning Bert dispatched a messenger to take a letter to Malissa. The note agreed to her terms and then said, *I am assuming there will be three of you. Any more than that could cause a problem. They can't carry much baggage, just a small bundle each.*

If the weather is bad, I will come on Sunday. If the weather is bad on Sunday, I will come on Monday.

The samples arrived safely. I think I know where to have the soil tested. The report should be back by the time you arrive in Blantyre. I shall be on the lookout for the report from Lilongwe.

Nine days is a long time before I see you again!

I love you! Bert"

There was a chance that it would not reach Mubi before Malissa left to go to Kulanji, but he had to try.

CHAPTER 73

Bert took a chance on Gui not being at The Farm office that Friday morning. Gui had bragged about the state-of-the-art laboratory that he had there. One time while he and Bert were waiting out a storm in Lusaka, Zambia, Gui had described in great detail how they tested the soil of each plot of ground for numerous factors, and then depending on the results, fertilizer or other elements would be added to the soil for better production. He had spoken of his laboratory technician, Yahara, commenting that Yahara was one of the best.

Bert knew Yahara because he had flown with them a couple times to corporate farms in other parts of Africa. He liked the man but had the feeling that there was tension between Yahara and Gui. Not surprising. The way Bert understood it, there was tension between Gui and everyone else he had anything to do with except, apparently, Carol.

If Gui was there, Bert had a reason ready for why he had come, but there was no sign of Gui's convertible. To be safe, Bert parked behind the lab building, out of sight of Gui's office. He had called ahead, and Yahara was expecting him.

Bert stepped into the small front office of the laboratory building. Through the door into the back room he could see rows of beakers, bottles and equipment. Yahara motioned for Bert to sit in the chair next to the desk.

"I need a little help that is right down your alley, Yahara," Bert began.

"I welcome something new to work on," Yahara replied. "Checking soil samples all the time gets old."

"Well, I have a soil and a water sample, but I want you to do absolutely every kind of test you can do on them, including anything you hadn't thought of before. I want to know everything there is to know about this bit of soil."

"Special samples of some kind?" Yahara asked. "Where are they from?"

"Just some I picked up on my last trip down south," Bert said quickly. "But they were growing the biggest ears of corn I have ever seen."

"We can check for growth elements, anything else?"

"Everything. Someone down there said they had medicinal properties. Any way you could check on that?"

Yahara looked doubtful, scratching his chin in thought. "There are some tests that are quite far-out and unusual, but I would be glad for a chance to run them. Haven't needed them with our usual samples." He reached for a journal lying on his desk nearby. "In fact, there is an article in here on some new tests for genetic alterations that they now say affect growth and health."

"I would very much appreciate whatever you can do. I'll pay whatever your going rate."

"Oh, I don't do custom work for anyone outside of the Farm. I'll just be glad to have something interesting to do. When do you want it?"

Bert wanted to say *today*, but settled for, "I'm in kind of a hurry, but just let me know as soon as you have exhausted the tests that are possible or that make sense."

"Well, this should be most interesting," Yahara said, lifting the carton of dirt to his nose and sniffing. "Smells like dirt," he said, grinning.

Bert lowered his voice as if someone might be listening. "I would like for you to keep whatever information you gather from Mr. Manieux. I really don't want him to know anything about this."

Yahara had had suspicions as soon as Bert walked in, but now he was sure that this had something to do with what Tomiko had told him about and certainly connected to Gui's search for a Green Country. The question was, where did Bert fit into all of this?

"Absolutely," Yahara assured him. "There is no reason Mr. Manieux should know anything about this. I will see to that." Then he added, "Actually he never comes to the lab. He leaves this up to me, says he doesn't like playing in dirt."

Bert made a face. "Not this kind of dirt anyway."

Their eyes met, and Yahara nodded, "Right."

CHAPTER 74

Back at his hotel room Tomiko called up his World.net E-mail and sent a message to Doctor Jim Harris at the lab in Lilongwe, asking if he had heard from Malissa Taylor and again reminding the doctor to process the samples immediately, and send him a copy of the report by E-mail as soon as possible.

Tomiko did not know for sure that Malissa was sending anything, but he wanted to cover all bases and hoped to luck out somewhere along the line. He would leave no stone unturned to find out about the Green Country. He could not be sure that samples she sent were from the Green Country or from her own hospital, but it was worth finding out.

As an afterthought, he sent another quick message to Jim, "Please let me know when any laboratory samples arrive from Miss Taylor, even before you check them out. It is important. You will be well rewarded for your trouble."

Tomiko turned off his computer and started out the door to get a sandwich for lunch when the telephone rang. It was Yahara.

"Bert McEwen was just here with a pint can of very black soil and a jar of water. He wants me to analyze them for everything imaginable. Do you think this would have anything to do with the Green Country?"

Tomiko thought for a moment. Soil analysis — soil and water? Of course, it was very possible that Bert had somehow managed to get a sample of the soil from the Green Country. How providential!

"Absolutely, absolutely! This could be it, Yahara! By all means, throw every test at them and then let me know the results! This may be the breakthrough I have been hoping for!"

"I thought it might be," said Yahara, very pleased with himself.

"But look, Yahara, you must absolutely make sure that Gui Manieux never finds out about this. It would be disastrous if he did."

"I agree," responded Yahara. "I shall keep it under lock and key."

"Yahara, for this I shall treat you to the finest dinner in Blantyre."

"If we can beat Gui to the punch, it will be reward enough," Yahara said firmly.

"Oh, and Yahara, don't be in too much of a hurry to get the report back to Bert. You are an expert in your field, but if there are some unusual things found, I may need time to run it past some scientists in some other areas of expertise."

"Right," Yahara said, "there is a lot I don't know about viruses, trace elements and the like. I would be glad for you to have someone else check it out."

CHAPTER 75

On Friday evening, June fourth, when Tomiko plugged in the telephone line in his room and turned on his computer, he found a message from Doctor Harris in Lilongwe.

A box just arrived from Malissa Taylor from Mubi in Wamba country. It contains fifty slides and some vials of blood to be tested. We will check them and let you know.Tomiko sent a reply: Please check for absolutely everything possible, not just what Miss Taylor requested. Please do any work on these slides yourself and do not share the results with anyone other than myself and Miss Taylor. Will you do that?

The answer was slow in coming and was not in Tomiko's E-mail until the next morning. It said, *I will do it as soon as I can.*

Tomiko sent another quick message. *I want you to run absolutely every test in the books and some that aren't if you can think them up,* Tomiko said. *Spare no expense. This is important!*

Jim had started to sign off when the computer announced he had a message. He read it and muttered to himself, "This guy isn't going to let go of this until I bow down and kiss his . . ."

But he responded with *How important?*

Tomiko's answer was terse, *It could mean life or death for millions of people.*

Jim returned a curt message that he would take care of it. Tomiko hoped that Jim planned to handle the process himself, he forgot to make that part clear. He knew the company was swamped with the new Soils and Waters lab being added to their Human Tissues lab that it was entirely likely the project could be turned over. Perhaps he had not stressed the importance enough.

Jim chose at random one of the vials of blood and automatically went through the various tests and slides for the genome of this individual, not really paying attention since these were routine tests and he expected routine results of malaria, anemia or any of the diseases prevalent in Africa.

If he did one complete genomic report on one of the slides, then his partner, Alhaji, could replicate the procedure on the others. He had been recording values and now had a neat list in the values column, which he quickly scanned.

A value that was out of line caught his eye. He paused and went back over the entire list. Something was definitely definitely wrong!

He checked his reagents, the scales, and the settings on the machines. Then he ran several of the tests again. Same results. He rubbed his eyes, as if that would make the values change. Tomiko was serious about this being important.

CHAPTER 76

On Sunday evening, June sixth, Bert had to wait out a heavy shower before leaving for Independence Arch. It was almost dark by that time. He had decided that he would tell Gui nothing, only show him the statement from Malissa about AIDS. That should take care of the thirty thousand. That would let him off the hook, and he would be through with Gui forever.

All he had to do was come up with another fifty-seven thousand dollars, and the plane would be his. But with thirty thousand dollars cash in hand, surely a bank would be willing to take a chance on him for a loan with the plane for security. Certainly he could qualify for that much. And he would be free of Gui!

Gui was late. Bert sat in his car for fifteen minutes before Gui's car came sliding in to stop in a swirl of splashing mud. Gui motioned for Bert to get into his car.

"Well?" Gui asked as soon as Bert sat down, not even caring about the mud he brought with him on his feet.

Bert thrust the paper toward him. "This should do it."

Gui read it, and a smile came over his face. "Good for you, Bert." He pulled an envelope from an inside pocket and held it out but did not release it when Bert grasped it.

Bert wanted nothing more than to be out of there. He pushed down on the door handle.

"Not so fast," Gui said. "It is not over. In fact, the next project is the most difficult, so . . . " he paused for emphasis, "So naturally you will be paid in proportion to the job."

"I don't want to . . . !"

"Wait until you hear what it is, will you? I do not imagine it will be too difficult for you, considering what you have already accomplished."

"No, Gui." He wanted nothing so much as to be done with this man.

"How does fifty-seven thousand dollars sound? I happen to know that is how much you are going to need to finish paying for your plane."

Bert clamped his jaw to keep his mouth from dropping open. "No, Gui."

"Bert, I have found out there are things more important than money. I am almost sixty-one years old. This may be my last chance. I do not care what it costs, do you understand?"

"I understand that you must be out of your mind to pay that kind of money. For what?"

"You bring me one AIDS-free young woman from the Green Country and the fifty-seven thousand dollars is yours."

Bert stared at him, unable to believe what the man had just said. No words would come.

"I stopped having other women in my life, because of AIDS, after my partner died, but it has not been easy. I am willing to pay whatever it takes to have one more chance to experience sex with a young woman who is AIDS-free and without using a damned condom. I cannot take chances, you see. But most important of all, I understand that she would also be a virgin. One last experience with a virgin, now that is worth the price!"

Bert was still speechless. He hoped he could keep his breakfast down.

Gui pushed on,. "What good is money if I cannot have what I really want?"

Bert's head was spinning, first with shock and then anger, and he could only stare at this man.

"Look, Bert, I know you have some reservations about this sort of thing, but surely your plane is worth it."

At last Bert found his voice. In quiet fury he said, "What makes you think this woman would want to go to bed with you?"

"Just give me an hour with her alone. That is all I ask. The rest is not your problem. Is it a bargain?"

Into Bert's mind came the vision of the young Kulanji woman, and it all suddenly came clear to him. Powerful Gui Manieux had put himself into Bert's hands. This was obviously something Gui wanted more than anything else in his life, which made him vulnerable.

Bert grimaced as he realized he too had made himself vulnerable to Gui by wanting the airplane desperately, but he knew some things Gui did not. Gui did not know how much Bert despised him. The fool thought Bert would do anything to get the airplane. Well, at this point it had become more than an airplane to Bert. It was also an opportunity to pay Gui back for the way he had treated his friend, Ahmed, two years before.

It was not long after Bert had arrived in Malawi and before he knew who Gui Manieux was. His very first customer was a man named Ahmed Amadu, a Pakistani who owned a huge tea plantation in Malawi. When Bert was still unknown in Blantyre, Ahmed gave him the contract to ferry in precious tea plant seedlings from Kenya. Somehow he and Ahmed hit it off right away. Before long they were playing squash at the local gym and meeting for drinks at the Mount Soche Hotel bar on Friday evenings after work. Bert was included in Amadu family celebrations. Through Ahmed Bert found other customers.

One afternoon Bert had returned with another load of tea plant seedlings for Ahmed and arrived at Ahmed's office for payment just as the police were arresting Ahmed. When Bert visited Ahmed in the jail, Ahmed told a tale of deceit and betrayal by none other than Gui Manieux. Gui had made an offer to buy the tea plantation then falsified documents and made it appear that Ahmed had done it. In the end, Ahmed was bankrupt and Gui had the tea plantation. Not long after that Ahmed suffered a major heart attack and died. Bert was not likely to forget his first, and only, close friend in Malawi.

Gui had admitted he wanted this more than anything else in the world, so Bert would make him pay and then leave him holding the bag. Just as Gui had done to Ahmed.

Bert knew he was not alone in this situation; he had allies. Malissa had said she would bring Saratu only if she would never be alone with anyone other than one of them. Saratu's mother or Malissa would always be with Saratu. Gui wouldn't have a chance.

He smiled at Gui. He could agree to anything. Bert would merely need to be paid ahead of time, but he didn't want to make this easy. He wasn't ready to accept the offer.

"It may not be possible, but I need something up front for expenses, say fifteen thousand." Bert hoped that would make Gui angry enough to call off the project.

There was a long silence while the rain splattered the windshield in whispering drops.

"Ten thousand, that's all."

"Twelve five."

Gui frowned but said, "Agreed."

"Have it delivered to me at my home by noon tomorrow," Bert said, "I'll bring a young woman from the Green Country to Blantyre. It will be up to you to make the arrangements after that."

"I can manage that," Gui said with assurance, relieved that Bert was even being so good-natured about it.

"But, I get paid as soon as she arrives at the Mount Soche Hotel."

Gui thought about that and started to shake his head.

"Look, Gui, getting a woman out of Kulanji and actually bringing her to Blantyre is no small miracle." Now Bert was deliberately cruel, "Surely you have what it takes to talk the woman into going to bed with you. If you don't . . . "

Gui's eyes flashed angrily. "You do your part, I will do mine! When she is in the hotel, call me on my cell phone, not at my home or the office. I will meet you at the hotel. I want to see her first. After all I don't want an ugly..."

Bert couldn't resist. "What difference does it make as long as she is a virgin?"

"When I am paying this much, I want a pretty one. When I have seen her, I will give you the rest of the money, and I will take it from there. When is this going to happen?"

"If all goes as planned, she will arrive on Sunday, June thirteenth."

"You already had this planned! Why, you, you greedy bastard!" Gui said loudly. "And you want me to pay you to do something you were already going to do."

"If you want to be included, you will have to pay for it." Calmly Bert continued. "If we are delayed by weather, it might be Monday. I'll have to call and let you know when, some time on Monday or maybe Tuesday, in the afternoon probably. Then the rest is up to you."

"There is one thing I need to know, Bert," Gui said firmly, now sure that he was going to get what he wanted. "What is her name?"

Bert just looked at him. It would be a sacrilege to let him bandy around Saratu's name until their meeting. He shook his head.

"Her name, Bert! How am I going to speak with her if I do not know her name?"

Reluctantly, in a low voice, Bert said, "Saratu."

"Saratu, Saratu. A lovely name."

"She is a lovely girl," Bert said emphatically.

"Bert, you're incredible, you know that? You know how to get things done. You can plan on having all of my business from now on. You have made it possible for me to have what will no doubt be the most memorable experience in my life, a virgin—at my age! I am not over the hill yet, by damn!"

"Sure, Mr. Manieux, sure." Bert grasped the envelope firmly and opened the car door. Then he turned around to add, "But the price will be a hundred thousand."

Gui stared at Bert as his handsome face contorted into angry ugliness. "You son-of-a-bitch. You have it figured out. You think I have to have this so you will stick me for it." His voice rose as did his level of anger. "You have not had a woman for so long you cannot remember what it is like, so you think you will make me pay through the nose just because I can have a woman any time. No, by damn . . . !"

Bert's voice was calm but clear. "What you are asking is worth what I will have to do to make it happen. You are asking me to compromise a young woman for your sexual pleasure, and you thought you could play on my greed. A hundred thousand or not at all. I don't have to have the money. I—I am getting a loan at the bank. But if I do this, I must be paid what it is worth."

Gui was obviously seething , unable to speak. Bert waited a few seconds and got out of the car.

As he started to close the door Gui said in repressed fury, "Okay, okay, a hundred thousand. But if you screw up, you will regret it." The last words were each emphasized one by one.

Bert was not inclined to show any mercy. "I believe you are the one who is screwing."

Gui was gone by the time Bert got into his car, screeching off into the night. Bert sat there, still in shock. What kind of a monster was this man? He had heard about men thinking that loss of sex drive was synonymous with death, but he had never actually met anyone who was living the idea.

But Gui would be in for a shock. It was payback time.

And, it answered the question of why Gui did not want Carol to know what he was doing.

Now, the next problem. Pray for clear weather on that Saturday.

CHAPTER 77

In Kulanji

Pindar caught up with Saratu as she was coming from the school where she had been working on her English.

"Saratu, will you go to the dance with me Friday night?" he asked.

Saratu glanced sideways at Pindar. One of the best looking men in the tribe, son of the chief, smart enough to be the top of his class, and he was polite and thoughtful. What more could she ask?

"If I am here Friday night, I will go with you."

"What do you mean—if you are here?"

"Oh," she tossed her head, "I thought maybe I would run over to Blantyre for the weekend or go visit the market in Higi."

"In your dreams," Pindar hooted.

"Sometimes my dreams come true."

"Not that one, no way."

She needed to glean some information from Pindar. She stopped and nonchalantly leaned against the neam tree beside the path.. "Did you get the assignment you asked for?"

"I start as gate guard right away; Friday will be my first day."

"But won't you be working Friday night?" Saratu asked.

"I go to work at sunrise and work until there." His hand moved upward and stopped at a point to indicate a mid-afternoon time.

"How do you know the time?"

"The supervisor has a watch," Pindar replied.

"Straight through, no breaks?"

"There will be two of us. We take turns stopping for food just before mid-day."

"Aren't you afraid someone will try to break in or break out?" Saratu teased. "They could hit you over the head or something."

"No one ever has, I don't think so."

Saratu started walking on down the path.

"Do you have guns yet?"

"Pretty soon, maybe next week, they say. Then I will have to learn how to shoot one."

"Learn how to not shoot your own foot, that is," Saratu teased.

"I'll be careful. Would you take care of me if I get hurt?"

"Your mother is very good at that," returned Saratu offhandedly.

Suddenly Pindar was serious. "Saratu, you are almost eighteen. It's time to . . . "

"To find out what the world is like, Pindar," Saratu turned to him and snapped. "Don't push me. When I am ready to get married, the whole world will know it."

"But how long will I have to wait? All the other guys my age are married."

It was her chance to ask the question she and her girl friends wanted to know about. "You can always sneak across the thorn barrier at night."

"Never!" His voice had an edge to it. "I wouldn't do that, Saratu . . . because I know you wouldn't like me if I did." He touched her arm gently. "I don't want anyone but you."

Touching was not permitted between unmarried people, but Saratu did not pull away.

"We shall see," she said, then danced off down the path not looking back.

Saratu walked quickly until she rounded a corner and was out of sight from Pindar, then slowed her pace. Surely there was more to life than marrying Pindar. It was well known that some of the young men sneaked out of Kulanji before they were married. She honestly believed Pindar when he said he did not, but who knows when he would get tired of waiting for her.

She knew why women could not take a chance on having sex before they were married, but her curiosity about the event was enormous. The feelings that were aroused when she danced with Pindar were intensely pleasurable, but she wanted to know more.

The idea of having sex with only one man all her life was stifling to say the least. What if Pindar was an inept lover? Given the social customs in her country, there was little chance of it ever being different. But that did not keep her from imagining what it might be like with someone who knew how to make it enjoyable.

CHAPTER 78

Jim Harris did not leave the lab until after eleven o'clock that night. The last thing he did before going home was send an E-mail to his friend, Clay Worthington, in Pennsylvania.

Hold on to your hat, Clay. I want your assessment of these values. I have checked and rechecked my reagents and gauges, they are okay. Tell me what we have here.

The head of the World Health Organization is asking for the report. I want to give him the correct answers. But more than that I want to know what these mean.

Please help me! I am in over my head here.

CHAPTER 79

Yahara had returned to The Farm Sunday afternoon and then stayed late Monday evening, running tests on the water and soil samples that Bert had brought. At first he thought he had really messed up, mixed up the chemicals or something. The results were skewed, crazy. So he had returned Tuesday night to run them all again.

He was tired and more than a little fearful that he was not going to be able to help his friend, Tomiko, if he didn't run the tests correctly. Admittedly, some of the tests were new to him, but even the old ones didn't seem to be coming out right.

But incredibly, when he re-ran them, they came out within a point or two of the original values. The night was very warm, and he sat down at his desk and sipped on a cold beer while he pondered the situation. He had checked and double-checked amounts, proportions, reagents, weights, everything. Why would the results be so different from anything else he knew? Why?

But, of course! Tomiko was expecting, hoping they would be different. And different they were! Tomiko picked up the phone on the second ring. Yahara gave the usual greeting, but Tomiko sensed the repressed excitement in Yahara's voice.

"The report, Yahara, the report!"

Yahara tried to sound nonchalant. "Just the usual growth elements, maybe a bit more ammonium nitrate than usual." He paused for effect.

"Yes, yes, Yahara, go on!"

"I can't tell you."

"What do you mean, you can't tell me? What else is there?"

"I don't know."

"You mean there are elements you don't recognize?"

"Yes, definitely, several. Their gene analysis is not like anything I have ever seen or heard of before."

"You don't say," Tomiko mused.

"Now what do we do?" Yahara asked.

"We take it to the experts," Tomiko said emphatically. "Bring me a sample of the water and soil as soon as you can."

" Tonight?" Yahara asked.

"Yes, tonight. I will get it to the lab first thing in the morning."

"A lab, where is there a Soils and Water lab?" Yahara asked.

Tomiko had to brag a little. "At my insistence, a Soils and Water lab has been added to the Human Tissues lab at the University of Lilongwe. It is quite new, open only about a month."

"But how will you get it there quickly?" Yahara asked. "There is no delivery service that I am aware of."

Tomiko had a sudden plan. "Yahara, this is so important that I don't want to trust this to anyone else. Could I possibly borrow your car tomorrow? I will take it to Lilongwe myself."

Rental cars were notoriously untrustworthy in Malawi, and anyway Tomiko would prefer to not leave tracks for someone to find.

"A Soils and Water lab by the UN," Yahara mused. "Mr. Manieux mentioned that this was likely to happen. He is not happy about the likelihood of the United Nations organizing conglomerates that will compete with him."

"Of course not," Tomiko said. "If he gets effective competition, he might have to lower his prices."

"Then certainly you may borrow my Mercedes."

CHAPTER 80

When Jim Harris had gone back to the laboratory on Saturday morning, there was no message from Clay. He really had not expected to hear from him over the weekend. Of course, Clay probably didn't even check his E-mail on weekends.

Jim did not usually work on weekends either, but he had been getting the new lab in order. This Sunday he barely took time to grab a bite to eat at noon and then was back at work, running and re-running tests on the samples from Malissa Taylor.

He had promised to do something special with his children that Sunday evening, so he quit about five o'clock. He checked his E-mail as he was getting ready to leave and quickly opened the message from Clay.

The message read: *Whew! I can hardly believe that your machines are accurate, but if you say so.*

I will give it my best and get back to you as soon as possible. If these values are correct, we have something out of this world on our hands.

Back to you later."

Now on Tuesday morning he was checking his E-mail again.

Clay's messages said, *Jim, I've run this past everyone here, and they think I have a polluted specimen. Tell me a little more about where this one came from.*

Jim replied in a quick note. *Clay, as near as I can tell, the samples came from a little-known country to the west of here. It seems to be some kind of a secret, which makes me believe there is something to it.*

The reply to that was a real surprise.

Jim, something in my bones tells me that this is a once-in-a-lifetime discovery. I've decided to take you up on your invitation to visit (I assume it is still open) and will be on the plane as soon as I can make arrangements for my classes and get a suitable ticket. I will let you know my arrival time. Clay.

That was the best news Jim had heard in a long time. He was losing sleep and had no idea what to do with what he had before him. He gave a long sigh of relief and returned a message.

He was going to have some help from an expert. Thank God!

CHAPTER 81

The next morning Tomiko left early to drive to Lilongwe. He needed to see the new lab so he could report on it when he returned to New York. possibly the report on the blood samples which Malissa had sent would be ready, making for an impressive first report.

The Mercedes purred quietly, and this was a beautiful country. He was glad for a chance to see it close up. Part of the highway edged Lake Malawi, and always there were the mountains in the background. He took few opportunities to see the local people, and he needed to be able to talk about them as if he were well acquainted with indigenous populations when he conversed with others in the United Nations. He saw several farmers ploughing their fields with oxen. He would remember to tell his wife about that.

Tomiko never wore shorts, and his long trousers were uncomfortably warm. At least he had taken off his suit coat. The morning was already warm enough to use the air conditioner. Tomiko did enjoy such *luxury. The car even had a short wave radio, and he tuned in to Rome for some classical music.

Gui's fears that the United Nations would consolidate many small farms into a corporate conglomerate was not without foundation, and in fact, to that end the United Nations had set about preparing for such an eventuality. They looked for a country in central Africa that had a fairly stable government, a livable climate, and transportation and communication systems that were reasonably reliable. They found it in Malawi, *The Warm Heart of Africa.*

If smaller farm units were to become more successful with help from the United Nations, a state-of-the-art laboratory was essential. The new genetically altered seeds for peanuts and yams had opened up a whole new area of research and experimentation. Unfortunately, the products had only met resistance, and other answers needed to be found.

It had been at Tomiko's insistence that funding for the research and development had been included in last year's budget, and now the fledgling lab was a reality. The logical location was in connection with the University of Lilongwe, the capital, near the farms where the tests would be conducted.

Hardly anyone knew about it. Jim Harris, an African-American from the States, who had been the director for the Human Tissues laboratory, was now in charge of the entire project. He had an African assistant and would be getting a couple more in the next couple weeks. Tomiko walked purposefully into the new lab building. There was not even a receptionist at the front desk yet so he wandered into the laboratory area.

"Doctor Harris, I believe," Tomiko said, extending his hand to the slightly sweating tall black man wearing a blue lab coat. "Tomiko Hirokamo."

"Welcome! Welcome," Doctor Harris exclaimed. "This is a pleasant surprise."

"Since this lab was my idea, I thought I should look it over."

"By all means. Come in, come in!" Doctor Harris led the way but paused long enough to say, "Please, call me Jim."

"Yes, Jim." Tomiko went on. "And to give you something else to work on, I brought a couple samples of water and soil to be tested." He held out the box. "Do you have all the reagents and testing equipment that you are supposed to have?"

"I've never worked in a lab with such up-to-date equipment," Jim said. "We got the spectrometer set up last week, and it works perfectly. I will be glad for a real live sample to try out on it. What are we looking for?" Jim asked.

"These samples are from the same location as the blood samples. Is that report ready?"

There was no way that Jim was going to give any kind of a report to Tomiko yet. In fact, he had nothing to give.

"Uh-h, well," he stumbled. "You wanted everything, and everything takes time."

"Not even an inkling of what it is going to be?" Tomiko queried.

"'Fraid not," Jim said off-handedly. "And now, with this new request, it's going to be a while."

"Oh," Tomiko was frankly disappointed. "Can you give me a guess as to when we might have some kind of report, even a preliminary one?"

"But shouldn't the report go to Miss Taylor?" Jim eyed Tomiko closely. Maybe there was more to this than a simple report.

Tomiko looked away as he replied. "Miss Taylor asked for my help. She lives a long way out in the bush, so I shall see that she gets the report."

Jim frowned. He did not see the connection, but there wasn't much he could do. Tomiko did appear to be in charge. Jim decided he might as well be honest with Tomiko.

"Actually, I am getting some help from a research lab in the States."

Tomiko interrupted, irritation in his voice. "Oh, news of this must not, I mean this report is not to go anywhere but right here!"

"Oh, it will be absolutely secure. My friend is a genomics specialist and will make sure it is not shared with anyone."

"Are you absolutely sure?" Again the displeasure in his voice.

"Of course! The man is a professional researcher." Jim turned and put his hand firmly on Tomiko's arm. "You know darn well that the report is going to be out of the ordinary, and for some reason, you want to keep this for yourself. The samples came from Miss Taylor, that is where the report is going."

Tomiko glanced around and lowered his voice. "This is an unusual situation. Miss Taylor asked for my help, which is why the sample has come to you, but I must have a copy of that report. It is of the utmost importance. And the report from this soil and water sample is to come to me."

Tomiko's tone of voice left no room for a difference of opinion. "Okay . . . I guess." Jim started toward a nearby table. "What are we looking for in the soil and water?"

"I don't know," Tomiko replied. "I just know it will be unusual."

"And I assume you wanted this yesterday also."

Now Tomiko grinned. "That's right, how long would you say it will take?"

"Give me, maybe five working days." He glanced at a calendar on a near wall. "Should have some answers by next Tuesday or Wednesday. Where do I send the report?"

"You have my E-mail address. Also please send a hard copy to my hotel in Blantyre. The address is on this paper. I will be waiting for it."

Jim lowered his voice. "So this is top secret."

"Unequivocally," Tomiko said firmly. "No one, absolutely no one is to receive a copy of this report other than myself. I will see that Miss Taylor gets a copy." At the sound of a door closing somewhere, Tomiko said in a low tone. "I assume your coworker is trustworthy."

"Doctor Okala has the highest clearance. You don't need to worry about his telling anyone about anything in this laboratory."

Tomiko left the laboratory feeling confident that the samples were in good hands. In five days he would have some answers. The Secretary General was expecting solid news of progress, and Tomiko had led him to believe it was forthcoming. It would be a long five days.

CHAPTER 82

Gui, what have you heard from Bert?" Carol asked as she poured each of them a glass of Zinfandel as they sat on the screened patio after dinner. A quiet rain was falling, cooling off the evening.

"Too bad I am not smoking," Gui said. "This would be a great time to enjoy a cigarette."

Thinking he had not heard her, Carol repeated, "Have you heard from Bert about the Green Country?"

He frowned. "No, I did not really expect to. I should not have asked Bert. He really is not reliable."

"But I thought you liked him," Carol said.

"Oh, I like him well enough. I just think he is not very responsible."

"What makes you say that?" Carol asked.

"Any man worth his salt would at least have a native housekeeper. He always looks like he was run over by a freight train. Hair a mess, clothes wrinkled."

Carol laughed. "I hadn't thought about, but you are right. But how about ... "

Gui interrupted quickly, "And I will bet he doesn't even keep a woman around, probably has not had sex in years."

Carol frowned. "I suppose that isn't important to him."

"Not important! Any man who does not have sex regularly is not to be trusted."

"Oh, Gui," Carol exclaimed, "don't be ridiculous!"

"A man's judgment, his ability to make decisions, even his physical strength is dependent on having sex regularly."

"Is that right?" Carol said teasingly. "Then you must be getting weak and unable to make decisions since we haven't made love for almost a week."

"Then we had better do something about that." He set his glass down. "Flora has gone to her quarters. I love making love to the sound of rain."

"Right here?" Carol asked in a whisper.

Gui slid out of his chair onto the cocoa-colored plush rug and beckoned to her.

As his fingers found her soft breasts, he closed his eyes and imagined what it was going to be like, when he was making love to a beautiful young virgin.

CHAPTER 83

Malissa had told Mallam Tomas, the dispenser in Kulanji, that she would probably be returning on Saturday, the twelfth of June. Since she normally came only every three months and it had been only two weeks, she explained that she expected a fresh supply of malaria medicine for him and would want to get it to him as soon as possible. That pleased him, and he asked no questions.

They left Mubi about nine o'clock Saturday morning, after seeing to the very ill patients in the hospital and checking the new mothers who came every Friday for blood pressure checks. She explained to Yusufu that she might be staying in Kulanji for a few days, but if she did that, he was to return to Mubi with the Jeep.

They arrived at the Kulanji gate about noon and were passed through the checkpoint without incident.

Shortly after starting to see patients in the dispensary, she noticed Saratu near the edge of the crowd. Saratu waved and smiled but did not come near.

"Mallam Tomas," Malissa said, "if you have any critical patients tomorrow morning, I can see them, but I need to leave about noon."

"I will call you if I need you," he said.

When all patients were gone, Saratu was still waiting some distance away but did not approach Malissa until Mallam Tomas had closed the dispensary and left.

"My father has asked to meet you, Miz Tayluh," Saratu said, "and my mother is preparing food for you tonight."

"Does your father know what is going to happen?"

"No, he knows nothing."

"Then why does he want to meet me?" Malissa asked.

"Because Ladu thinks you are an important person."

"How are Ladu and the baby?"

219

"The baby is doing fine. Ladu would like for you to take a message back to her husband. She does not know that you are not going back."

"We can send it with Yusufu. He will be returning to Mubi tomorrow. In fact, they could ride back with him if they are ready to go."

They left the main road and turned off on the path toward Saratu's compound.

"You won't believe how well Laraba looks and feels," Saratu said. "But I doubt they will want to leave just yet. Mother and Ladu do so enjoy being together. They do everything together and share everything, just like sisters."

"Saratu, are you sure you want to do this? You can change your mind any time, even when the plane comes."

"Never! I want this more than anything!"

"Do you think Pindar will have anything to do with you when you return?" Malissa asked.

"Maybe not, but so what? Maybe I will be a nurse like you, and never marry, like you."

"Would it surprise you if I were to get married?" Malissa asked.

"Oh, no, Miz Tayluh. I think a man would be very lucky to have you for a wife."

"Thank you, Saratu."

"Will I get to meet your man in Blantyre?"

"Actually, he will be flying the plane."

At the compound gate, Malissa called out a greeting, "Sallam."

Asta came, almost running, and took both of Malissa's hands in hers, the expression of close friendship. .Almost immediately Ladu called for Malissa to come to where she was sitting under the shelter made of mats over poles at the door of the house holding her new baby on her lap. Asta returned to her evening meal preparation.

What a happy baby," Malissa said, stooping to make little noises to the infant.

Laraba came from inside the house and said, "Hello."

It had been only two weeks since Malissa had seen Laraba last, but the change was marked. The color of her face was pink instead of gray; her eyes were bright instead of dull; she was smiling. It would certainly appear that the HIV was not progressing.

"How are you feeling?" Malissa asked.

"I can't believe how well I feel. The sores are almost all healed; my cough has gone away. I am sure I am gaining weight."

"What have you been doing?" Malissa asked. "Have you been taking any medicine?"

"Only the sacred powder every day which Birama sent for me to take."

"You may go home to Mubi with Yusufu today if you like," Malissa offered.

"Is the famine finished?" Laraba asked.

"I'm afraid not."

"Then I will stay as long as they will let me stay here. I am afraid if I go back to Mubi I will get sick again."

In a few minutes Malissa excused herself and motioned to Saratu to come.

They found Asta at her cooking house, and they pulled up small stools close to the fire where Asta was cooking goat meat with onions, tomatoes and peppers. They sat close so no one could hear their conversation.

Malissa peered into the steaming pot. "Ummm, smells good."

Asta motioned toward Saratu. "Saratu chose the menu.

Malissa went immediately to the problem at hand. "What is your plan for getting through the gate, Saratu?" she asked.

"I'm still working on that, some way to distract the guards," Saratu said. "If Pindar is on duty tomorrow, it might be more difficult."

"I suggest we play it by ear," Asta said. "Something will turn up; we just have to be ready."

"Are you going to tell Ladu, and when are you going to tell your husband?" Malissa asked.

"I have told Ladu, and she has offered to take care of the compound while we are gone," Asta replied.

"Sounds like a good arrangement," Malissa commented. "And Yamta?"

"He senses that something is going to happen," Asta said, "but he isn't asking any questions. I will tell him as we leave in the morning."

"What is it like to ride in an aeroplane?" Saratu asked.

"Most people say airplane, Saratu. I think you will enjoy flying in an airplane, although it will probably be scary at first."

"Mama," Saratu said, "Malissa is going to marry the man who flies the airplane."

"Oh, not so fast," Malissa said quickly. "I said maybe."

"I am eager to meet him," Saratu said. "I wonder what kind of man you like."

Malissa grinned. "I will be interested in your opinion of him,"

"Let's go over the plan once again," pleaded Asta. "I can't believe I am doing this, but since I am, I want it to succeed."

"What do you think will happen to you when you return, Asta?" Malissa asked.

"Oh, there is no doubt about it," Asta replied, "we will be severely punished, most likely by shunning. The only question is for how long."

They went over every step of the plan for the next day.

At the meal, Yamta, Asta, Saratu and Malissa sat around the fire on small stools. Usually each person would use their fingers to pick off pieces of guinea corn mush to dip in a meat sauce in another bowl. But for company, the guest had a small bowl of rice and another smaller bowl of the sauce. It was a well-seasoned peanut and sweet potato sauce that Malissa found very tasty. She had become quite adept at using her fingers in this way, but Asta insisted that she have a spoon.

The conversation was lively as Yamta questioned Malissa about many things in the Outside. Asta and Saratu said little but missed nothing. Yamta made no mention of the pending trip.

After the meal Saratu walked Malissa back to the guesthouse. Malissa fell into a troubled sleep, waking numerous times with a scared feeling in her stomach.

Then she was abruptly awakened by Yusufu's voice. "Breakfast will be ready soon, Miz Tayluh." He knew she liked to have a meditation time each morning before she ate. This morning she really felt the need of it.

CHAPTER 84

B ert did his usual plane check and then repeated it. He was still getting used to his new plane and certainly did not want to miss anything this time.

He was so excited at the prospect of getting to see Malissa again that he made himself check and double check every procedure. He realized that would be to his best interest after his discovery that morning. When he had gone to get milk out of the refrigerator, he had found it where he had put it the night before, in the cupboard. The glass he had used was in the refrigerator. The milk had soured, of course, so he had skipped breakfast.

What should he take for snacks for his passengers? Definitely bottles of water. Cokes for everyone might be a good idea. Saratu and her mother might as well get used to modern ways immediately. He added a couple sacks of potato chips, salted nuts, and some candy bars. Then as an afterthought, he had stopped at a drug store and bought some toothbrushes, toothpaste, combs, several small towels and washcloths. If they were traveling light, they would need those things. He had thrown in several T-shirts of his. They could use them for nightgowns.

It was the beginning of rainy season when clouds would pile up during the day and produce thunderstorms by mid to late afternoon. It would be hot, in the nineties, before the day was over which would make takeoffs and landings trickier.

He did file a flight plan. Not that anyone would come looking for him if something happened to him, but he just liked to play by the rules.

If he left at nine o'clock, three hours should be about right to arrive at Kulanji at twelve o'clock. He didn't like landing on dirt roads as they often had potholes in them, or animals. He would do a flyover first to get the lay of the land.

At nine o'clock sharp his plane rose into the morning air, already hinting of the heat that was in store.

CHAPTER 85

Malissa washed her face at the washstand in the guesthouse and brushed her hair which simply would not lie down and behave. The curls insisted on popping up again. It was already humid and would be hot later, her hair always knew that.

She took her book of meditations and walked a short distance away to where she could see the low hills and the eastern sky as it was lightening. She could hear She leaned against an mbula tree and thought about the day. Nothing on the written page could really prepare her for what was ahead.

Was she doing the right thing? If she did not help Saratu, someone else would. Thorn barriers could not keep these people isolated forever, and yet, was what was out there any better than what they had? Of course it wasn't, but that was not the question that was being asked here. The question was when would their lives be impacted by the outside world? If whatever knowledge they gleaned would make life better for more people, would that be worth it? And at the cost of their present culture?

She did not know the answer to that. She knew only that this seemed the right thing to do at this moment.

She went back to the guesthouse and waited for Yusufu to prepare her breakfast. He had found two fresh guinea eggs which tasted delicious fried in a bit of peanut oil with a slice of the bread held on a fork and toasted over the fire. As she drank the tea made with water which Yusufu drew from a nearby well, she wondered if she was drinking long life and good health in the water.

There was no question that this group of people were unique, different from any other on earth. They were connected to something out of the distant past which still impacted their lives. She clearly recalled the feeling she had the morning they had gone to The Gathering Place. She had felt connected to something beyond herself, something very powerful, and wonderful. She would like to know more about it.

She was not to go to the dispensary that morning unless Mallam Yusufu called for her. She tried to read the Time magazine she had brought with her, but she found herself staring at the page unaware of what she was seeing. At nine-o'clock a messenger came asking her to come to the dispensary. Thank goodness. She would go crazy with nothing to do.

Mallam Yusufu wanted her to see a little boy with a severe infection of his leg. Interesting, Malissa thought, it seems these people are not immune to bacterial diseases but do not seem to be susceptible to AIDS, a viral disease. What could be in the soil or water that could account for this?

Being Saturday, the dispensary was especially busy, so Malissa stayed to help out, glad for something to occupy her mind.

Finally ten o'clock came, and as agreed, Saratu, Asta and Malissa met under the mbula tree a short distance from the main gate. Malissa was carrying the small suitcase she had brought with her and her medical bag.

The look on Asta's face told Malissa that something had happened that morning. She greeted them but did not ask, just waited for Asta to speak.

"My husband could not believe we had found a way to leave Kulanji without going by motor of some kind," Asta said. "At first he forbade us to go, but we reminded him of his statement."

"What did he do then?" Malissa asked quickly.

Saratu answered, "He just got up and left. He will say that we left without his knowledge."

"He won't try to stop you?" Malissa asked.

"No," Asta said. "He will keep his promise."

"I honestly think he wants to know what is out there as much as I do," Saratu said. "Remember all the questions he asked about the Outside last night?"

Malissa reached over and touched Saratu's hand. "I still have great reservations about the wisdom of this trip, and you may still change your mind, Saratu."

Without hesitation, Saratu said, "Absolutely not."

"Then we wait here until the plane comes. No doubt he will fly over and look for the best landing spot, then land on the road. It must be done just right."

Suddenly Saratu shivered visibly.

"Are you all right?" Malissa asked.

"I have never been so excited about anything in my life. It is just my body's way of saying so."

Malissa wondered if she should give Saratu a Valium but decided against it. She smiled to herself. Maybe she was the one who needed a Valium. She didn't usually take drugs to get through difficult situations and wouldn't start now.

They chatted or sat in silence as the minutes dragged by. They moved deeper into the shade as the sun reached them. They were already perspiring profusely.

They heard it at the same time, the sound of a motor approaching from the east. They scanned the eastern sky.

"There!" Saratu said, pointing to a speck that was getting larger as they watched.

As the noise grew, people came running to look up into the sky. When the plane was visible to everyone, the mothers scooted their children back into their houses or under shelters, and then they all peeked through cracks at the oncoming sound.

"Okay," Malissa said, getting up slowly, "the time has come."

They stood just outside the shade of the big tree, their eyes trained on the plane. It was flying in a line to the north of them perhaps a half mile and continued until it banked and turned, this time returning to the south of them. It was so low that Malissa could see Bert's face. She waved, but he was too interested in his approach to wave back.

The plane sailed over the gatehouse, now only a few hundred feet above the ground. It continued until it was out of sight behind trees. Malissa could tell from the sound of the motor that Bert had gone several miles east and then returned to land on the road as planned. Apparently he was not going to fly over again. He must have thought the landing spot was okay.

"Will anyone go check to see what is going on?" Malissa asked as they started off down the path at a leisurely pace.

"That is what I am banking on, that no one is ready to do that," Asta said. "We don't have a special person in charge of investigating something like that."

"What will you tell them?" Malissa asked.

Saratu answered, "That you are leaving in the plane, and we are going to walk with you. Do you think we can get into the plane and escape if one of the guards goes along with us?"

"Yes," Malissa said, "I think we can manage that, if you do exactly what I tell you."

The three of them sauntered slowly into the main path and turned toward the entrance.

As they walked Malissa tried to prepare them for the flight, what it would feel like, the noise, the fear the first time. But she knew there was really no way to prepare these two bush women for what was about to happen to them.

As they approached the guard station, they saw Pindar and another young man standing at the pole gate peering down the road toward where the plane had disappeared.

"Aren't you going to see what is happening down there, Pindar?" Saratu asked when they reached the gate.

"We aren't supposed to leave our post," Pindar replied.

Asta spoke. "Miz Tayluh is going to go in the plane, and we are going to walk down there with her."

Pindar frowned. "You can't leave. We aren't supposed to let anyone in or out without permission."

"Just to walk with Miz Tayluh down the road a little way?" Saratu asked. "Don't be silly."

"Then I am going along," announced Pindar.

"You just want to see the airplane, Pindar," the other guard accused.

"Someone needs to go with these women to see that they get there and back safely," insisted Pindar.

Saratu was walking around the gate through the opening left for foot travelers. Asta and Malissa followed closely behind her.

"I'm going," Pindar told the other guard.

"You aren't supposed to leave your post," the other man repeated.

"Yeah, well I'm doing it." Pindar moved quickly to catch up with the women, now walking at a leisurely pace down the road.

The three women exchanged glances. Malissa nodded slightly, trying to show more confidence than she felt. What if it didn't work? What if someone tried to stop them?

Malissa listened intently. She did not hear the engine noise. She had said he should leave the motor running, but perhaps with his new plane he could start it quickly enough, and it was certainly safer not to have the propeller going until they were ready. The women laughed and joked in loud voices. Pindar walked beside them, silent and straight, a worried frown on his face.

As they came close enough to see, Bert was standing on the wing and waved, and Malissa waved back.

The plane was pointed down the road away from Kulanji. Bert came to meet them some distance from the plane.

They stopped as he reached them, and Malissa proceeded to introduce Asta and Saratu. Bert bowed awkwardly and said, "Pleased to meet you." Malissa explained in a loud voice that they wanted to get a closer look at the plane.

"And this is Pindar," Malissa went on. "He is a gate guard, but he would like to see the airplane too."

"Of course," Bert said with enthusiasm. "But, Malissa, please make sure they understand they must stay behind the wings. People who aren't used to airplanes don't realize there is a propeller as it is invisible when it is whirling so fast. It isn't going right now, but it will be when we start to take off." Malissa explained in Kulanji. Pindar's eyes were wide with wonder and not a little fear.

"Let me show Pindar first," Bert said, motioning to Pindar. "The rest of you stay here."

Pindar followed Bert closely. The rest of them watched unmoving.

Bert touched various things on the plane, obviously explaining to Pindar who no doubt understood very little since it was in English. But Pindar listened with rapt attention, glancing back now and then and grinning. He obviously felt very important. Bert helped him into the cockpit.

Malissa was nervous. She was not at all sure how they were going to accomplish this feat, but she was eager to get it over with. Asta and Saratu were fascinated with watching Pindar's progress around the plane, but Malissa was getting very anxious. Bert needed to get Pindar out of there.

Fearfully she looked around, glancing back toward the gate and saw a group of people milling around. Then suddenly one person left the group and started down the road toward them. Malissa's anxiety level rose even higher. The more people involved, the more complicated this was going to be. She looked back at Bert, and when he glanced their way, she waved and the pointed behind her. He nodded.

Bert guided Pindar back to where the women were standing.

"Now it is your turn, ladies," Bert said evenly, although his hurried glance at Malissa belied his calm demeanor. "You stay right here, Pindar. It isn't safe to get any closer," Bert said as he pointed to a spot on the ground at Pindar's feet. Malissa repeated the instruction in Kulanji.

As they walked toward the plane, there was a cry from behind them as now several people were walking rapidly toward them, shouting and waving their arms.

"Quickly!" Bert said as they reached the plane, taking Asta and Saratu by the hand. "Asta first, then Saratu."

The group behind them were running now. Pindar looked back and forth between the approaching people and the ones at the plane. The look on his face indicated he was not sure what was happening, but whatever it was, he wasn't happy about it. He waved for the oncoming group to hurry.

"In you go," Bert said as he boosted Asta into the plane, "into the back seat, quickly now." He was really glad for the wide doors on the plane which made getting in much easier for people not used to airplanes.

Turning to Saratu, he reached to help her, but she was already scrambling into the plane. Bert glanced at the people who were now very close and still shouting.

Bert did not want the plane to be surrounded by people who did not understand that a whirling propeller could kill. "Can you manage?" he said to Malissa.

"Yes! Get going!" Malissa exclaimed as she hoisted herself into the front seat of the plane while Bert raced around the plane and jumped in, slamming his door and automatically reaching to check the lock on Malissa's door.

"Fasten their seatbelts, Malissa!" Bert yelled as he turned the key. The motor came to life instantly. Bert did a swift check of the gauges.

At the sound of the motor starting Pindar began jumping up and down, screaming to the people running toward him to hurry. The scene was bedlam.

Bert pushed on the throttle and released the brake at the same time. Now a short distance behind the plane Pindar was shouting, "Stop! Stop!"

CHAPTER 86

Malissa turned around in her seat and got up on her knees to reach back and fasten the seatbelt around the two ashen-faced women, their eyes mirroring the terror that they felt.

Malissa patted each one, mouthing calming words, but the incredible noise of the roaring engine, the shouts of the crowd now in full chase, and the lurching of the plane as the wheels hit bumps in the uneven road turned the scene into one of absolute chaos.

Fortunately, both Malissa and Bert wore faces of studied composure, although his eyes were fastened on the gauges before him. Malissa sat back down in her seat and fastened her seatbelt but continued to stay turned in her seat in order to reassure the two women.

By this time the plane had gone a considerable distance. Bert had planned to use a long takeoff roll, but that changed abruptly.

"Oh, my God!" Bert said. Fortunately, it was only loud enough for Malissa to hear, and she turned to look out the front window. Sauntering onto the road from the left was a wild pig followed by two piglets.

"Get ready to go up!" Bert shouted. Thank goodness his new plane had STOL wings because he was going to have to test them right now. He waited until absolutely the last second before pulling back on the wheel and lifting abruptly off the road and into the air. The mother pig and babies oinked in panic and bolted.

The two in the back seat could not see the pigs but the sudden lurch upward was shock enough. Saratu screamed, and Asta covered her eyes. Malissa reached into the pockets on the back of Bert's seat for sick bags. Surprised but gratified to find some, she opened one and handed it to each of the women and pantomimed what they were to do with it.

Suddenly the whole scene was so funny and the tension so great that Saratu began laughing hysterically. It was the perfect reaction, and Malissa and Asta joined in.

Bert took the plane up smoothly a few hundred feet and began to level off a bit so that some of the noise was reduced.

"Shall we go around and wave at them?" Bert asked.

"Let's do," Malissa responded, reaching back to pat the women who were still in paroxysms of fright and laughter.

At one thousand feet he turned the plane and headed it back toward where a large crowd now stood. "Tell them to get ready," Bert instructed.

Malissa called out to the women, "Bert is going to wave the plane's wings at the people down there, so don't be afraid."

That brought Asta and Saratu to attention, and each peered out her window to the ground below.

"There they are!" said Asta. "Look, Saratu, they look so small!"

Bert dipped the right wing, then the left and then turned the plane's nose southeast.

"Mama," Saratu said, "we did it! We did it! Poor papa, now he is going to have to explain."

"For better or worse, Saratu, we did it," Asta said. "Remember what the Wiseman says, 'When the gods want you to be miserable, they give you what you ask.'"

"I don't believe that, Mama. Look at me, do I look miserable?"

"You did a few minutes ago," laughed Asta.

"Well, now I am going to enjoy every minute of this trip."

"You might as well because when we get back, we will both be miserable."

Malissa turned back to face forward. The plane was climbing again but at a slower rate. Bert was methodically checking the gauges again as was his routine. He was an extremely careful pilot. But now he paused long enough to reach over and squeeze Malissa's hand and smile at her.

Saratu poked Asta and they smiled knowingly.

Before long their flight took them over Malissa's village, and Malissa proudly pointed out her house, the hospital, the school.

"They look like play houses," Asta exclaimed.

As they headed toward Blantyre the drone of the plane was soothing and hypnotic, and Malissa was pleased to see that both Asta and Saratu were calm and seemed to be fascinated by the scene unfolding beneath them.

Malissa kept her eye on the gauges, especially the gas gauge. She tapped on the gas gauge and looked questioningly at Bert.

"This plane gets excellent gas mileage, shouldn't be a problem. Just pray we don't have any detours."

Malissa was already praying.

As they moved eastward, Bert continued to scan the skies. This time of year the weather was likely to change without notice, and he peered ahead now at clouds on the horizon. They were perhaps forty-five minutes away from Blantyre. As they neared the cloud formations, Bert could see that they were thunderheads, huge, billowing dark forms. The question was, were they between Bert's plane and Blantyre or beyond. The usual pattern at this time of year was for afternoon thunderstorms, but he had hoped to slip in before they formed. He knew enough about flying in this country to know not to take a chance. If those clouds were between them and Blantyre, he would have to come up with a plan of what to do.

On Saturday, the twelfth of June, Tomiko left his car parked a block outside the gate of Agricole Internationale headquarters. Since it was Saturday afternoon, he didn't know if Gui would be at the farm, but he didn't want to take a chance on running into him.

Just on a hunch, he had checked at the airport that morning to see who was coming or going, and because of what he had learned he needed to talk with Yahara.

Yahara was expecting him and motioned him into the office, which was closed off from the rest of the plant, and firmly closed the door.

"It sounded urgent, Tomiko. What's going on?"

"If you will help me, we may be able to stage the biggest coup in modern history."

"I'm listening."

"I just came from the airport. Bert McEwen, Gui Manieux's pilot, has just filed a flight plan for five hundred miles northwest of Blantyre with a return also scheduled for today."

"Yes?"

"I don't know what he will be bringing back, but I will bet everything I own that it has something to do with the Green Country."

"And what do you want me to do?"

"Do whatever you need to find out what Manieux knows about this and what is coming down. Will you be talking with him tomorrow?"

"Not likely. He never comes in on Saturday afternoon or Sunday. But I am sure he will be here Monday." Yahara ran his hand through his hair, but met Tomiko's gaze unflinchingly. "I'll do my best," he said. "I'd sure like to see us beat Manieux to the draw."

"If you learn anything, call me immediately on my cell phone. I plan on going back to the airport this afternoon to wait for Bert to come back. I want to see what he brings."

As Tomiko started to leave, he turned back and said, "I would like to have another copy of the tests you ran on the water and soil samples. I gave what I had to Jim Harris."

Yahara reached behind a file cabinet to where he had placed the files for safekeeping and made a copy.

"Thank you," said Tomiko, folding the papers and tucking them in his jacket pocket.

CHAPTER 88

Gui considered going to the Health Club for a while that Saturday after-noon, but he really did not feel like working out. He could go to the Mount Soche bar, but it would be hard to not smoke with the guys. He would just go to The Farm and work on accounts. Ever since Roger's death, he had had to make sure that the accountant was doing things right. There was plenty he could do. Anything but go home, until he was so tired he could go right to sleep after dinner.

Carol had been trying to get him to try lovemaking again after his fail-ure on Monday, but this close to the arrival of Saratu he was not taking any chances on not being ready.

When he arrived at the Farm, he noticed that Yahara's car was still there. Although Yahara put in odd hours, he was not usually there on Saturday afternoon. They routinely met on Monday afternoon to go over things, but last Monday had been Gui's doctor's appointment, and there had not been opportunity for another meeting. He would just drop in and see how things were going. Yahara was doing an outstanding job of keeping the workers in line and maintaining production schedules. Thank goodness he still had Yahara.

As he stepped into Yahara's office, he saw the room was empty, but Gui could hear water running in the bathroom. He wandered over to the desk and glanced at papers lying there. Yahara was very well organized, never a messy desk.

One of Yahara's main tasks was to run periodic soil samples to see how the soil was maintaining the elements necessary for maximum production. On the desk was one of the usual report forms with *SOIL SAMPLE REPORT* at the top of the sheet. Gui glanced at it idly without really seeing it, reading it but not paying attention to what he was reading.

Gui heard the bathroom door opening and greeted Yahara as he came into the office.

"Mr. Manieux! It's Saturday!"

"With Roger gone I have a lot of extra work so thought I would do some of it this afternoon and I saw your car. Why are you here on Saturday afternoon?"

Yahara answered quickly, "Just, just some catchup work."

"Soil samples, I see," Gui gestured toward the report on the desk.

"Uh, just the usual reports."

"Put them on my desk, I want to see them."

"Sure, sure, I will."

"When will the Bangari fields be ready for planting?" Gui asked. "It is almost the middle of June."

"My foreman tells me they will be ready to plant next week."

"Good. Even a day or two may make the difference between a good crop or a mediocre one."

"Yes, that's right, Mr. Manieux."

Gui hated the way Yahara said, Yes, Mr. Manieux, all the time. He turned toward the door.

"Mr. Manieux," Yahara said to stop him. He was trying to think of how to ask about Bert's flight. "I guess I was surprised to see you today as I thought you must be flying with Mr. McEwen today."

"Why would you think that?"

"Well, a pilot friend of mine said that Mr. McEwen had filed a flight plan to be gone most of the day today."

"Did it say to where?"

"I thought you might know."

Although he was irritated by Yahara at times, they had been together for many years, and Yahara was easy to talk to.

"Do you remember when I asked you to find out about a place called the Green Country?"

Yahara nodded offhandedly.

"Bert found it for me."

"Is he bringing something from it, something that will help us to know why it is green?"

"I hope so, I surely hope so."

"I will get to see this... this miracle?" Yahara asked.

"When I get the answer, you will most certainly know about it." He paused. Gui did not have many men friends, and he would like to share this event with a man who could understand the importance of it. "But there is more, much more."

Yahara waited for Gui to go on. When he did not, Yahara said, "Yes?"

Gui shook his head. Yahara might not understand. "Just something that most men would die for, that's all."

When Gui left, Yahara hurried to his desk and looked over the soil sample report frantically as if trying to figure out how much Gui had read. It did not look any different from a normal report except for the elements listed there, which were anything but the usual ones. The column for *Gene status* contained some values that were different from anything Yahara had ever seen.

He did not think that Gui really understood anything about the report, and his manner did not seem to indicate that he did.

Yahara picked up the phone to call Tomiko. Maybe Tomiko knew what it was that *most men would die for.*

CHAPTER 89

Tomiko picked up the phone on the first ring.

Yahara spoke quickly. "Bert flew to the Green Country today and will be bringing back something very important. Gui wouldn't say what it was."

"Thank you for trying, Yahara. I will find out what he is bringing." Tomiko was almost breathless.

"Oh, Tomiko, Gui said something about this being *something that most men would die for*. Do you know what he means?"

"If he is talking about the Green Country, then yes, the knowledge of what keeps the country green would be worth dying for."

"Yes, I am sure that is what he means. But he is the last person who should have that bit of information," Yahara said emphatically.

"Let's see that he doesn't get it, Yahara."

"Right!"

CHAPTER 90

"Malissa," Bert said as he leaned over so only Malissa could hear. "Those clouds don't look good. They may be beyond as I figure we are about forty minutes out. We might be smart to land on a road this side of town. What would you say?"

"My dad told me that a smart pilot doesn't take chances." She stared at the clouds, trying to read them. "It seems to me we could go a little closer and look and still have time to land somewhere else if necessary."

This woman is not afraid of anything, Bert mused. Just his type! He was ready with some persuasive arguments as to why she should marry him right away and move to Blantyre.

Now, Asta and Saratu were awake and were intently watching out the windows, commenting to each other on the scene below. But they were far from relaxed. Any slight movement of the plane from level made them exchange worried glances.

"How long?" Saratu asked.

Malissa relayed the question to which Bert replied cheerfully, "We should be there for dinner." But the sweat on his forehead belied his confidence. Now Malissa began staring out over the fuselage, hoping for signs of a town. The countryside became more populated with small villages.

Bert called on the radio to the tower at Blantyre and flipped the switch so that only he could hear the reply.

"Do not attempt to land at the Blantyre airport," came the voice. "The storm is within a few minutes of the airfield. I repeat, do not attempt to land at Blantyre. Find another landing place."

His superb avionics were of little assistance at a time like this. They only made it possible to hear bad news better.

"What did they say?" Malissa asked.

"It will be a tight squeeze," he replied evenly.

Malissa was not fooled by his words. She had not known him long but long enough to read his eyes, and they were worried.

Malissa made a point of leaning back in the seat as if she hadn't a care in the world.

Bert watched Malissa out of the corner of his eye. He had not seen her under duress, and he wondered how she would handle it. *Thank goodness, she doesn't fold under stress, Bert thought. Good girl!*

Ordinarily his Position Finder would tell him how far he was from the airfield, but for some reason it had gone crazy, with the needle bouncing around like a rubber ball. Apparently the VOR which sat to the far side of the field was in the midst of the storm and had been adversely affected or even damaged. He was on his own.

"According to my calculations," Bert said evenly, "Blantyre is right over—there." He pointed. "Let's see who can spot it first."

Malissa sat up and relayed the message to the back seat. The two women sat up as tall as they could and searched the horizon ahead.

The threatening clouds were closer now, towering high above them. They could see the roiling movement in the heart of the blackness. Bert had been in such a situation before, and he did not like what he saw. If he were alone, it would be different, but he had three other lives to think about. This was not the best introduction for Saratu, he thought grimly.

Bert leaned closer to Malissa. "Can you distract them? This could be difficult."

Malissa pointed out compounds below and a main road that obviously led somewhere important, as it was not just a bush trail. She continued in a stream of conversation, pointing and talking about figures and houses they could see very clearly now. Asta and Saratu watched, fascinated.

Suddenly the plane dropped precipitously straight down for perhaps fifty feet, and everyone lost their breath. They could not even scream. But then the plane continued on as if nothing had happened.

"Just an air pocket," Bert said jauntily. He didn't feel jaunty. The sudden drop indicated that they were in the front trough of the storm where there could be invisible wind shear, the deadly violence that could smash a plane into the earth in seconds.

The women's eyes were wide with terror, now fastened on Malissa for a sign that they were not on the verge of death. They were no longer looking ahead but grasping each other's hand. With her other hand Asta held the airsick bag, which she had used earlier. Incredibly, Saratu's stomach did not seem to be bothered by the plane's chaotic movements.

Malissa smiled as relaxed a smile as she could muster and waved her hand nonchalantly. "Nothing to worry about," she said in Kulanji.

They were very low now, but ground winds caught the plane and shook it hard. Bert held tightly onto the wheel, gauging his wings against landmarks to keep them level and alternately watched the gauges.

"There, " Malissa said, "it has to be over there. See that main road filled with people leading to somewhere? I'll bet they are coming home from market."

"I think you are right," Bert said, "That should be the road into market which is west of town, so the airport should be just beyond. There it is! I see the tower!"

Indeed the tower was silhouetted against an ebony backdrop, and it was like a lighthouse to a sailor. He headed straight for it as the wind tossed the little plane like a toy. His hope was to get down on the ground before the storm actually hit. It would be a close call. The alternative of landing on a road was equally dangerous.

Saratu's face was white now, and Asta looked like she was praying.

"Put your head between your knees," Malissa instructed in their language, "and don't come up until I tell you."

They obeyed instantly.

Suddenly lightning flashed from a cloud to their left, then another in front of them. Malissa was glad the women could not see it.

Barely over the treetops now, they could see the runway. Bert headed straight for it, scanning the skies all around for other planes that might be as frantic as he.

Malissa did not have to be told what to do. She too was searching for planes. Her stomach was going up and down with the plane, but she swallowed hard and tried to ignore it.

"I think we can sneak in ahead of it," Bert said. "Just hang on."

"We are going to land," Malissa told the women, "but don't be afraid. Bert is a good pilot."

Abruptly Saratu raised her head, and with ashen face and saucer eyes, she stared out the window.

"Don't watch the ground, Saratu," Malissa told her. "Fasten you eyes on a spot inside the plane."

But Saratu was determined. She might never get to leave Kulanji again, and she did not want to miss anything. She could not hide the apprehension in her eyes, but her face carried a look of determination, and she made no sound, only gripped her mother's arm tightly.

The storm was at the far edge of the airfield, black and ominous.

The little plane was buffeted by crosswinds as the plane came even with the end of the runway. Bert was holding the wheel with an iron grip, and yet the plane was being pushed off the runway. He managed to get it back onto the tarmac only to be blown off again. With masterful control, he finally set the wheels down on the tarmac with a couple of bounces.

"We're down," Malissa announced to the back seat. Saratu was trying to smile. Asta finally raised her head but leaned back with her eyes closed.

As soon as he had the plane pointed toward the terminal, Bert wiped his brow in the sultry heat of Blantyre. As he swung around to stop, the rain arrived with a vengeance with the wind right behind it.

"Run for the terminal, Malissa. I'll put the plane away and bring the car."

As soon as the motor died, Malissa motioned for the women to come. She helped them out, and then they ran hand in hand with the rain drenching them instantly and the wind whipping their clothing and hair.

CHAPTER 91

Inside the terminal the clock on the wall showed four o'clock, but it was dark enough for anyone to think it was much later. Malissa asked if they needed a bathroom. Sharp relief was obvious in Asta's face as she nodded. Malissa led them to the restroom and explained what the little booths were for and showed them how to flush the toilet. Then she left Saratu in one of the cubicles and turned to guide Asta into another, but Asta refused, stark fear in her face.

When Malissa asked her what was the problem, Asta could only point at the stools in the toilets. Malissa realized Asta was afraid that perhaps she would be sucked down when the stool was flushed.

"I will stay with you, Asta," Malissa offered. "Come."

When she was through, Malissa had Asta leave the cubicle before flushing the toilet. Apparently Saratu had no problem, as she came out smiling, as if ready for the next adventure.

In a corner of the waiting room, Tomiko sat behind a newspaper and had watched the three women stumble in out of the storm. So that was what Bert was doing. But why bring two African women to Blantyre today? Their clothes told him they were straight from the bush, and the frightened look of the older woman told him that this was the first time she had been there. No doubt the younger one was her daughter.

Bert normally did not put his plane to bed without first filling it with gas. He never knew when someone would request immediate departure for some distant destination. But this time he guided his plane to the first available tiedown spot and leaped out to secure the plane. Then leaning into the whipping wind, he ran to where he had left his Landrover and drove it to the entrance of the terminal lobby.

The women had been watching for him, and Saratu jumped nimbly into the vehicle, but Asta climbed in carefully, reluctantly. Asta had already seen more than she really wanted to see. Malissa sat in front with Bert.

In the blinding torrent of rain Bert drove slowly and carefully, navigating as much by memory as by sight since the street signs were obscured by the driving rain.

Behind him, Tomiko tried to follow them, but there was no way he could keep track of their tail light. Finally he gave up and made his way back to the Mount Soche Hotel.

To his surprise and delight, as he pulled into the parking lot, he saw Bert's Landrover. His luck was holding out!

CHAPTER 92

A ll four of them were thoroughly soaked by the time they reached the Mount Soche Hotel entrance. Bert held the door, and Malissa herded Asta and Saratu into the lobby.

Bert went immediately to the check-in desk, while Malissa stayed close to the women, pointing out things they should know about the hotel. Saratu and Asta stood in the middle of the lobby, rooted to that spot, turning around slowly. They did not really hear what Malissa was saying.

Then Saratu's gaze came to the chandelier suspended from the two-story ceiling far above. Always lighted, it shimmered in the room dimmed by the dark clouds outside. Saratu's mouth hung open as she stared in fascination.

Keys in hand, Bert led the way to the elevator, but half way across the room Malissa suddenly stopped and called to Bert. As he turned, she motioned toward the stairs. Smiling, he nodded and moved to the stairs. After that plane ride, an elevator ride might be just too much.

Saratu had missed nothing from the time they entered the hotel lobby, but Asta was clearly in shock, dumbly following directions.

At the door to room number twenty-four, Bert paused. "This is their room, and yours is next door, Malissa."

Malissa smiled. Number twenty-six was the room she had stayed in the last time.

Malissa led the way into the room and motioned for the women to follow.

"I stuck in a couple of my T- shirts for them to sleep in, but what do they do for clothes?" Bert asked.

Malissa grinned at the image of the women in Bert's tee shirts. "They are used to sleeping in their clothes, so I don't think it is a problem. But first thing tomorrow . . . "

"What time shall I be here?" Bert asked.

"We should be through breakfast by nine o'clock. But actually, Bert, you don't need to go shopping with us. It will be terribly boring."

"I will be here at nine o'clock sharp. I am going to spend every minute with you that I can." He turned toward the door. "I'll get your suitcase."

"Thank you, Bert."

He spoke close to her ear, "When do I get to see you—alone?"

She laughed her ascending scale laugh, and kissed him quickly on the cheek. "Soon enough."

"Never soon enough," he replied.

"I am not letting these women out of my sight until we take them back to Kulanji," Malissa said.

"Well," he paused. He had to set up the meeting. "I could help you with that, Malissa." Immediately he felt ill at ease that he was going through with the charade in order to let Gui see Saratu. What if something went wrong? But he could not back down now. He would just have to make sure it went according to his plan.

"There is something I want to show Saratu tomorrow, say about three o'clock tomorrow afternoon." He hastened to add, "If that would be all right."

"I'm not sure exactly what we will be doing, but we could put that on our list of things to be done. Where do you want us to go?"

"I will come here for her," Bert said quickly.

Malissa thought about that. "You mean I don't get to see it?"

Bert tried not to stammer as he replied, "I... I just thought Saratu would enjoy this, and I wanted to show it to her."

"Should I be jealous?" Malissa laughed, squeezing his hand.

"Absolutely," Bert said, glad for the change in topic and even more pleased to have an excuse to put his arm around her.

"Well, I would guess that perhaps Asta would be ready for a rest about that time," Malissa said.

Relieved, Bert headed for the door. "I'll be right back," he said.

Malissa showed the room to Asta and Saratu. There were two regular-sized beds, a dresser, a desk and chair. Malissa demonstrated how to use the shower, the sink, and again the toilet. Asta just shook her head and refused to go into the bathroom. Malissa pointed out their towels, soap and toilet paper.

"You may each have a bed, or you may sleep together, as you wish," Malissa said.

But Saratu was not interested in sleeping. "Where does one eat in Blantyre?"

"As soon as you are dried off, we will go to the dining room for dinner,"

Malissa explained. "I'm sorry I can't offer you any dry clothes."

"Rain is something we are used to," Asta said, seeming to come out of her fog somewhat.

Bert arrived with Malissa's suitcase and the sack of things he had prepared for them. He held up one of the T-shirts and explained what it was for. Asta and Saratu exchanged embarrassed grins.

He also explained each toilet item, the toothbrushes, and the toothpaste. Saratu and Asta took the items he handed them, but their faces registered only bewilderment.

"I will demonstrate these things later," Malissa said. "I suggest you lie down for a few minutes and rest. You have had quite a day."

As she started toward the door Malissa stopped. "I want to remind you that neither of you is to leave this room unless Bert or I is with you. Will you promise me that?"

"What is to promise?" Saratu asked. "We would be crazy to go out there alone."

CHAPTER 93

It was agreed that Bert would go to dinner with them at six o'clock. In the meantime, he told Malissa he had some loose ends to tie up. But he stayed long enough to follow her to her room where he took her in his arms for the long-delayed kiss.

Now bold, he said, "Do I get to come back tonight?"

Malissa looked at him in dismay. "After what we have been through today? All I want tonight is a good night's sleep."

"Without you, I won't get a good night's sleep."

"Not until this is all over, Bert. I am still under too much stress to relax. And I want to enjoy our being together."

Funny thing about women, Bert thought as he went downstairs to find the telephone. For him, sex was the way to relax. For Malissa, she had to relax first. Well, whatever . . .

CHAPTER 94

Gui answered at The Farm on the first ring. He had told Carol he had catch-up work to do.

"We arrived safely," Bert said.

"When do I get to see her, now?"

"We had a pretty rough ride, and all of this is exciting to say the least. I have arranged it for three o'clock tomorrow afternoon, in the hotel garden at the fountain. I will tell her to sit there and wait for me. The rest is up to you. You will have fifteen minutes."

"Now, wait a minute. Fifteen minutes, no way!"

"That is as long as I can be sure Malissa will let her out of her sight," Bert assured him.

"What if you tell Malissa she is with you?"

"Malissa feels very responsible, and if she gets a glimpse of you two together, she will kill me." And, Bert said to himself, it will be all over between Malissa and me.

"Malissa does not know me. She will think I am just a kindly man being nice to Saratu."

"Fifteen minutes. I thought you wanted to check her out first, see what she looks like. That will be enough for you to decide if she is the woman for you."

"Then when can I set up a time to be with her?" Gui asked.

"Well, her English isn't the best, so you will need to make it very clear when this is to happen, like write it on a piece of paper."

"And have her show it to Malissa? Hardly."

"I suggest you set it up for nine o'clock Tuesday evening. Have her meet you at the fountain again or something like that."

"In the garden? I don't think so. But I will decide that after I see her."

"I will be watching. Don't try to leave without paying me. Bring the money with you. Remember, if you decide you really don't like her looks, you still owe me the hundred thousand."

"What does she look like, Bert?"

"I think you are used to black women." It was just a statement.

"Oh, yes, I guess you could say I am a connoisseur."

"I would say she is attractive, in fact, very attractive."

"Bert, I owe you more than money if you pull this off."

"Good night, Gui." Bert hung up before he lost his nerve and told Gui go to hell. Gui had no idea what this could cost Bert if Malissa found out, and even Bert did not want to think about that.

CHAPTER 95

The three women descended the stairs together at six-fifteen. Bert was waiting in the foyer. Saratu and Asta's clothes had dried, but were wrinkled. They wore plastic sandals. Malissa had changed into a cotton dress, and her hair had dried, twisting into curls all over her head. Impatiently, she had tried to straighten them to no avail.

"I like your hair like that," Bert said as they waited to be seated in the dining room.

"I'm glad someone does," grimaced Malissa.

Malissa carried on a running commentary, explaining everything in sight, alternating between English and the Kulanji language. Bert listened, impressed by Malissa's ability to speak yet another language besides Wamba.

Malissa asked if Asta and Saratu would like fish to which they gladly agreed. Malissa ordered baked fish for them, broiled for herself. Malissa tried to explain about salad dressing, but a green salad was not in Saratu and Asta's experience. When the salads came, Malissa demonstrated the use of salad dressing, and also which fork to use with the salad.

When Saratu tasted the vinaigrette dressing, she said to her mother that it tasted like their own lemon herb sauce. Asta thought so too.

Asta was a bit more alert by this time and was as interested in how to use the silverware as Saratu was. The ice in the glasses was of special curiosity to Saratu, but when she took a big drink of water, the cold hurt her teeth, and she held her face in pain. Malissa explained how to drink ice water to keep it from chilling the teeth.

Absolutely everything was new to the visitors from Kulanji, and Malissa patiently explained, using some English and some Kulanji. She wanted them to learn as much English as possible quickly. She told them how to use napkins, how to cut open the buns and spread butter on them, where to place the knife when not using it. Saratu watched people at other tables, but Asta kept her eyes on her plate most of the time.

Tomiko had paid the Head Waiter to seat him near the table where Malissa and Bert sat with their guests, but shielded from them by a plant stand. He had entered unnoticed by a roundabout route. But he was just close enough to hear the murmur of their voices and a word now and then. It was extremely frustrating. He still did not know why the two women had been brought by plane to Blantyre.

Surely he would hear from Jim in Lilongwe on Monday. Somehow all that was happening was part of the same story. He had the feeling that the various parts of the puzzle were all there; he had only to put them together.

CHAPTER 96

Before she left Asta and Saratu alone in their room for the night, Malissa demonstrated how to use the telephone in their room. She went to her room and called them. In spite of her instructions, they did not pick up the phone. When she returned and asked them why, Saratu said she was afraid the phone would ring again when she picked it up and it would hurt her hand. Only after extensive explanation was Malissa able to convince them to pick up the phone when it rang.

At first Asta refused to believe that it was Malissa on the other end of the phone until Malissa had Saratu go with her into Malissa's bedroom and speak to Asta over the phone.

It was not until they returned from dinner that Malissa showed them how to use the television set, the bathtub, and the overhead fan. She demonstrated how to lock the door and made sure they did that as she left.

Saratu experimented with the bathtub until she had run a tub half full of pleasantly warm water.

"You first, Mama," Saratu said. Asta did not argue. A bath such as this was something to tell the others about when they got back home.

Saratu was glad for some time to herself. She was fascinated with the television remote control device, and with her mother soaking in the bathtub, Saratu explored the real outside world, the one beyond the borders of Malawi. After flipping through the channels several times, she stopped at one which showed beautiful young women and young men, mostly white but a few with dark skins. She was surprised by that and told herself she would ask Malissa about that.

Suddenly there was before her the picture of a swarthy-complexioned man, not a young man. He was gazing at her with disarming, almost sad eyes, but totally engaging. There were stars all around his picture and written across the screen were the words, "Enduring and endearing movie star!"

Saratu did not understand the meaning of the words, but she could not look away from the picture. She was completely charmed by his face. She could understand only a little of what was being said, but it didn't matter. This man was looking at her!

Then the scene changed, and the wonderful man was gone. She remained staring at that channel, hoping for another glimpse of the man, until Asta came from the bathroom.

"Anything interesting?" she asked.

"Yes, I am learning a lot," Saratu replied.

In her own room Malissa collapsed on the bed and almost didn't wake up to change her clothes. She could still hear the TV distantly through the wall as she drifted off to sleep.

It would have been so nice to have Bert with her, but it would not have been a very high quality night. Her exhaustion was complete, and she slept soundly through the night.

CHAPTER 97

Tomiko was getting impatient. He had sent an E-mail to Jim Harris in Lilongwe when he arrived home Sunday night, but rather than wait for a reply, he called Jim's office Monday morning a couple minutes after eight o'clock. It wouldn't hurt to put a little pressure on Jim.

When he asked for him, the newly hired secretary told him that Doctor Harris was in the laboratory and had asked not to be disturbed.

Tomiko had been so sure he would know something by this time that he had told the Secretary-General that he would have an answer by Monday. Well, maybe he would yet.

He would go hang around the Mount Soche Hotel and not be available on his phone when the Secretary-General called. He just might find the answer with those two women who had arrived yesterday.

CHAPTER 98

On the third ring Malissa finally come out of a stuporous sleep to answer it.

"Good morning, Miz Tayluh," Saratu proclaimed. "Could we eat now?"

"What time is it?" Malissa asked, then realized it was a dumb question. Neither Asta nor Saratu had watches.

"Seven o'clock," Saratu responded.

"How do you know?" Malissa asked.

"A little red light here says seven-zero-zero."

Apparently there was a digital clock in the room that Malissa hadn't noticed. Surprising that Saratu had figured out it meant the time of day. She was even smarter than Malissa had thought.

"Give me a few minutes to get dressed. Do not leave your room. I will come for you."

"Okay."

Okay was almost the first English word that Africans learned to say, and somehow they loved using it.

Malissa wore the same clothes as last night. At least her shoes were dry now. As she picked up her purse to leave, the phone rang again. It was Bert.

"How did you sleep?" he asked.

"Like the dead," she replied.

"So it is breakfast and shopping today."

"Yes, they desperately need clothes."

"But you will be back by three o'clock?"

"I've been thinking about that, Bert," Malissa said. "Asta is beginning to adjust a little better and should be included in whatever happens."

"I don't think this would interest her," Bert hurried to say. "It's a young person's thing."

"I guess that puts me in my place," Malissa said pretending to be angry.

"You know where your place is, right here with me."

"We were talking about Saratu."

"I would like the fun of watching Saratu with this. You get all the fun."

"All right," Malissa conceded. "Asta and I will have afternoon tea in the garden while you show her whatever it is."

Bert had not planned for that, but he thought quickly. "Well, actually, I happen to know that the little tearoom just down the street from the hotel is a great place to go for afternoon tea."

"Oh, that would be nice. But wouldn't Saratu like to go there too?"

"She can't do everything. Maybe tomorrow afternoon." He hurried on. "Why don't you all meet me in the lobby about two forty-five, and we will wait for you there when you get back." He added, "Or if we finish early, we will walk down to the tearoom. It is just a couple of blocks."

"That would work," Malissa said. "Let's do that."

"When do we get some time together, alone?" Bert asked. "I have thought of new reasons why you should move to Blantyre."

Malissa laughed. "I am sure you have. But I thought Saratu was your priority."

"From now on, for the rest of my life you are my priority. Everything else comes second."

"Well, right now I have no choice but to stick with these two women. Saratu is like a child in a candy store. I can't leave them to fend for themselves."

"Of course not," Bert said. "But what do we do next to find out why these people are so healthy?"

"I have not received the lab report, and goodness knows when it will come. So I am at a loss as to how to proceed next. I think Saratu should be checked over by a medical doctor. That should tell us quite a bit. Did you make the appointment, Bert?"

Bert answered quickly. "Actually, I didn't. I frankly wasn't sure when we would get to Blantyre. But I will call my doctor and see when we can get her in."

"I hope it isn't too late to get in," Malissa said with a worried frown.

"I will call as soon as his office is open. I should know by the time I meet you for breakfast."

"Good. See you in a little while." She started to hang up the phone. "Bert,"

"Yes?

"I love you."

"I love you too, sweetheart."

She stood for just a moment as she actually allowed herself to feel the surge of excitement that was welling up inside her. Her whole life was on the verge of being completely turned around. But first, she had a responsibility to Saratu. Her own happiness could wait a little longer.

This time the women went to the hotel coffee shop. Saratu was hungry and asked about every item on the menu, what it was and how to pronounce its name. Asta was in better shape this morning and asked questions too. They settled on scrambled eggs, bacon and toast.

In Kulanji they drank herbal teas but had never had coffee. Malissa ordered green tea for both of them and coffee for herself. Bert arrived just as they finished ordering and added his order to theirs.

"The doctor's appointment is this afternoon," Bert said.

"This afternoon!" Malissa exclaimed, "How did you manage that?"

"It is because I am such an important person," Bert grinned. "Actually they had a cancellation."

"What time?"

"Four o'clock," Bert replied. "I will meet you here and take you to the office."

Malissa turned to Saratu, speaking in Kulanji. "Do you remember that I said you would need to have a physical examination if you came to Blantyre?"

Saratu nodded.

"We will go to the doctor's office this afternoon at four o'clock. It will not be upsetting or painful, just to look you over. I will be with you all the time."

Saratu frowned but nodded. Asta put her hand on Saratu's and squeezed it. Mother and daughter exchanged an anxious look.

Bert caught the glance, and his guilt multiplied. What was he doing to these two innocent people?

Malissa frowned. "It is too bad that the lab work will have to be repeated as of course, the doctor will want that information. I sent it to Lilongwe a couple of weeks ago."

"Malissa, I just thought of something. As I was coming through the lobby, I caught a glimpse of Tomiko. Remember him, the . . . "

Malissa interrupted. "Yes, of course, I remember him. He was the one who told me about the lab in Lilongwe."

"I remember your telling me that. Maybe he could check on your lab work," Bert said.

"Of course!" Malissa exclaimed. "He should be able to get that information. Where is he now?"

"I'll go see if I can find him."

Bert left, returning almost immediately with Tomiko in tow.

"Good morning, Miss Taylor," Tomiko said, then bowing to the women.
"Do we have guests to Blantyre?"

"Saratu, Asta," Malissa said, "this is Tomiko Hirokama, Special Assistant
to the director of the World Health Organization. Mr. Hirokama, this is
Asta and Saratu."

Saratu was trying to digest the unfamiliar words and could only nod, as did
Asta.

"And what tribe are these lovely ladies from?" Tomiko asked innocently.

Malissa paused, wondering if she should answer that. "They are from my
neighboring country, Kulanji."

Bert was cringing, wishing Malissa would not be so forthcoming. He
still did not trust Tomiko.

Malissa hurried on. "Mr. Tomiko, would it be possible for you to help me
obtain the results of the lab tests that I sent to the Lilongwe lab? Saratu will
be seeing a doctor this afternoon, and we need those lab studies or else they
will have to be done again, which will take several days."

"Of course, I will do whatever I can. I would just need to know the names
to ask for." Tomiko reached for a pen in his shirt pocket and pulled a small
notebook from his inside jacket pocket.

"Actually there is no name but mine on the blood samples in the vials,"
Malissa said, "but they are actually for Saratu."

"I will make a call as soon as I get to my room. What is the name of the
doctor who needs this report?"

Bert pulled a piece of paper from his pocket. "Doctor Boyer on
Independence Street."

"I will see that it gets there as quickly as it comes in, in fact, I will deliver it
personally." He was still curious. "And what will you ladies be doing today?"

"When we finish breakfast, we are going shopping," Malissa replied.
"Saratu and Asta just came in from bush and need clothes to wear."

Tomiko bowed again. "If you will excuse me, I will go make a phone
call."

"Goodbye," Saratu said, pleased with herself for remembering the word.

When their meals arrived, Malissa explained what food they had and
how to eat it.

CHAPTER 99

Tomiko went to his room in the hotel and immediately put in a call to Jim Harris' office, relieved to find the man in.

Almost breathless in his haste, Jim said, "I'm glad you called. I just this minute received a message back from my colleague at Pennsylvania State University. I sent him an E-mail and fax last night."

Impatiently Tomiko interjected, "What did you find?"

"Nothing like it on the face of the earth, Tomiko. Where on this earth did the water and soil samples come from?"

Tomiko shrugged his shoulders. "I think it was just a routine sample."

"These findings are nothing short of astonishing," Jim exclaimed

"When can I have them?" Tomiko asked quickly.

"I want to wait until I hear from my friend in Pennsylvania. He sent me a quick response but said he wanted to do some research and would get back to me by tomorrow morning."

"So you think this is something pretty spectacular, Jim," Tomiko said eagerly.

"No doubt about it!"

"But how about the blood sample Miss Taylor sent? What did you find in it?"

"That's another surprise, Tomiko," Jim said. "I've never seen a sample like it. I figured it had been altered somehow."

"What do you mean, what was wrong with it?"

"Nothing wrong with it exactly. It was just.., just different."

"We need a copy of those lab results for the doctor they will be seeing this afternoon. Could you at least send me that by E-mail right away?"

"Yes, I could do that, but you might want to warn the doctor that it is an unusual report."

"Yes, Jim, I will do that," Tomiko said breathlessly. "You will send me your friend's opinion as soon as you get it, won't you." It was a statement.

"You bet. My friend was excited enough about it that I have no doubt but that he will be contacting me as soon as he knows something."

"Thank you, Jim, thank you very much."

"Tomiko, I do have some questions I would like to ask Miss Taylor about the people who gave the samples. Would it be possible to talk with her?"

"Fortunately, she is in Blantyre right now, staying at the Mount Soche Hotel. I am sure she would not mind answering questions. But, Jim," he lowered his voice, "until we know the ramifications of this, please don't get Miss Taylor too excited."

"Sure, Tomiko, sure. We just want to ask some questions."

Tomiko dropped onto his bed and hugged himself. At last! He could stop avoiding Mr Oboji. In fact, he would call him right then and tell him he had a breakthrough in technology that would revolutionize crop production and the health of all humans.

Not only would he, Tomiko, keep his job, he would be acclaimed as the person who changed the face of hunger. He reached for the phone but stopped. First he would call Matsuko. Her opinion meant more than anyone's, and she would tell him how wonderful he was.

And he would deliver a copy of the report to the doctor, in exchange for the doctor's opinion about Saratu.

CHAPTER 100

Malissa had decided not to take Saratu and Asta to the boutiques or the bigger stores that had clothing departments. It made more sense to go to the market, as the women would be more at ease there.

She was right. As they approached the market from a small rise above it, Asta and Saratu halted in amazement. They had never seen a market so vast. But they wasted no time in making their way down the small hill and into the maze of little covered stalls where all kinds of wares were displayed.

Malissa just followed them, listening to their cries of surprise and delight. They stopped at a stand surrounded by blouses hung from wires, with matching lengths of cloth for the wrap-around zhebi, which was the style all women wore.

"Do you see something you like?" Malissa asked, intending to buy several outfits for each of them.

Asta replied quickly, "Oh, no. We will make the rounds of all the stalls and then decide where to buy."

Malissa smiled. "Well, we have until about three o'clock. Saratu has an appointment at four o'clock."

"I do?" Saratu asked. "What for?"

"Mr. McEwen has something he wants to show you."

"Oh-h-h," she cooed. "It will be something very nice, I think. I really like Mr. McEwen." She went on, "But he likes you. I can tell by the way he looks at you."

Malissa flushed. "Just tell me when you find something you like."

"'Too bad we can't speak their language," Asta said. "You will have to do the bargaining for us."

"Most of the traders understand English. Here is a good opportunity to try out your English, Saratu."

"All right, but I may need your help," Saratu replied.

"I will be right beside you at all times," Malissa promised.

CHAPTER 101

By one o'clock Malissa was exhausted and had sweat running down her back. Asta and Saratu did not appear to notice the heat. They had each chosen two outfits of a blouse and zhebi combination plus headscarves to match. Matching headscarves was a new fashion to them.

They found a place in one of the stalls where they could change to their new outfits. It was quite a transformation from the wrinkled soiled clothes they had worn from Kulanji. Asta wrapped her headcloth in the twisted-up style she usually did, but Saratu folded hers in the way she saw a young woman do it in the market, wrapping it around her head at a saucy angle. They had already donned new sandals.

Malissa could not help but think that Saratu was a beauty in any country as she watched men follow with their eyes as she passed. At first Malissa thought Saratu was unaware of their attention, but as she observed Saratu, it was interesting to see her begin to walk a bit differently, to swing her hips ever so little, but just enough.

Asta caught Malissa observing Saratu and whispered, "Girls are the same everywhere, aren't they?"

Malissa smiled. "Yes, I am sure they are. But few are as attractive as Saratu." They were silent for a moment. Then Malissa said, "I think we should get her back to Kulanji soon. She might decide some man here is more interesting than Pindar."

"Oh, I don't think she would do that," Asta said but with a question in her voice.

"Mama, how do you like my scarf tying?" Saratu asked, striking a pose.

"That is clever. We will start a whole new trend when we get back home," Asta said.

"When we get back home," Saratu said. She turned to Malissa. "I have been too excited about getting here to ask how and when we will go home. I figured you had that all planned."

"It will depend on the weather and on Bert's schedule, but as soon as your medical exams are complete, you could go home."

An anxious glance went between Asta and Saratu.

Seeing it, Malissa said, "Do you think there will be a real problem with your returning home? Is it possible that they won't let you back in?"

"I don't think so," Asta replied, "but the real question is what they will do with us once we get there."

"And what might that be?" Malissa asked.

"No doubt we will be shunned for a period of time," Asta said, "I just hope they put us both in the same place. That would at least be bearable."

"For how long?" Malissa asked.

"Depends how upset they are probably," Asta said. "Could be a month, could be a year."

"Poor Baba," Saratu said, "he is the one who will be punished for our actions. I am really sorry about that."

"Are you sorry you came?" Malissa asked.

Saratu shook her head and said firmly, "Whatever happens, I am glad we came."

"I know a great place for lunch," Malissa said, taking an arm of each, and propelling them toward the little restaurant where Carol had taken her.

It was slow going as Saratu or Asta had to stop every few steps to look at something or to ask questions.

It was after one-thirty when they finally sat down. Even Saratu was ready to rest.

Malissa ordered for them, grilled cheese sandwiches and cocoa, with ice cream to come later.

Here at last was Malissa's opportunity to ask the important questions. "Asta, can you tell me why your people are so much healthier than other people?"

Asta spoke slowly in a low voice. Malissa leaned forward so as not to miss a word. "Our storytellers repeat the tale of a time when a great cloud appeared over Kulanji, darkening the sky for many days, and ever since then the crops grew better, people did not get sick as much, and flowers flourished everywhere. That is all we know."

Saratu chimed in. "Every child must learn that story by heart and be able to repeat it to a younger child once a year at the Festival of the Cloud."

"What do you think is going to happen as the world encroaches on your country?" Malissa asked. "More people are going to want to see the Outside."

Asta shook her head sadly, "We are caught between wanting to preserve what is good in our culture and enjoying what is good in the Outside."

Saratu tossed her head. "But keeping us all prisoners will only makes us more curious."

"And what would you suggest, Saratu?" Asta said with a hint of anger in her voice.

Saratu was adamant. "They should tell us what is important in our culture and how to protect it but trust us to go into the Outside and do that."

Asta shook her head. "We have talked about this so many times. Do you really think you are the first person who wanted to see the Outside? We have discussed it over and over, but always came back to the belief that any dilution of our culture would mean the end of it."

"I don't see why . . . " Saratu began.

"Inevitably our young men would find wives in the Outside. According to the storytellers, that actually happened many, many years ago, and the children of the families of mixed parents did not have the immunity and good health that others had. So they went back to prohibiting marriage with someone from the Outside."

"There would just have to be rules that were enforced," Saratu said.

"What kind of rules?" Asta asked.

"Rules about who you could marry and . . . "

Asta interrupted, "And about who you could have sex with?"

"Of course," Saratu answered emphatically.

"Silly girl," Asta said, shaking her head. "You can't set such rules in that kind of a society.. In our tribe there is a place provided for men to go, but they may not go there until they are married."

"How can you be sure they are married?" Malissa asked.

"Our tribe is not so big but that everyone knows who is married and who isn't. Or the women have only to ask."

"And where do these women come from, these—what do you call them?" Malissa asked.

"They are called 'the unlucky ones' because they cannot have children. They are considered the most unfortunate of all women. But on the other hand, they are treated very well, even having some comforts that the rest of us do not have."

Malissa had to ask, "And you don't mind, if your husband goes to one of these women?"

"Do we have a choice?" Asta laughed. "It is important to have children a safe distance apart, and the only way to do that is to not get pregnant, so during the time that a woman is still nursing her baby, but could get pregnant, the husband goes to the House of Women."

"But the other diseases that both men and women get, like the one you call *kokal*, 'the man's disease,' you do get them."

"Yes, and people get very ill."

Bacterial infections, Malissa thought to herself. Somehow it is the virus causing AIDS that has been altered .

That reminded her that she had agreed to give Carol Walters some information. She had said she would make it available to her, through Bert. But maybe, instead, she would talk to Carol herself. And make sure what information was given only to Carol. It wasn't that she didn't trust Bert, only that he might have a different idea of what was appropriate to tell Carol.

The sandwiches arrived, and Malissa showed them how to dunk the sandwich into the cocoa. It had been a favorite of Malissa's as a child. Cheese was a new taste and texture to the women, but they liked the sandwich. They had tasted chocolate before but never in a hot drink.

"Can I take some of this back with me?" Saratu asked. "I think Pindar would like to taste this."

"Pindar!" Asta exclaimed. "Now it is Pindar you want to do something nice for. It is about time. You would hardly give him a look at home."

"Pindar is okay," Saratu said grinning. "I like him better when he is far away."

They all laughed.

It was the first ice cream the women had ever had. Malissa tried to caution them about how to eat it, but they did not understand, and with the first bite, they were both holding their faces in pain.

"Don't let it touch your teeth," Malissa instructed. "Just let it slide over your tongue and then down your throat."

After a couple more tentative tries, they got the hang of it.

"I'd like to take some of that home too," Saratu said.

Malissa laughed, "Afraid not. It would melt."

"What do I need to make it not melt?" Saratu asked.

"Something that would change your whole world," Malissa replied. "Are you sure you want to do that?"

Saratu was silent, pondering the possibility.

CHAPTER 102

The three women walked back to the hotel, arriving a couple of minutes before three o'clock. Bert was waiting for them, clasping and unclasping his hands in front of him but unaware of his motions. Malissa noticed the nervous movements and wondered why Bert was tense. But she smiled to herself, assuming it was because she was there. And indeed, his face lit up when he saw them coming through the door.

"Bert!" Saratu said, then added stiffly in English, "How are you this day?"

Bert bowed and replied, "Very well, thank you, and how was your shopping?"

Saratu did not recognize the word *shopping*, but Bert pointed to the clothes they were wearing. Saratu gave a saucy bow, grinning broadly.

"Pretty," she said and waited for Bert's response.

"Very pretty," he said. In fact, he was struck by the beauty of this young woman whose molded features and smooth milk chocolate skin was a classic in any country. This was more than Gui had bargained for and certainly more than he deserved, but with Bert's plan, Gui's little téte-a- téte would be aborted. But until his plan was accomplished, a niggling doubt remained.

Gui was waiting in the garden, and Bert turned to Malissa, trying to appear nonchalant. "So you and Asta are going to the coffee shop down the street now?" he asked.

"Actually I think not," Malissa replied. "We are tired and I am sure Asta would like a rest."

An alarm went off in Bert's brain. He had checked out the view from Asta's and Malissa's rooms in the hotel. A huge tree obscured the view from Malissa's window, but the place where Gui was to meet Saratu was clearly visible from Asta's window. He could not object to their going to their rooms without raising suspicion. All he could do was hope that even if Asta did look out her window, she would not think anything unusual was going on to tell Malissa about. And especially, he hoped Malissa would have no reason to look out the window in Asta's room.

Bert tried to sound casual as he said, "Saratu probably would like to rest too. She will be back in a few minutes." He took Saratu's arm. "This way."

Saratu waved as they moved away, the same pleased look of anticipation on her face that had been there since arriving in Blantyre. She was ready for any new experience.

Bert glanced back as they neared the door to the garden to make sure they were not following for some reason. But Malissa and Asta were already at the stairs and not even looking in his direction.

Trying to be nonchalant, Bert walked slowly, pointing out flowers and objects as they moved down the steps and into the garden. Saratu repeated the words after him. The path wound through flowering trees, shrubs and potted plants beside the path. Bright-colored birds flew as they neared. Saratu said the Kulanji name for things, and Bert would say the English.

Gui was standing off to one side of the fountain watching them approach. For a moment Bert paused, and Saratu looked up to see why he had stopped. The look on Gui's face made Bert absolutely nauseated. Gui was gazing at Saratu with a frank look of lust. Bert had seen that look in Gui's eyes before, but this time was different.

Something told Bert that he should turn around and hurry Saratu back into the hotel, but Gui came strolling over, his eyes on Saratu only. "My God, Bert, you didn't tell me this!" The man was wearing navy blue slacks and a knitted light pink silk polo shirt under a powder blue cashmere jacket. He would have turned any woman's head.

What Bert did not notice was the way Saratu was looking at Gui. This was the man she saw on the TV! The charming, handsome man who had almost spoken to her from the screen.

Bert gulped and said, "Saratu, this is Mr. Manieux."

Still without looking at Bert, Gui said, "It would be easier for her to say Gui."

"This is Gui, Saratu."

So that was his name, Gui, Saratu thought. And incredibly, he was look-ing at her just like he had on the TV.

Gui motioned for Saratu to come to the stone bench that surrounded the fountain. Bert followed but with alarms going off in his head like crazy. This man was dangerous! Why had he consented to this? Was his plan going to work?

Saratu sat at Gui's invitation, no longer aware of Bert.

"Saratu," Gui said in his seductive gentle voice, "you are very beautiful."

Saratu was charmed by his voice and his smiling eyes, and relaxed a bit, leaning back against the stones.

Without looking at Bert, Gui said, "I think you can leave now, Bert. We will come in in a few minutes."

"But..." Bert tried to protest.

Gui ignored him as he pulled from his jacket pocket a small box.

Bert did not move. Still without taking his eyes from Saratu's face, Gui reached into his other jacket pocket and brought out a plump brown envelope, which he held out to Bert.

The money, his money, and now hush money. Like a man in a trance, Bert accepted the envelope and walked away, full of loathing for what he had just done, but with the knowledge that the fat envelope made it necessary.

How could any single action be so right and so wrong at the same time? Furtively he glanced up at the window of Asta's room and was relieved to see no one there.

He stepped into the seclusion of a corner of the building and looked at the contents of the envelope. Quickly he counted the stacks of hundred kwacha bills, ten stacks, one hundred thousand dollars.

Suddenly a spot of moisture fell from above his head landing on the bills, and for an instant he had the incredible feeling that it was blood. His guilt was complete.

Abruptly he knew he could not leave Saratu with this monster. He turned to hurry back down the path and rescue Saratu, but there they were, walking slowly toward him. Saratu was looking into Gui's eyes as Bert had seen many women do, fascinated, snared.

"Gui," Bert began.

"Bert, Saratu has said she would like to see my farm tomorrow afternoon. Shall I have someone pick her up or will you deliver her to me?"

Bert hated those words, *deliver her to me.* Like a lamb to the slaughter. But he had his plan.

"That's not my problem, Gui."

"If it does not happen, Bert, the hundred thousand comes back to me." Gui was smiling that rapturous smile of his but his eyes were stone cold and dead serious.

"Wrong, Gui. I have done my part of the bargain," Bert said. "Now you are on your own." He looked straight at Gui unflinching. "You can pick her up here at three o'clock tomorrow afternoon."

Surprised at what appeared to be capitulation, Gui frowned but then turned to Saratu and said, "I will be here precisely at three o'clock tomorrow afternoon, Saratu."

Gui bowed, taking Saratu's hand and kissing it ceremoniously. Gui gave her a brilliant smile, then turned and walked quickly away without looking back, but with Saratu watching until he disappeared into the garden.

Saratu now turned to Bert, her eyes shining as she showed Bert the cameo that now hung at her throat. Of course, it was the real thing, Bert sneered to himself.

"Beautiful!" Saratu said in stilted syllables.

"Nice man," she said nodding and smiling.

How was he going to explain the cameo? He could take it away from her.

"Saratu, better let me keep that for you." Bert reached out his hand for it. Saratu backed away, shaking her head. "My beautiful thing," she said.

His mind was racing to think up a story to explain how Saratu could have come by such a beautiful cameo as they waited for the elevator. By the time they reached the second floor, he thought he had it figured out.

Saratu knocked lightly on her door, and Asta opened it. Saratu turned and waved goodbye, saying, "Thank you, Bert, thank you very much."

The door closed behind her, and immediately he heard animated conversation in Kulanji as Saratu obviously described her encounter with the handsome man who gave her a beautiful gift.

Malissa would be furious, and right now he did not want to see Malissa. He would take the hundred thousand and put it in a safe place. Then he had to be back about three forty-five to take Saratu to the doctor's office. Damn, damn, damn, damn! All he did was push himself further into hell. But his plan was in place; he was still going to outsmart Gui.

CHAPTER 103

Malissa was downstairs in the lobby of the hotel when Bert returned a few minutes before four o'clock. He dreaded having to see the anger in Malissa's eyes, but he deserved it. He had allowed Saratu to be put in harm's way, and Malissa would certainly figure that out.

"Bert!" Malissa called to him across the lobby. "What a beautiful gift to Saratu! Who in the world . . . ?

He decided the best answer was the truth, at least part of it. "I ran into Gui Manieux last week, who had talked with Carol Walters about bringing Asta and Saratu here. He told me he wanted to do something nice for Saratu. I didn't know what it was going to be." Now he rushed on headlong. "But it is beautiful, isn't it? I am sure it is authentic, and very expensive. Gui has good taste."

"It is exquisite," Malissa said. "Obviously not a plastic imitation. I suppose Saratu doesn't mind that it is the bust of a naked woman."

"Oh?" Bert had not looked closely at the cameo, but he was not surprised that Gui would have given something like that.

Relieved that Malissa had not objected to Gui being the one involved, Bert hurried them out to his Landrover and drove quickly to the doctor's office a few blocks away, pulling up to the door.

"I'll wait here," Bert said as he helped Asta and Saratu out of the Landrover. Malissa never waited to be helped.

"It is likely to be a while," Malissa said, "but as you wish." She started to walk away then turned around. "I have forgotten the doctor's name?"

Bert grinned, "Oh yeah, I guess you do need that. Doctor Boyer."

When Malissa announced to the receptionist that she had come with Saratu Sheria, the young woman behind the desk said, "Just a minute," and disappeared through a door behind her. Almost immediately a middle-aged man appeared. He held out his hand to Malissa, who was nearest. "I am Doctor Boyer. Are you Miss Sheria?"

"I am Malissa Taylor." She turned to Saratu. "This is Saratu Sheria, doctor. So good of you to see her this afternoon."

"Well, we were glad to do it." He motioned toward the door he had come out of. "This way, please."

He led the way as they followed to his office where he motioned them to sit in overstuffed chairs in front of his desk. Then he sat in the chair behind his desk.

He leaned forward, speaking intently but somewhat breathless. "Saratu, what country are you from?"

"Kulanji," Saratu replied.

He looked to Malissa. "Where is Kulanji? I have never heard of it."

"A small area northwest of here, quite secluded actually."

"Miss Taylor, I see they don't speak much English, and I don't speak their language. Tell me more about Kulanji."

Malissa wanted to tell the doctor the least amount of information necessary in order to acquire the answers to her questions. "It is just a small country near where I live and where I go to supervise the dispensary. I became acquainted with Asta and Saratu, and now we would like for Saratu to be checked over."

"Has she been ill?"

"No, doctor, we talked about her coming to Blantyre, and she said she would like to have a complete physical. She thinks she would like to become a nurse or a dispenser herself. She is a very good student."

The doctor was knitting his brow as if confused. "I have looked over Saratu's lab results. They were delivered to me a little while ago. I have used the United Nations laboratory in Lilongwe before and have had what I felt to be accurate readings, so I am going to assume for the moment that Saratu's lab report is correct. But I must tell you that the values are, shall we say, off the scale."

"Doctor," Malissa said, "I am aware that Saratu is extremely healthy, and she is here today for your evaluation. We would like to know why she is so healthy."

"Tell me about the other people in her tribe. Are they healthy too?"

"Yes," Malissa admitted, "but they have some rules and taboos that help to keep them that way."

"Such as?"

"Young women are not allowed to have sex before marriage. They know how to raise fruits and vegetables so have a healthy diet. They remain almost completely isolated from other tribes so do not have the usual diseases. They have a fairly high level of sanitation and water purity."

"But that would mean that they have little immunity to such things as measles and would be decimated if they come in contact with such diseases, is that true?"

"Not really, doctor. They seem to have resistance to many diseases, at least some viral ones."

The doctor looked at her for a long moment. "Are you saying that this tribe does not have AIDS?"

"That appears to be the case, doctor."

Doctor Boyer stared at Malissa now, then turned to gaze at Asta and Saratu, fascinated by what he had just heard.

"Well," he said, standing up, "let's take a look."

Saratu was ushered into an examining room by the nurse while Malissa and Asta stayed in the waiting room.

Half an hour later Doctor Boyer asked Malissa to come into his office. Asta and Saratu were told to wait in the waiting room.

It was an opportunity Saratu had been hoping for. They had been so busy that she had not had time to read much of anything such as newspapers or magazines. She flipped through the magazines on the low table next to the upholstered couch, choosing one called, *The Movie World*.

She glanced quickly through the pages, noticing the lovely young people, again mostly white, but a few with dark skins. Again she reminded herself to ask Malissa about that.

Suddenly there was the handsome man again. It had to be Gui, the same well-trimmed mustache, silver hair, and the same beguiling smile. A warm flush moved up her body, a sensation not quite like anything she had ever felt before. And he thought she was beautiful!

CHAPTER 104

Clay Worthington knew a miracle when he saw one. There was no question but that the lab report from Jim Harris in Malawi was that kind of a breakthrough. Here was genetic altering occurring naturally, and he wanted to be there on the spot to see it.

But there was so much more going on. Something told him that this was the portent he had been waiting for, the opening of a door for him. Africa was an unknown, even a scary unknown, but it beckoned to him and he went gladly. He felt like this was what he had been waiting for all his life. Nothing could have stopped him from getting on that plane.

He found someone to cover his classes and had bought a ticket to leave on Monday, the fourteenth of June.

The plane was already over New England heading for Amsterdam, then to Nairobi and finally to Lilongwe. He had sent an E-mail to Jim notifying him of his arrival.

He waved away the evening meal by the stewardess; he was much too excited to eat. If this was what he thought it was, it was the breakthrough he had been waiting for, a facet of genomics that no one had explored because it simply had not been possible before.

He could make a name for himself all right, but more importantly, he just might be able to help a lot of people to live longer, healthier lives. It was his opportunity, the chance of a lifetime.

CHAPTER 105

I have to say, Miss Taylor, that I am amazed and completely mystified by what I have seen. Saratu has no evidence of the usual maladies I find in virtually every African woman I see. You did say you think she had a light case of measles when she was small. Otherwise she has none of the many intestinal parasites or diseases I would expect to find."

"What do you think accounts for her exceptional health, doctor?" Malissa asked.

"It is an absolute mystery to me, but I must tell you that I would like to know the answer to this puzzle. I would like to pass it on to all my other patients."

"We hoped you could help us find the answer, doctor.

"I am sorry to not be of more help, but I would like to keep in touch with you. Would that be all right?"

"Of course, doctor, although I am a little hard to contact as I work in bush country."

Malissa wanted out of there and rose to leave. If he was not able to give them any idea from the lab report as to why Saratu was so healthy, she was not going to promise to give him the information when they did find it.

"Thank you, doctor, for your time. I will pay for the visit as I leave."

"There won't be a charge, and I am sorry not to be of more help." The doctor hurried from behind his desk and stood at the door they would be going through. "I really would like to know what you find out, and would most appreciate your letting me know."

Malissa was making no promises. "Thanks again, doctor," she said as she guided Asta and Saratu ahead of her, and out the door of the clinic. Bert was there waiting, and as they got into the car, Malissa noticed that the doctor was still standing at the door staring after them.

"Sorry, Bert, we struck out again," Malissa said as she climbed into the front seat beside him.

"Where do we go from here?" Bert asked.

"I'm not sure, but I think we need someone who can interpret those lab results and tell us what they mean."

"Who would that be?"

"I have an idea," Malissa said. "Take us back to the hotel."

CHAPTER 106

Tomiko was walking on air. The Secretary-General had been so pleased with Tomiko's report that he told him to plan on returning to New York immediately to provide them with full details.

Just as importantly, when he had called his wife, Matsuko, she told him to hurry home so they could celebrate properly. He knew what that meant, and just thinking about it caused an erection. He had been away too long. It was time to go home, and he would, just as soon as he knew some answers for sure.

Jim Harris had promised to call him the moment he heard from his professor friend at the Pennsylvania State University.. In the meantime, he would like to know what Malissa had learned from the physical exam for Saratu that afternoon.

In fact, he would go directly to Doctor Boyer for that information. Tomiko had made it plain when he delivered the laboratory report to Doctor Boyer that he would expect a report.

"I'm sorry, Mr. Hirokama," Doctor Boyer said over the phone. "I am completely mystified by this young woman. She is obviously extraordinarily healthy, but why is something I cannot explain."

Tomiko quickly ended the conversation, making no promises to get back to Doctor Boyer in spite of the doctor's repeated requests that he do so.

Remembering to take his cell phone, Tomiko went down to the lobby to stand in an inconspicuous spot and wait for Malissa.

He did not have to wait long. As Malissa came in the main entrance, he pretended to be coming from the elevators.

"Ah, Miss Taylor, how nice to see you."

"Mr Hirokama,, I was just going to look for you and here you are!"

"Yes indeed, here I am." He smiled his most gracious smile.

"Asta," Malissa said, "you and Saratu go on up to your room. I will be up shortly."

The two women were glad to go rest. It had been a tiring afternoon, and they were not at all sure what had happened.

In their room, they stretched out on the wonderfully soft beds and talked about the incredible things they had seen, but soon the talk turned to what was now becoming uppermost in their minds, what was going to happen when they returned home.

"Well, Saratu," said her mother, "you wanted this more than anything in the world. How do you feel about it now?"

Saratu did not answer immediately. "I'm not sorry we came. I am sorry if Baba gets into trouble because of this. And probably Pindar won't want me any more."

Asta asked quickly, "How would you feel about that?"

"I never had any great feeling for Pindar. How did you feel before you married Baba, Mama?"

"I guess I never really asked whether or not I had any great feeling for him. He was the one I was to marry. I was lucky; he turned out to be a good husband."

"How do you feel about getting him into trouble?" asked Saratu.

"I figure he is strong enough to get himself out of trouble or to handle what he has to. I learned long ago not to worry about your father. He can take care of himself."

"Mama, I have the feeling he feels the same way about you."

Asta laughed, "Yes, I think you are right."

They were quiet for a while.

"Mama?"

"Yes."

"This may be crazy, but I think Mr Gui, the guy who gave me the cameo, was wanting more from me than thanks for the cameo."

"In that case, you should not have accepted the gift," Asta said firmly.

"I guess I thought people in the Outside gave gifts just to be giving gifts."

"Not hardly," Asta said. "Most gifts have some kind of return expectations, in Kulanji or Outside."

"Then what do I do about it?" Saratu asked worriedly.

"Well, you didn't respond. I guess that is the end of it."

"Not really," Saratu said quietly. "When he offered to show me his big farm, I thought that would be a great idea. Maybe I could learn something about farming to take home to Baba."

"You mean you are going to see his farm?"

"Tomorrow afternoon."

"Is Bert going to take you?"

"No. Gui is going to pick me up."

"I will not allow you to be alone with that man. I will be there and make sure it doesn't happen. What time is he coming?"

"I...I'm not sure," Saratu stuttered. She felt guilty for not being honest with her mother, but somehow she really wanted to go to Gui's farm. She had to admit that the thought of being close to Gui again engendered some feelings that she had never felt when she was with Pindar. This was a part of the Outside that she did not want to miss.

CHAPTER 107

Down in the foyer, Tomiko and Malissa were headed toward comfortable overstuffed chairs when Bert came in after parking the car. He followed them and chose a big chair.

"Tomiko," Malissa began, "we need to know what you have found out from the lab results that went to Lilongwe."

Tomiko would rather have kept that bit of information to himself, but at heart he was an ethical man, and after all, without this woman and the young woman from Kulanji, he would never have had the opportunity to discover the secret of the Green Country.

"I am waiting for a response from the lab technician who runs the lab in Lilongwe. He was surprised at the lab values but did not know what they meant. So he contacted a friend of his at the Pennsylvania State University Research Department, and we are right now awaiting his expert opinion."

"That is wonderful!" exclaimed Malissa. "That is just the kind of response we are looking for."

"Yes," Tomiko said solemnly, "this information could revolutionize the way we farm and the way we treat AIDS."

"Will you promise to let us know the moment you hear anything from the States?" asked Malissa.

"Yes, I will do that," replied Tomiko.

"If we are not here at that moment, please, please leave a message for us to find you. Will you do that?"

Again Tomiko promised. He excused himself and went toward the elevators.

"Are we ever going to have even a few minutes alone, Malissa?" Bert asked. "There are so many things . . . "

"Bert, I can't even think about anything else until this matter is settled."

"I could sure use a hug," grinned Bert.

"All right," Malissa returned, smiling at him, "you may come up to the room for a few minutes, no more."

As he entered Malissa's room, Bert flipped the lock on the door. Then he scooped Malissa up in his arms and carried her to the bed where he kissed her passionately. She responded playfully to his caresses.

But when his hand moved up her leg to her thigh, she sat up. "Not now, Bert. This is not the time."

"Malissa, I hardly get any sleep for wanting you. You do incredible things to me. Couldn't we just . . . ?"

"No, Bert, when this is all over, then maybe . . . "

"Maybe! What is with *maybe*? Marry me, Malissa, now, today."

She laughed her happy laugh and kissed him on the lips.

"All in good time, my love, all in good time." She stood up. "Now, are you taking us to dinner or not?"

* * *

They were awaiting their orders in the only French restaurant in Blantyre.

"Is there any restaurant in Blantyre that serves guinea corn mush?" asked Saratu. "I didn't know that other people could live without eating guinea corn mush."

Malissa laughed. "I believe it is available in market, and I promise you we will go there tomorrow morning and get you some guinea corn mush."

"Thank goodness," laughed Asta. "I never thought I would be desperate for guinea corn mush, after eating it every day for most of my life."

"Every day?" asked Bert incredulously. "Didn't you get tired of it?"

"Oh, we serve it many different ways," Asta replied. "With many different kinds of vegetables, different flavorings, thin mush, thick mush, with meat, without meat."

"I'll bet your husband will be glad to have you back, or does he cook his own guinea corn mush?"

It was the wrong thing to say, and Bert was immediately sorry, judging by the look on Asta's face.

Saratu jumped into the conversation. "Poor Baba, he may never want to see us again. We have caused him great pain."

"Sorry I brought it up," Bert said and quickly changed the subject. "If the weather is good, we should be taking you home the day after tomorrow, Thursday. What else would you like to see in Blantyre?"

"I want to go back to market and get some things to take back to people in Kulanji," Saratu said.

"I saw some things in market I would like to take back—for me," Asta laughed. "There was something that you can hold with one hand while you sweep with the other, a pan to sweep into."

"That is called a dust pan," Malissa said.

Asta went on, "And I would like to take Ladu's new baby one of those warm bags to wear. They look like a great idea. I wish I had had one when my children were small."

Malissa smile. "Unless she also starts using diapers, I am afraid a sleeping bag would not be a good idea."

"I hadn't thought of that," Asta said.

"To market tomorrow morning then," Malissa said. "Hopefully by tomorrow afternoon we will have some answers for which we brought you here, and then it will be time for you to go home."

"How will you get home from Kulanji, Miz Tayluh?" Saratu asked.

Malissa looked at Bert questioningly.

Bert shrugged. "If there hasn't been too much rain, I should be able to land on the road in your village, Malissa."

Suddenly Malissa remembered something. "Bert, you told me you were having trouble raising the money for your new airplane, but you haven't mentioned that recently. Have you found the money?"

Bert closed his eyes and let out a short sigh. "Yes, I have found the money."

"Then the plane is yours!" exclaimed Malissa.

"It is mine," he nodded but without a smile.

"Isn't that something to celebrate?" asked Malissa. "You don't look very happy, Bert." She placed her hand on his.

"I may have lost my soul in the process," he said without a smile.

"What does that mean?" Malissa asked.

"I'll know tomorrow. Until then I would just as soon not talk about it."

"At least let us toast Bert's new plane," Malissa said as she raised her glass of wine. "Without it, we would not be here."

"Toast?" Saratu asked. "Didn't we have toast for breakfast?"

"It just means to celebrate, and we lift our glasses to that." They all raised their glasses and touched each other's.

Bert felt like a sinner, but he lifted his glass anyway and let a prayer slip from his lips that his plan would work. If it turned out badly, no one was to blame as much as he. How would he ever explain to Malissa?

"Look!" Saratu exclaimed, pointing with her chin toward a woman holding a small baby in her arms, and apparently waiting for someone to come. "What is in that baby's mouth?"

"That is a pacifier," Malissa replied.

"What is it for?" Asta asked.

"It has a nipple on it which the baby sucks. It is to keep the baby from crying."

"That is what I want to take to Ladu!" cried Asta.

"Please, no!" Malissa exclaimed, appalled at the idea of African children using pacifiers. "The pacifier drops out of the baby's mouth and lands on the ground, and . . . "

"You would spend all your time picking it up," interjected Bert.

"It seems to me that the healthiest solution to a baby crying is the way you handle it now, give it a real nipple," Malissa observed.

Asta shook her head. "You just don't know the times when you would rather not have that baby on your back, and something to quiet it would be welcome."

"If we see any in market, we will get a couple," Saratu stated firmly.

Malissa prayed that there would be none in market.

CHAPTER 108

Clay arrived at the Lilongwe airport at eight o'clock in the evening, forty-five minutes late after eleven hours in the air. Jim Harris gave him a bear hug and hustled him to the waiting car.

"We will get your luggage in the morning," Jim said.

"Shouldn't we check at the baggage place?" Clay asked.

"Oh, it never comes at the same time you do," Jim assured him. "I will check later."

Jim herded the car around bicycles and women with babies on their backs, tooting his horn over and over at goats that darted into the street.

"Clay, I can't tell you how much I appreciate your coming right now."

"It seemed just the right thing to do and just the right time to do it."

"We haven't really talked for a long time, Clay. What's going on in your life? Found a woman crazy enough to have you yet?"

"I just decided this very week that it was time for me to do something about that. I think I am ready."

"It's about time," Jim grinned. "Marriage is scary but so is the thought of spending your old age alone."

"I could use a little help on that project, you know," Clay said slyly.

"Here, in Africa? Lotsa luck!"

"At least there are black women here," Clay said. Then he asked, "Can we go straight to the lab?"

"I was hoping you would not be too tired to do just that," Jim said.

"Jim, this has to be the most bizarre genomic results I have ever seen. I assume you have other tests?"

"We are testing the water and the soil from that part of the country, and the results are just as outlandish as the first set."

"What do you make of it?" Clay asked.

"I'm stumped. I am hoping you have some answers since you've been closer to all of this."

"Let's go put our heads together."

CHAPTER 109

When Bert awakened on Wednesday morning after a restless night, he felt a cold dread in the pit of his stomach. Even if his plan worked, and Gui was disgraced, Bert would still be held responsible for putting Saratu in danger.

On the way home the night before, after kissing Malissa goodnight at the hotel and wanting desperately to spend the night with her, he realized that it was inevitable that she would find out what he had done, and without question, she would leave him. What he had already done was certainly reprehensible. Now he knew that having Malissa in his life was more important than the money, the plane, his job, even more important than the secret of the Green Country.

He lay there, going over and over what he could possibly do to undo what he had caused to happen so far.

He could simply refuse to let Gui get close to Saratu again. He could take Saratu and Asta back to Kulanji that very day.

Then a thought came to him, how did Gui think he was going to get the secret of the Green Country? Through Carol, of course. But if Bert told Malissa what Gui had in mind, Carol would not be given that information. Of course, he could not reveal to Malissa what was really going on, so what if he offered the laboratory results to Gui in exchange for Saratu?

Surely Gui wanted the information badly enough to give up his tryst with Saratu.

That was what he would do! It was his way out of this. Of course, he would not give Gui the real information, only an inconsequential part of it.

It was early, but he would try The Farm. He was sure Gui went to work early.

Gui answered on the second ring.

" You called to confirm our appointment?"

"No," Bert said. "Actually I called to tell you that the information about the

Green Country that you want so badly is available only through me. Carol is not going to receive that information if I say so."

"What? Now wait a minute!" Gui exploded. "Carol said Malissa Taylor was going to get that information for her."

"Only if I say so."

"And . . . ?"

"I will let you have the secret if you leave Saratu alone."

"And if I refuse?"

"You don't get the secret."

There was a long silence.

Suddenly Gui shouted, "You son-of-a-bitch. You never were going to do this. You just wanted the money!"

"You can have the money back, all of it," Bert said.

"I don't believe you!"

"The secret in exchange for Saratu and your money back. Take your choice."

"I will talk to Carol about this!"

"You do that, Gui. And be sure to tell her you are planning to go to bed with Saratu this afternoon."

"How do I know you have the secret?" Gui demanded.

"We have it all,, soil sample reports, expert opinions, the works. We have the answers, and they are unbelievable!"

Soil reports! Glancing down, Gui's eyes fell on a lab report lying on his desk, and a light came on in his brain. The day he was in Yahara's office there was a soil sample report on the desk with strange elements and strange values. They were using his lab, and Yahara would have the results!

"So, flyboy," Gui's voice was sarcastic, scorn in every word. "Suddenly you are tired of playing pimp and you want out. To hell with you, Bert! No bargain! And I will still get the secret!"

Gui's words reached deep and stung like fire, but Bert managed to say, "Lots of luck!"

"They do not call me Lucky Gui for nothing. I have been lucky all my life, and it is not going to stop now. You have Saratu at the front door of the hotel at three o'clock this afternoon, or you will give all the money back. And besides that, I will tell that girlfriend of yours exactly what you are doing."

"But . . . "

"Three o'clock, Bert!"

Bert stood staring at the receiver in his hand. He would have Saratu there all right, along with everyone else, including Carol. If he had to give back the money, so be it.

CHAPTER 110

G ui stormed out of his office and across the yard to Yahara's office. He could not talk to Carol about this, but he damned well could talk to Yahara.

"Yahara!" he yelled as the door banged back against the wall.

Yahara came running from a back room.

"Yes, Mr. Manieux?"

"Where are those reports I saw on your desk that morning, the one with the strange elements and strange values?"

"I don't . . . " Yahara began.

"Do not lie to me, I saw them!" Gui was ranting now, his eyes wild, his arms flailing. "You used my lab for someone else's work!"

Yahara scurried behind the desk. He did not trust Gui not to become violent.

"I did not think you would mind, Mr. Manieux. It was for Mr. McEwen. I knew you and he were friends and . . . "

"It does not matter who it was for, you do not use my lab! Do you understand?" He was still shouting.

"Yes, Mr. Manieux, yes."

"Where are the reports?"

"I gave them to Mr. McEwen," he lied, trusting that Gui was unaware of how the computer worked or that it retained a copy of all reports. "I didn't think we had any need for them."

"Oh, really! Just the most important bit of information in a million years!"

"I'm sorry, Mr. Manieux. I didn't know."

"You must have thought that the results were a bit off!"

"I—I guess I really didn't pay that much attention. I just gave him the report."

"Well, get it back, now!"

"Yes, Mr. Manieux, I will try."

"Not just try, get it!" He put his hands on the desk and leaned across it. "And if you do not, you are fired! Do you understand? If you do not get that report for me today, you are fired!"

"Yes, Mr. Manieux!"

"And quit saying *Yes, Mr. Manieux!*"

Yahara gulped and nodded.

"I want you to leave here right away and do not return until tomorrow morning."

Gui started out the door and turned back. "If Carol calls while you are still here, asking if I am here, tell her no."

"Yes, . . . " Yahara cut off in mid-sentence.

Yahara stared after Gui, unable to move even after he heard the door to Gui's office slam.

His only thought was to call Tomiko. He would know what to do. The one thing he did not want to happen was for Gui to get his hands on the secret of the Green Country.

He called Tomiko on his cell phone and found him as he was leaving for breakfast.

"Stall him, Yahara," Tomiko advised. "Tell him you haven't been able to get hold of Bert."

"Yes, all right, I will do that."

"And, Yahara, don't worry. I am the one who has all the reports, all the results. I will see to it that Gui does not ever get to see them."

"Thank God, Tomiko. I would never forgive myself if he were to get hold of them, even if I lose my job."

"Mr. Manieux will not receive the information from me."

CHAPTER 111

Saratu did not even wake up until eight o'clock, something she could rarely do at home. Asta did not want to awaken her so sat looking out the window across the rooftops of Blantyre, pondering what they had done and what was likely to happen to them. But Asta was not a worrier and pushed the problem out of her mind. Right then she was enjoying this lovely room where someone else provided clean towels and there was always water available for drinking or bathing. It would not be easy to return to life in Kulanji, but on the other hand, she was eager to see Yamta. Somehow she would get across to him how important this journey had been to Saratu. And she hoped she could tell him that now Saratu was willing to settle down in Kulanji and live the normal life of a wife and mother. But there was a nagging doubt in the back of her mind that would not go away.

Malissa even slept in that morning but awoke with a start, wondering where she was for a moment. She had been dreaming of long lines of patients waiting for her to see them. She lay there for just a moment longer, but the image did not go away. She was sure there were long lines of patients waiting for her to return to Mubi.

She ran through the day ahead of them. Breakfast of guinea corn mush in the market, lunch somewhere, in the market perhaps. She had an uneasy feeling about Saratu's visit to Gui Manieux's farm, but nothing she could put her finger on. Bert was to take them to the market and leave them, coming back for them later. She didn't want to be gone too long, in case Tomiko called.

Then Malissa remembered, she was going to call Carol Walters. She would do that when they returned at noon. She simply did not want to do it right then. Anyway, maybe it was too early. She might as well wait until she knew something more definitive, although she had not decided whether she would tell Carol everything about the Green Country. That would depend on what they learned about Saratu's laboratory results.

Malissa was glad to hear that Saratu had slept in. This was a grueling experience for both women, and Saratu had begun to develop circles below her eyes. It was time to bring this to a conclusion and get the women back home, regardless of what waited for them. Surely these two remarkable women would not be severely punished for doing something so natural. Besides, Asta was as important in the tribe as was her husband.

Asta and Saratu wore their second new outfits. Saratu proudly fastened the cameo around her neck.

This time Saratu sat in the front seat, clutching the new purse she had bought in market the day before. It was actually a woven bag in shades of green and orange.

While Bert was checking something in the engine with the hood up, Saratu opened the door of the glove box and idly examined what was in it. She was still very curious about the trappings of a modern civilization. Matches, a flashlight, aspirin, part of a package of peanuts. And something else she did not immediately recognize. Then she remembered Laraba telling her about things like this, called condoms. She dropped one of them into her bag, something to show the girls back home.

Bert dropped them off at the entrance to the market. It did not take long in market to find the sellers of guinea corn mush. Saratu and Asta chose to have mbula bean sauce, which has a clear sour flavor to go with the mush. Malissa had to smile to herself to see with what pleasure the two women devoured their bowls of mush. Malissa chose to have little deep-fried bean cakes, actually made of ground black-eyed peas. She chose the medium pepper-hot ones and was glad she had not chosen the hot ones as these were almost more peppery than she could stand.

Then they wandered around having a wonderful time choosing what they would take back with them to Kulanji. Saratu spied a large-faced wind-up alarm clock with big numbers.

"I think I should take this to Chief Inuwa," Asta said. "His eyesight is getting so bad that he has trouble seeing. This way he would be able to read the time easily."

"Mama, he would love it!" cried Saratu. "Take it to him. And it just might soften his heart a little."

Asta bought two of the clocks, one for her husband. "Maybe he will leave it out where we can all use it," she said.

"Here they are!" Saratu cried, pointing to an array of pacifiers. Malissa stood back and reluctantly watched them pick out two of the things. The last thing an African baby needs, she said to herself.

As they approached a stall that looked like a rainbow with all the colors of scarves, Malissa looked up and saw Carol Walters who was fingering one of the scarves.

"Good morning, Carol," Malissa said.

"Malissa! How nice to see you!" Carol said. "I was going to call Bert today and see what news there was about our project. And here you are!"

Malissa indicated the two women behind her. "Carol, this is Asta and Saratu from Kulanji." To the women, "This is Carol Walters, a friend of mine."

The two women held out their hands. Saratu said, "Nice to meet you." Asta said, "Hello."

"Malissa, what a beautiful young woman Saratu is! And have you learned anything about why they are so healthy?"

"I was going to call you this evening, Carol. We went to the doctor's office yesterday, but he could not tell us anything. He was merely surprised at the lab values, that's all."

Carol turned to Saratu and Asta and spoke slowly. "How do you like Blantyre?" Then seeing their obviously new clothes, "Did you enjoy shopping? What have you done that was fun?"

Saratu held up the cameo at her throat and said with obvious pride, "My beautiful gift."

Carol purred, "A gift, how lovely. And how nice of someone to give you such a special gift." Carol peered at the cameo closely, and reaching out her hand to touch it, turned it over. She recognized it as an authentic hand-carved cameo, no doubt from Italy.

Saratu was eager to try her English. "Beautiful gift from Mr. Gui."

Carol did not understand, but wanted to. An alarm was going off in her head. She turned to Malissa. "Who gave her the gift?"

Malissa had no reason not to tell Carol where the cameo had come from. "Mr. Gui Manieux, I believe."

"Are you sure?" Carol asked incredulously. "When?" Anger was in her voice.

"Yesterday afternoon," Malissa replied.

At that moment Bert appeared, not noticing until too late that Carol stood there.

Carol turned to Bert as soon as she spotted him. "Bert, did Gui have anything to do with bringing Saratu here?"

It was a pointblank question; there was no avoiding it. And Bert was tired of dodging the truth. "Actually, he did help in making it happen."

Carol's voice was deadly quiet. "Do you have any idea why he did not tell me?"

"He said it was to be a surprise."

The anger in her voice was seething. "He was right; it is a surprise."

Holding herself tightly under control, Carol said goodbye to Asta and Saratu and excused herself, walking away with determined step.

Standing beside Malissa, Bert said, "I think Gui Manieux is in deep trouble."

CHAPTER 112

Tomiko checked his cell phone every few minutes just to be sure it was still working okay. What was keeping Jim Harris so long?

Tomiko was pacing in the garden of the hotel where it was still somewhat cool, although the day promised to be hot. There might be a chance of rain by afternoon, but until then it was warm and sticky.

Even though he was expecting a call, when the phone rang its peculiar buzz, Tomiko jumped.

"Yes, yes, hello!" he said, then realized he had not pushed the talk button. "Yes, hello," he said again.

"Tomiko, this is Jim."

"Yes, Jim! What do you know?"

"My friend from Pennsylvania is here. He thought it was important enough to make the trip. He is quite excited about what he thinks is in the samples and is going over all our data. He expects to have some answers by this afternoon, surely by three o'clock. I will call you then."

"This suspense is killing me, Jim," Tomiko said.

"I know, me too. But he promises no later than three o'clock today."

"All right, I will be waiting for your call."

Tomiko had a feeling his blood pressure was high, very high. He had a pressure sensation in his head and a headache. He always took his blood pressure medicine faithfully, but these past few days had been stressful enough for anyone to have high blood pressure. What he needed most of all was Matsuko's healing hands on his body.

Well, at least it would not be long now. He would have a quiet light lunch, rest for a little while and wait for he phone call.

CHAPTER 113

Clay Worthington stared at the figures before him. They were black and white numbers on a page, but they represented real people, people who had had major changes in their DNA, something that had not happened to anyone else on the face of the earth as far as anyone knew.

Now, it had. Something had happened to alter their DNA, to make them immune to some diseases. He understood that, that was his job, but he wanted to see these people. He desperately wanted to talk with them, if that was possible. He had a million questions to ask.

He left his work station and looked for Jim, who he found uncrating a machine that looked impressive with its gauges and movable arms.

"Jim, I want to talk to some of the people who gave these samples. Is that possible?"

"Tomiko told me that Malissa Taylor is staying at the Mount Soche Hotel in Blantyre. She might be able to put us in touch with some of them."

"Let's do it," urged Clay.

Malissa had lain down for just a minute, wishing she could take a nap. She was exhausted.

The phone's shrill ring broke her reverie.

"Malissa Taylor here."

"Malissa, this is Doctor Clayton Worthington at the University of Lilongwe laboratory. We are working with the samples that you sent us, and we have some questions. Would you be able to answer them for us?"

He sounded authentic enough. "Doctor Worthington? What kind of questions?"

"I would like to talk with some of the people who gave those samples. Would that be possible?"

"One of them is here. She speaks some English." Malissa laughed, "Unless of course you speak Kulanji."

"I would like to learn it," Clay responded quickly. "Who is this person and when could I meet with her?"

"She is Saratu, a seventeen-year-old Kulanji woman, here with her mother, Asta. They will be returning to their home in Kulanji tomorrow or the next day, so it would need to be soon."

"How about later today?"

"I think that would be possible. Would you like to go to dinner with us?"

"Sounds great. What time and where?"

"Mount Soche Hotel at six-thirty. Meet us in the lobby.

CHAPTER 114

Carol paced the veranda of her house, getting more and more upset and agitated with each passing minute. Now she realized why Gui had been evasive the last few days, not answering his phone, giving excuses about why he could not keep an appointment with her. He had been planning this all along.

And Carol knew why! As sure as she knew anything, she knew why he was bringing Saratu to Blantyre. Gui had made excuses for avoiding making love with her since last mid-week, and he claimed to have to go to Lilongwe the morning before, not to return until Thursday. But instead, he had been in Blantyre the previous afternoon, giving the cameo to Saratu.

She thought Gui had matured, grown up so that he could make a commitment to a relationship and keep it. But his need to have other sexual encounters had never really disappeared, in spite of his claim to the contrary.

She remembered his strange response to the news that young women in Kulanji were free of AIDS, but just as important, were virgins. It had come back to trouble her over and over, but until this moment she had not figured out what it meant. And now she understood his reaction to Roger's death. Gui wanted sex with a virgin who could not give him AIDS!

How juvenile, immature, and despicable. The list of adjectives went on and on as she stormed around the house, not able to sit down at all.

But what was most difficult to understand was that he would jeopardize his obtaining the secret of the Green Country by doing this. But of course, he thought she was securing the information for him from Malissa, and as long as she didn't know about his perfidy, he was safe. Well, he was safe no longer!

She kept trying his cell phone number, but he had turned it off— of course.

She had called Yahara at The Farm, but he said Gui had not been there.

But the way he said it didn't sound convincing. It could mean that Yahara had been told to say that. She did ask Yahara to call her if Gui came in, that it was important, but not to say anything to Gui about calling her. She made sure he had her number.

She could drive out there, but if he were there, he would see or hear her coming and disappear.

At long last she had Gui Manieux figured out. He never had any intention of being faithful to her! And now he was going to use that beautiful young woman for his own self-indulgent needs.

There had to be some way to find him and stop him! There had to be!

CHAPTER 115

At two thirty Bert arrived at the hotel and called up to Saratu's room, asking her to come down. He also called Malissa and without telling her that he was at the hotel at that moment, asked her to bring Asta downstairs a few minutes before three, and be sure to be there herself. If all of them were on the front porch, there would be no way that Gui would be allowed to take Saratu.

Earlier he had called Carol, who had answered breathlessly and then seemed disappointed that it was Bert. He told her it was important for her to be at the hotel promptly at three o'clock. When she asked why, he said it had to do with Giu and he was sure she would want to be there.

"You bet I'll be there," she said in a husky voice that sounded as if she had been crying.

Bert led Saratu to the front porch of the hotel and indicated she should sit in one of the white wicker chairs. He sat in one nearby.

His plan was in motion, but he felt like he needed to say something to Saratu about the matter.

"Saratu," Bert began, not at all sure what he was going to say. "Mr Manieux is not . . . Mr. Manieux is a man who . . . " He stuttered and stopped. What could he say to a beautiful young girl from the bush about not having sex with Gui Manieux?

"Bert," Saratu said, "stop."

Bert looked at her in surprise as she did not usually speak so sharply or tell a man to be quiet.

"Look, Saratu," he began again.

"No," Saratu said, her hand on his arm. "My mother has talked to me about men, especially men like Mr. Manieux. I understood yesterday that he gave me the gift because he wanted to have sex with me." She stopped. *"Have sex*, that is how you say it, yes?"

Bert nodded uncomfortably. He was not good at this.

"I do not think I want to have sex with Mr. Manieux, but, maybe, just maybe I might."

"But, why?"

"I'm not sure, maybe to see how a man such as Gui treats a woman. He is so good-looking and really very nice. I am sure I will never have such an opportunity again."

"But you could get hurt!"

Saratu ignored that. "You are the one who brought us together, so you can't say no now, right?"

"This is not going to happen, Saratu. I will not let him take you away when he comes. I just thought I would make it clear that . . . "

Saratu interrupted, "My cousin, Laraba, told me about the truck that came to her village to show the people how to prevent AIDS. I have one of those . . . things."

"Things?" Bert stared at her uncomprehending.

"The little rubbery things for a man to use when a man and woman have sex . . . "

Bert flushed, sure his face was bright red. How did she know about these things, and talk so glibly?

"Condoms," Bert said barely audibly.

"Condoms," Saratu repeated firmly.

"You would insist that he use one?" Bert asked unbelieving.

"Of course," Saratu said matter-of-factly.

Reaching into her bag, Saratu brought out the condom package. "I found this in your car."

Bert stared at the packet. He had not used condoms for years but he remembered Gui having put a package in there.

"Good ones?" Saratu asked innocently.

Oh God!. "The best," he said.

For just a moment Bert thought it was a shame that they were not going through with this because Gui would be in for the surprise of his life.

It was twenty minutes before three o'clock, and Bert was very nervous.

"Could I have a drink, Bert?" Saratu asked. "Some lemonade?"

Bert checked his watch. There was time, but he would hurry.

Bert stepped inside to get drinks at the bar and was gone at the most five minutes. Carrying two glasses of limeade, he pushed open the big front door of the hotel. The wicker chairs were empty. He glanced quickly around for Saratu.

Panic welled up in his throat as something told him that Gui had outsmarted him. Turning quickly to peer down the drive that led to the main street, he saw what he knew to be Gui's Mercedes just turning onto the main thoroughfare.

CHAPTER 116

In spite of orders to leave, Yahara was still at The Farm. He had moved his car some distance away where it would not be seen by anyone coming to The Farm and returned to the lab through the rear door.

Gui had left The Farm soon after his confrontation with Yahara that morning. Obviously something was coming down, and Yahara was going to be there to see what it was. Then he would pass it on to his friend, Tomiko.

At three-fifteen that afternoon, Yahara watched Gui drive into the yard and park in his usual spot near his office. Gui hurried around the car and opened the door for a beautiful young black woman who gracefully stepped out of the car, and taking Gui's arm walked with him into his office.

What in the world? He had seen this happen numerous times before, but this time something told Yahara to keep watching.

CHAPTER 117

Tomiko logged onto his laptop computer and breathlessly waited for the E-mail screen to come up. His heart took a flying leap when he saw a message from Jim Harris.

After a glance at the first few lines, Tomiko let out a shout and jumped up, dancing around the room like a dervish.

Then he turned on his little portable printer and told the computer to print out the message. His job was safe!

CHAPTER 118

At the hotel, Bert raced to the house phone and called Malissa's room, but there was no answer. Obviously she was on the way down. He stood at the bottom of the stairs, agitatedly watching first the elevator and then the stairs, but Asta and Malissa did not appear.

Five minutes dragged by.

He called Malissa's room again. No answer.

They must be on the way down!

Another five minutes.

Suddenly the thought came to Bert that something terrible had happened to Malissa. He told himself it was crazy, but what other explanation could there be?

After another five minutes, he was beside himself. Should he just leave and go catch up with Gui? For his plan to work, he needed to have Asta, Malissa and Carol with him when he confronted Gui.

Again he called Malissa's room with no answer.

When Malissa went to Asta's room to get her a few minutes before three o'clock, Asta told her she had a very bad headache. Malissa returned to her room for aspirin, but could not find any. Quickly, she ran downstairs to the giftshop for a bottle of aspirin.

She hurried back upstairs to Asta's room and found Asta in the bathroom vomiting into the sink. Malissa gently guided her to the stool and pulled a small chair over for her to sit on. Malissa kneeled on her knees and held Asta's head as she continued to retch.

After some minutes, Asta indicated that she thought the vomiting was finished. Malissa helped her up, and practically carrying Asta, moved her to the bed and sat down beside her.

Malissa glanced anxiously at the clock. It was almost three-fifteen. Bert would be waiting for her. Well, it wasn't to be helped. Asta was obviously in no condition to go anywhere.

She heard the phone ringing in her room next door, but figured Bert would come upstairs if he really wanted her.

Downstairs, Bert was frantic. Maybe she was in Asta's room. He wouldn't call; he would just go upstairs.

Two steps at a time he raced up the stairs and pounded on Asta's door.

"Malissa! Are you there?"

"Bert, what in the world is wrong?" She hurried to the door and opened it.

"You've got to come, Malissa! Right now! Gui has spirited Saratu away, and goodness know what will happen!"

Asta heard the tone of voice and the name of her daughter spoken, and in spite of being wobbly, she made her way to them.

"Asta, you can't . . . " Malissa began.

"If Saratu is in trouble, I am going!"

Bert was already starting down the hall, motioning for them to follow. Malissa pulled the door shut behind them and put her arm around Asta to steady her.

Bert chose the stairs and started down when he realized that something was wrong with Asta. Quickly he returned and put one arm around her as the three of them made their way down the broad staircase to the first floor.

"I'll bring the Landrover," he said as he raced for the front door, almost knocking Carol down as she was opening the front door.

"Carol, come with us! Gui has Saratu with him!"

"Oh, God!" Carol said, "That bastard! I knew it! I knew it!"

Malissa heard Carol's statement and asked, "Knew what?"

"Is there a problem?" Tomiko asked, arriving on the scene.

"We will soon find out," Malissa said. "Maybe you should come along, Tomiko. We might need some help."

Bert tooted the horn of the Landrover as he drew up to the entrance, and they scurried down the steps and climbed in with Malissa helping Asta. But Asta had seemed to recover at the news of danger to Saratu.

CHAPTER 119

At The Farm, Gui escorted Saratu into his office and guided her to a chair.

"I will be right back," he said. Hurriedly, he hid the car behind the laboratory building.

Back in the office he bowed, kissing Saratu's hand. He listened intently, pleased that there was no sound of motors. He had made good his escape. Even if Bert followed, he did not know about the special room in his office. Even Carol was not aware of it. The only one who knew was Yahara, and he had been told to leave and not come back.

Now gazing at the beautiful young woman before him, he muttered under his breath, "I will have it all, Bert, including the secret of the Green Country!"

Gui gently took Saratu's arm.

"I have some lovely gifts for you," he purred. Guiding her to the sideboard he lifted the lid of a ribbon-bedecked box of candy. "I bought this just for you."

Saratu stared at the unfamiliar sight. "Take one," Gui urged.

"What is it?" Saratu asked, her senses alert for whatever was going to happen next.

"Candy, chocolates, chocolate candy. Here, I'll show you" He picked up a chocolate and bit into it then showed her the soft raspberry center.

She saw no reason not to have a sample. She chose one and tasted it tentatively. The chocolate she was acquainted with, but there was another flavor, but not unpleasant.

Saratu glanced quickly around the room, apprehension gathering in her dark eyes. Gui saw the look and hurried to keep her attention. He was well versed in the protocol for such situations and now turned on the charm full force.

Gently he propelled her to a false panel in the wall, which slid open to reveal the door to the bedroom. They stepped inside.

He turned back to slide the panel back in place as Saratu cried out, "How beautiful!" and reached out to touch the crystal boudoir lamp beside the bed. It sparkled like diamonds.

He shut the door and moved quickly to her side. He put his arm around her gently. The walls were soundproofed. No one could hear anything that went on in that room, and there were no windows.

Boudoir lamps gave a delicate glow to the room which was decorated in warm peach and cinnamon tones. Thick fluffy ivory carpet underfoot absorbed all noise.

Gui wanted to take his time for this experience. Bert would no doubt be showing up, but they were safe behind the hidden panel. No one would find them there.

"Before I show you The Farm, I thought you would like to see an elegant bedroom."

Saratu was dazzled by such a beautifully appointed room. She moved about touching the materials and inhaling the fragrances. Every table held a bouquet of flowers—roses, gardenias, night-blooming jasmine. She touched each one, naming their names.

Saratu remembered Pindar's awkward, stumbling advances and wondered how Gui would proceed. But she only continued to murmur about the exquisite colors and textures. Gui stood and watched, drinking in the curves of her body, her throat, her delicate ankles. She was indeed beautiful., Gorgeous skin color, like milk chocolate. He had known many women, but none more desirable than this one. This one he would have liked even if she were not a virgin.

This was his moment, the one he had paid dearly for, and he was going to savor every second of it.

As she touched something and remarked about it, he responded with an explanation or a description of where it had come from and why. Peach silk from Italy, brocaded wall hangings from France, embroidered curtains from Belgium.

"This is for you," Gui said, holding out a gauzy pale cocoa-colored silk negligee, the very color of her skin. Such feminine accoutrements turned him on, and he wanted to see Saratu in this.

She touched the silky softness of the gown and then held it to her. She did not seem to be afraid, In fact, appeared at ease. For just a second he wondered if perhaps it was not true that she had never made love before.

Then he came to her, and standing behind her, placed his hands gently on her arms, moving down to her fingers and caressing them one by one.

Saratu relaxed against his body and closed her eyes.

As he felt Saratu's body leaning into his, the incredible sensation he had been praying for began, filling his groin with a warm glow, spreading slowly up and down his body. He felt his face flush, and his breathing changed to short inhalations. The glorious stir of beginning passion quickly gathered momentum. But he would not hurry this, for either of them.

As his hands found her waist and moved upward, he realized she was not wearing a bra, and his libido soared.

"Saratu, you have a rare beauty, as unique as these lovely furnishings." His voice was husky, muted as always when he was aroused.

He pulled off her headscarf, and instinctively she turned her face upward. He kissed her on the lips, just once, gently but lingering. Then his lips touched her eyes, her face, her cheeks, moving to her throat. He found the little cave beneath her right ear with his tongue, then moved slowly up to her ear lobe.

His loins were on fire, but he moved deliberately.

"I would like for you to put the gown on."

He moved away, stepping into the walk-in closet.

Saratu had had warm feelings when she was with Pindar but never anything like this. It had begun low in her groin, then between her legs, as she felt herself swelling, almost painfully, but also most pleasurably.

Apparently a man provides expensive gifts and a lovely gown for the woman to wear, she thought. Kicking aside her slippers, she slipped out of her wraparound skirt, blouse and panties and into the elegant gown.

Gui emerged wearing only a chocolate velvet robe. His arms encircled her, and this time his moves were urgent, compelling as he found her lips, his hands moving down her body, his fingers catching on the flimsy silk.

She fought the desire to melt into the moment, to give herself completely, but in spite of the incredible sensations moving in her body, an alarm was going off.

She pulled away and sat down on the bed, a huge expanse of peach silk.

Gui was not surprised. Even women who were experienced often pulled away momentarily. But there had never been one that did not eventually give in. And obviously this inexperienced young woman was going to be a fairly easy conquest.

Now for the element that would ensure success. He poured two glasses of wine, Special Harvest from South Africa, he had paid a king's ransom for.

Smiling at him, she accepted the glass and sipped a little of it.

"Good wine," she said.

"The best."

Then taking the glass away, he sat down beside her on the bed and pulled her into his arms, the longing that filled him was declared in his kiss. Her mouth responded, as did her body as they dropped back onto the bed, two bodies seeking each other. His fingertips found her breasts, and she caught her breath at the pleasure of it.

It was important to always remain in control, so he moved to the center of the bed and beckoned for her to join him. This was what he had been waiting for, the delicious enjoyment of a virgin's body. The incredible thought that he would be the first to enter this woman brought his sensations to a high he had never known. But he would not hurry.

She moved with liquid motion to his side and stretched out, her head resting on one hand.

Her breasts stood up high and firm with nipples hard. When his tongue touched her nipple, he felt her shudder in response.

In spite of the wondrous sensations coursing through her body, Saratu was still in control of her thoughts. The one thing she did not know was when to offer the condom. It was still firmly clasped in her left hand.

CHAPTER 120

The Landrover screeched tires and brakes as Bert rounded the corner onto the main street. Dark clouds were piled up in the southeast as on the day they had arrived in Blantyre, moving fast and covering more and more of the sky. Thunder growled from the blackened sky. Everyone held on as Bert drove like a demon was after him.

"What is it, what is it?" Asta asked urgently.

"We aren't sure," Malissa replied. "Saratu may be in danger."

"Oh, no! Yamta would never forgive me!"

"Where are we going?" Tomiko asked.

"To The Farm. Saratu is with Gui Manieux."

"That is bad news," Tomiko said warmly. Then, "The Farm! I think Yahara could be a great help to us."

He quickly dialed a number on his cell phone.

A muted voice answered, "Hello."

"Yahara, hello. Are you all right?" Tomiko asked.

"Yes, but something is going on with Gui," Yahara replied.

"Yes, we know. We are on our way."

"I will watch for you."

"Carol, we should not park . . . " Bert began.

"Yes, I know just where to go," Carol said quickly.

The streets were busy as people were hurrying to get to their destinations before the storm unleashed its wind and rain. The gusts had already begun, whipping through the car windows.

Bert swore as the light turned red at the last intersection. One more curve before the open road that led to The Farm. They were almost there!

They rounded the curve and cries went up of "Oh no!" and "Not now!" An accident had happened long enough ago that the police were there, and were not letting anyone through.

Quickly Bert tried to think of another way around, but this was the only road that would take them there in time. Any other would be much too far around.

Bert slid the Landrover to a halt. "Maybe I can bribe them to let us through," Bert said as he jumped out of the car and started toward the policeman dressed in dark blue uniform of shirt and knee-length shorts with a high pillbox hat sporting a red tassel.

Bert spoke to the man briefly, but the shaking of his head left no doubt as to the response to Bert's request to go through.

As Bert reached into his pocket, Carol said, "Don't do it, Bert, don't try to bribe the officer!"

The officer leaned down to hear what Bert was trying to say to him, but to no avail as at that moment there was great pounding as someone tried to separate the two cars whose bumpers were entwined. The officer raised his hand to Bert in dismissal and walked away.

Bert returned swearing.

Bert's watch said four-fifteen. "I've had enough of this!" Bert said. He started the car and said, "Hang on!"

To the right of the accident was a steep embankment, and he headed for it.

Malissa saw what he intended to do and cried, "Bert, don't do it! We'll be killed!"

"Just hang on!"

All four wheels were pulling as they started up the embankment. Bert knew his Landrover almost as well as he knew his airplane. With a sure sense of how much speed and how much tilt the Landrover could take, he guided the car over the distance, returning to the road on the other side of the wreck.

"Bravo!" "Good boy, Bert!" "Thank God!" and some words in Kulanji were offered up.

It was slow going because of the cars lined up on the other side of the wreck, many of them in the wrong lane as they tried to get around the others.

At last they could see The Farm up ahead.

CHAPTER 121

G ui," Saratu said.

His eyes were closed; he was absorbing every bit of the extraordinary sensations that were coursing through his body. He did not hear her.

"Gui!" she said again firmly.

"Yes?" he replied from out of his hazy world where his tongue was languidly enjoying the indentation at her umbilicus and moving downward.

"You must use this."

"What?"

She didn't know her body could have such feelings. It would be so easy to just let him take over.

She held up the condom packet. "This!" She spoke urgently.

He opened his eyes but could not believe what he saw. This bush girl with a condom packet in her hand!

He sat up. "What in the world?"

"You must use this," she repeated.

"Are you out of your mind? We do not have to use one of those damned things, you are a virgin!"

"That is why . . . "

Although the soundproof room kept sounds out as well as keeping sounds in, suddenly there was the unmistakable sound of pounding and shouting.

"Damn!" Gui said. "Damn!" But they would not be able to find the false panel.

But Gui had been so sure they were safe and so wrapped up in enjoying his virgin that, unbelievably, he had been distracted and had shut but not locked the door to the bedroom, the secret panel known to no one else but Yahara.

Suddenly the room was full of shouting people. One of the them was Carol who began beating Gui with the umbrella she had picked up in the outer room and calling him names that were not translatable into Kulanji.

Asta was not shouting; she was covering Saratu with her wrap-around cloth and pushing her from the room. Her mother had tried to get her to exchange the silk gown for her wraparound cloth, but Saratu was not about to give it up, so Asta covered her with the wraparound cloth. And as she passed the box of chocolates, Saratu grabbed that too.

The whole crowd surged toward the door with Saratu and Asta leading and Gui desperately trying to hold his dressing gown around his body as Carol gave him one last blow across the back of his knees, causing him to crumble to the floor.

Above him stood Bert, a triumphant smile on his face. "Do you remember Ahmed, Gui? Of course, you do. Well, this is for him from me." In one swift motion, Bert grabbed Gui's head and shoved it to the floor, blood gushing onto the ivory carpet as his nose hit with enough force to fracture it.

CHAPTER 122

G ui lay there without moving until he heard them drive away.
"Damn! Damn!" He said it over and over. If only they had come a
few minutes later, if only he had locked the door, if only . . . But how did
they get in? Who knew about the secret panel? It was Yahara, of course!
The bastard.

Suddenly the truth hit him—hard. Carol knew, Yahara knew, everyone knew, and they were not going to let him have the secret to the Green
Country! But Bert had said "Ahmed." Had Bert planned this all along?

As desirable as had been his tryst with Saratu, it suddenly dimmed when
he realized he had just lost access to the most important bit of information
to appear in a million years, the secret that would make him the most powerful man in Africa.

Why did he not see this coming? And if he had, which would he have
chosen—Saratu or the secret?

That was not even a contest, he said to himself. Any man would have
chosen one last experience with a beautiful virgin. Through his mind went
something he read once, *He can die, he who has once been happy.*

Well, he was not going to die. He had failed to get what he had bargained
for, but now he at least needed that secret. His future depended on it.

He staunched the blood from his nose, and despite the pain he lay there
going over every possible thing he could do that might still make it possible
for him to have the secret.

Finally he crawled to his feet, poured a glass of whiskey and sat on the
edge of the bed concentrating every fiber of his brain on finding a solution
to his problem.

He was Gui Manieux. He had solved incredibly difficult problems, set
up elaborate systems that worked. Surely he could find a way to obtain the
secret.

Maybe it was the whiskey, maybe it was just his superb mastery, but suddenly he knew the answer.

Of course! It was the most logical, the most practical, and the most obvious way to go. He would have to summon all the skill and talent for persuasion that he possessed. But he was a master at persuasion; he could do it! For what was at stake he could do anything, even beg. Well, begging wasn't exactly his style, but if that is what it took . . .

From a small box on the dresser he lifted a handcrafted silver cross, held it up, smiled and dropped it back into its box.

He poured another glass of whiskey and reached for a pen and paper.

CHAPTER 123

Outside Gui's office the group milled around, not sure what to do next. Asta had pushed Saratu toward Bert's car where she sat waiting for the rest of the group. Malissa was concerned about getting Saratu out of there and back to the hotel, but she also wanted to have a serious conversation with Bert about how this could have happened.

But Bert was organizing the group to return to the city. They were almost as eager to leave as they had been to get there, and they were piling into the Landrover. There was little chatter. The group seemed reluctant to talk about what had just happened, so they said nothing.

Malissa stepped up on the running board of the Landrover and spoke loudly to get their attention. "We need to get together this evening and make some decisions. Eight o'clock at the Mount Soche Hotel? Can you be there?" There was a nodding of heads.

Bert placed his arm lightly around Malissa's waist and said, "Malissa, could you drive the Landrover back to town? I need to make sure my plane is fastened securely with this weather moving in. I am going to ask Yahara to take me to the airfield."

Malissa turned to look at him sharply. She couldn't imagine he had left his plane not tied down securely, but she really could not challenge him on that point.

"I... I guess I can. We need to talk. Will you be back later?"

"Of course," Bert said lightly.

Yahara agreed to take him to the airport, and Tomiko went along with them.

Bert had to get away from Malissa. He had decided it was best to disappear until the eight o'clock meeting tie. He was not ready to explain to Malissa just yet. In fact, he had to sort out some things in is own mind.

CHAPTER 124

A sta sat in one of the big armchairs in the hotel lobby. Exhausted from the last few hours, she collapsed against the soft cushions and wished she could walk out the door and be home in her own compound.

But Saratu was energized. Back in her hotel room after her encounter with Gui, she had carefully folded the silky gown and tucked it away in the small canvas bag they had bought in market. The box of chocolates, too, was safely wrapped in paper and then in one of her zhebis. She had smiled as she thought of trying to answer Pindar's questions about where the candy came from.

Asta had plied her with questions, but Saratu simply remained silent.

She was wearing one of her new matching blouse and wraparound skirt combinations. Her mother had re-braided her hair the night before, and she had used some of the moist powder that she bought in market to highlight her eyes. She looked attractive and knew it. Her rendezvous with Gui had left her feeling like a real, grown-up woman. The thought of going back to Pindar was not at all appealing. On the other hand, returning to her own home was a most welcome thought. She had had enough of the Outside.

Malissa was watching the front door, curious to know what questions Dr. Worthington would ask of Saratu.

Bert's sudden departure had left her a bit miffed There was no way she believed his story about having to check on his plane.

Saratu had wandered over near the front door and was leaning idly against a pillar. As the door opened, she turned and observed the two men coming in.

The first person Clay saw as he stepped through the door was Saratu, and he knew instantly that this was the young woman he had come to see. Unaware of anyone else, he walked over to her and said, "Miss Saratu?"

Saratu gave him a gentle smile and curtsied in the Kulanji fashion.

Malissa hurried to Saratu's side and said, "Saratu, this is Doctor

Worthington. Right?" she asked him.

"Right, but my name is really Clayton, Clay, please."

"Clayton Clay," Saratu repeated solemnly.

"No, just Clay," Clay said grinning.

"Clay," Saratu said, matching his grin with her smile.

"And I am Jim Harris." Jim put out his hand to Malissa and then to Saratu who curtsied as before.

Asta had watched this and now slowly pulled herself out of the low chair. Malissa motioned them all over to greet Asta. "Asta, Saratu's mother," she explained.

"We can go into the dining room now," Malissa said, looking at the door again to see if Bert was there.

Clay chose a chair next to Saratu, and the two of them began a conversation, which continued all through dinner, to the virtual exclusion of everyone else. But Malissa and Jim did not lack for things to talk about, and Asta was pleased to be left alone to enjoy her meal. Malissa kept one eye on the door, her concern growing as time went on and Bert did not come.

Just as the lime sherbet was being served, Bert appeared and took the empty seat beside Malissa. He did not respond to the question in her face except to say, "I got delayed."

This was not the time to demand explanations so Malissa introduced Bert to Clay and Jim.

"Bert is the one who flew to Kulanji to bring us to Blantyre," Saratu explained.

"Bert," Clay said, "I have made a decision. I want to see the Green Country, and I want to see Saratu's home and meet her father. In fact, if possible, I want to move my research to Kulanji."

Jim gasped in surprise and said, "What in the world?"

Malissa smiled, "It may sound like a great idea, but I can't imagine they will let you in."

"We won't know if we don't ask, will we?" Clay said. "Besides, I have decided I want to know more— much more about Saratu, her family, and the Green Country."

Jim was suspicious now, remembering Clay's statement about there being black women in Africa.

"What do Saratu and Asta think of that?" Malissa asked.

All eyes turned toward the two women.

"Saratu?" Malissa said.

"Mama and I will talk about it," she replied.

"And your father," Asta said firmly. Then she turned to Saratu with a grin.

"And maybe even Pindar?"

Saratu made a face.

"Pindar may not want a woman of the world," Malissa said.

"A woman of the world may not want Pindar," Saratu said firmly, then her voice softened, "And then again . . . "

"It is time for our meeting," Malissa said. "We can talk about this later."

As they walked toward the door, Malissa took Bert's arm, and noting that, Saratu did the same with Clay. and gave Malissa a knowing smile .

At the door to the room where they were to meet, Clay stopped. "I don't think we belong in your meeting. Saratu, could you and I have some coffee when your meeting is finished?"

"Okay," she replied with a smile and walked on into the meeting room.

"Clay," Jim said, "we need to get back to Lilongwe tonight. We have work to do."

"Jim, I have been waiting for something like this all my life. I'm not leaving, at least not just yet."

"I can't believe this. You've just arrived here."

"So?" Clay said.

"These people live in Africa in the Garden of Eden, and you live in Pennsylvania. Doesn't that sound just a bit strange to you?"

"Not at all. I have been looking for a challenge in my life; this is it. I want to follow this to its natural conclusion. I want to explore the secrets of the Green Country and see what they hold for the rest of us."

Jim frowned, "Is that all?"

Clay flung his arms wide. "Who knows?"

Jim shook his head, "I give up. You are crazy."

They returned to the lobby to wait.

CHAPTER 125

A short time later Malissa, Bert, Saratu, Asta, Tomiko, Yahara and Carol gathered in a small meeting room off the lobby of the Mount Soche Hotel. Tomiko was the center of attention and loving it. "The story goes like this. Centuries ago there was an asteroid that struck earth, bringing with it elements not found on earth. The people who lived downwind of that asteroid have benefited from extraordinary health and robust agriculture because of those elements. The very dirt contains a factor that prevents AIDS from getting started. It counteracts the AIDS virus with its own genetic code."

"And the crops that grow so well?" Carol asked.

"Again, a bit of protein found in the asteroid causes the guinea corn and other crops to be resistant to disease."

"Is that transferable?" Malissa asked.

"We will proceed to immediately begin to research the possibility of synthesizing these factors so that everyone can benefit from them."

There was a general buzz of excitement as they talked about the possibilities.

Tomiko spoke again. "We have a hero in our midst, ladies and gentlemen. Yahara was in the thick of battle with Mr. Manieux but refused to give up. He lost his job as a result, but he will be starting a job at the World Health Organization laboratory in Lilongwe right away."

Yahara's face lit up with the news, and he reached for the bottle of sake among the collection of liquor on the sideboard.

Saratu spoke up. "That is all very well, but because of Mama and me, you know the secret of our country. Now what happens to us? We have to go back to Kulanji to people who do not know or care about these things."

The group was hushed.

"Sorry, Saratu," Malissa said. "We have been very insensitive." She turned to the others. "What are we going to do for Saratu and Asta? According to custom, they will be shunned for six months, a terrible punishment for the gift they have given the world."

"Couldn't they stay here?" Carol asked.

Asta and Saratu replied in chorus, "We want to go home!"

Saratu went on, "We were snatched from our village and . . . "

"That's it!" cried Bert as he jumped to his feet. "That's it! You didn't run away. Look, you didn't take anything with you. You just walked down the road to be with Miss Taylor, and you were kidnapped!"

"Kidnapped!" cried Malissa. "Of course! Bert kidnapped you!"

"Now wait a minute, Malissa," Bert objected. "It wasn't just me!"

"Sounds reasonable to me," Malissa said grinning.

"Wait, wait, wait!" Saratu cried. "What is this *kidnapped*?"

"Sorry," Malissa said, rushing over to Saratu and hugging her. "Kidnapped means we stole you away against your will."

It took a moment for the meaning to register with Saratu. "I like that!" she exclaimed.

She turned to Asta and spoke in Kulanji. "Mama, listen! They forced us to get into the plane and brought us to Blantyre!"

It was like the sun had just come out from behind a very dark cloud. Asta hugged Saratu, saying, "Yes! Yes! Yes!"

Suddenly Saratu was not laughing. "But what if Baba has told them that we went willingly?"

Asta shook her head vigorously. "I know your father better than that. He would never admit that we went willingly."

Saratu was reassured. "Maybe he has already made up a story about how we were forced to go."

Asta walked over to Bert and demanded, "When can we go home?"

"Tomorrow morning bright and early if the weather is good."

"Okay!" Saratu shouted. "Tomorrow we go home!"

Bert had his arm around Malissa and said softly in her ear, "But not before I get to spend the night with my sweetheart, right?"

Malissa ducked out of his embrace and said, "Bert, I have a feeling there are some things I don't know about all this. When are you going to explain?"

"I will, I will," he replied. He pulled her to him again and this time spoke loudly. "What I want to know is when are you coming to live in Blantyre."

"Yes, Miz Tayluh," Saratu said, "when will the wedding be? I want to be there."

Asta pushed her way into their midst. "Don't be silly. They will never let us out again, even if they believe we were kidnapped this time."

"Then the wedding will be in Kulanji," Malissa said with a smile.

"When?" Bert asked quickly, grateful that she had at least agreed to the marriage. "Next week?"

"At the beginning of dry season, in November," Malissa replied. "The mission board will have to have time to find a replacement."

Bert dropped onto a couch and moaned.

"Nonsense," Carol said. "Why not get married here, today or tomorrow? Bert will just have to fly out now and then to see you. That way Asta and Saratu can attend the wedding and so can the rest of us."

Malissa held up her hand. "I have to know something first." The tone of her voice stopped conversation, and all eyes turned to Malissa.

"Saratu, Bert, I want to know how it happened that Saratu was left alone with Gui Manieux."

Silence hung over the group as they waited for the response.

"Bert?" Malissa said.

"Uh, uh," Bert stammered, looking everywhere but at Malissa. "Saratu?"

Saratu shrugged. "When I saw him in the garden and he gave me the lovely naked lady necklace, he invited me to see his farm."

"In the garden?" Malissa swung back to Bert with an ominous look in her eye.

"Gui said . . . he wanted to meet Saratu, and . . . " He was definitely stumbling.

The frown on Malissa's face deepened.

Carol's voice was shrill. "Meet her! That was not what he was doing."

Saratu grasped Malissa's arm for attention. "I knew what he wanted, or at least I thought I did." Her eyes sought those of the group surrounding her as she looked from one to the other. "You have no idea what it is like to live in a closed society. I am to have little choice as to who I marry or what I do with my life, other than marry and have children. I want that too, but Mama understood that first I wanted to see the Outside. Now I know a lot more than I did, thanks to Bert."

"You set this up, Bert?" Malissa's voice was incredulous. "You did this?"

"If I had not been able to buy the new plane, we could not have been able to get away from Kulanji safely. Gui's offer made that possible."

"Offer to what?" Malissa demanded shrilly.

Bert looked at his feet then suddenly straightened. "Saratu is not a weak little girl without defenses. In fact . . . " He moved over beside Saratu and put his hand on her shoulder. "In fact, she handled the situation with intelligence and grace. If we had not interrupted, I think Saratu would have taught Gui a lesson."

"And that is supposed to be your explanation?" Malissa asked.

"It was for us, Malissa, you and me. That plane means the difference between being able to come to see you in Mubi or not. It means I can make a living, enough to support us both."

"But Saratu was put in jeopardy . . . "

Saratu broke in. "I don't know what that word means, but if you had not brought me out, I would have found a way, somehow. And who knows what I would have done, on my own." She turned to Asta. "Tell them, Mama."

"She was determined," Asta agreed. "It would have happened, but not with such helpful people as you."

Bert again moved to encircle Malissa's waist with his arm. "How about it? Any reason we couldn't get married tonight, or tomorrow morning?"

Everyone crowded around Bert and Malissa, laughing, talking, shouting. "Yes! Today! Why not!" They were all waiting for her reply.

Malissa looked around at all the eager faces, thoughts racing through her mind. So much to consider.

Then she felt Bert's arm around her, loving, safe, secure.

"I don't have anything to wear," she said finally.

"I have a feeling there is something in my closet that would fit you," Carol offered. "How about in the hotel garden, in the morning, say nine o'clock?"

"Wear that pretty peach dress," said Bert. "I'll get the orchid to go with it." Then to the others, "Will you all be there?"

In the midst of the chorus of responses, a waiter was frantically trying to get someone's attention, and finally Tomiko realized it and asked who it was he was looking for. "Miss Walters," was the reply.

Tomiko literally pulled Carol out of the crush of people, and the waiter handed her a box and a note. She opened the note first, and as she read it, Carol's face flushed.

"Listen, listen all of you!" She finally got their attention. "I have just received this message from Gui, and I need your help."

They gathered around, quiet now.

She read, "I have come to beg your forgiveness for jeopardizing our love. Nothing in this world is as important to me as you. Even this gift is not as precious as your love, but please accept it as evidence of my abject apology."

All eyes were on Carol as from a small box she took a necklace, and as she held it up, the whole room gasped at the exquisitely crafted silver cross of most unusual design, suspended on a heavy chain. As it swung it caught the sun from the window and shot a delicate beam of light upward.

Carol caught her breath. The Maria Theresa silver cross! Gui had found one, for her! The look on her face reflected her indecision with the realization that Gui had given her this most precious of crosses. It could not have been easy to find this cross, nor inexpensive. He must be really serious this time. Looking at it, through her mind went pictures of Gui's kindness, his vulnerability, his lovemaking.

"He wants the secret of the Green Country pretty bad, doesn't he?" muttered Bert quietly but loud enough for Carol to hear.

"A greedy man," Malissa said.

"Does he really think that Carol will . . . " Yahara began.

"Of course, you could forgive him, Carol," Saratu said. "He sounds truly sorry."

"I am sure he is," Carol said but with an edge of bitterness in her voice.

"He was very sweet," Saratu said softly.

Carol closed her hand around the cross, then opened it again and held it up to where the light caught it. "I think he does truly care for me, he spent a lot of effort and money to get this for me," she said almost wistfully. "Maybe he really has learned his lesson."

Asta now touched Carol's arm. "No, Miz Carol. He has learned only how to get your sympathy." Suddenly her eyes sparkled with impishness. Asta motioned to Malissa to come close and said something to her. Malissa translated.. "Asta says I should tell him that I will think about it and that he should wait for me in the lobby."

Carol looked questioningly at Asta, and Asta again whispered in Malissa's ear. Malissa relayed another message.

Carol grinned and asked for a pen, which Tomiko supplied.

The group stood silent as Carol wrote and handed the note to the waiter who disappeared toward the lobby.

Carol turned to Malissa. "Malissa, this is your wedding present from Gui," she said, placing the cross around Malissa's neck.

Then moving quickly, Asta led the way as one by one they moved quietly to the door leading from the room to the garden outside. Tomiko was the last one out, and he quietly closed the door behind him..

www.ingramcontent.com/pod-product-compliance
Lightning Source LLC
Chambersburg PA
CBHW062109170626
46813CB00002B/380